Lost Paradise:

Book One

Francine Quesnel

YellowRoseBooks
a Division of
RENAISSANCE ALLIANCE PUBLISHING, INC.
Nederland, Texas

ISBN 1-930928-12-2

First Printing 2001

9 8 7 6 5 4 3 2 1

Cover art by Carla van Westen
Cover design by Mary A. Sannis

Published by:

Renaissance Alliance Publishing, Inc.
PMB 238, 8691 9th Avenue
Port Arthur, TX 77642

Find us on the World Wide Web at
http://www.rapbooks.com

Printed in the United States of America

I'd like to thank my original Beta readers, Pat, Dawn, Carole, Trish and my latest friend Sharon. You guys really helped a lot.

I would also like to thank a very special person, Cindy. Throughout this project, you have been a solid shoulder for me to lean on. Your help, great suggestions and ideas were and still are very precious to me. You're the best!

— Fran, a.k.a. WolfDragon

Chapter 1

"*Cut,*" a man yelled, and then took a deep breath to relax as he glanced around him.

Montreal, Canada, a place as far away from Hollywood as could be, but a location that was quickly becoming more popular with the moviemakers than the crazy atmosphere of Tinseltown. In the past few years, it had seen the number of movies filmed there growing steadily as productions from all over the world discovered this rich location. With the newly built studios, the excellent technical crews available, and the European look, the old section of Montreal had lots to offer with its unique flavor and desirability.

One of those movies currently being shot was a joint Canadian/Austrian production. A number of the exterior shots had already been filmed in and around Montreal, including some done in the Laurentians, which were only two hours north of the city.

The week's schedule had the crew filming in the south section of Montreal, a few blocks away from what people called the Old Port, also known as Old Montreal.

A small group of people stood in front of a small color monitor on the set to watch the replay of the stunt that had just been performed. The movie director, a man in his mid forties, nodded as the scene played through under his studious inspection. He had never worked with the Austrian stunt people before but knew of them through other directors who had worked with the professionals. The most highly recommended was Kristina Von Deering. It was her stunt of a very tight rollover in a police car that they watched on the screen.

Nodding his approval, he gave Kristina a thumbs up, indicating that the stunt was a good take. "Great work, people. That's a take." He then took his leave to attend to other pressing matters. A tall, dark-haired woman separated herself from the rest and walked over to a nearby bench. She dropped down onto the hard wooden surface, put her racing gloves into her helmet and then placed it down on the bench beside her. The protective padding she wore under the police uniform made the warm day even more difficult to manage. She unbuttoned the shirt all the way, pulling it out of the uniform's dark blue pants, and pulled at her soaked T-shirt. She then spotted a young man acting as gopher, moving around the set, offering bottled water. Since her throat was parched from the heat, she waved the gopher over.

The young man quickly approached. "You want one?" he asked with a smile and handed her a bottle, which was accepted with a nod.

She twisted off the cap and drained half of the bottle's contents before putting it down beside her helmet. She rubbed the tiredness from her face then leaned her elbows on her knees and rested her head in her hands, closing her eyes for a moment.

It was Kris' second day in Montreal, working for a project that started to look like it would be a very long one. She was alone in the city since none of her siblings had been chosen to work with her, and she was already bored out of her mind. Then, there was the hotel room. She had to find a house to rent so she could have her own place and get comfortable while she was there. Even though she spent a lot of time in hotels, she hated them, no matter how big and luxurious they were.

Once settled, she would connect her computer directly to her house in Innsbruck and keep in touch with her Arabian horse breeding program. As long as she kept working, everything was fine.

The sound of loud voices off to her left caused Kristina to

lift her head and open her eyes to see a scrawny looking man groping at a young woman. She caught sight of the man's hand as he tried to reach for the girl all the while making lewd comments.

"I told you to leave me alone!" the young blonde said as she backed away from her assailant, trying to put some distance between them as she batted his wandering hands away but to no avail. "Can't you take no for an answer?" she asked as she stopped, taking a stand.

Kris got to her feet and silently walked up behind the woman without her knowing. She casually crossed her arms over her chest and gave the man a dangerous glare that promised nothing but pain. His eyes narrowed as he opened his mouth to say something but her strong stance and size quickly made him change his mind. At the sight of the tall Austrian's smile, devoid of any humor, he reconsidered his actions and quickly turned and walked away.

A slight frown of confusion crossed the blonde woman's features at the man's sudden departure. "That was easy," she sighed in relief, realizing that the jerk had decided to finally leave her alone. She took a deep breath and turned to leave. She didn't get very far as she walked right into a wall of muscle and flesh that stood directly behind her, causing the files she carried to rain down to the ground.

"Oh! Excuse me, officer," the smaller woman exclaimed nervously as she bent down and gathered the fallen papers. "I didn't see you behind me. I'm such a klutz sometimes."

Long, slender fingers came into view as they helped in gathering the files. She concentrated more intensely on picking up the papers, too embarrassed to look up at the police officer helping her.

"No, I'm the one who's sorry. Are you okay?" the woman asked, concerned.

At the sound of the slight German accent, the voice a warm contralto, the blonde looked up and was engulfed in the most beautiful eyes she had ever seen. "Wow...huh, I mean, yes. I'm okay," she murmured as she stared at the woman crouching down with her. Her long, dark hair was tied back in a tight braid and the bangs that hung loosely just above her perfect eyebrows were a beautiful contrast to her sapphire colored eyes.

Kris bit back a smile, as the younger woman stared at her all slack jawed. She was pretty, Kris decided as she looked into her bright green eyes and at her long blonde hair. She was petite but not to the point of being fragile. The girl kept staring as she blindly picked her papers up. Kris noticed that papers were missed and the blonde searched with her hand to find them, unable to tear her eyes from Kris' own. "Are you sure you're okay?"

"Hmm? Oh. Yes. I'm fine, thank you." She blushed as she looked down, put the papers back into the files and got to her feet at the same time as the officer. She took a good look at the person in front of her, and realized why the jerk had left so suddenly.

The woman was at least six feet tall, towering above her five foot four frame. The tight T-shirt underneath the opened police shirt showed an incredibly flat abdomen. Even the protective padding could not hide the broad shoulders and trim waist, which made for a very impressive sight. Only then did she notice that the "police officer" wore no gun and that she was halfway out of uniform. "Yeah, I'm okay," the young woman stated, smiling.

Satisfied that the young woman was unharmed, Kris nodded then turned around to go back to the bench and pick up the equipment she had left there. Her day of work was done and now she had to find something interesting to do.

Seeing that the woman was about to leave, the blonde thought furiously of something to say to her, not knowing why she didn't want to see her leave. Spying the helmet on the bench, she blurted out the first thing that came to her mind. "Are you one of the stuntmen...I mean, stuntwomen for the movie?"

Kris stopped walking and turned to look back at the woman. "I'm not a police officer, that's for sure," she teased. "My name is Kristina Von Deering," she said as she held her hand out.

"Nicole McGrail." She stepped forward to shake the outstretched hand. "Nice to meet you." She smiled a little nervously, wondering where all the butterflies in her stomach had come from. Never before had she felt this way towards anyone.

A raised eyebrow from the stuntwoman made Nicole realize that she still held her hand. "Oh. Sorry." She pulled back her hand and blushed even more as Kristina flashed her a beautiful smile.

"Are you from this area?" Kristina asked, wanting to put the young woman at ease.

"Yes." Nicole nodded, glad that the woman wasn't angry with all the staring she had been doing. "I live in Montreal."

Kris wasn't upset. In fact, she seemed a little amused.

"Where are you from?" Nicole asked as they walked to the full-face helmet left on the bench.

"I live in Innsbruck, Austria." Kris grabbed her helmet and gloves and tucked them under her arm. Not wanting to go to her hotel room and stay alone, she looked around for a place to go and relax for a while but nothing caught her eye. She turned to the blonde woman. "Is there any place near here where I could get a cold beer?"

"Sure," Nicole exclaimed excitedly. "We have lots of clubs and bars around here. There's..." She hesitated then remembered that she hadn't set foot in a bar yet. Thinking furiously, she tried to remember a place that was popular by name. "There's...hmm, I know. Hmm, no..." *I'm making a fool of myself in front of her,* she thought as she quickly went through bar names in her head while stealing a glance at the older woman. Kris stood there watching her with a slight grin on her face. "I know a place, just...Oh. There's *Les Deux Pierrot,* a couple of streets away," she said triumphantly. "It's a very popular Francophone bistro. We could go...I mean," she paused, "I could show you and your friends where it is."

"I'd like that." Kris smiled and tilted her head to catch Nicole's green eyes. "Maybe you could have a beer with me?"

Oh God. Did I hear right? Did the stuntwoman just ask me to come with her? "Really?" Her heart beat faster at the thought of spending more time with the raven haired Austrian. "I'd like that. Have you ever been to Montreal before? Do you know anybody here?" she asked with a smile.

Kristina shook her head. "No, this is my first time in Montreal, and no, I don't know anybody here. Actually, you're the first person I've really spoken to since I arrived." She frowned a bit as the smaller woman grinned.

"Well, what would you say if I showed you the sights?" she asked hopefully. Then noticing that the woman was about to say something, Nicole quickly added, "I know you must be very busy but I'd be happy to do it if you want."

Kris was surprised that the girl would volunteer to guide a total stranger all over the city. *Either she's a naive young woman or she figures I'm harmless,* she thought with a chuckle and smiled. *Yeah, me harmless. But what harm could be done by accepting the offer and playing tourist?* "Thank you for offer. I'd like that very much."

"Great."

"Nicole! You have my file?" the movie director called out from a distance.

"Well, I guess a gopher's job is never done." She shrugged and smiled. "I finish at six. Meet me here then?" she asked enthusiastically as she walked away backwards.

Kris couldn't help but laugh at the happy bounce in the young girl's steps. "I'll be here." A bright smile answered her, and she watched as Nicole turned around and sprinted to the waiting director.

After handing the files to the man, the young gopher looked back at the tall stuntwoman walking away to the trailer that served as a dressing room. She took a deep breath and let it out slowly, wondering what had possessed her to appoint herself as tour guide to a total stranger.

"Are you hiding something from me, Nick?" her cousin and best friend, Alex, stepped up beside her and asked with a smile. She was the same height as Nick, but with a more muscular build. "I didn't know you knew her."

Nicole turned to her friend with a confused look on her face. "Huh?"

"The tall, blue-eyed beauty that you were talking to...hello?" She grinned as she mimed knocking on Nicole's head.

"Oh...that." Nicole smiled as they walked to the director's

office near the dressing room trailer. "Samuel was trying to grope me again," she said with a disgusting shiver. "She just kind of scared him away."

"Ooh, she came to your rescue. And? Go on," the brunette prompted with an encouraging elbow to the ribs.

"Alex!" Nicole exclaimed, laughing. "And, we just chatted a little bit, that's all." A tug on her arm stopped her from walking any further.

"Kristina Von Deering isn't known for her conversational skills, Nick," Alex told her friend as she brushed her fingers through her short hair. "In fact, I heard that she's very antisocial. A loner...though a damn good looking loner, but she..." She stopped talking as the dressing room door opened and Kris walked out.

While closing the door behind her, the tall stuntwoman caught sight of Nicole and gave her a smile as she walked past. "See you tonight," Kris purred as she put her sunglasses on and swung the black leather jacket she carried over one shoulder.

See you tonight? Alex mouthed and looked at her silent friend who had a silly grin on her face as she watched Kris walk away. "Earth to Nick?" Alex teased, making the young woman blush. "Care to explain this latest development?"

"There's nothing to explain, Alex. We're going for a beer, that's all," she said as they continued walking. "She doesn't know anybody here so I thought that maybe I could show her the sights."

"And will you be one of those sights?" Alex grinned. *How I love to tease her. It's so easy to make her blush.*

"What?" Nicole turned to her friend. "What do you mean by that?"

"You know, a nice walk, a drink somewhere, a visit to her hotel room later?" Alex chuckled. She was having too much fun.

"Why would I go to Kris' hotel room?" she asked, confused.

"You can be so dense sometimes, Nick," Alex exclaimed, and then a thought crossed her mind. "How much do you know about Kristina?"

"That she's a stuntwoman from Austria," the young woman replied as if that answered everything.

"Aside from knowing her job and where she comes from, what do you know about *her*?"

Nicole thought for a moment and realized that she didn't know much. "Nothing really," she responded, shrugging. "She was kind enough to come and help me with that creep. I just want to thank her."

"You obviously like Kris." Alex grinned. "Your face lit up when you looked at her. You weren't able to keep your eyes off of her and that smile of yours..."

"What's wrong with my smile?" Nicole asked as she crossed her arms over her chest and stared at the brunette.

"I've never seen you smile like that at anyone before, Nick," she said, imitating her cousin's pose, then smiling. "She's a very beautiful woman. I wouldn't mind getting to know her better, and I think you wouldn't mind either."

"Well, sure, she seems nice enough." Nicole smiled, as she thought about the stuntwoman. "I don't see any reason why we can't be friends."

"You just want to be friends?" Alex lowered her voice as more technicians walked pass them. *Poor girl, you have no idea what Kristina is really like, do you?*

The blonde slowed her pace then stopped and took a deep breath. She brushed her hands through her long hair and sighed. "I don't understand how I feel. I only talked to her for five minutes, but it feels like I've known her forever." She took another breath and closed her eyes. "When she smiled at me, I thought that my knees were going to buckle from under me. This is so silly."

"Well, she does have a beautiful smile." Alex lightly poked her cousin in the ribs, trying to make her laugh. "And incredible blue eyes...so tall and muscular...and a very nice, tight b..."

"Alex!" Nicole laughed. "You're incorrigible, you know that?"

"Yeah, that's why you like me." Alex laughed, glad to see her friend in a less confused mood.

Chapter 2

Six o'clock came and found Nicole sitting on the same bench where she had met Kris earlier. Taking a deep breath to calm her nervousness, she brushed her fingers through her long hair for the third time and picked at nonexistent lint on her pale green tank top. She stood up and paced.

What if she doesn't show up? Did she really mean that she would meet me here? She shook her head to get rid of those doubts and let out a nervous laugh. "I can't believe I'm doing this." Looking down at her watch, she saw that it was twenty minutes after six. "Don't think she'll show up," she told herself. *What would she be doing with a girl like me? She probably found somebody more interesting to be with.* The sound of a motor coming closer made Nicole turn around.

A beautiful motorcycle approached slowly. The rider was dressed in faded blue jeans covered with black leather chaps, black boots, and a zipped up leather jacket. Dark sunglasses hid part of the face, and the black and gold helmet framed the rest of the head. Kris stopped in front of Nicole and her easy smile made the blonde relax.

"Sorry I'm late, I got lost," Kris said loudly over the sound of the Harley's motor before shutting it down and then taking her sunglasses off. "Thanks for waiting for me."

"I'm just glad you made it." Nicole smiled shyly at the

leather-clad woman.

Kris raised an eyebrow, a grin appearing on her lips. "Thought I wouldn't show up, didn't you?" Seeing the blush covering the young blonde's face, Kris knew she had hit the bull's-eyes.

"Well, I...hmm, I...humph!" Nicole mumbled, then looked down at her hands, trying to find a good comeback. She heard a hearty laugh and was sure that the tall woman was laughing at her. She lifted her eyes to give an angry retort, but only saw good humor in the blue eyes and an easy smile showing perfect white teeth.

"Let's go for that beer, shall we?" Kris suggested as she put her sunglasses on, not getting off the motorcycle. She waited for another couple of seconds, but saw that the woman wasn't moving. "Are you coming?" she asked and offered her left hand as support.

Nicole hesitated for a moment, not knowing exactly how to approach this new mode of transportation. "I've never been on a motorcycle before."

"It's just like riding a horse..." she began, but seeing that this didn't help, added, "You've never been on a horse either." This was said more as a statement than a question. "Okay, there's a first time for everything, right?" Kris gave the extra helmet to Nicole. "First, put this on," she instructed, making sure Nicole tied it securely under her chin. Then Kris clasped Nicole's hand to help her onto the bike. "Just swing your right leg over the bike and sit close to me. Then, hold on."

Nicole followed Kris instructions and found herself fumbling with her hands, not exactly sure where to place them. Kris reached back, took both hands and wrapped them around her waist. The gesture surprised Nicole, but she soon found the position very comfortable and pleasant. The motorcycle rumbled to life, sending deep vibrations through the young woman's body. "Where to?" she heard the stuntwoman yell back. She pointed to the left, and Kris nodded. She grasped the muscular body harder as the motorcycle sped along.

The death grip around her waist made Kris smile. Not wanting to scare the poor girl half to death, she decided to take it easy. They quickly made their way to the bistro, guided by Nicole's accurate hand signals and finally parked in front of the terrace.

Nicole beamed at the older woman as they got off the motorcycle and took their helmets off. "That was so much fun," she said. "I never thought riding a bike was so exciting." A silent nod was her only answer. Nicole walked into the establishment first and looked around the room for an available table. A strong arm guided her towards a table near the open window that had a clear view of the Harley. It was only seven o'clock, so the place wasn't crowded yet.

Kris put both helmets on a vacant chair at their table then slipped out of her leather jacket and, out of habit, looked around the room before sitting down.

In fascination, Nicole watched the woman across from her. Without the blue uniform shirt Kris had worn earlier, her broad shoulders and muscular arms under the tight, white T-shirt were even more impressive. She already knew what Kris' waist felt like because her hands had accidentally slipped under the leather jacket when trying to get securely settled on the motorcycle. She blushed at the memory of feeling the warmth of Kris' body under her touch.

"Will you be standing all evening?" Kris asked, amused. Obviously, this girl was going to go through a lot of firsts that evening.

While she pulled her chair out and sat down, Nicole looked around the room with big, curious eyes. Sensing that she was being watched, she shyly smiled as she looked into incredible blue eyes. "You must think I'm such a twit," she murmured.

A slight frown crossed Kris' features. "A twit?" she asked, not understanding the term.

"It means stupid or an idiot," Nicole explained, playing with a napkin. "Here you are, visiting from another country, doing an exciting job, riding a motorcycle, and I don't even know how to sit on one."

Kris chuckled, shaking her head a little bit. "I don't think you're a twit. You never had a chance to ride one before, right?" Nick shook her head silently. "So, now you can say that you've done it, and you'll know what to do next time."

Nicole started to feel better. Not only was this woman not making fun of her inexperience, but she was offering her encouraging words. She smiled brightly at the Austrian. "I never thanked you for helping me out this afternoon. So...thanks."

"It was my pleasure." Kris nodded and noticed a waiter approaching their table. "What will you have?"

"It's my treat," she offered and quickly added, as Kris was about to protest, "Just to say that I appreciate what you did. So, what will it be?"

"I'll take a Guinness," Kris said and listened while Nicole spoke in French to the waiter. She took the opportunity to get a good look at her companion and she saw that she was in fact a very beautiful young woman.

Her long, blonde hair was tied back in a ponytail, making her look even younger than her eighteen years. Nicole's age was the first thing Kristina had asked about after parting company with her earlier. The wardrobe mistress had sworn that the young McGrail was in fact of legal age. The last thing Kris wanted was to be accused of being with an underage kid. She had seen this happen to too many people, and she didn't want to get caught up in that kind of trouble.

But what Kris had in mind for the evening and maybe the night quickly lost its appeal. She had been looking for somebody to share her bed but found that what Nicole offered her was much better than a night of sex with yet another nameless face. This young woman helped her relax. She found her presence calming in ways that she thought she could never feel again. Nicole looked back at her and smiled, her emerald eyes shining with happiness. Kris was not prepared for her reaction to this simple gesture. She usually knew what the other wanted. Usually, it was her money or her body. But what came out of this young woman was pure friendship. Her breath caught as Nicole gently patted her hand and looked like she was waiting for an answer.

"I'm sorry, what did you say?" Kris blushed at being caught staring at the young blonde.

"I asked if you are staying in Montreal for a long time?"

Nicole repeated and leaned back slightly as the beer, a can of Coke, and an empty glass were put on the table. She paid the waiter and turned her attention back to the woman.

"I'm here for three months, then I'm going back to Austria."

"But there's not three months of stunt work to do on the film," Nicole stated before taking a sip of her soft drink.

"You're right." Kris nodded, taking her beer and drinking a good portion of the cold brew. "I'll also be teaching at the Canadian Stunt School not too far away from here." She chuckled as Nicole closed her mouth, her next question answered.

If I didn't know better, I'd think that she's teasing me, Nicole told herself. "Are you going to visit outside Quebec?"

Kris took another sip of beer. "Nope."

"You mentioned riding horses. Do you have one?" Nicole couldn't help but think that she sounded like a police officer interrogating an unwilling witness. The woman wasn't much of a talker that was for sure. The word "loner" came floating back in her mind, one of the terms Alex had used in describing Kris. *But she didn't seem to be antisocial,* Nicole thought, *she's sitting here with me, right?*

"A few." She answered but immediately felt guilty as the young woman's shoulders slumped. Nicole was doing her best to start a conversation and all she got in return were a few short responses. Hardly what she would call "holding up her half of the conversation." She just wasn't used to idle chitchat. She usually went in, did her job, and got out.

Meeting people was usually all the same to Kris. Talking business or doing an interview, asking or answering questions the most direct way as possible.

But this girl wasn't like the others. She didn't ask the standard questions Kris was used to answering. There was no mention of the famous people she had met and worked with, nothing about her celebrity status back in Europe, and especially nothing about the large fortune and estate that belonged to her.

Why did I think that spending some time with her was going to be fun? Nicole thought sadly as she stared with an unnatural interest at the glass she held. All Nick wanted was to talk to her but she didn't even seem interested in doing that. *Maybe I should just get up and leave. I thanked her for helping me and paid for her beer. I shouldn't embarrass myself even more. I'm obviously not somebody she's interested in talking to.*

Watching Nicole play with her glass with downcast eyes, Kris mentally berated herself. This young woman didn't deserve the cool facade she usually reserved for people she didn't know. *But why is this girl any different? I hardly know her.* She made an effort to think of something to ask the young blonde. "What about you?"

Nicole's head snapped up when she realized that the older woman had spoken to her. "What?"

"Have you been working on the set for a long time?" Kris asked, fascinated by the way Nicole's facial expressions conveyed various emotions. She seemed on the verge of tears, and then, with one simple question, her face lit up with an exuberant smile. The emotions playing on Nicole's face seemed so honest and open. Kris was actually touched for being responsible for the beautiful smile that now graced the young woman's lips.

"Oh! No, I haven't," she confessed and straightened in her chair. "The only reason I'm allowed to work here is because of my uncle," she stated, unconsciously playing with her straw. "He's the second unit director. I would love to work behind the camera one day. Uncle Robert said that he would teach me all that I needed to know. It's so cool. I love doing that. I always..." Nicole stopped as she realized that she was babbling, but the easy smile on the dark-haired woman's face made her relax. "I'm sorry. I talk too much sometimes."

For some strange reason, Kris didn't mind listening to the young woman. It was so refreshing to hear real thoughts and plans for the future. She was so sick and tired of the artificial show business crap she heard all the time. Somehow, she knew Nicole spoke from her heart, and Kris found it endearing.

"You seem to like it a lot," Kris said. "Will you be going to camera school to learn more?" Kris didn't miss the slight change of humor on Nicole's face before it was quickly replaced by a small smile.

"I'm afraid not. My father only allows me to work on the set because I'm helping his brother, and Robert promised him to keep me near." She chuckled at the thought of where she was now. "Robert's okay. He trusts me more than my own father does," she mumbled and was relieved when Kris didn't push the subject.

"You mentioned before that this place was a Francophone bistro," Kris stated, looking around. "What do you mean by that?"

"Ah. Well, even though most of the Canadians speak English, French is the language we mostly use in Quebec, and its been this way for hundreds of years," Nicole explained.

Listening to the group of people seated next to their table, Kris noticed their accents for the first time. "It sounds different from the French from France."

"It's very different," Nicole insisted and jumped into the history of the Province of Quebec. A flash crossed her mind as she looked at her watch. "Oh my God, I'm going to be late." Nicole got up from her chair.

Seeing the look of pure panic on her companion's face, Kris gently touched her arm. "Late for what? It's only nine-thirty." She frowned at the look Nicole gave her. She looked like a deer frozen by a car's headlights.

"I have to be home by..." *What are you going to say? That your daddy won't allow you to play outside passed ten?* She shook her head. "I have to go. I'm sorry. I'm already late." Nicole made her way towards the door.

"Hey...hang on." Kris took the helmets and her leather jacket and followed her outside the bistro. She reached for the young woman's arm and stopped her. "I'll drive you, come on." *There is something going on here,* Kris thought. *Eighteen years old and she has to be home before ten? Besides, she looks too damn scared for it to be just a house rule.* Nicole hesitated. "I'll drop you off wherever you want." Kris smiled, trying to calm the girl. "It doesn't have to be at your door step if you don't want."

Nicole looked up into the blue eyes that were filled with understanding. *Does Kris know? How could she know?* Taking a deep breath, she nodded. "I'd appreciate that." She took the helmet that Kris held out for her.

Looking at the green tank top that Nicole wore, the Austrian offered her leather jacket and held it for the smaller woman to slip into. "It's going to be cold riding. You'll be more comfortable wearing this."

Smiling her thanks, Nicole slipped into the oversized jacket, breathing in the smell of leather and Kris' perfume. She waited until the dark haired woman sat down on the motorcycle before she climbed aboard. Both secured their helmets and before Kris had a chance to start the engine, Nicole tapped her on the arm and waited until the stuntwoman turned and looked at her. "Thanks," she said softly. A beautiful smile answered her, making Nicole's heart skip a beat. Wordlessly, they made their way to her home.

When they were near the house, Nicole motioned for Kris to stop. She stole a look at the driveway and noticed that her father's car wasn't there. Letting a relieved sigh escape her lips, she indicated the right house and let Kris drop her off at the end of the driveway. Once stopped, the older woman shut the motor off.

"Thank you. That was very nice of you." Nicole fumbled with the chinstrap, took the helmet off, and handed it back. Before she took the leather jacket off, she breathed in a lungful of Kris' scent, trying to burn it into memory. *I'm acting like a real groupie,* Nicole chastised herself before handing it back to Kris.

"Are you gonna be okay?" the stuntwoman asked as she slipped into her jacket. Something was going on, and Kris was surprised by the urge to find out what and help the young woman.

Nodding, Nicole smiled and turned towards the house. She took a few steps then stopped and looked back at Kris. "I'll see you tomorrow?" she asked with hope in her voice.

"I have a stunt to perform, but I'll be on the set around lunch time." Kris smiled as a big grin spread on Nicole's face. "See you then." She watched as the girl made her way to the house, a light bounce in her walk. She waited until Nicole waved goodbye and got into the house before she started up the engine and rode back to her hotel.

Chapter 3

The stunt Kris performed in the morning was fairly easy but took a long time to rehearse. It consisted of a fight between gang members with the police breaking things up. Once again dressed as a police officer, Kris and a couple of other stuntmen threw some punches, got thrown around a few times, and then she crashed through a glass window. Aside from a few bumps and scrapes, everything went as planned.

Kris sat beside the movie's director, Robert McGrail, working on her second bottle of water. She looked over the plan for a more complicated stunt that was scheduled for the following week, trying to figure out the best and safest way to perform it.

Kris frowned and traced the notes with her finger. She shook her head slightly and mumbled something in German under her breath.

"Did you find something wrong?" he asked.

Kristina handed the plan back to him and waited for him to take it. He never did. "A couple of things," she replied and lifted an eyebrow at the man, trying to figure out what he wanted.

"Would you perform the stunt the way it's written?" Robert asked, knowing her answer already.

"Exactly as is? No, I wouldn't. Too many errors." Kris wasn't the type to refuse to perform, unlike certain people. But when there was a risk of somebody getting hurt by poor planning, she wasn't afraid to speak up. "Why are you asking me this?"

Direct and to the point...I like that. Robert smiled. It was no secret that the stunt people were having problems trusting their current stunt coordinator. Seeing him coming on the set drunk and unprepared didn't muster trust from the stunt crew whom he was supposed to keep relatively safe and unharmed. "You are well aware of the trouble we've been having with our current SC. It's no secret. I'd like you to re-work the stunt."

"Why me?" Kris asked. "Why not one of the other stuntmen?"

"I heard them talk, Kristina. They trust you. Sebastien and Paul worked with you before, right?" He tilted his head, indicated the stuntmen sitting beside the tree having lunch. "Some of them actually volunteered you for the job of stunt coordinator. You interested?" he asked with a grin.

Whoa. What's going on here? Kris silently thought. More stuntmen, watching her expectantly, gathered near the tree. So much work needed to be done in taking up the job. She had to study the planned stunts, make the adjustments if necessary, study the expertise of each stuntmen, and plan for rehearsals. *Where's Franz when I need him?* Kris wished for her brother's presence. He was the Von Deering's stunt coordinator, especially for Kris. She sure could use his guidance right at that moment. "Can I think about this?" she asked the movie director.

She's going to say yes. I know it. "Don't make me wait too long," was all he said. At least she didn't say "no" outright. "So, how was last evening?" Robert asked.

Kris looked up in surprise at the director. "It was nice...why?"

"Well, Nick couldn't stop talking about it all morning." He chuckled at Kris reaction.

She told him? Kris thought. Obviously, Nicole could talk to her uncle.

"It's been a long time since I've seen Nick smile this much," Robert said a bit sadly. "Maybe if things were different for her at home, we'd see her smile a lot more." He got up and reached for a thick file and handed it to Kris. "Take a look at what's ahead. I hope you'll agree to what I proposed." Without waiting for her answer, he walked away.

Kris stared speechless at the director's retreating back. She had guessed that something was wrong between Nicole and her father; she just didn't expect Robert's little slip to confirm her suspicions. Her temper rose at the thought of someone harming the young woman, and she became confused by the strong feeling that suddenly took over, especially wanting to protect her and keep her safe. *Where did that come from?* Kris surprised herself by the thought. Sure, Nicole was nice, funny, and had a very charming smile, and the fact that she was a beautiful young woman didn't hurt either. She smiled as she remembered Nicole's emerald eyes dancing with delight as she looked at her.

With a sigh, Kris stood up and walked away from the hectic activities going on around the set and away from the other technicians. Passing by a mobile canteen, she made a brief stop to buy a can of Coke and a chocolate bar to snack on for lunch and then she headed towards a large old elm tree to clear her head. After getting comfortable, she hauled out the stunt plans and began reviewing them.

Not too far away, Nicole chatted with Alex as they swerved and weaved their way among the crew. Everybody had stopped their activities for the lunch period and both women were looking for a place to sit down and eat. Alex could see that Nicole was searching for something or someone. She didn't miss the sudden smile light up her cousin's face. As she swiveled her body around to look in the direction that Nicole was staring in, she noticed the tall, dark-haired stuntwoman sitting by herself. *Interesting.* Alex smiled to herself as she followed Nicole, who was moving towards Kris.

"Hi," Nicole said cheerily as she flopped down beside the woman. She had been looking forward to talking to her again. Since she got out of bed that morning, all she could think about was the time they had spent together the evening before. Aside from her uncle and Alex, Kristina had been the only one to spend time with her. *Maybe there was a chance of them becoming friends,* she thought hopefully.

Kris looked up from the paper she was studying and smiled

at Nicole. "Hi, yourself. How are you today?" A warm feeling coursed through her body when she looked at the young woman. It seemed like such a long time ago since Kris had greeted anyone, other than her family, this way.

"I'm doing great," Nicole replied and recited a recap of her morning.

Alex sat down on the grass in front of both women, watching the scene with interest. She had never seen Nicole so relaxed or smile so much, not even with her. Kristina wasn't what Alex had expected at all; especially if one went by the rumors they heard about her. The woman in front of her was smiling, almost social, and seemed very interested in what Nicole had to say. So very unlike the cold and distant woman people made her out to be. At least, she wasn't where Nicole was concerned.

"Anyway, so that's basically my morning so far," Nicole finished and cast a glance at Alex. "Oh! Kris, I'd like to introduce you to my cousin. Alex, this is Kristina," she said as the women shook hands. She opened her lunch bag to take out her sandwich and noticed the half-eaten chocolate bar in Kris' hand.

"Nice to meet you, Alex," Kris said politely with a slight smile. She lifted her chocolate bar to take another bite but stopped midway when she noticed Nicole staring at her. "What?"

"Is that your lunch?" she asked and frowned as Kris nodded. She reached into the brown bag, pulled out half of her sandwich and handed it over to the dark-haired woman. "This is much better. I hope you like chicken salad."

"But..." Kris started to protest.

"No buts. Eat," Nicole ordered and grinned at the look of disbelief on Kris' face. Then a small tug at the corner of the Austrian's lips turned into a smile as she nodded her thanks and bit into the tasty sandwich. Happy that Kris had accepted her offer, Nicole took the other half and ate it hungrily, following her new friend's lead.

Unknown to both women, Alex stole glances at them every chance she could. She could barely hide her amazement at how at ease both of them seemed to be together, even though they had known each other for only twenty-four hours. Alex chuckled lightly as Kristina let a hearty laugh escape at a joke Nicole had just told. She also caught the twinkle in the stuntwoman's eyes as she looked at her cousin and smiled. Alex suddenly felt she was witnessing the start of something beautiful and she didn't want to intrude. She got up to leave and smiled at Nicole and Kris as they turned to her with questioning looks.

"Well, it was nice meeting you, Kristina," Alex said as she shook her hand again. "I have to be on my way. Sophie's waiting for me." She grinned at Nicole. "You remember what happened last time I was late meeting her?"

The blonde nodded. "What a scene that was. She really has you wrapped around her little finger, doesn't she?" Nicole giggled, as a slight blush crawled over her cousin's face.

"Just wait until you fall in love, you'll find out how it is." Alex grinned as she pointedly looked at both Nicole and Kris. "Well, have fun, you two." She winked at her friend and walked away.

Kristina watched the brunette leave and turned to Nicole. "You two seem very close," she said before finishing her can of Coke.

"We grew up together. She's like a sister to me. We talk to each other about everything. I always know what Alex is doing and where she's going and vice versa." Nicole smiled.

"She doesn't talk much," Kris stated.

"Knowing Alex, she was probably studying you like a hawk." She laughed as she took an apple out of her bag and bit into it.

"Why would she do that?" Kris asked with a lifted eyebrow. "She doesn't trust me with you?" She grinned.

"Oh, that's not it. She just can't keep her eyes off a gorgeous woman when she sees one." As soon as it was out, Nicole realized what she had just said, causing her to blush furiously. "I meant that she...I mean, that you...I just...oh boy," she sighed.

Another booming laugh from Kristina made Nicole lift her head and look into pale blue eyes.

"Well, you are beautiful," Nicole whispered, relieved that she had not embarrassed the stuntwoman.

"Thank you." Kris smiled at the blonde. "You're not too bad yourself." She watched in amusement as the blush already on

Nicole's face got even deeper in color. Not wanting to make the younger woman uncomfortable, she handed Nicole the paper she had been looking at before the cousins showed up. "Do you have any idea where these houses are located?"

Thankful for the change of subject, Nicole took a look at the paper. According to the addresses, they were spread across the island of Montreal. "Are you looking to buy a house?" she asked, as Kris stretched out on her side, her head comfortably resting in her hand.

"No, I just want to rent for the time I'm here," Kris explained as she pulled at a blade of grass and played with it. "Are there any areas you would recommend?"

Nicole looked at the paper again and scanned the addresses. "This area is nice." She indicated one number then tapped a second one with her finger. "Stay away from there." She suddenly thought of a house that would probably please Kris but she had no idea how much she wanted to spend. "There's a nice place two blocks away from where I live. It's right on the lake with a beautiful view, but I think it may be very expensive to rent."

"I'd like to see it," Kris said, looking up into green eyes. "Maybe we could go and visit it?" she asked hopefully. The bright smile on Nicole's face at the suggestion warmed Kris all over.

"I'd love to." The blonde woman beamed. "How about tomorrow? I can't today, I..." She let the sentence trail.

"We'll go tomorrow then," Kris said softly, as Nicole's smile resurfaced.

"Thanks." Noticing that the activity on the set had started up, Nicole took a deep breath and reluctantly stood up. "Gotta go back to work." She looked back at Kris. "See you later."

"Have a good day, Nick. Thanks for the sandwich." She smiled back.

"My pleasure." Nicole waved and headed for the director's trailer.

Kris watched the young woman leave and a pang of loneliness grabbed hold of her. She enjoyed the time spent with Nicole. She was honest and very friendly. Maybe it was time for Kris put her loner days aside and make the effort to act like a friend. Maybe taking a look at the house for rent not too far away from Nicole wasn't such a bad idea.

Having no other stunts to do for the day, Kris sat up and leaned her back against the tree. She studied the future stunts that were planned for the movie, knowing she still had to let Robert know if she accepted the stunt coordinator job or not.

****

Nicole spent most of the day following her uncle around while she studied his way of working. While things on the set weren't too busy he supplied her with all kinds of helpful information that she eagerly soaked up. She hoped that she could learn a lot more and would be able to work full time as part of the technical crew someday. What she really wanted to do was work behind the camera. The time she usually spent at her Uncle Robert's house was filled with improvised lessons on how to handle the camera, advanced camera techniques, and tricks of the trade.

She kept thinking about her uncle's offer to go live with his family and continue her studies in school rather than being content with just taking notes that her uncle supplied. He had already talked to a few friends of his whom were more than willing to teach the young woman. All Robert needed was for her to make the decision and take him up on his offer. Nicole could still hear the last conversation on the subject she had with her uncle.

"You can't continue to live this way, Nick. You're eighteen years old. How long are you going to let your father control you this way?" Robert asked, wiping a tear off his niece's cheek.

"But he's my father. He wants what's best for me," Nicole replied, not believing her own words.

"By insulting you and telling you that you're worthless? That's not what loving fathers do." He gently lifted her chin to look into her watery eyes. "Until you can find your own place, you're more than welcome to come and stay with us."

The idea was so tempting. She would no longer have to be

afraid of her father and finally be free to do what *she* wanted to do.

Nicole shook her head. She knew that she had to leave someday, she just needed to gather all of her courage to do it. She also knew that when she finally made the decision to leave home, there would probably be an awful fight with her father. How she envied her cousin, Alex, for having such a loving family. She also envied Kris for her independence and getting to see the world at such a young age. She smiled as a picture of the dark-haired stuntwoman entered her mind's eye. Kristina had been so nice to her. *Sure, she doesn't talk all that much, but she's a great listener.* Even if a lot of what she talked about probably wasn't of much interest to Kris, she still sat there and listened to her with a knowing smile or a comforting look.

The phone rang, bringing Nicole back to the present, and she scrambled to answer it before her father did. He was in a bad mood...again. Being a stockbroker wasn't one of the easiest of jobs going. It involved tremendous amounts of pressure and lots of stress. She only wished that he would leave his problems at work and not bring them home with him and take them out on her.

She grabbed the phone on the second ring. "Hello?"

"Hey, girl. How was your lunch date?" Alex teased.

"It wasn't a date, Alex." Nicole smiled into the phone. *But it sure felt like one.* She smiled inwardly. "We just had lunch together."

"She looks like she's a very nice person. You like her?" Alex asked bluntly, already suspecting what the answer would be.

"I do. We have so much fun just talking with one another. Today, we looked at a number of possible houses to rent. We'll be going out tomorrow to look at them." Just the thought of spending more time with Kris made her happy and giddy inside.

"You mean the two of you will be renting a house together?" Alex asked, certain that she had misunderstood what Nicole had said. Either that or she had definitely missed a very important detail.

"No, silly," Nicole quickly corrected, even though the

thought did seem very interesting. *Whoa. Where did that thought sneak in from?* "It's for Kris. We're just..." She stopped as a movement near her caught her attention. She quickly glanced over and saw her father standing in the doorway. "I have to go," she said and rapidly hung up the receiver.

The tall man, wearing a stern and tired look, had his arms crossed over his chest.

Nicole flashed her father a smile and tried to inconspicuously move around him towards the only way out, but he didn't budge.

"Who was that on the phone, Nicole?" Her father's voice thundered in a dangerous tone.

Nicole knew her father had had an awful day. One of his major stock accounts had taken a nosedive on the market, putting him in a nasty mood. That coupled with the fact that he had barely slept in the last two days didn't help matters. "No...no one, daddy...I was..."

"Don't lie to me, you little tramp," her father yelled, his neck veins appearing as he slapped his daughter on the back of her head with enough force to throw her into the wall. "You were on the phone with some bastard weren't you? WEREN'T YOU?"

"N—no, Daddy." She bit her lip trying not to panic but crouched a little in fear of her father's next attack. "I was on the phone with Alex, really. I wouldn't lie to you."

He grabbed her by the shoulders with his strong hands and shook her. "You were talking to Alex? Didn't I tell you to stay away from that dyke? She's nothing but trouble. Who's this boy you were talking about? Who's Chris?" His deep voice thundered through her heart as his massive hands shook her vigorously.

"It's not a boy, Daddy, Kris is a woman. She's one of the stunt people working on Uncle Robert's movie," she explained, still caught in her father's painful grip.

McGrail's eyes narrowed to tiny slits as his deranged mind processed the information. An unnatural rage built up inside of him. His grip on his daughter's shoulders increased, shooting more pain through her. "You're moving in with her? You said you were looking for houses to rent."

"Please, Daddy, let go...you're hurting me," she whispered

pitifully, her eyes mirroring the increased pain in her body.

"No daughter of mine will be known as one of those dykes," he hissed as spit hit her in the face.

She looked back at him, confusion dancing through her mind. "What? I don't understand..."

"You know damn well what I'm talking about, you little slut. I will not allow you to become some freak like your cousin."

"But, Daddy, we're just friends. Nothing is..."

"I forbid it! You will do as I say."

McGrail drew his hand out aimed to strike across her face. She managed to twist her body at the last minute so that the powerful blow struck her on her shoulder blades rather than her face. Still, the force of it knocked her into the brick wall with a thump. She cried out as the pain of the impact shot through her shoulder, causing tears to fall down her cheeks. "Daddy, please," she begged.

He would hear none of it. He picked her up by her injured shoulder, causing another painful cry to escape Nicole's lips, and held her firmly, looking her in the eyes. "You do as I say. Stay away from her and everything will be fine," he spat out, his breathing labored.

Nicole didn't even hear his words through her pain before she was thrown down onto the hardwood floor, her knee hitting the side of the coffee table. Her trembling body crumpled to the floor, and she wrapped her arm around her injured leg and rocked back and forth.

McGrail stared down at his daughter, emotionless. "I do this for your own good, Nikki. You'll thank me later on." With that, he turned and left his daughter alone on the floor, crying softly and in pain.

Chapter
4

The next day at noon, anyone looking for Kristina would have found her sitting in the same spot under the elm tree where Nicole had found her the previous day at lunch. She lazily stretched her long frame out as she rubbed her tired eyes from all the reading she had to do after agreeing to take on the job as the new stunt coordinator. Robert McGrail had agreed to let her work her own way as long as the stunts were spectacular and within budget. She liked the freedom he offered her in this new position. She felt that this was going to be a good experience and that her working relationship with Robert wouldn't be all that stressful as long as she did her job.

Kris looked around for the fourth time trying to spot Nicole. She looked at her watch and noticed that it was past lunchtime. They had planned to eat and then go visit a few houses for rent. Thinking that maybe Nicole had forgotten about it, she decided to take a walk around the grounds to try and find her. She got up from her comfy spot under the tree, grabbed her large binder with all the stunt plans and went in search of her new friend.

Kristina checked most of the grounds and still Nicole was nowhere in sight. Another gopher passed by and she stopped him. "Do you know Nicole McGrail?"

"Yeah, I do."

"Have you seen her today?" she asked. He shook his head

and continued on his way. Frowning at this latest information, Kris headed off to find Robert and caught sight of Alex sitting alone, eating her lunch. As she got closer, she noticed the forlorn look on the brunette's face.

"Hey, Alex," Kris greeted the young gopher. "Have you seen Nicole lately?" she asked in a neutral voice.

Alex looked up and smiled briefly. "Not lately, no," she replied and looked back down, concentrating on her sandwich.

Finding Alex's reaction intriguing, Kris said, "We were supposed to meet at noon. Do you know where she was assigned to work today?"

"I'm sorry, I don't know." Alex kept playing with her food, unable to look into Kris' suspicious eyes.

"All right. Something's up. What is it, Alex?" she asked the woman who looked up.

"What makes you think that something's wrong?" Alex asked defensively.

Kris crouched in front of the young gopher. "You barely answer my questions, you can't look me in the eyes, and you have no idea where she is. Nicole told me you guys always know where the other is."

Alex took a deep breath and started to say something but changed her mind. Her shoulders slumped slightly, and she turned her attention back to her half eaten sandwich.

"What's wrong, Alex?" Kris asked softly. "Is Nicole okay?"

Alex debated with herself about whether she should answer or not, then let a defeated sigh escape. "She wants to be alone for a while, Kris. She's gonna be okay, she just needs time." She looked up, afraid that she had said too much.

"Is somebody bothering her?" Kris asked as her temper rose at the possibility. "Where is she, Alex? Maybe I can help."

"And what are you going to do?" she asked with anger in her voice. "Hit the bastard? Don't you think we didn't think of doing that already?" *Oh God. Forgive me, Nick,* Alex thought as she realized what she had just said. The last thing Nicole wanted was for people to know the stuff that went on behind closed doors in her home. "There's nothing we can do if she doesn't want to help herself."

"Who is it, Alex?" The deep timbre of Kris' voice rumbled through the air and the muscles in her jaw danced under the bronze skin.

Alex briefly hesitated between spilling it all and keeping the information away from the stuntwoman who looked at her with narrowed eyes. Just the thought of the bastard being pummeled by the muscular woman was enough to make up Alex's mind. "It's her father," she said, just above a whisper.

Kris got up and scanned the area once more in hope of seeing Nicole. She spotted Robert not too far away and looked down at Alex who hadn't taken her eyes off the dark-haired woman. "Thank you, Alex." She smiled briefly. "I know there's something we can do."

"I hope so," Alex said. "She's working for my father today."

Kris briskly strode over to the director. What kind of trouble was Nicole's father giving her? All Kris had heard was that he was a very strict man. She approached the director and waited until the technician he was talking to left. "Where's Nicole?" she asked Robert in a tone that bore no argument.

He hesitated briefly then turned his attention to the papers he held. "I gave her some books to study. She wasn't feeling too well today."

"Robert, I know about her father." Kris knew she was walking a thin line. Not only didn't she know exactly what had happened, he could tell her to mind her own damn business. "I just want to talk to her. Maybe there's something I can do."

He relaxed a little, seeing in Kris' eyes an honest wish to help. He didn't know why but he had a strong feeling that he could talk to her. That she really cared about Nicole. "You know, it would be a hell of a lot easier if Nicole wasn't of legal age," he sighed, scratching his jaw. "We could just ask the court to take her out of there. But she's an adult now, it has to be her decision." He shook his head, frustration evident on his face. "I only wish I had known what was going on a long time ago."

So many images went through Kris' head. She wanted to press Robert for more information but knew that it was up to Nicole to tell the whole story when she felt like it. She only hoped that the young woman would come to trust her enough to confide in her one day. "Where is she, Robert?" she asked. "I promise that if she asks me to leave her alone, I will."

"Maybe you'll have more luck getting her out of my trailer."

The stuntwoman nodded her thanks and jogged to the movie director's trailer. She slowed down as she approached and took a deep breath before knocking lightly on the door. "Come in," came Nicole's soft invitation. She slowly opened the door and stepped inside, not knowing what to expect.

The blonde sat behind a wooden desk with many opened books scattered in front of her. She looked so tired and worn out.

"Hi." Kris smiled, trying to look cheerful, but the sight of an exhausted Nicole tore at her heart.

Seeing Kris however did wonders for Nicole's mood. She smiled at the stuntwoman and put her pen down beside her note pad. "Hi. Are you looking for Robert?"

"No. Actually, I was looking for you," Kris said, holding herself back so she wouldn't just blurt out her questions. *If she wants to talk, she'll do it in her own time.* "Did you eat yet?" she asked as she sat down on a chair beside Nicole.

A surprised look crossed Nicole's face as she noticed the hour for the first time. "Oh my God, I'm so sorry. I didn't think it was so late." She moved to get up but hit her injured knee on the edge of the desk, causing her to suck in a sharp intake of air. She hid the wince as best as she could before reaching for her knee and discreetly rubbing away the pain.

The motion hadn't gone unnoticed by Kris, who grasped Nicole's shoulder, squeezing gently. "Are you okay?" she asked with genuine concern.

Nicole winced in pain, not bothering to hide it this time. Her hand reflexively shot up to her injured shoulder.

"I'm sorry," Kris exclaimed as she knelt by Nicole's side. "What happened?" She wanted so much to take Nicole in her arms and let her know that she wasn't alone, that she was there to help her through whatever was happening. But she knew it was all up to the young woman to ask for that help. Kris' hands were tied until then.

"I'm okay," Nicole lied as she took a deep breath to ease the pain a little. "I'm just a klutz that's all."

Kris looked at the young blonde and frowned. "What do you mean?"

"I fell down the stairs yesterday and hurt my shoulder," Nicole told her, using the line she had used many times before.

Disappointment spread through Kris at the obvious lie. *What did you expect?* Kris thought to herself. *That she would tell you the whole story and let you help? She barely knows you.* "Did you have a doctor check it out?"

Nicole shook her head and smiled more for Kris benefit than anything. "It's only bruised." Looking into the intense blue eyes, she could see that Kris had seen past her lie. She sensed that the dark-haired woman wanted to say something more, and she feared that Kris would pressure her into admitting what really happened. Nicole didn't want to burden the Austrian with her problems. Maybe one day she'd feel comfortable enough to speak to Kris about it. Tension filled the air as the stuntwoman kept silent and Nicole became a little nervous. Kris then smiled, breaking the tension, making Nicole relax a bit.

Respecting her choice of not wanting to talk about it, Kris changed subjects. "I'm hungry," she stated. Nicole breathed a soft sigh of relief. "Would you care to join me?" Kris stood up and stepped away from the desk.

Nicole looked up and smiled. She was so thankful that Kris had let things be. Alex had pushed her until she told what had happened the night before, then it had been Robert's turn. But Kris just accepted her answer and that was it. She was bothered that she had lied to her, and she was sure that the stuntwoman knew it. *When the time is right, I'll tell her everything,* Nicole silently promised.

"I'd love to. I'm starving," Nicole replied as she got up, being careful not to hit her injured knee again.

They left the director's trailer and were quickly joined by a smiling Robert. "Well, I see you've succeeded in getting Nick out for some fresh air." He beamed at both women.

"We're going out to lunch. We'll be back in an hour," Nicole told her uncle, wondering why he was smiling.

"Before I forget," Kris said as they headed for the parking lot, "I'll be looking at a few houses to rent for the time I'm here.

You can reach me on my cell phone, if you need to contact me."

"Why don't I assign Nicole to you as guide for when you drive around?" Robert said, seeing the perfect way to have his niece relax and use the time to calm down a bit. "I wouldn't want my new stunt coordinator to get lost in Montreal."

Kris stopped walking at Robert's suggestion. *Subtle,* she thought with a smile. "If Nicole doesn't mind..." She trailed off, waiting for the young woman's reaction and was saw pleased with what she saw.

If not for her injured knee and shoulder, Nicole would have jumped into her uncle's arms. "I'd love to."

"Go on," Robert laughed at the excitement on his niece's face. "Good luck with your house search."

"Thanks." Kris nodded at the second unit director. "Is there a car I can borrow?" she asked quietly. "Long rides on a motorcycle can be tough for the passenger."

Aware of Nicole's injuries and Kristina's interest in keeping Nicole comfortable, his respect for the Austrian stuntwoman climbed another notch. He nodded, handing Kris the keys to the company car.

"We're using your car?" Nicole asked Robert then turned to Kris. "What's wrong with the bike?"

"I thought it would be nice and comfortable," Kris explained, not giving the director time to answer. "Besides, it's a little hard to chat while riding a Harley." She smiled as she guided Nicole towards the parking lot. "Come on, let's make the most of our day."

****

Kris let Nicole make the choice of where to eat. She chose a French Canadian restaurant with the intention of introducing Kris to Quebec's traditional foods and ambiance. They knew that Robert wasn't expecting either of them back on the set until the next day, which gave them plenty of time to hang out and talk. Or rather, Nicole talked while Kris listened in rapt attention with a smile of pure contentment.

Nicole was very expressive with her hands, unconsciously

touching Kris frequently as she talked. Much to her surprise, her reaction to Nicole's constant touches was pleasant and she wanted more. Usually the dark-haired woman hated the unwanted physical contacts. But there she was, allowing Nicole to touch her freely and she was enjoying it. The gentle squeeze of Nick's hand on hers as she laughed at one of her jokes felt so right.

Nicole excused herself to go to the washroom, lightly rubbing Kris muscular shoulder as she got up. She had to take a moment to relax and get her heartbeat back under control. She knew that she was a touchy kind of person and had even been teased a lot because of it, but she hadn't expected her intense reaction when she touched Kris' hand. She just wasn't able to break contact, and more importantly, didn't want to. Nicole knew a lot of people, some were good friends, but no one, not even Alex, compared to the way she felt when she was in Kris' presence.

The blue-eyed woman made her feel like somebody, not just a little tag-along, the feeling she sometimes got when she was with others. Kris listened to her and much to her surprise, the older woman even asked questions about her dreams and plans for the future. Nicole didn't understand her strong feelings for Kris, but they weren't unpleasant, she decided with a smile before going back to their table and to the beautiful stuntwoman.

After lunch, they left in Robert's BMW and visited some of the houses for rent, the addresses of which were scrawled on a piece of paper. They were beautiful homes located in nice neighborhoods, but Kris only looked at them half-heartedly, having already made up her mind at the restaurant. Nicole had spoken of a house near where she lived, and according to the younger woman, it was a beautiful place. But the main reason she decided to take the house was simple. Kris wanted to be closer to her, just in case something else happened between the young blonde and her father.

Kris was starting to care a lot more about the young woman than she wanted to admit. She never had any close friendships because of her busy schedule. Between her stunt career and her Arabian horse breeding project, which she started only two years earlier in Innsbruck, she had very little time for much else. Now, Nicole was settling into her life, claiming the role of the closest friend she ever had.

The only reason they were still looking at the houses was because Kris didn't want to see the day end too fast. Nicole probably had to be home early, making a normal evening spent between friends somewhat difficult. They would just have to do things together during the day.

They finally arrived at the house Nicole had unknowingly talked Kris into renting. It was located on the western edge of the island of Montreal. The 150 year old house, which was of Canadian style, had been built along Lake St-Louis. The numerous trees in front offered plenty of privacy as they obscured the main part of the house from the road.

Kris drove the car up the drive where a Grand Cherokee was already parked. Nicole had called the owners from the restaurant to inform them that somebody wanted to visit the house. As soon as Kris turned the motor off, a smiling woman with shoulder length salt and pepper hair walked out of the centennial house.

"Hello. You must be Nicole and Kristina," she greeted, shaking both women's hands. "Would you like to start the tour now?"

Kris nodded and the woman led the way with Nicole following close behind. The first thing they saw was the large furnished living room with a full-length sliding door. Through the glass of the sliding doors was a breath taking view of the lake. Its calm waters reflected the silent image of the trees along the shoreline of its crystalline surface. A fish jumped toward the sky sending ripples through the water and distorting the mirror reflection for a few moments before returning to its calm perfection.

"Oh Kris, it's so beautiful," Nicole exclaimed. "Look." She reached for her hand and pulled her towards the doors. She slid them open and stepped onto the wooden deck with an amused Kris trailing behind. "What a view." Nicole wrapped her hands around the stuntwoman's arm and gave it a squeeze.

Kris chuckled at the young woman's enthusiasm and especially at the soft squeeze that she was receiving. Standing on the deck with Nicole, looking out at the wide lake with the wind gently blowing their hair, mixing the blonde with the raven locks, Kris couldn't think of a better place to be. She looked down at her companion and smiled, gently placing her hand on Nicole's. "You like this place?"

Blushing furiously, Nicole tried to pull her hand away, but the tall woman simply held on to it. "Its a beautiful place, Kris, but it must be so expensive," Nicole murmured.

Hearing the smaller woman's words, the owner described the house to them. Three bedrooms, one of them offering the same beautiful view of the lake as the living room, two bathrooms, a modern kitchen, and a large dinning room. There was also a Jacuzzi and a room that served as an office. An added section to the house had been transformed into a playroom with a pool table. There was even a two-car garage on the other side.

After hearing what it would cost the stuntwoman to rent for three months, Nicole almost choked. "I knew it would be expensive but not that much," she whispered to Kris, but the dark-haired woman just smiled and nodded to the owner.

"I'll take it," she said, looking at a speechless Nicole. "I had some money put aside, don't worry." She chuckled. "It's a beautiful place you found, Nick, thank you."

Getting over her shock, she smiled back, beaming with the knowledge that she had done something to please her new friend.

Chapter 5

The first thing Kris tackled after she moved all her belongings into the house was installing her powerful laptop computer in the spare room that she decided would serve as an excellent office. Once everything was all hooked up, she logged on and accessed the Arabian horse breeding program's computer in Innsbruck. This way, she was able to manage her business affairs even while she was overseas. Kris could keep in touch with the daily reports from the full time veterinarian working there, potential buyers, and everyday problems. She knew her staff was the best and could probably handle any problems that came up, but she took comfort in being able to keep an eye on things while abroad.

Once Kristina had checked things out with the stables and was satisfied that everything was running smoothly, she concentrated on finding a place where she could re-work the stunts for the movie. The previous stunt coordinator had done a poor job by getting cheap equipment, giving improper assignments to the numerous stunt people, and God knew what else. Because of all that, a lot of work needed to be done.

Kris looked about the room. Save for her laptop computer on the big wooden desk in a corner, there was enough room left for her to make it into a planning area.

By having her own quiet place, she could peacefully re-work all the gigs, starting with the easiest ones and working her way to the larger ones. She knew that there would be long evenings and that she'd possibly have to pull some all-nighters to get them all done on time. She was thankful for this small room instead of the trailer they gave her on the set. Kris also managed to talk Robert into doing all the physical stunts first that needed very little to no equipment like fights, falls down stairs, high falls into water, etc. His cooperation bought her a little more time to fix up the more difficult ones scheduled for late the following week.

The days passed with a semblance of a routine. Kris met with the crew at five a.m. to prepare for the coming day. They rehearsed and coordinated the fights and falls. Then Kris divided her time between re-vamping some of the stunts and coaching the less experienced stuntmen in how to improve their performances by supplying them with tricks of the trade. No matter the grueling hours and possible risks, Kris loved her job as both a stuntwoman and stunt coordinator.

For the first time in a long while, she looked forward to taking her lunch break with someone else, namely a young blonde gopher who went by the name of Nicole McGrail and continued to meet under the tree where they met for their first lunch together. Kris didn't have much chance to see her during working hours, so these times together were nice.

A couple of times, Robert assigned Nicole to Kris, to help the stunt coordinator in anyway necessary. The young gopher not only excelled at any assigned task given to her, but she also managed to lighten any atmosphere. They liked to tease each other and left the crew in stitches, especially with the practical jokes they played every once in a while.

Montreal's Old Port was the site of the day's performance. The stunt itself was a relatively easy one if everything went according to plan. A speeding car was scheduled to jump off one of the docks and into the St-Lawrence River where boats and tow trucks on the shore would pull the vehicle out of the water once filming was done. The one drawback wasn't the stunt itself, but the time at which it would be done and because it needed to be performed in the late evening, Kris knew that Nicole wouldn't be there.

Kris sat in her trailer reviewing the gag one more time. A part of coordinating stunts involved crowd control and being a Friday night, she knew that they'd be dealing with a fair amount of tourists, curious onlookers, and wandering pedestrians. She made a quick call on her cell phone to confirm they had adequate security personnel to deal with the crowd. She glanced at her watch and saw that it was nearly six o'clock, the time when Nicole usually quit work for the day.

Kris stepped out of her trailer and scanned the area, spotting Robert not too far away. She knew that where he was, Nicole usually wasn't too far away. And she was right. A balding man, talking to Robert, shifted slightly and revealed the petite form of Nicole scribbling away on a notepad.

Kris walked up to them with a grin. "Hi."

Robert smiled and nodded to the other two men as they departed.

"Kris." Nicole smiled brightly. "Taking a break?"

"Well..." A blushed crepted over Kris' cheeks and she couldn't believe that she was reacting this way. "I...just wanted to see you before you left for home," the dark-haired woman explained shyly as she lowered her eyes. "I wanted to make sure that you'll be okay...going home." She sheepishly raised her blue eyes and was greeted by a huge grin on Nicole's face.

What a surprise this will be, Nicole thought. "There's been a change of plans," she announced, delighted by the confused look on Kris' face. She looked at Robert then with a smile, returned her attention to Kris. "I've been assigned to work with you this evening."

"Really?" Kris smiled, but then thought of her father. *How much trouble will this change of plans cause for the young woman?* Kris thought with a slight frown.

Robert caught Kris' expression. He smiled at her before turning to his niece. "So, remember, Nick, I left a message on your father's answering machine about your working late. If you have any problems, let me know, okay?" The director waited until Nicole nodded before he smiled at them and walked away.

Kris turned to face her companion. "Listen, the meeting's about to start. Why don't we go there, and afterwards, I'll treat you to a nice dinner?" She almost laughed at the change of expression on the younger woman's face at the mention of food. "How about Kiomi's?"

Nicole just stared at the tall woman, not sure if she had heard right. "Kiomi's?" she asked with a touch of doubt. "But...that's such a... I'm sure we could go to a less expensive one like..."

"You like Japanese food, right?" Kris asked.

"Yes, but..."

"I heard you mention to Alex that you would love to eat there one day," the older woman stated. "Is that true?"

"Yes, it is, but..."

"Then it's settled," Kris said, crossing her arms over her chest. "Do you have any more objections?" She raised an eyebrow and watched in amusement as Nicole tried to speak, her mouth going through the motions but with little sound coming out. "Good." Kris gently guided her companion to the meeting place, chuckling to herself at the unusual sight of a speechless Nicole.

****

Dinner had come and gone too fast, much to Nicole's chagrin. It thrilled her that Kris was much more relaxed in her presence than a few days earlier. The stuntwoman was even participating in the conversation, laughing, and managing to crack a few good one liners.

Kris had opened up to her, talking about her early start as a stuntwoman, her trips to Japan where she learned to speak the language, and her horse breeding program amongst other things. But Nicole had been surprised or maybe a little disappointed that Kris hadn't mentioned anything too personal like her parents, her friends, or if she had anyone in her life right now. With a slight shake of her head, Nicole remembered the hint of jealousy that gripped her heart at the thought of someone being intimate with the dark-haired beauty.

For a fleeting moment, she imagined Kris as more than just a friend and wondered what it would feel like to be held in those long, muscular arms or even to kiss her full lips.

A light tap on the shoulder brought Nicole out of her reverie, and she blinked up into blue eyes. "Wha...Oh! Sorry."

"Daydreaming?" Kris teased. "If I go by the smile you had, it must have been a very pleasant one."

"I...hmm, yeah." A blush crawled up her neck and Nicole was thankful for the semi-darkness in the parking lot. She took a deep breath and coughed lightly, trying to get her emotions under control. "Just thinking."

"Huh uh." Kris smiled. "Listen, we're about to get ready for the stunt. There're a few things I need to check before that. You want to come with me?"

"Sure. I'd love to." Nicole nodded. "I could take notes if you need me to."

"Alright. Come on."

Walking by a table, Nicole grabbed a clipboard and pen, then ran after Kris who inspected the equipment needed for the performance.

She was amazed at the amount of energy and life that radiated from Kris as she immersed herself into her stunt preparation. Not a single detail escaped her attention, even making sure that all the bolts were secure on the ramp.

Kris fixed her headset and peered at the river. "Are all security boats ready?" the stuntwoman, turned coordinator, asked into the microphone then nodded at the reply. "Okay, get them all into position and make sure they're out of camera range." She approached the stunt driver. "Dale, you want to go over the plan once again?"

"Yeah." The driver nodded as he finished his own inspection of the car. "I was told it's pretty deep where I'll be landing."

"It is, and with the angle you'll be hitting the water, the car will sink very fast," Kris explained. "Just remember what I told you. The air tank behind the seat is big enough to give us plenty of time to pull you out. Just stay calm and everything will be fine." She grabbed the breathing apparatus and made sure that it was working properly. "Good. Let's go over the scene once again."

The sight of Kris so commanding in her work mesmerized

Nicole. She was so much the professional in every aspect of the word. She cared deeply for the welfare of her crew, and it showed. Some may think that she didn't trust her people with the safety checks, but truth was, as the coordinator, her stuntmen trusted her with their lives, and it was her job to make sure that everything was perfect.

After her conference with the stuntman, Kris walked up to the second unit director. "Everything's ready, Robert."

"Great. Let me check a few things, and I'll let you know when we're ready to start."

Kris pulled a chair over for Nicole to sit in. "You might as well be comfortable," she said as she rotated her aching shoulders and neck. "Everything is up to Robert now and that might take some time."

The stretching exercises weren't lost on Nicole and she tugged on the woman's leather jacket. "Come on, sit down, and just relax."

Kris turned and was quickly guided to sit on the chair. "Wha...Nick, you need it more than I do. You look exhausted," she tried to argue.

"Your shoulders ache, and I just want to ease the stiffness a bit," Nicole explained as she helped her friend out of her jacket.

"Nick, I'm okay, really," Kris started. "Its not that bad, I...ouch!" she blurted as Nicole's gentle fingers barely began their ministrations.

"Not that bad, huh?" she teased as she gave Kris a shoulder massage. "What did you do to earn yourself such knotted muscles?" she asked as her fingers tried working through the multiple knots in the broad, tense shoulders.

"You don't want to know," Kris replied softly as she closed her eyes, blissfully enjoying the younger woman's touch once she got past her initial shock of yearning for Nicole's contact.

"And what if I do?" She smiled with a hint of curiosity as Kris' body relaxed beneath her fingers and her head tilted back into the soothing touch. Nicole stepped closer to the chair offering Kris a place to lean against. "What happened?"

Kris took a deep breath. "Don't say I didn't warn you," she half joked. "I wrapped a car around a tree, pretty much totaling it," she stated matter-of-factly. Nicole's hands momentarily stopped as she digested this revelation. "That was one of the stunts that went wrong."

"Were you badly hurt?" Nicole asked with a mixture of curiosity and concern.

Kris shrugged. "Broken ankle, broken arm, three cracked ribs, whiplash, and four days in a coma." She chuckled at Nicole's gasp. "Well, you told me you wanted to know...now you do."

Any professional worth their reputation could have given Kris an excellent massage but with less satisfaction than the amateur working on her sore shoulders at that moment. The soft and surprisingly strong hands that worked through her tense muscles were so warm and caring. It had been a long time since anybody had shown her such kindness and gentleness that she was surprised at how much she enjoyed the attention.

Kris shut her eyes as the soft hum of Nicole's voice vibrated through her chest where her head rested against it. She smiled as she imagined herself under the woman's caring hands, feeling them slowly glide over her bare back as soft lips trailed small kisses up her spine. Slowly, those same lips brushed against her sensitive neck, nibbling slowly at her ear...

"Kristina, show time!"

Kris broke out of her reverie at the director's voice, and she hopped out of the chair, fumbling to get her leather jacket on. "Uh...thanks for...loosening my muscles." Kris blushed furiously as her mind went over the residual images of her imagination. "That was very nice." *Where's that damn sleeve?* she thought with frustration as she fought a losing battle with her leather jacket. "Thank you...yes...hmm."

"Kris, are you okay?" Nicole asked worriedly. "I didn't hurt you, did I?"

"No!" Kris blurted, shaking her head to assuage Nicole's misplaced fears. "No, you didn't." She nervously coughed before smiling at the blonde who watched her with wide eyes. "Have to go back to work," she said, walking backwards and pointing with her thumb at the stunt site behind her. "Have to make sure everything's okay." Kris nodded. "Yep, lots of work to do." Then she turned around and disappeared in the darkness.

What have I done? Nicole shook her head, cursing her stupidity. She turned at a movement beside her and faced her grinning cousin.

"What just happened here?" Alex asked as Nicole fell into the chair Kris had just vacated.

"Alex, I think I just did something really stupid," Nicole said as she rested her elbows on her knees and dropped her head into her hands. "I think I just freaked her out," she mumbled through her fingers.

Alex took her hands out of her jeans' pockets, crouched down beside Nicole, and rubbed her cousin's back with a comforting touch. "If you ask me, that wasn't the look of someone who was freaking out, Nick," she said as she tried to hold back a chuckle. She had caught the look of total bliss on the stuntwoman's face before she got up.

"Then...why did she take off like that?" Nicole looked up as Alex smiled at her.

"You'll have to ask her yourself," the brunette said, then looked out and spotted the tall Austrian standing beside the stunt car. "I have my own ideas, but..." Alex stood up and shoved her hands back into her pockets.

"Alex, I know that look of yours. What aren't you telling me?" Nicole demanded.

"Will you relax?" She laughed. "All I'm saying is that maybe Kris cares a lot more about you than she thought. Did you know that she walked all over the set today trying to find you? She seemed to be awfully worried about you, Nick."

"She did?" Nicole asked. "She was worried about me?"

"Yes, she was." Alex gently squeezed Nicole's uninjured shoulder. "You seemed to have found a very good friend in Kris. Just talk to her." The brunette walked away with a smile on her lips.

****

The stunt had gone much better than what was originally planned and was performed efficiently and with precision. The security teams and divers had gotten the driver out of the sinking car with no problems. Nobody had gotten hurt, and Robert had been very pleased at the results. The new stunt coordinator had just proven that she could work under pressure by re-working a gag from scratch and have it performed with a minimal schedule change.

Kris stood apart from the others as she watched the crew pull the car out of the water. She couldn't tear her mind away from the wonderful massage Nicole had given her earlier or her own stupidity when she abruptly ran away from her. Since first meeting, they had spent pretty much all their free time together, talking and just having fun. Kris had grown very comfortable with Nicole around, but tonight...tonight, she had gotten just a little too comfortable.

She knew that if she hadn't fled from Nicole, things might have gotten out of hand. She needed friendship at the moment and that's what Kris would give her, even if it meant swallowing down her own growing feelings for the blonde. With her leaving for Austria soon, any relationship other than friendship was out of the question. She couldn't and wouldn't do that to Nicole.

At least tell her you're sorry for the way you acted, she scolded herself. Turning around to go and find Nicole, Kris almost walked into Alex who was standing behind her.

"Hi." Alex smiled at the surprised stuntwoman. The brunette leaned on the guardrail with her arms crossed over her chest.

"How long have you been standing there?" Kris asked gruffly, upset that she had been caught off guard.

"Long enough to hear you mumbling to yourself." She chuckled and handed Kris a folded piece of paper. "I'm just here to deliver a message."

She took the note and read it. *Hi. Robert offered to drive me back home so don't worry, okay? See you at work tomorrow. Nicole.*

Kris had taken it upon herself to drive the girl home each day after work and this sudden change of plan made her wonder if she was the cause of it. She carefully folded the paper and slid it into her pocket.

Hearing the older woman's soft sigh, Alex took a step

closer. "You can tell me to mind my own business, but if you think that you're the reason why my father drove Nicole home, you're wrong." Kris remained silent and looked out over the river. "My father wanted to make sure that Nicole wouldn't have any trouble when she got home."

"Why would I think..." Kris started but was stopped by Alex.

"Kris, I know you care about Nick. Your body language is a dead giveaway if someone paid enough attention. I also know that she cares a lot about you because she told me so. But she's afraid that she made a terrible mistake a few hours ago, and she thinks that she may have lost you as a friend."

"Why would she think that?" Kris asked with a confused look on her face. "I'm the one who made the mistake. I shouldn't have run off like that without talking to her first."

"If all those show business magazines tell the truth, you've had a few girlfriends in your life, right?" Alex asked, and continued without waiting for the answer. "Then it means that Nicole's touch isn't what made you panic," she stated as she unwrapped a stick of gum and put it in her mouth, chewing a couple of times before continuing. "Nicole has no idea you're gay, and she's afraid she freaked you out by the massage she gave you. Just talk to her, she might surprise you." Alex smiled and tilted her head sideways a bit, then winked at the silent woman and walked away.

Kris watched the smaller woman leave and wondered what had just happened. She appreciated the straightforwardness the young woman had offered but Kris hadn't planned to talk about her sexual preference to Nicole, since their relationship was one based on friendship. But following tonight's misunderstanding, maybe it would be a good idea to just tell Nicole and be done with it. She just hoped that it wouldn't be Nicole running away, completely freaked out. Then she remembered Alex talking about her girlfriend, Sophie, and Nicole seemed comfortable with the concept. *Well, maybe she won't freak out after all.* Kris smiled to herself, feeling better already and walked to her Harley to go home.

Chapter 6

Once she arrived at the house, Kris slipped into an old, worn pair of jogging pants and T-shirt, and then she grabbed a bottle of water out of the fridge and drank it all in a few swallows. She tried to work on the scheduled stunts for a while but accomplished little as her mind kept wandering to the gentle massage Nicole had given her and the feelings she had for her.

"I've only known Nick for a week. I can't believe I feel this way."

She walked to the patio doors in the bedroom and slid them open, letting in the breeze from off the lake and took several deep breaths of the fresh air as it filled the spacious room. Kris then walked over and fell limply onto the inviting bed. She got into a comfortable position, closed her eyes, and let the sounds of the gentle waves lapping at the shoreline lull her into a fitful sleep.

Even in sleep, she couldn't fight off the images of Nicole running through her mind. She kept seeing the younger woman trying to protect herself from her crazed father as she vainly avoided the blows that rained down on her.

Kris woke up with a start from the nightmare, sweat glistening off her tanned body, her heart beating furiously against her chest. The dream had seemed so real, especially the sound of Nicole screaming for her father to stop, then with a shaking voice calling out for Kris to help her.

The dark haired woman sat on the edge of the bed and shakily brushed her fingers through her disheveled hair. "What was that all about?" she breathed as she looked at the clock on the nightstand. It was four o'clock. No use going back to sleep. Taking a deep breath, the stuntwoman got up and changed her sweatpants for a pair of shorts and took another T-shirt out of the drawer.

After brushing her teeth and tying her hair back into a thick ponytail, Kris decided that a good, long run would help her relax. She tied the laces of her running shoes and went through a long series of stretching exercises before leaving the house twenty minutes later.

She chose the paved path that went along the lake, sharing it with a few runners and the occasional biker all out for their own early morning exercises. Making a detour from the path, Kris ran by Nicole's house, seeing nothing special except that there were no cars in the driveway. Maybe her father was away, leaving her alone in the house with a chance to relax without fear. Kris hoped that the nightmare she had was nothing but a bad dream, but she couldn't shake the feeling that it was real, almost as if it were a premonition of things to come for the young woman.

Half way through her run, Kris stopped to buy a bottle of water and sat down by the shore. She watched as the sun rose higher in the sky, and the path became busier. More runners appeared along the shoreline, and the number of bikers doubled by that time. She even noticed a few people rollerblading along the paved path while others chose to take a leisurely walk with their dogs.

Kris briefly debated whether or not to go by the McGrails' house again and see if everything was okay, or continue on her way and call Nicole on the phone later, giving her more time to sleep. *I'll call her,* she decided as she finished her bottle and threw it into the trashcan, then continued on with her run.

About ten minutes away from her rented house, Kris spotted a blonde woman sitting by herself, facing the lake. She had both of her arms tightly wrapped around her bent legs, her forehead resting on her knees. Kris slowed her pace and tried to see the woman's face.

"Nick?" she called out and the blonde jumped in surprise at the sudden sound of a voice. Nicole looked like she hadn't slept at all. "Hey, what happened?" Kris sat down on the grass beside her friend, last night's dream rushing back to her.

Nicole shook her head. "I thought everything was okay." She said as she concentrated on a blade of grass she had just pulled from the ground. "He greeted my uncle in a nice way, but when Robert left..." She sighed and closed her eyes, trying to forget.

Kris didn't know what to do. She reached out to brush Nicole's hair but stopped midway, not sure how to proceed in a situation such as this. She let her hand drop to her muscled thigh instead. What she wanted to do was to take the smaller woman in her arms and just hold her, to let her know that she was there for her.

"I'm sorry I lied to you, Kris," Nicole said and looked up into the stuntwoman's blue eyes. "I told you I fell, that I hurt myself. I didn't...want to burden you. My father..."

Kris silently opened her arms to let Nicole in. She didn't waste a second as she wrapped her arms around the trim waist and rested her head on Kris' chest. "Shhh, I've got you. It's gonna be okay," she promised and hesitated briefly before wrapping her arms around the blonde.

They sat there for some time, neither one speaking, letting the peace and calm surrounding them ease away some of the memories and not make them so painful. Kris gently rocked the younger woman back and forth as she rested her cheek on the blonde hair and closed her eyes.

She could have stayed that way for hours, her arms protectively around Nicole. She gently kissed the top of her head and smiled as Nicole acknowledged the gesture with a small squeeze around the waist. She heard a soft sigh and was disappointed when Nicole sat back, no longer in her arms.

"Thanks." Nicole smiled shyly. "That was nice. Sorry about your T-shirt, though."

Kris frowned and looked down, seeing nothing out of the ordinary, then looked back up into emerald eyes studying her.

"It's kind of wet because of my tears," Nicole explained as she wiped her eyes with the edge of her sweater.

"Oh. Don't worry. You didn't do the original damage," Kris stated with a chuckle. "I've been running for a while. I'm just thankful that you didn't pass out from the smell."

"Nah." Nicole grinned, her good humor returning. "I was too comfortable to notice." She gently laid her hand on Kris' and gave it a squeeze. "Thank you."

"For what?"

"For being a friend." She smiled.

"You're welcome."

They continued staring at the lake in silence until a thought crossed Kris' mind. "Nick, why didn't you come to the house instead of staying here alone?" she asked gently and looked at her companion. "You know you can talk to me."

"I didn't want to worry you or burden you with my problems," Nicole replied honestly, bending her head, unable to look at Kris. A strong finger slipped under her chin and lifted her head and made her look into pale blue eyes.

"I'll say this once," Kris spoke softly. "You don't burden me, Nicole. I want to help you and be there for you, but I can't do that if you don't talk to me." She brushed her hand on Nicole's cheek, wiping a tear with her thumb. "I'm gonna give you my cell phone number, so whenever you need me or just want to say hello, call me. Okay?" Kris smiled as the blonde closed her eyes and leaned a little into the touch before she pulled her hand away.

Nicole nodded. She could still feel Kris' soft touch on her cheek and wanted more. The woman was so gentle, so caring and she felt privileged to see that side of Kris. So many people talked about her as if she was a machine, devoid of emotions but Nicole knew otherwise.

A rush took over her body as soft lips kissed her forehead, causing her whole body to tingle. She opened her eyes and stared into Kris' eyes, wanting to say something, anything, but her mouth refused to work. So, she just sat there with a silly grin on her face until her stomach rumbled to life.

With a chuckle, Kris stood up and offered a hand to Nicole.

"Ready for breakfast?" she asked as her friend got to her feet. "Why don't we go to my place, and I'll try to make something edible for us to eat?" Kris joked and laughed when Nicole nodded vigorously. She wasn't the best cook, but she guessed that she could probably handle a few eggs, bacon, and toast.

Once in the house, the first thing Kris did was to prepare a fresh pot of coffee. "I'll go take a quick shower, and then I'll get breakfast ready," she told the small woman who walked around the living room. "Just make yourself comfortable. There's some orange juice in the fridge if you want."

"Thanks." She smiled and caught a glimpse of Kris muscled back as the stuntwoman pulled her T-shirt off, causing a huge grin to grow on her face. *What a beautiful woman,* Nicole thought as she sat on the large sofa in the living room. She closed her eyes, remembering how it felt to have Kris' arms around her.

Kris stood under the hot water, letting the water jet massage her tired muscles, wishing it were Nicole's hands doing the job instead. The smaller woman hadn't said anything about her sudden departure on the set the evening before, and she wondered if this was a good time to talk to Nicole, at least let her know why she had run away like that. She didn't want her to think that she had done anything wrong. In fact, she had done everything right, much to Kris' discomfort. If they were in Austria, things would be so much different.

After rinsing her hair and shutting off the water, she slipped into her bathrobe and stepped out of the bathroom rubbing her hair dry with a towel. She had gathered her courage to speak to Nicole, and she was about to when she saw her lying on her side, sleeping peacefully on the sofa.

With a smile, Kris took the soft blanket from a chair and covered her, then bent down and planted a soft kiss on the blonde woman's temple. "Just rest easy, my friend," she whispered. A mumble was her only reply, but the gentle smile on Nicole's face was the greatest gift for Kris.

****

Nicole slowly opened her eyes. She felt disoriented as she looked around the living room, seeing the unfamiliar furniture. It took a moment for her to realize where she was and quickly rose from the sofa, unable to believe that she had fallen asleep on Kris' couch. She looked at the blanket that had partially covered her and frowned. She couldn't remember any blankets...heck, she couldn't even remember lying down on the sofa. The blanket could only have been Kris' doing. The smell of coffee brewing and of bacon cooking guided her to the kitchen, and the sight that greeted her put a smile on her face.

Kris was making breakfast, unaware of her visitor, who leaned quietly against the kitchen's doorframe. She padded around the kitchen barefoot, wearing shorts and a T-shirt that was cut at mid stomach, giving a clear view of the trim waist. Her raven hair tightly braided fell down her muscular back.

She stopped once in a while to look out the window and watch as some people sailboarded not too far away on the windy lake. But what made Nicole smile the most was the sound Kris made as she hummed softly. She had such a beautiful voice.

Sensing somebody watching her, Kris turned around. "Hi there." She smiled in greeting. "Did you have a nice rest?"

"I'm sorry I fell asleep," Nicole said as she walked into the kitchen and noticed the time. She had been sleeping for over three hours. "Why didn't you wake me up?"

"You looked like you didn't get much sleep last night, so I let you rest." A grin played on the dark-haired woman's lips, and she winked at Nicole. "Besides, you're so cute when you're asleep," she said, then turned to finish making breakfast. "Coffee's ready if you want some."

Nicole blushed at the older woman's comment. "Thanks." She took the pot and refilled Kris' mug before filling her own, then walked to the sliding doors and looked outside. It was amazing how relaxed she felt in this house with Kris. It had been such a long time since anybody had cared for her this way. Just the simple act of being covered by the blanket almost brought tears to her eyes.

"What are your plans for this weekend?" Kris asked, startling Nicole. "I'm sorry, I didn't mean to make you jump."

"No, it's okay." Nicole quickly smiled. "I was just lost in thought." She helped with taking the plates to the table and then sat down when Kris motioned for her to do so. "I don't have anything planned really," she finally answered. "You can say that I'm pretty much on my own for the next two weeks."

Kris looked at her smaller companion in surprise. "What happened...I mean, where's your father?"

"He left on a trip that had been scheduled some time ago. So, I guess it'll be quiet around the house." This was greeted with a grin and a twinkle in Kris' blue eyes.

She realized it was her best chance to get Nicole to really enjoy herself. It was also the best opportunity to get to know her. "Well, since Robert gave us the weekend off, I was thinking that maybe we could go for a motorcycle ride, and you could show me around Montreal?"

"Really?" Nicole exclaimed. "That would be great."

Kris laughed. "Where would you like to go?" It was wonderful to see her so happy about doing something so simple. Her enthusiasm was contagious.

"There are so many places I would like to show you. I don't know where to start."

"What about the mountains?" the dark-haired woman asked. "I heard you talking to Alex, saying how much you missed going there."

"The Laurentians are beautiful." Nicole smiled, remembering the trips with her mother when she was younger. "But it's about a three hour drive to go to Mt-Tremblant," she said, disappointed.

"So? You just told me you had nothing planned."

"I don't, but..."

"It's settled then." The stuntwoman grinned. "We'll eat, then we'll stop by your house for you to get something warmer, and we'll be on our way." Kris winked at the speechless woman and started eating her breakfast.

Nicole didn't know what to think. What began as another typical day with her father's insults was turning into a very exciting day. Not only was she having breakfast in Kris' house, but they were about to go for a long motorcycle ride together.

Spending several hours sitting behind Kris, her arms tightly wrapped around the taller woman's waist was an especially pleasing thought. *Things are looking better,* Nicole thought as she finished her breakfast with a big smile plastered on her lips. She met Kris' eyes. "Thank you."

A blush rose on Kris' cheeks at having been caught staring, but she didn't lower her eyes. She couldn't get enough of seeing Nicole happy. She was such a beautiful woman when she smiled and she loved the way the blonde looked at her, with her green eyes shinning with excitement and her grin making her nose wrinkle a little bit. Kris nodded to her companion, pleased that Nicole was looking forward to their little trip together.

The dishes were cleared and put in the dishwasher, and then Kris left to change into something more appropriate for a motorcycle ride. She came back wearing her usual black jeans and boots, but this time, she wore a white silk blouse. Nicole couldn't help the smile as she took in the dark-haired woman.

"You look real nice," she said, as her eyes roamed over the muscular body. She reached for Kris' arm and brushed her fingers on the smooth blouse then pulled her hand away, realizing what she was doing. She looked up at Kris, who smiled down at her, seemingly not disturbed by the show of affection.

"Thank you. I'm glad you appreciate it." Kris smiled as she casually put her hand on Nicole's shoulder and guided her to the garage and the Harley, grabbing her leather jacket on the way. "I'll make sure to wear it more often." She chuckled, as the young blonde blushed.

They were soon at McGrail's house, and Kris quietly waited in the main area until Nicole called to her from her room. "Don't just stand there. Come on up."

She climbed the stairs to the second floor and approached the room, not wanting to catch Nicole half dressed. *Would that be so bad if I did?* Kris thought with a smile.

"What kind of jacket should I wear?" Nicole's muffled voice called out. "I don't have anything made of leather."

Kris peeked inside the room and saw that Nicole was digging into her closet. "I guess we'll have to do something about that," she said as she sat on the edge of the bed.

"What did you say?" Nicole asked, taking a worn winter jacket out of the closet to show her friend.

The stuntwoman shook her head no at the jacket. "You could always wear a windbreaker. I'll be shielding you from most of the wind anyway."

"Oh, okay." She put the jacket back into her closet and closed the door.

Kris looked around the small, Spartan room. It was furnished with a small bed, a colorful comforter, a small TV set on top of a large desk with drawers, and a rocking chair in the corner. The only personal items on display were a few books, a couple of CDs beside the CD player, and a few photographs under the lamp on the small nightstand beside the bed. One of those caught her attention, and the taller woman stood up and reached for it.

"That's my mother," Nicole said, feeling the familiar tightening of the heart every time she thought of her.

"Is that you with her?" Kris asked, studying the small blonde child smiling in the woman's arms.

"I was ten years old when that picture was taken. She died a few weeks later," Nicole said sadly. "Are we ready?"

Kris nodded as she put the picture back. "She's a beautiful woman, just like her daughter." She smiled and walked out of the room, respecting Nicole's wish not to talk about, what seemed like, a touchy subject.

Did she just call me beautiful? "Wow." She grabbed her windbreaker and rushed down the stairs after her friend.

Before leaving for their little trip "up north," Kris made a quick stop at a leather store that she had discovered one evening. She got off the motorcycle and steered a confused Nicole inside, prepared to deal with her arguments.

The sale turned out to be one of the easiest the salesperson had ever made. Kris walked in with Nicole, went to a specific rack and pulled out a precise size for her to try. The jacket fit perfectly. The stuntwoman handed her credit card to the clerk and paid for the jacket, then reached for her companion, who still wore the new purchase, and walked her out of the store.

Everything happened without a sound from Nicole, the

young blonde was stunned speechless.

As Kris was about to sit on the bike, Nicole tugged at her arm and she turned around to look at her companion. "Hmm?"

"Kris?" Nicole asked, getting her voice back. "Why did you do that?" She glanced down at the jacket, gliding her fingers on the smooth black leather, then looked back up at the stuntwoman.

"Because I wanted to give you a gift," Kris replied. "Besides, you needed one for riding the bike."

"But I...It's so...That's too..." Nicole tried to speak, but the words just wouldn't come out. She closed her eyes and took a deep breath, then looked back at the taller woman. "Do you realize how expensive that was?" she finally blurted, but the only reaction she got from Kris was her biting her lip so she wouldn't laugh. "You have the house to rent, then you talked about renting a car, then you invited me to a very expensive restaurant, and now this? Kris, you'd better..."

"Do you like the jacket?" she asked simply.

"Yes, I love it, but..."

Kris put a finger on Nicole's lips, silencing her. "Don't worry about the money, okay?" she said softly as she brushed her finger on the soft lips before letting her hand drop to her side. The small gesture caused the blonde to close her eyes momentarily. "I didn't do this because I can afford it. I did it because I wanted to buy you something nice and make you happy."

Nicole couldn't believe how soft Kris' finger had felt on her lips and how the simple touch had sent a shock wave coursing through her body from her head down to her toes. She stared into pale blue eyes that were fixed on her and the beautiful smile on Kris' lips that was meant only for her. For a moment neither spoke and just looked at each other.

"I don't know what to say," Nicole finally said, her voice cracking with emotion. "Nobody ever did anything like this for me before."

Kris stepped forward and gently kissed her forehead. "Just say thank you."

Not caring how it looked, Nicole wrapped both arms around the dark-haired woman's neck and gave her a hug. "Thank you," she whispered in Kris' ear as the stuntwoman wrapped her arms around her waist and hugged back.

"You're welcome." As she was about to let her go, Nicole gave her a small kiss on the cheek and stepped back, her green eyes sparkling. Surprised by the sudden gesture, Kris looked at her companion and smiled. It had felt so nice. She couldn't remember the last time she had hugged somebody outside her family. One thing was for sure, she was getting used to Nicole's little displays of affection and even found herself wishing for more.

After giving the blonde's shoulder a light squeeze, Kris sat on the Harley and invited Nicole to do the same. They strapped their helmets on, zipped their jackets closed, then Nicole wrapped her arms around Kris' waist.

The stuntwoman turned and grinned at her friend. "Ready?" she asked as she put her sunglasses and gloves on and chuckled when Nicole nodded vigorously, smiling from ear to ear. She then faced forward and started the motorcycle.

Chapter
7

Kris and Nicole went to Mt-Tremblant, visited the very popular ski resort, which looked a lot like a European village, and took a chairlift all the way up to enjoy the scenery of the surrounding mountains. Even though Kris had lived most of her life in the Alps, she was pleasantly surprised by the different panorama the Laurentians offered. Instead of the jagged peaks of Austria, the Laurentians offered mountain after mountain of high rolling hills filled with maple, pine, spruce, and oak trees. After a stop for dinner at a restaurant and a much-needed stretch of the legs, they continued back to Montreal.

The long day seem to end too soon when Kris parked the Harley in the garage of her home and guided Nicole into the house.

"That was wonderful." Nick stretched her sore back. "I can't remember when I had so much fun."

Kris walked to the closet, slipped out of her leather jacket and put it on a hanger then reached for Nicole's to do the same. "I'm glad you enjoyed yourself. I had fun, too." She watched in amusement as the petite woman walked to the sofa and dropped heavily on it, barely stifling a yawn. "Are you tired?"

"No, I'm fine. I'm just not used to being outdoors this much."

Kris nodded and headed towards the kitchen. "Want something to drink?"

"A Coke would be nice, thanks," Nicole called back. "So, what are we doing tonight?"

With a smile, Kris shook her head at her friend's enthusiasm as she took two cans out of the fridge and grabbed a bag of chips from the pantry. "I thought that maybe we could take it easy for tonight," she answered as she walked back into the living room and handed her guest the drink along with the bag. "It's been a long day. You're not used to going on long rides like the one we just finished." She put her own can on the coffee table and sat down beside Nicole to take her boots off. "Maybe we could just watch a movie or something?"

"Good plan," Nicole agreed, not wanting the day to end, and it seemed that Kris wasn't in a big hurry to see it end either. Nicole knew that the time she spent with the older woman was going to have a special place in her heart. Kris took her can and lazily put her feet on the table and leaned back. Following her lead, Nicole took her running shoes off and settled comfortably on the sofa. "Anything good playing tonight?"

Kris reached for the remote beside her and clicked the TV on, turned the lights off, and started channel surfing. "Ooh, *The Fly* is playing." She grinned and laughed as the blonde made a big show of shuddering. "Not that, huh?" She continued surfing and stopped at another movie classic. "Hmm, how about Aliens?"

"Ew, I hate those things." Nicole laughed, as she poked Kris lightly in the ribs and grabbed the remote. Clicking past a few channels, she finally stopped on the movie *Gremlins*. "Here are a few ugly creatures I'm sure you'll like," she teased.

"Ugly creatures? Those are cute," Kris replied. "They're so small and cuddly," she started, then looked at her companion with a grin. "Just like someone I know."

"Cute and cuddly?" Nicole exclaimed. "They're green and slimy and they..." Surprised, she looked up at the taller woman watching her. "Like someone you know?"

"Hum hmm, small, cute, and cuddly, just like you," Kris teased as a blush formed on Nicole's cheeks. "You're smaller than I am, and you sure like to cuddle, I noticed that on the bike..." She lightly tapped her friend's small nose. "But I really liked it," she finished with a smile.

"You did?" Nicole whispered. "You forgot about the cute part." She surprised herself by saying that.

"I didn't forget that part." Kris said with a wink and took the remote from Nicole's nerveless fingers, switched channels, and stopped on another movie.

"*X-Files*!" both women exclaimed at the same time, then laughed.

"I guess we'll watch this," Kris said as she put the remote on the table and took a long swallow of her Coke. *Is it getting warmer in here?* She was pretty sure that the weather had nothing to do with the way she was feeling. She watched Nicole from the corner of her eye and noticed that she was still blushing furiously. She briefly wondered if she had gone too far with her teasing, but a hint of a smile tugged at Nicole's lips. Satisfied that she hadn't made her uncomfortable, Kris settled back on the sofa to enjoy the movie, only wishing that her friend would sit closer to her.

After three deep breaths, Nicole could feel the flush that warmed her face slowly go away. She couldn't believe that Kris had teased her that way. *It almost sounded like she was flirting with me*, Nicole thought, trying to hold back a giggle. *So you think I'm cute and cuddly, huh? If you only knew that cuddling is the only thing I want to do right now. Just to be able to lean on that muscular body and have another chance to wrap my arms around your waist.* Nicole stole a glance at the taller woman. When she saw the smile on Kris' lips, she turned her attention back to the movie. *Whatever she's thinking about sure seems nice.*

Kris suddenly opened her eyes at the strange sound and noticed that the TV station had gone off the air. She blinked a couple of times then looked down to see Nicole comfortably nestled against her. The blonde head rested against the crook of her shoulder with her right arm loosely draped across Kris' stomach. While asleep, the stuntwoman had brought her arm to rest across the smaller woman's shoulder, cradling her against her body.

Nicole was sleeping soundly. Kris could hear her regular

breathing and feel her warm breath through the satin shirt she wore. *What do I do now?* she asked herself, and wondered if she should wake Nicole up and invite her to sleep in one of the guest bedrooms, or just enjoy this moment and stay as they were.

Not wanting to disturb her young companion and most importantly, not wanting to break contact with Nicole, she decided to stay the rest of the night in that position. She brought the coffee table closer to the sofa with one foot and put her feet up on it. The slight movement caused Nicole to stir and tighten her hold around Kris' waist.

Kris held her breath, hoping that Nicole wouldn't wake up, but she cuddled even closer, mumbling in her sleep. She softly kissed the blonde head and closed her eyes with a smile on her lips. She soon joined her companion in sleep.

****

Nicole couldn't remember being so comfortable. Feeling the chill of the morning air, she unconsciously reached for the blankets that she must have kicked off during the night. All she succeeded to grab was something warm, and she sleepily opened one eye to investigate. She wasn't in her room and obviously not in her bed. She was leaning against Kris, who was still sleeping and what she had grabbed was Kris' thigh. She lifted her hand off the muscled leg and tried to untangle herself from the warm body, being careful not to wake Kris up. *What would she say if she saw me like this?* Nicole thought. She became aware of something resting across her waist and she looked down to see that it was the older woman's arm. *Great! Now what do I do?*

"Good morning."

Nicole looked up into a pair of blue eyes, and she swallowed nervously. "I'm sorry. I didn't mean to...I just..."

Kris lazily stretched her tall frame. "You looked so comfortable last night that I didn't want to wake you up." She grinned. "I hope you don't mind."

"...I should apologize. I don't know what came over me. I..." Nicole stopped and frowned. "Don't mind what?" she asked as she sat up.

"That I didn't wake you, that I let you sleep against me like this." Kris sat up on the edge of the sofa, giving Nicole an uncertain look. "It was kind of comfortable and nice," she admitted softly.

That caught Nicole off guard. Understandably, she was nervous about how Kris would react to being cuddled against her this way, but she didn't expect to see her friend look so uncertain. "I...yes...it was nice." She smiled shyly. "But are you sure about being comfortable? I know I was." The words were out of her mouth before she realized what she said.

A laugh escaped Kris' lips, and she smiled at her companion. "Yes, I was very comfortable, Nick." Then she got up and stretched. "Are you hungry?"

Nicole's stomach took care of answering her question, and both women looked at each other. "I guess I am." She stood up and headed for the kitchen. "How about pancakes for breakfast?"

Kris hesitated for a moment before answering. "Ah, my kitchen skills are somewhat limited," she mumbled. "Why don't we just go out and eat. That's what I usually do."

"Did I ask you to make breakfast?" Nicole mock-glared, then smiled. "I asked you if you wanted pancakes?"

"I do, but..." she started, but was gently turned around and guided out of the kitchen.

"No buts. You go have a shower or whatever, and I'll make breakfast, okay? Now go." Nicole gave her a small pat on the butt and turned back to the kitchen, missing Kris' surprised look.

I decided a few times what to do or where to eat. I guess it's her turn to decide, Kris chuckled as she headed to the bathroom.

****

Le Café des Berges was a nice little bistro located by Lake St-Louis near Montreal. It was also only a few streets away from Kris' house. The café's clientele were young people, most of them taking a break from a long ride of bicycling, rollerblading, or having tied Seadoos and small boats to the café's marina. Sitting at a table on the terrace, four people sipped drinks and exchanged jokes in a light banter.

Alex McGrail lazily stretched her neck and shoulders and tilted her head back, soaking in the sunshine. She briefly wondered what Nicole was doing. She had called at her house earlier only to get the answering machine. It wasn't like Nicole to be out that early on a day off, especially when her father wasn't home. More often than not, her cousin used that time to sleep in late.

"Ah, *merde,* Alexandra! Are you listening?" Sophie exclaimed. She poked her girlfriend in the ribs with her finger, forcing the brunette to break out of her thoughts. The redhead had a heavy French accent, causing her to pronounce every word precisely. "Sometimes I wonder where you're drifting to."

"Daydreaming again?" Anne, the other woman sitting at the table, asked a little sarcastically.

"Sorry. I was thinking about Nick." Alex smiled and sat straighter in her chair, bringing all her attention back to the conversation.

"I was saying that maybe we could all go to Quebec City next weekend," Sophie repeated. "Neilson has to go back Monday night."

"I'm leaving for Los Angeles on Tuesday morning," Neilson corrected.

Alex scratched her head, frowning a bit. "I don't know if I'll be able to go. There was a fire last night and a good section of the movie set got damaged. We might have to do some major work to make up for lost time."

"Was anybody injured?" the young man asked as he flagged the waiter for another round of drinks.

"No, but the carpenters have a lot of work ahead of them to rebuild. That set was the one they were going to use for tomorrow's shoot." Alex shook her head as she remembered the phone call her father had received about the fire. "Dad sure was angry as hell."

"*Quel vacherie*!" Sophie said, pouting, her French tending to get out more often when she was upset. "And I was looking forward to a nice weekend together."

As the waiter arrived with their drinks, Neilson said, "I'm sure we'll have another weekend. I'm only in L.A. for two weeks." He paid the waiter before turning to Alex. "You can..."

"It would be so much nicer if we could spend more time in L.A," Anne cut in as she sipped her ice tea.

"I told you, Anne, this is not a vacation. I'm going there to work," Neilson explained, starting to lose patience with his grumpy girlfriend.

"Yeah, whatever," Anne said as she got up and walked away.

Sighing, Neilson turned his attention to Alex. "You mentioned Nicole. How is she doing?"

"Nicole's got a girlfriend," Sophie sang, making a big show of winking at Neilson, and giggling.

"They're only friends," Alex stated, allowing a slow grin. "At least, they are for now."

"Oh? And your instincts tell you that it will develop into..." he trailed off, grinning at Alex, who wagged her eyebrows at him as she took a sip of her beer.

"Nick looks very happy with her. They both do as a matter of fact. I wouldn't be surprised if things got a little more, hmmm, intimate between them?" She smiled at Neilson, who seemed to be happy with the news.

"That would be real nice. Nick needs to have somebody in her life who cares for her," Neilson agreed. "She's got enough crap from that bastard who calls himself her father." He took a sip of his drink and shook his head. "She's a good woman. She deserves to be happy."

"Talking about the devil, and there she is." Alex grinned as everybody turned to the terrace's entrance.

Nicole and Kris had walked in, taking their motorcycle helmets and leather jackets off. Kris bent close to whisper something in Nicole's ear, causing the younger woman to burst out laughing. She turned a bit and backhanded the stuntwoman in the stomach.

Alex was so happy to see them together and having fun. She waited until Nicole looked their way to wave them over. "Hey girl!" Alex got up and hugged her cousin, then smiled at Kris, who kept her sunglasses on. "How are you doing, Kris?"

"Things are good," she replied, looking at the others sitting at the table.

"Why don't you join us?" Alex invited. She pulled two chairs over to the table and fingered Nicole's jacket. "Cool leather. You bought this?" she asked as she sat down and watched her cousin as she put the jacket on the back of one of the available chairs.

Nicole shook her head and turned to her tall companion. "It's a gift from Kris." She smiled and looked back at Alex and her friends. She nodded to Sophie and then saw Neilson. "Neil!" She laughed and hugged the young man. "How are you?"

"I'm doing great, kid." He kissed her on the cheek and stepped back to get a better look at his friend. "You look great," he said as they sat down.

"Hey, I'd like to introduce you to my friend, Kristina. Kris, this is Neilson. We grew up together."

After lifting her sunglasses and putting them on top of her head, Kris reached out and shook his hand. "Nice to meet you," she said as she sat down, putting her motorcycle helmet on a chair beside Nicole's and her leather jacket on the armrest.

"It's an honor to meet you, Ms. Von Deering," Neilson gushed, star struck.

Nicole frowned, looking from Neil to Kris and back. "You know her?" the blonde asked him, confused.

"Please, call me Kris," the stuntwoman said.

"Okay, Kris it is," he replied. "This is so cool, Nick. Ms Von...I mean, Kris is one of the reasons why I became a stuntman. You did a wonderful job in the movie *Law & Revenge* by the way. The full burn you did was so incredible."

"Thanks. Have you been a stuntman for a long time?" she asked, and then turned to the waiter who had just arrived. "A Guinness and a Coke for the lady here, please." She winked at Nicole.

"I trained at the Canadian Stunt School in the suburbs of Montreal and graduated five years ago," he said proudly. "I was lucky enough to get myself hired on a movie project in L.A."

"The school, that's where you'll be teaching, right?" Nicole asked Kris.

"Yes, right after I'm done with the movie we're doing in Montreal."

"Can I ask a stupid question?" the blonde asked. "What's a full burn?"

"That's a very spectacular stunt," Neilson exclaimed, a little too enthusiastically. "You set yourself on fire."

"What?" Nicole turned to Kris with an alarmed expression. "You were on fire?"

Kris reached for Nicole's hand and gently squeezed it. "It's more complicated than that." She smiled reassuringly at her companion. "There are a lot of precautions to take before that. Lots of fire retardant gel, special clothing, a breathing apparatus..."

"Still...I'm not sure I could stand the sight of you in flames." Nicole shuddered.

"Especially someone you care about," Alex whispered in Nicole's ear then spoke with a louder voice. "Kris, did I introduce you to my girlfriend, Sophie?"

"No, you didn't. Nice to meet you, Sophie." Kris reached out her hand and the redhead held it longer than necessary.

"No, it's nice to meet *you,* " Sophie purred before letting go of Kris' hand.

The stuntwoman's cell phone rang, and Kris excused herself as she got up to answer the call. She stopped briefly to pay for both drinks as the waiter returned with their orders.

"Oh, boy. I can't believe you're going out with Kristina Von Deering," Neilson said to Nicole then winced when Alex kicked him on the shin under the table. "Ow! I mean, that you get to spend time with her." He looked at Alex, who glared back at him.

"Why are you acting so weird, Neil?" Nicole asked. "You act like Kris is some kind of superstar or something."

"She is, Nick," he explained. "Kristina is very famous in Europe. She's one, if not, the best stuntwoman in the world. She broke so many world records, I mean, the press hounds her everywhere she goes. She's traveled all over the world; she's met and worked with famous actors. She's also a very rich woman. They say she's got so much money, she doesn't know what to do with it."

"That's enough, Neil," Alex warned, observing Nicole's withdrawn silence.

Somehow that image of Kris didn't make sense. She didn't act like a snob like most famous people were rumored to act like, and Nicole hadn't seen any signs of the press following them around Montreal. And as for the money, at least now she understood why Kris was so easy going about spending it. A hand on her shoulder made Nicole look up at worried blue eyes watching her.

"Are you okay?" Kris asked as she sat down.

"Yeah, I'm fine," she replied softly, taking a sip of her Coke.

Kris looked at Alex, who had an angry scowl on her face, then at Sophie, who found her glass of wine very interesting, then finally at Neilson, who looked like he had made a big mistake. Turning back to a silent Nicole, Kris bent down and whispered in her young companion's ear, "Can I speak with you for a minute?" She rose to her feet and said to the group, "Excuse us."

"Sure." Nicole followed the taller woman down the three steps that led to the marina. They walked to a bench and sat down in silence.

"Something's bothering you, Nick. What is it?" Kris asked softly.

"It's nothing." Nicole smiled shyly. "Nothing important." She looked out at the numerous boats moored at the marina, feeling so stupid to be reacting this way.

"Nick, when I left, you were all smiles and happy, now you look like your best friend died." She gently lifted the blonde's chin so she would look at her. "What's wrong?"

"I didn't know you were so famous," Nicole blurted out. "Neil told me that you're some kind of celebrity in Europe, that you're often seen with the rich and famous."

"I see." Kris' body tensed. For once, she thought that she had met someone whom didn't care if she was famous or not. Now it seemed like it did matter to Nicole.

"Why didn't you tell me?"

"Would it have made a difference?" Kris asked tersely.

"No, it wouldn't, but...I don't know." Nicole sighed. "I mean, you've met actors and celebrities. I'm just wondering why you would want to spend some time with an ordinary girl like me," she said as she stood up and walked closer to the water.

"What are you talking about?" Kris asked as she also rose and approached Nicole. "Did it ever cross your mind that maybe I like spending time with you? You're an intelligent young woman, you're funny, you're caring, you make me feel so alive." The dark-haired woman gently cupped Nicole's face in her hands and looked into her watery green eyes. "I love...being with you."

"You do?" she whispered, cursing her lack of self-confidence.

"Yes, I do." Kris smiled, as the tension ebbed away from her body. "I don't know why people are so impressed by celebrities," she said as she wiped a tear away from Nicole's cheek with her thumb. "A lot of them are so full of themselves." She grinned, causing her friend to chuckle a little. "I thought you knew that I was...you know..."

"Rich and famous?" Nicole replied, a grin tugging at her lips.

"How I hate those two words," Kris sighed, but smiled. "Yeah, that."

"No, I didn't know. It was a shock to find out. I mean you act so...normal."

"Normal? Are we supposed to act differently because of it?" Kris grinned.

"You know what I mean." She poked the Austrian in the stomach. "No matter how rich you are, I still think you spent too much money on me."

"Nicole, I'll tell you something. I'm not the type to buy friends. I bought you that jacket because I wanted to. I just wanted to please you."

"You don't need to buy me anything to please me, Kris. Just your presence makes me happy."

Kris smiled, feeling warm all over. "Really?"

"Really." Nicole smiled back and threw her arms around the stuntwoman's neck, giving her a hug.

Back on the terrace, Alex, Sophie, and Neilson hung over the railing watching the scene at the marina and sighed. "Isn't this wonderful?" Neil grinned, then frowned as Alex elbowed him in the ribs.

"No thanks to you. God, I thought Nicole was going to start crying," Alex exclaimed.

"I thought Nicole knew the facts about Kris."

"Everything's back to normal." Sophie grabbed her two friends and made them sit down in their chairs. "So, let's change subjects, *oui*? Here they come."

Kris and Nicole walked back to the terrace, both of them smiling. Alex had feared that the knowledge of the stuntwoman's fame and fortune would have intimidated Nicole to the point of walking away from her. She was glad that whatever they had discussed seemed to have calmed her cousin. The brunette smiled as the women sat back down at the table. "Did my father call you about the fire they had yesterday?" Alex asked Kris.

Nicole looked up at Alex in total surprise. "What fire?"

Kris took a long swallow of her beer before nodding. "That's the phone call I just received," she answered the brunette and looked at Nicole. "It seems that a worker doing welding repairs was the cause of the blaze. Tomorrow's schedule has been postponed to a later date until they can rebuild the set."

"So, we have tomorrow off?" Alex asked hopefully. "I sure could use another day like today." She grinned wistfully.

"I don't know about you guys, but we have to move one of the scheduled stunts earlier than planned." Kris looked back at Nicole and smiled sadly. "I'm sorry, I have unexpected work to do. Do you want me to drive you home or are you going to stay here with your friends?" the stuntwoman asked, disappointed that this day was over so soon. She took one last swallow of her beer and stood up.

"No, I'll go back with you." Nicole smiled as she got up and slipped into her leather jacket. "I've got a lot of house cleaning to do." She turned to Neilson who stood beside her. "You be careful in L.A., okay?" she said as she gave him a hug and a kiss on the cheek.

"Always," he replied, nodding. "Listen, I'm sorry about earlier, Nick. I didn't mean to..."

"I know. Don't worry about it. Everything's fine." She smiled and gave Sophie a hug, then Alex. "So, see you at work tomorrow?" she asked her cousin who rolled her eyes.

"Yeah, I guess. Unless we get word that we're not working."

"It was nice meeting you all," Kris said politely, then shook Neilson and Sophie's hands. "Guess I'll see you at work, too," Kris teased Alex before putting on her motorcycle helmet.

"Yeah, yeah. Whatever," Alex grumbled, but grinned at the tall woman. "You take care of her, alright?" she told Kris, a hint of seriousness in her voice. "I really care about Nicole. I'd like to continue seeing her this happy."

Kris smiled. "Of course."

Alex watched them leave with Kris gently guiding Nicole through the crowd and to the black Harley-Davidson.

It was a short ride back. Having gone past Kris' house, they continued until they reached Nicole's. They drove up the driveway and turned the motor off. For a moment, neither moved. The petite blonde stayed behind Kris, her arms still wrapped around her waist. With a sigh, Nicole finally disembarked from the Harley, took her helmet off, and stood in front of Kris. She silently handed her helmet to the stuntwoman who tied it at the back of the motorcycle.

"Will you..." Kris started.

"Are we..." Nicole spoke at the same time and laughed. "I'm sorry, you start." She smiled as Kris took her sunglasses off.

"Will you be having lunch with me tomorrow?" she asked.

"I was going to ask you the same thing." Nicole chuckled with a twinkle in her eyes. "Same place, same time?"

"I'll be there." Kris smiled.

"I'll be bringing the lunch so don't buy any chocolate bars to eat, okay? It's not healthy." As Kris was about to protest, Nicole added, "Let me do this, please?"

Kris nodded, making the smaller woman smile. She took a deep breath, wanting to tell Nicole something, but after the little conversation they had at the marina, Kris wasn't sure how she would react to the news. Obviously, her friend didn't know much about her past, and if there was one thing she didn't want to lose, it was her friendship with Nicole. Better to have it in the open now than to risk having it brought out in the most embarrassing moment.

"Nicole," Kris started, swallowing with difficulty, nervousness taking hold. "The talk we had at the marina made me realize how little you know about me." She had Nicole's undivided attention as the green eyes watched her intently. "We've been spending a lot of time together, and well, I'm afraid you might hear a few things concerning me."

Nicole had never seen Kris so nervous before. "What is it?" Nicole asked softly, trying to reassure the older woman. She laid her hand on the muscular arm and gave it a light squeeze.

Kris looked at the small hand, hoping that Nicole wouldn't pull it away in disgust. *Just say it,* she thought and took another deep breath. "Nicole, I'm gay." *There, I said it.*

Nicole released the breath she held. She was so relieved to know it wasn't anything serious. Her biggest fear was that Kris would tell her that they wouldn't be seeing each other anymore. "So?" she asked, then smiled as Kris lifted surprised blue eyes. "Is that what was making you so nervous?" Kris nodded still looking unsure of herself. "I've seen my cousin with a string of girlfriends in the past few years. You'll have to do better than that to shock me."

"I didn't want you to find out...the same way you did about..."

"About you being rich and famous?" Nicole grinned as Kris smiled a little. "I'm glad you told me, and it doesn't make a difference at all. I want you to know that I loved our unplanned weekend together," Nicole stated shyly. "I'd really like it if we could continue this way."

"There's nothing I'd like more than that." Kris was so happy she wanted to hug Nicole.

"Great. So, I'll see you tomorrow then." She leaned forward and kissed the tall Austrian on the cheek. "Bye," she said, then turned to leave.

A speechless Kris sat on her motorcycle, watched the young woman walk away, and reached up to touch her cheek. She knew she had a stupid grin on her face. That had gone better than expected. Nicole opened the door, and Kris waved before the blonde walked into the house. Her heart beating furiously, she started the Harley and backed it out of the driveway.

Riding back home, Kris whistled a tune, something she hadn't done in ages.

Chapter
8

The damage done to the set wasn't as bad as they initially thought. The technical crew had cleared the area and rebuilt everything as soon as possible. The schedule was re-worked to adjust to the change in filming locations and instead of shooting in Old Montreal, the crew, along with Nicole and Alex, had moved to the countryside while Kris was at another location, preparing for a stunt that would be performed later in the evening.

Taking a break from the hectic schedule, the cousins sat apart from the others on the grass and chatted amicably.

"I still can't believe that Kristina came all the way from Montreal just to have lunch with you," Alex said as she shook her head. Nicole had looked so happy when the tall Austrian rode up on the black Harley. "You even made a lunch for the both of you," she continued, smiling. "Isn't that cute."

"Well, I told her that I would prepare something to eat." Nicole grinned at her cousin. "I just didn't expect her to show up after Robert split the crew in two."

"So, how are things between you two?" the brunette asked as she lay down on the grass.

"We're good friends. She's...really nice." Nicole looked around to make sure they were alone and took a deep breath to relax. "Alex, how do you know when you're in love with somebody?"

Alex looked up to see green eyes studying her. "You're in love with Kris?"

"I didn't say that," the blonde quickly defended. "I just want to know, well...you know..."

You don't have to say it, my friend. It's written all over your face, Alex thought, smiling. "How can I explain this." She thought for a minute while Nicole silently waited. "You know you're in love when all you can think about is the other person. You long to be with them every waking moment. A simple touch or smile from them gets your heart beating so hard against your chest it hurts. All you want to do is hold them in your arms and never let go."

"But..." Nicole sighed a little frustrated. "How do you know if it's more than just friendship you're feeling?" She looked down at her fingers, nervously pulling at the grass. "You know I've never had any relationships before. How am I supposed to know?" she whispered.

"Do you feel like you want to kiss Kris?" Alex asked bluntly. The crimson color on Nicole's face answered her question.

"Why would you think it's Kris we're..." she started.

"Don't play games with me, Nick." Alex smiled to take the edge out of her words. "Since she came along I've never seen you so happy." Her cousin relaxed a little and she saw the beginning of a smile form on Nicole's lips. "You laugh more, smile a lot. Damn, Nick...you look alive." She chuckled. "Of course, you have strong feelings of friendship for her and that's good. She's nice to you and obviously cares a lot about you."

Alex took a deep breath. "Did you have that talk with Kris? About how worried you were that you may have freaked her out?" Seeing no recollection on Nicole's face, Alex pushed on. "About the massage you gave her?"

"Oh, that. Well, I didn't exactly talk to her about that, but I think I know what you're getting at." Nicole smiled. "I know that she's gay. She told me herself."

"She did?" Alex asked, surprised. "How did it come to that?" She sat up and faced her friend.

"Well, after seeing my reaction to her being a celebrity, she was afraid that I might find out about her being gay from strangers, so she told me herself."

"And how do you feel about that?" Alex pressed.

"Relieved?" Nicole smiled shyly at her cousin. "I mean, I thought I freaked her out when I gave her the massage. At least now, I know it wasn't that."

"But how do you feel about her being gay?" Alex asked again.

"Why would I feel differently now that I know she is?" she asked. "I love being with Kris, I love the way she looks and smiles at me...I love the way she makes me feel." Nicole smiled at her cousin. "That's a good enough reason to me."

"All I can say is go with your feelings, Nick. I know Kris really cares about you, but if you want to know how she feels, you'll have to find out by yourself." Alex winked at her. "Talk to her." She gave her cousin a light squeeze on her shoulder before getting up. "Time to go back to work."

****

Kris grew more tired as the days went by. She had been working almost non-stop since Sunday night, the day Robert announced the new stunt schedule caused by the fire on the set. Many outdoor scenes and stunts had to be shot earlier than planned, and Kris had to work overtime trying to get the final adjustments ready for filming. Kris often awoke on the office desk at her rented house, plans and calculations littering the surface and floor. More often than not, she would spend the night drinking coffee and taking cold showers just to shock her body awake.

The latest stunt was the explosion of a convertible car, rigged in a way that the stuntman sitting in the driver's seat was propelled out and into the air amidst the flames of the explosion. The stunt was done perfectly; the stuntman having only suffered minor bruising from the harness solidly attached around his body. Once the stunt was performed, the crew cleared the burned-out car and debris out of the area.

Kris watched the clean-up crew as she ran shaking fingers

through her long, raven hair. It had been more than forty-eight hours since she last slept. The crew had finally caught up to the schedule, but she was exhausted because of it and wondered how long she could keep it up before falling down.

A soft hand stroked her back, and she looked down at Nicole, who watched her with worried eyes. *Damn, I'm glad to see her back with me*, she thought.

"I hear the stunt went well," Nicole commented, giving the muscled back a small pat. "That was the last one until next week, right?"

"Yes, it was," Kris replied as she rubbed her fists into her burning eyes. "What I have to do now is get the next stunts ready so that when..." she stopped when Nicole stepped in front of her, frowning.

"No, you won't," she stated. "You're so tired you can barely stand." She lifted one of Kris' hands. "See how you're shaking? You need to relax and get some sleep."

"But I have so much work left to do, Nick. We're finally on schedule, and I don't want to get behind like we were."

"What good will it do if you get sick, or worse, what's going to happen if you're too tired and there's an accident? Will your reflexes be good enough to do something about it?"

Kris knew that the young woman was right. "I've got too many things on my mind, I just can't seem to relax."

Nicole had slowly been guiding the stuntwoman towards the dressing room trailers and she finally stopped in front of one of them. She unlocked the door and smiled at Kris, inviting her in with a motion of her hand. She knew that her friend was running on very little sleep, and had had arranged, with the help of her uncle, for the use of one of the trailers.

"What's going on?" Kris asked, confused as Nicole gently pushed her up the steps.

"You need to relax, and I'm going to make sure that you do." Once inside, Nicole locked the door behind her and indicated the small bunk at the end of the trailer. "Take off your shirt and lie down."

"Take off my..." Kris repeated, giving Nicole a raised eyebrow.

Nicole chuckled at the expression on Kris' face. "Unless you want massage oil all over your shirt," she said as she held up the bottle.

So many conflicting emotions ran through Kris' body. She needed to relax, and a massage would surely do the trick, but she was afraid of her reaction to it. It was getting hard to keep the feelings she had for Nicole tucked down. Logic clearly stated that a relationship with her was impossible without Nicole being hurt by her departure in a little less than three months. Kris would be back home in Innsbruck, leaving her friend behind.

But every smile she gave her, every gentle touch she received brought the walls she had built around her crashing down, piece by piece. To feel Nicole's gentle hands on her once again was what Kris had dreamed about ever since the first and only time she had given her a massage. But she knew that it was only a matter of time, if they continued this way, before her walls were down fully. Then, she would give in to her feelings, and finally let Nicole know how she truly felt.

Looking at Nicole, who was patiently waiting, Kris silently nodded and walked up to the small bed, pulling her shirt out of her jeans and undoing it. "I might fall asleep on you," she warned.

"I'm kind of counting on it." Nicole winked as she shook the oil bottle and urged her friend to lie down. She turned around, twisted the bottle cap off and poured a good amount of oil into her hand. After putting the bottle back on the small table, she rubbed her hands together vigorously to warm the oil. The thought that she was about to massage Kris, letting her hands roam over the muscled flesh, had Nicole excited but also a bit worried.

After her talk with Alex earlier in the week, she had paid more attention to how she reacted to the stuntwoman and discovered that what Alex had described was exactly what she felt for Kris. *But how do I broach the subject with her? Would it be better to just come up and say, "Kris, I love you." And hope she feels the same? Or just try to hint as much as possible and hope that she picks up on the signs and acts on them?* So many questions.

Nicole didn't know what to do. All she knew was that she didn't want to be apart from Kris. She longed to lean against her while watching TV like they did the week before, to wrap her arms around her, or give her a hug for no reason. She found herself wanting and hoping for more.

"You can turn around now, I'm ready," Kris teased, trying to hide her nervousness.

Nicole turned around and smiled. "Sorry. I was just thinking." Taking a deep breath, she sat on the edge of the small bunk.

"Thinking about what?" Kris asked, closing her eyes as Nicole gently rubbed the massage oil over her tired muscles.

"About all the things we've done since we met. I really had a lot of fun." She slowly shook her head, knowing that she had done more exciting things in the last two weeks than she had done in her entire life.

The motorcycle rides, going to the movies or renting videotapes to watch at Kris', and the nice dinners at fancy restaurants. Kris had even agreed to a dinner at her uncle's house including a late swim with her cousin and friends. Nicole remembered with a smile the jokes the stuntwoman had told and the stories of practical jokes that most crewmembers were fond of playing on the various movie sets.

Both her uncle and aunt had really enjoyed the Austrian's presence that night, her aunt having only heard about Kris. "I never expected all this to happen."

"I'm glad you enjoy it. It's been a very special time for me, too." *You have no idea how special it is,* she silently added.

Nicole slid both her hands up Kris' back, gently but firmly trailing her thumbs on each side of the spine then gently massaged the neck and broad shoulders. The small woman took her time, enjoying the liberty of being able to move her hands anywhere she wished. *Well, almost anywhere,* she thought. She let her eyes wander all over the bronze skin, seeing for the first time the numerous scars on the muscled back. She noticed more scars on Kris' shoulder blades and a nasty cut that started on her left side, right below the first rib and continued down towards the front.

"When did you get this?" Nicole asked, trailing her finger

along the scar, curiosity getting the best of her.

Kris held her breath as the small woman's finger traced the old injury. Such a simple action, but it brought out such a strong feeling. "That happened three years ago," Kris explained, trying hard to get her racing heart under control. Nicole traced each and every scar on her body, ever so slowly; it was driving Kris insane with desire. "We had a stunt to do, a simple fight," she continued, trying to get her mind off what her friend was doing. "We had rehearsed the scene but when it came time to film it, the stuntman I was working with came in too close and hit me. I landed on a metal pike fence." Nicole sucked in a sharp intake of air and stopped her hands for a second before continuing with her massage.

"Were you seriously hurt?"

"The pike went right through my left side. But I was lucky, it was only a flesh wound."

That's no flesh wound, Nicole told herself as she inspected the scar more closely and breathed in a hint of Kris' perfume mixed with the soft smell of the massage oil.

How she wanted to just curl up and feel Kris' strong arms wrapped around her. Sitting straighter, she took a few deep breathes to calm herself. Bringing both hands up and along the woman's waist, Nicole brushed her fingers on the sides of Kris' breasts. For a moment, she didn't know what to do and so she just left her hands there. Her heart beat furiously against her chest, the blood rushed through her veins creating a buzz in her ears. Kris turned onto her back and gazed at Nicole.

Nicole blinked a couple of times, swallowing convulsively as her eyes trailed up the taut abdomen, up to Kris' firm breasts then ended up looking into the blue eyes watching her. *She's not running away. She's not saying anything. She's smiling at me.* Kris lifted her hand and gently brushed Nicole's cheek then slid it into the blonde hair.

Don't do this, Kris heard a little voice say. *You're not staying here, remember? You're going back home. She'll stay behind. She'll just end up getting hurt.* Nicole bent her head, hesitated, and then continued down to Kris' lips. *But I want this so much,* Kris silently replied. *You'll regret this,* the voice said. *I don't care,* she stubbornly argued with herself. *I love her.*

This is it, Nicole thought. *Either I'm making a fool of myself or...*She let her thought trail off as she hesitated. Seeing that Kris was making no move to get away, Nicole continued before she lost all nerve. Kris' hand guided her down, inviting her.

Nicole softly kissed her and her heat beat twice as fast when Kris responded in kind. She knew that the older woman could be gentle, but she had never expected anything like this. Kris' hands slowly slid down her back, sending thrilling chills down her spine, leaving her breathless.

Kris couldn't believe how happy she felt. Not only was she finally letting Nicole know how she felt, but she now knew that her friend felt the same way. She softly kissed Nicole's lips, cheek, and worked her way up to the delicate ear, then left a trail of small kisses down her neck to end up where she had started.

Nicole's heart and breathing were out of control. She tried to calm herself, but each kiss the taller woman gave her only got her more excited. Feeling Kris' tongue sensually run along her lips, Nicole kissed her more passionately, giving Kris' tongue access into her mouth.

There was a knock on the door and they froze, hearing Robert's voice coming through the locked door. "I'm leaving in ten minutes. I'll be waiting by the car."

"Thanks, Uncle," Nicole called out, her voice shaking with emotions. She put her head on Kris' naked chest, and wrapped an arm around the tall Austrian's waist.

"Talk about a mood killer," Kris said, taking in deep breaths. She wrapped her arms around the smaller woman and kissed the blonde hair. "Are you okay?" she asked her silent companion. Nicole nodded and lifted sparkling green eyes.

"I've never been better." She kissed the stuntwoman, gave her a squeeze, and then got up. "We better get to Robert before he leaves."

"I knew I should've taken my motorcycle this morning," Kris grumbled good-naturally. "We wouldn't have to rush this way." She sat on the edge of the bunk and slipped into her shirt, fastening it closed.

"You were too tired to ride it, remember?" Nicole said as

she put the oil bottle back into a small backpack and slung it over one shoulder. "That's why I asked Robert to pick us up this morning."

Before unlocking the trailer door, Kris tenderly wrapped her arms around the smaller woman and gave her one more kiss.

"Do you know how many times I wished for a moment like this?" Nicole smiled as she locked her hands behind Kris' neck. "How long I've been waiting for this?"

"Since this afternoon?" Kris grinned and laughed when Nicole slapped her butt. "I've been wishing for this, too." She let go of Nicole and became more serious. "But we have to talk about this. You know I'm going back to Austria."

"I know," Nicole whispered, then looked up into Kris' pale blue eyes. "But it doesn't change the way I feel. I want to spend as much time as possible with you."

"We will, I promise." The stuntwoman opened the door and they stepped out into the darkness and their waiting ride.

****

Nicole walked along the lake for some time. She had been unable to sleep all night; images of Kris and the massage were still fresh in her mind. She only wished that her uncle hadn't insisted that Kris go and get some sleep once he dropped her off at her house. She knew Robert was right, but she didn't want to be apart from her friend. She wondered what went through Kris mind once she was home. *Maybe she was so tired she just fell asleep, not thinking too much about our kiss. Or did she think about it as much as I did? How does she feel about it?*

Nicole sat on the grass, absently looking out across the lake. So many questions went through her mind. Kris had said they needed to talk about what had happened last evening between them. Was she going to say it wouldn't work out? She did say they would spend as much time as possible together, but did she mean as friends or as something more?

She looked in the direction of Kris' house and sighed. How she wished she was with her, but she wanted the stuntwoman to get as much sleep as possible. She would wait until noon and then she would give Kris a call on her cell phone.

Some distance away on the paved bicycle path, Kris was running back to her house. She had been able to get some sleep, but not as much as she would have liked. She had gotten out of bed and aimlessly walked around the empty house, wishing for Nicole's presence. But it had been too early in the morning to see or even call her.

Kris could still feel her lips on hers, remembering how she had felt when they first kissed. She had never felt that way before. That intense feeling of really loving someone was a whole new experience for her. She didn't want to lose that feeling, but what was she going to do? Nicole didn't deserve to have her hopes of a lasting relationship with her be destroyed by her return to Austria, and Kris couldn't stay in Montreal. She wished she didn't have so many responsibilities back home.

Spotting a lone figure sitting at the edge of the water, Kris slowed her pace to a stop. Nicole was watching a few seagulls fly and dive above the calm waters. She quietly walked to an empty bench some distance away, sat down, and just observed her. The stuntwoman was amazed at how quickly her heartbeat sped up once she spotted Nicole. After a few more minutes watching her friend, Kris stood up, walked to her and sat down.

"Good morning."

"Hi," the petite woman exclaimed, smiling from ear to ear. "Did you get some sleep?"

"Some," she said with a nod. Nicole looked so tired, and Kris wondered if she had as little sleep as she did. "What time did you go to bed?"

"Not too long after we dropped you off at the house," Nicole said as she played with a blade of grass. She lifted her eyes to the dark-haired woman, who watched her intently with one eyebrow lifted in question. "I did. I...just didn't fall asleep right away," she murmured, looking away from Kris. "I kept thinking about last night." Nicole took a few deep breaths before looking up at her friend again. "Do you regret what happened?" she asked.

The question caught Kris by surprise. "Of course not," she exclaimed. "Do you?"

"No!" Nicole quickly said. "It's just that...well, I..." *This is so embarrassing,* she thought as she took a calming breath. "You've had...relationships before, right?"

"If you mean have I been with women before, the answer is yes."

"Well...what I'm trying to say is...I...hum..." Nicole let out a frustrated sigh and Kris smiled.

She had an idea what Nicole wanted to say, but it seemed important to the young woman to say it, so she waited patiently until Nicole gathered her courage.

"I've never felt anything like this before," she quietly admitted. "But...I don't know what to do."

"What do you mean?" Kris frowned. "I thought you liked being with me."

"I do...I love it," Nicole insisted as she lay a hand on Kris' thigh and gave it a squeeze. "What I'm trying to say is, you have experience in...having girlfriends...and stuff. I don't," she finished in a whisper. "I've never been with...anyone...before." She looked down and played the grass again. "I don't know what to do...well, you know..." Nicole expected a comment or maybe a chuckle from Kris, but heard nothing. She looked up and found the woman smiling gently at her.

"Nicole," Kris said softly as she brushed her hand against the young woman's face, her right thumb gently caressing her cheek. "There are no instruction manuals that go with new relationships." She smiled as Nicole chuckled. "You just do what comes naturally for you, what feels right."

"But..."

"Don't worry so much. You give me something I've never had before, Nick. Pure friendship and love, and that's very precious to me." Kris waited until a few people walked by before she continued. "I love being with you, too, Nicole, but I'm afraid...I don't want to see you hurt when I go back home."

Nicole looked into Kris' eyes. "I know you'll eventually go home, you told me that from the start. But like the saying goes: It is better to have loved and lost than never to have loved at all." She smiled shyly. "I want to be with you. I want to share every moment we have together. Kris, you're the best thing that ever happened to me."

"I'm glad to know how you feel. I want to be with you, too." Kris did a quick scan around them, then kissed Nicole.

This feels so right, Nicole thought as she closed her eyes, loving the feel of Kris' soft lips on hers. How she wanted so much more than just a kiss. "This is so new to me," she shyly said. "I want to get closer to you, I want..."

Kris put two fingers on Nicole's lips and smiled. "I want it too, but I want our first time together to be special. We'll take our time, go at your own pace, no pressure, okay?"

The young blonde nodded. "No pressure," she agreed.

Kris stood up and helped her friend to her feet. "What would you like to do today?" she asked as she put her arm across Nicole's shoulders.

"Hmm, how about some breakfast first?" Nicole grinned as she wrapped her arm around the taller woman's waist.

"Okay, we can't have you starve to death, now can we?" Kris chuckled, getting a slap on the stomach.

"It's not my fault if I'm always hungry." Nicole stuck the tip of her tongue out at her companion.

"Hey. Don't stick that out if you don't intend to use it," Kris teased, getting a good laugh from Nicole.

"Oh, believe me. I intend to use it real well." She winked at Kris as they walked towards the house.

A huge grin on the stuntwoman's face was Nicole's only answer.

Chapter 9

The day's destination was Old Montreal. When they first met, Nicole had promised to act as Kris' tour guide and she had been racking her brain for the best sights. After all, the tall Austrian had so readily accepted being a tourist that Nicole felt compelled to show her everything worth seeing. Problem was, there was just so much to do and see that she wasn't sure where to begin. A little history was always a good place to start.

"Did you know that Montreal was founded in 1642?" Nicole asked as they walked along the cobblestone roads and passed in front of an ancient building. Her tall friend shook her head no. Nicole pointed to the twelve-foot high rock wall that surrounded the building. "That's the Saint-Sulpice Seminary. The walls were built in 1658, and the Seminary dates back to 1683. It's the oldest building in Montreal."

"Impressive." Kris nodded approvingly. "Is the clock on top as old?"

"Not really," Nicole said, smiling mischievously. "There's a big difference in age. It's actually quite a few years younger than the building. It was built in 1701."

Kris nodded before realizing that she was being teased. "Oh, I guess eighteen years is a big difference in age." She smiled as she shook her head.

"Hey, it's a big difference to me. It allows me to enter bars legally." She looked up at her friend. "How long have you been...legal?"

Kris burst out laughing. "Now, that's a most original way of asking my age." She winked at the smaller woman. "I'm twenty-three years old for your information."

Nicole smiled, satisfied at how directly her question had been answered. As they continued walking, Nicole pointed out other sights. "That's the Notre-Dame Basilica," she said as they stood in front of a neo-Gothic church. "It houses one of the largest organs in the world, and its wooden interior creates outstanding acoustics. Did you know that Luciano Pavarotti recorded his Christmas concert here? So did the Montreal Symphony Orchestra."

Kris shook her head. "No, I didn't. You seem to know a lot about your city."

"Am I bothering you with all the historical facts I've been throwing at you?" Nicole asked in a worried tone. "I'll stop if..."

"No, it doesn't," the tall woman quickly said. "I was just thinking that if the roles were reversed and you were in Innsbruck, I would have to do a lot of research to play tour guide for you." She shrugged and switched her backpack to her other shoulder, then looked back up at the church. "We usually know so little about our own cities. It's pleasant to see somebody who does. I like to learn things."

"Don't feel bad." Nicole smiled as she patted her friend's arm. "You've visited a lot of cities and countries. All I have are history books and travel brochures. But I'm thrilled to be able to teach you something that I know first hand." She tugged on the taller woman's hand. "Come on. Let's continue on our little tour. I've got tons of information just itching to tell you."

"Lead the way." Kris smiled as they walked down to the St-Lawrence River.

While just over two kilometers had been turned into a tourist attraction, the Montreal Port was still a working one with one hundred berths and five container terminals spread along twenty-five kilometers of shoreline. About forty commercial shipping lines used the port as well as a large number of cruise companies, which provided a colorful backdrop to the other attractions at the Old Port.

They stopped at the marina and watched with interest the pleasure boats moored in their slips, the vessels ranging from small cruisers to powerful jet boats to huge luxurious yachts. A three-mast sailboat caught their attention as it headed out of the harbor.

"I've always dreamed of being aboard a tall ship like that," Nicole said as she leaned against the guardrail. "I can only imagine what it must feel like to cross oceans that way." She turned to Kris, who had one elbow on the metal fence, her chin comfortably resting in her hand. "Were you ever on one of those?"

"Never," Kris replied. "I've been on all kinds of speed boats and spent a few hours on a Catamaran, but nothing as huge as that." She straightened and they continued their walk. "Did I thank you for taking the time to show me the sights?"

"You're welcome. I thought that it would be a nice way for you to take it easy for a while. You've been working hard lately," Nicole said as they strolled past another dock. "Now, that would be a better way for you to relax." She grinned and pointed to a few paddleboats in the shape of small tugboats as they circled the small man-made island in the middle of the second harbor.

"There's no way in hell I'd be caught in one of those," Kris growled at her giggling friend.

"I don't know, I think you'd look cute in..."

"Nicole..." Kris warned, a small smile tugging at her lips. "I've been called many things, but cute isn't one of them."

I think you're wrong, Nicole thought. *You are cute...no, you're right. Not cute but beautiful.* "Hmm, well anyway, the Bonsecours Basin always has something to offer, no matter the season. Ice skating in the winter or paddleboats during the summer. On the small island, we have the International Beer Festival once a year."

"Now, that's something I know." Kris grinned, thinking of their festival in Innsbruck.

"Is the circus in town?" the stuntwoman asked as she spied a huge blue and yellow big top next to the St-Lawrence River.

"Oh, not really. That's the National Circus School. They have their annual show at the old port. The school itself is a few streets further down. It's the only one of its kind in North America."

"Hmm, interesting."

"Are you hungry?" Nicole asked.

Kris nodded. "A little bit. You want to sit somewhere and eat?"

"I thought you'd never ask." The young blonde grinned and led the way to a pier that stretched deep in the river. Having stopped previously to buy some cheese, cold cuts, bread, and cocktail carrots, they headed for the long public expanse surrounded by trees at the foot of the Clock Tower.

Many years before, the tower served as a lighthouse, while navigators set their chronometers by its clock, legendary for its accuracy. It was the perfect place to relax, soak up some sun, and have a picnic.

The women took their time, enjoying the fresh air, watching the children play, and laughing at the antics of a couple of dogs running after balls and sticks, catching them in mid flight.

Kris glanced at the shore some distance away, and noticed some interesting structures. "What's on the other side?" she asked.

Nicole stretched her neck to see what her friend was pointing at. "Oh, that's Saint-Helen Island. That's where Montreal had its Worlds Fair in 1967." She indicated a giant geodesic dome in the center of the island. "That used to be the United States Pavilion during Expo 67. Over there," she pointed to the islands to the extreme left, "is *La Ronde.* A big amusement park with all kinds of rides and a great roller coaster. During the month of July, the International Fireworks Competition is held there."

"What about that?" Kris asked, as she pointed to a white building that looked like a giant flying saucer surrounded by spikes.

"That's the Casino," Nicole explained. "It used to be the French Pavilion during the Expo. But that's on another island named Notre-Dame. It was man-made especially for the World's Fair. All around the island is the Gilles-Villeneuve race track, used for the Formula 1 Grand Prix."

Nicole finished drinking her Coke, stood up, and gathered the remnants of their lunch to put them in a trash can. "Ready to continue the tour?"

Kris chuckled as she got up and slung her backpack on one shoulder. "Sure," she said. She couldn't remember the last time she had enjoyed herself this way. How different this outing was compared to the activities and social gatherings she usually attended. The atmosphere at those functions was often artificial and hypocritical, a huge contrast to the open freshness that Nicole offered.

Place Jacques-Cartier was in the heart of Old Montreal. The gentle slope down from the Admiral Nelson monument and City Hall next to it afforded a superb view of the Old Port. It was a major gathering place and entertainment site where passers-by and visitors enjoyed street artists, roving entertainers, jugglers, mimes, face painters, and caricaturists. Sidewalk cafés and lively restaurants, established in century old buildings, lined the square with Victorian street lamps creating a festive atmosphere day and night.

Nicole stopped to watch a woman sitting behind a young girl. The artist took a small lock of the girl's hair and braided it with colorful strands.

"This looks so cool." Nicole inspected the threads.

"You have long hair," the woman said studying the blonde. "A braid would look real nice. All you have to do is chose four colors." She took in the tall, dark haired woman standing next to Nicole. "It would be impressive in yours, too," she said with a smile. "I'll make you a special price if you both decide to have one."

Nicole looked up at her silent friend with pleading eyes. "How about it?" Kris hesitated, seemingly not impressed at having bright colors in her raven hair. "She only takes a very small lock of hair. You can always cut it later if you don't like it. Please?"

"Humph..." she growled softly, wanting to refuse but she couldn't resist Nicole's pleading expression. She looked at the spools of thread and spotted a few that were softer in color and not as bright as the other ones. "Alright," she sighed, and Nicole clapped her hands enthusiastically.

"Can I pick your colors?" the young blonde asked.

"I want those," Kris stated, pointing to a red and blue thread.

"But you can have four different colors," Nicole said as she trailed a finger along the bright colored spools.

Kris gave in. "Okay, add the green to it."

"Can I at least choose one?"

Kris knew that she should say no. The small grin on her friend's face could only mean trouble. *What damage can she really do anyway?* she thought and sighed again. "You can pick one."

"Great."

Kris impatiently sat for twenty minutes, having a small lock of her hair braided. She didn't mind it too much, but she had trouble with the attention she was getting as people stopped and watched her. She spied Nicole hiding a smile behind one small hand. Kris frowned.

"All done," the woman sitting behind her announced. "It looks very...interesting."

At the sound of Nicole's giggling, Kris grabbed her hair. The colors she had chosen had been artfully braided with her dark hair. *Not bad,* Kris silently approved, until she saw the color Nicole had chosen...a fluorescent orange.

"Nicole..." Kris growled at her laughing friend. "I'm gonna get you for this," she said, trying hard not to laugh herself.

"You're next," the artist told the blonde and took the spools Nicole had chosen.

With a smirk on her face, the tall woman handed the artist a different set of threads while Nicole settled into the chair. The mischievous look on Kris' face stopped the woman from saying anything.

When the artist finished, Nicole stood up and looked at her newly braided hair...and frowned. Those weren't the colors she had chosen. She turned to Kris. "Wha..."

"Two can play this game." Kris smirked at the fluorescent green, yellow, pink, and purple threads. "I think you look kinda cute with them."

"Yeah, you're right. It does look cute."

"Liar."

"And you're so dead," Nicole breathed and then laughed.

As the day wore on, the young woman guided Kris along Saint Paul Street where many of the buildings, dating from the nineteenth century had been renovated and served as boutiques, artists' studios and even homes. They visited one boutique after the other, with Kris following close behind, an amused grin on her face. At times Nicole seemed more the tourist than Kris was. The different Inuit and Native American pieces of art caught the blonde's attention, from the sculpted seals in soapstone, the Dream Catchers, the suede moccasins, to the native jewelry.

The street overflowed with warm, inviting restaurants offering traditional *Québécois* fare. They decided to stop at one of them for dinner with Nicole choosing to have dessert someplace else.

"So," she announced as they walked out of the restaurant an hour later, "how about if we head over to eat some beaver tails?"

"Beaver...Wh..." Kris looked at her friend as if she had lost her mind. "Huh?"

"Beaver tails," Nicole repeated seriously. "The English have their blood pudding, the French frog legs. Canadians have beaver tails."

"Ah...I don't think..." Kris started.

The smaller woman smiled as she took the stuntwoman's hand in hers and tugged. "Come on. Trust me."

"Yeah, famous last words," Kris grumbled under her breath.

They stopped at a small kiosk where a light scent of oil reached their noses. Nicole left Kris and went to the counter and held two fingers up, then came back, holding two long, flat pieces that looked strangely like beaver tails.

Kris swallowed worriedly as Nicole handed her one of the tails.

"Go on, it won't kill you." Nicole grinned as she took a huge bite.

Kris looked down at her hands and laughed. The "beaver tail" was a lightly fried pastry shaped into a tail and dunked in a mixture of sugar and cinnamon, then sprinkled with a bit of lemon juice. She took a small bite then gave Nicole a surprised look.

"This is good," she said.

"Told ya to trust me." Nicole winked. "So, you liked it?" she asked after she swallowed the last of her pastry.

"Yes, I did." Kris grinned. "Do you always eat everything with the same attack plan?"

"Yep, everything." Nicole nodded and looked up. "Well, almost everything," she added with a wink. "I suppose some things I would just take my time and savor the moment."

Kris bit her lip so that she would not laugh out loud. "I can't wait to find out what those things are," she teased.

Nicole couldn't help the blush that heated her skin. "Well, some of them you already found out about."

They walked down the cobblestone streets crowded with horse-drawn carriages, passed busy bistros and jazz clubs that all added spice to the neighborhood nightlife.

"Kris?" Nicole asked, stopping at the corner of the street.

The tall woman turned away from an artist working on a painting. "Hmmm?"

"There's something I'd like to do, but I want you to promise me that you'll let me do it, okay?" Nicole said.

"What is it?"

"Just promise me you'll say yes, okay?"

Kris took a moment before finally nodding her head. "Sure, I promise."

"You've given me so much, I just want to be able to give you something in return and..."

"Nick, you don't have to..." she started.

"You promised," Nicole stated and Kris nodded again. "It's not much, but I thought it would be a special way to end our evening in Old Montreal," she continued as they walked towards several horse-drawn carriages. "It's a very nice ride through the old streets, and we get to visit a lot, too."

Kris smiled at her young companion and bent to whisper in Nicole's ear. "And it's also very romantic," she said as she gave the blonde a soft kiss on the temple. "That's very nice of you. Thank you."

They walked up to an available carriage and climbed aboard. The driver got the horse going and guided the two women through the streets of Montreal.

"If you ever come to Austria for a visit, I promise you that we'll do the same through the streets of old Innsbruck," she said in Nicole's ear.

"I'd love that very much." She smiled and nestled her head against Kris as the stuntwoman wrapped her arm around Nicole's shoulders.

Kris half listened to the guide as he recited the history of the buildings they passed by and concentrated on the wonderful feeling she was experiencing. She wanted to commit to memory every sight, every smell, and every sound of this perfect day she had spent with such a beautiful woman.

****

The ride home was uneventful. Neither woman was in a hurry to part, and after a brief conversation, they had decided to head back to Kris' house and relax. They stopped at a video store to rent two movies for the evening. Once inside the house, Kris changed into a pair of sweatpants and T-shirt. Remembering Nicole's dress pants and blouse, she reached into a drawer and called out for her to come into the bedroom.

"Would you be more comfortable wearing this?" she asked, holding up a large T-shirt. "It might be a bit big for you though."

"Oh, that would be great, thanks." Nicole took the offered shirt and studied the words written on the front. "Is that German?"

Kris closed the drawer and opened the bathroom door so Nicole could change in there. "That's a joke my crew did after a small incident that happened last year."

"What does it mean?" she asked.

"It means: Tall, Dark, and Deadly."

"Deadly?" Nicole repeated, both eyebrows nearly at her hairline.

"While performing a stunt, a seagull had the misfortune of crossing the car's path and hit the windshield. That's where I got the deadly from."

"Oh!" The thought of the bird crashing against a racing car gave Nicole shivers down her back. "What a mess that must have been."

"You can change in here," Kris said and Nicole entered the small room. "Would you mind if we watch the movies here?" Kris asked loud enough to be heard through the closed door. "I installed the video player in the room last week. But I can put it..."

"No, watching the movies here is fine," Nicole replied then opened the door and walked out. "How do I look?" she asked, tugging at the shirt, which came down below her knees.

"You look real cute." Kris grinned as she popped a videocassette into the VCR then sat on the bed, leaning against a couple of pillows. "Comfortable?"

"You bet," Nicole said and got onto the bed and cuddled against her friend. "This looks like a slumber party. You know, like the ones we see on TV? I never had one of those."

After reaching out to turn off the light, Kris wrapped her arm around the smaller woman's waist and smiled down at her. "There's a first time for everything." She lightly kissed Nicole's lips and brought her closer against her.

A few minutes passed in comfortable silence.

"Kris?"

"Hmmm?"

"Thanks for inviting me over for the night. I didn't feel like going home alone." She gave the taller woman a squeeze before burrowing herself more comfortably against her.

Kissing the top of Nicole's hair, Kris closed her eyes and relaxed against the pillows. "I'm glad you're here."

Nicole never saw the ending of the first movie. She fell asleep, pressed against her friend.

Kris watched her companion sleep, hearing her regular breathing, hoping that sleep would claim her too, but she had no such luck. Having finished watching the movie, Kris decided to get up and do some work in the office. Only a few stunts remained to be performed. By the end of the week, the first project would be finished, and Nicole would continue working with her uncle until the movie was completed. Kris would have one week of free time before she started her second project, teaching at the Canadian Stunt School for one month. *Now that should be fun,* Kris thought with a smile.

A small noise caught Kris' attention. She held her breath and listened more closely. *There it is again.* She stood up from her desk and walked out of the small office. The sound seemed to be coming from the bedroom. She worried that Nicole was in trouble when she heard a quiet whimper and hurried into the room.

The young woman was caught in a nightmare, her legs kicking out and her arms pushing at an invisible assailant. "No! Please, Daddy, no!" she mumbled in her sleep.

Kris sat on the bed and reached out to Nicole, gently brushing away sweaty blonde locks from her face. "Shhh, it's okay," she said softly. "It's just a nightmare."

"Daddy...NO!" Nicole screamed and sat up, breathing heavily. She could feel strong arms holding her, preventing her from escaping. *He's here!* Nicole's sleepy mind told her and she fought even more, trying to push away the arms around her. "Please, stop!" she cried.

"Nicole. It's me...Kris," she said softly as she held the trembling woman in her arms, gently brushing her fingers through her hair. "Shhh, it's okay. I've got you."

"Kris?" she called out with a shaky voice. "I'm sorry." Remembering where she was, she threw her arms around Kris' neck.

"Everything's gonna be okay now, shhh." Kris rocked the smaller woman, humming softly. Nicole's body slowly relaxed in her arms, her breathing going back to a more normal rhythm. Kris' temper rose at the thought that Nicole's father was responsible for these nightmares. Thoughts of how she could make the bastard pay for the pain he caused his daughter rushed through her mind. "Better?"

Nicole nodded silently. She felt safe and protected in Kris' arms. "I'm okay now," she said softly as she finally let Kris go.

"Do you want to talk about it?"

"It's always the same thing." Nicole tiredly rubbed her eyes.

"My father comes home, he's upset, I manage to do something wrong, he hits me," she explained in a quiet voice.

"He's got no right to hit you." Kris tried to reason. "No matter the situation."

"But he's not always like that. Sometimes..." she started.

"It doesn't matter, Nicole," Kris insisted. "You can't go on like this, you deserve better." A small shrug from Nicole was her only answer. "You need to get out of his house. He'll continue to terrorize you if you stay there."

"But where would I go?" Nicole asked. "I have very little money, most of it goes to my father, and after the movie is done, I'll have no job."

"Your uncle offered to give you a room, right?" The blonde nodded. "Or you could stay here, with me." A hint of hope on Nicole's face appeared and quickly disappeared.

"I couldn't do that," she said in a whisper looking down at the bedspread. "I wouldn't want to become a burden for you."

Kris lifted Nicole's chin to make her look into her eyes. "You keep saying that. You are not a burden. I'm offering this because I want you to...I'd like..." Kris took a deep breath to steady her heartbeat. "I'd like for you to stay with me, Nicole," she admitted. "You don't need to say anything right now, but think about it okay?" Nicole nodded again. "Get some sleep now. I'll be in the living room if you need anything."

"Please," Nicole said, grabbing Kris' hand, "stay here with me?" With a smile, Kris slipped under the blankets with her. The small woman cuddled against Kris, resting her head on a strong shoulder. "Thank you," she murmured before falling back to sleep.

Kris softly kissed the blonde head under her chin and soon, joined her companion in sleep.

Chapter 10

The day at work seemed to go so slowly for Nicole. Kris, after giving her a ride to the set, had gone back home to finish work on the next stunt. Most of the planning was done, but Kris wanted to make sure that everything was perfect. She would be on the set tomorrow, ready to have the next stunt performed, but it didn't help Nicole feel any better. Their daily lunch together had been fun, but she wished that the tall Austrian had stayed longer. She shook her head, not believing the way she was reacting towards her friend. She always hoped to fall in love one day but had never expected to fall for a woman.

Nicole sat under a tree munching an apple as she remembered what it was like to wake up in Kris' arms, comfortably nestled against the taller woman's body. The light breeze that blew in off the lake through the patio doors, the gently fluttering curtains, and the sweetly singing birds had made it very difficult to crawl out of bed. *Why did I have to get up this morning? I was at peace and comfortable.*

"Hey, girl," Alex said, sitting beside her smiling cousin. "You seem to be in a good mood today. What's up?"

"Hi." Nicole smiled and took another bite. "Nothing much."

"Well, your nothing much is making you blush," Alex teased. "Does it concern your tall, dark, and extremely gorgeous friend?" she asked before taking a sip of her Coke.

"Alex!" Nicole blushed even more.

"Ah," the brunette exclaimed slapping her thigh. "I knew it. Details, girl, details."

Nicole laughed. "Yes, it does concern Kris." She glanced at Alex who was grinning from ear to ear. Her cousin would understand the way she felt. "I'm in love."

"Of course you are. I could have told you that a long time ago." She gently poked Nicole in the ribs. "Do you know how she feels about you?" she asked but already knew the answer to that question. Kris looked as in love with Nicole as she did for the stuntwoman.

"I kissed her," she stated, causing Alex to nearly spew a mouthful of soft drink in her direction.

"*You* kissed *her*?" Alex exclaimed. "This is getting better by the second. And?" she pressed as she put the can of Coke on the grass.

"Yeah, I did. And she didn't run away this time." Nicole smiled.

"Nick!" Alex threw her hands in the air and stared at her cousin. "Do I have to torture you to get all the information? Details. I want details."

"Okay, okay," Nicole chuckled and then told Alex about the massage she had planned for Kris in the dressing room trailer. Then she described their day in Old Montreal, her sleeping over at Kris' place for the night and the nightmare.

"She asked you to live with her?" Alex asked.

"For the time she'll be in Montreal," Nicole explained. "I still haven't decided what I want to do. I'd eventually have to find a place of my own after she leaves. I couldn't go back to living with Father." She sighed. "I want to stay with her so much, but I feel like I'll just get in her way."

"Nick, listen to me," Alex said, squeezing her friend's hand. "From what I know about Kris through all those European magazines, she's not the type to make offers like this just for the hell of it. She really cares about you, you know."

Nicole nodded. Why was it so hard to believe that somebody could love her and would want to be with her? Maybe after all the times her father had told her she was worthless, she had started to believe him. "That's what she said."

"And I believe her. Nick, you deserve better than the way he treats you. It really looks like Kris loves you and she wants to help you. Why don't you let her?"

"I'm scared, Alex," she said softly.

"Of what? Moving in with Kris?"

Nicole silently shook her head. "Of my father. He'll go nuts if I move out."

Alex knelt before her cousin and cupped Nicole's face in both of her hands. "He's already nuts," she said bluntly. "I never liked the bastard. Nick, you're not alone. There are a lot of people who want to help you. Please, let us?" Nicole hesitated for a moment then nodded, making the brunette smile. "Since we're talking seriously, there's just one thing I worry about," she said as she looked into Nicole's green eyes. "How do you feel about Kris leaving to go back home?"

Nicole knew that this question would come out sooner or later. "I wish that she could stay here. I don't want to see her go, but I understand," she explained as she looked out at the people rushing past them. "Falling in love wasn't in our plans, but it happened, and I'm not sorry," she added defensively.

"I'm just worried that you'll get hurt when she does leave, that's all."

"Were you ever hurt in any of your relationships?" Nicole asked, looking her cousin straight in the eyes. "Things happen, Alex. I'll get hurt just like everybody else, if not by Kris leaving, it'll be by something else," she stated and took a deep breath, letting it go slowly. "I finally know what being in love feels like. I want to live that to the fullest."

Alex quietly nodded. She understood her friend so much. What both women had was special, the type of love not too many people got a chance to have. "Okay, my friend," she said happily. "You convinced me. You're a lucky woman you know that? I just wish I was in your shoes." She winked at the blonde, grabbed her can of Coke, and stood up. "Come on, we have to get back to work."

Nicole smiled at her cousin's remark. Yes, she was lucky. Lucky that such a beautiful woman like Kristina would want to spend time with her, or better yet that she would fall in love with her. Nicole nodded and stood up. *Live every day to the fullest. My new game plan.*

****

Kris nervously walked about the area, absently playing with her headset. The last stunt was ready to be performed. Everything had been checked and rechecked, making sure that the smallest of details had been reviewed. No matter how well a stunt was planned, anything could go wrong, especially when dealing with explosives. She scanned the area around her for the tenth time, making sure that the security on set had cleared enough space between the building they were about to blow and the growing numbers of curious onlookers standing behind the barricades.

The space they were working in was minimal. The old, abandoned factory was located in the industrial park of Montreal, with other buildings right across the street, giving the crew very little space within to work. Kris nodded to the explosive experts as they walked back from setting the charges. Everything was ready; the rest was up to the director.

It looked like most of the management had shown up for the final performance. The director, Gary Watts, was talking with the second unit director, and Kris could see that Robert was nervous, judging by how he was chewing his half destroyed pencil. She spotted the two stunt people that were about to perform and headed for them.

"It promises to be one hell of a bang. Right, boss?" The young stuntman grinned at Kris.

"If it's anything like the one she did in *Law & Revenge*, just be sure to tighten your belt or you'll lose your pants, pretty boy," Claudia, a stuntwoman, teased him. "Everything ready?" she asked Kris.

Kris nodded, looking out at the still arguing directors and saw the producer approaching the little group. "If they can make up their minds, we should get going soon." Robert seemed to be more agitated than before, his hands pointing at different locations, shaking his head. Watts had his arms crossed over his chest and kept silent. The director spoke briefly then he and the producer left, leaving a fuming Robert behind.

"Doesn't look good," Claudia said as the second unit director walked to a small group of technicians and dispatched them in different locations. "What's he doing? They're going too close to the explosion site."

"I don't like this," Kris said between clenched teeth. "Take your positions and wait for my signal," she told the stunt people and headed to Robert.

When he saw Kris heading his way, he held a hand up to stop the stunt coordinator. "Don't you say anything," Robert said as he planted his feet solidly in front of Kris and ran his hands through his gray hair. "Bunch of stupid assholes," he spat, furious. "They didn't like the camera angles I chose for the shot, they changed the whole plan."

"But the cameramen will have less protection from the blast where they're standing now," Kris argued. "This is insane."

"I know," he replied, sounding defeated. "The big boys want it this way." He gave Kris a half smile. "You wouldn't happen to have any army helmets or flak jackets for the crew, would you?" He shook his head and scratched his jaw. "Everything ready on your side?"

"Do you want me to talk to Watts? Maybe I can change his mind, insist on the fact that it's not safe for the crew..." Kris started.

"I already tried. I argued as much as I could." Robert shook his head. "He says they have enough protection where they are and will get better shots that way." He looked around and spotted the rest of the technical crew standing a few feet away, among them Nicole and Alex. "They look excited about the blast."

Kris turned and saw her friend who waved enthusiastically at her. She smiled and waved back. "It's not everyday that you get to see a building blow up," she said as they walked to the explosive experts. "I just wish Nick...that they wouldn't be so close."

Robert looked at the stuntwoman and smiled. "They're far enough, don't worry." he reached out and stopped the tall woman by her arm. "Kris, I never thanked you for all that you've done for Nicole. I've never seen her so happy, especially when you're around."

"I'm only trying to..."

"You don't have to explain." Robert held a hand up. "I know that you care a lot about her, and that she cares about you, too. She's happy, Kris, that's what's important to me." He gave her a small pat on her shoulder. "Come on, let's get this show going," he said.

Kris quietly walked behind the director as he made his last round among the different department supervisors, making sure that everybody was ready. *Does it show that much on my face what Nicole means to me? Even Robert noticed,* she thought as she glanced one more time at Nicole, who was engaged in an animated chat with Alex.

"Kris, you ready?" Robert asked. She quickly scanned the area one last time, seeing both stunt performers waiting at their marks, the firefighters and medic units waiting on the side.

"We're ready," she confirmed as she lifted her hand with fingers extended in the air and looked at the stunt people.

"Okay, people!" Robert called out. "Everybody get ready!" He glanced at the explosive operator whose hands were already on the controls. "Okay, start rolling cameras!"

"Cameras rolling!" somebody called back.

"Stuntmen ready in five, four, three, two, one...GO!" Robert yelled as Kris ticked off her fingers with every second and then brought her hand down in one swift motion.

Coming out of the explosive rigged building, the pair of stunt people ran away from the factory. Following Kris' plan, the male character stumbled on the ground holding on to his wounded leg. The female character stopped running and turned back to help her fallen comrade, pulling him back on his feet to keep running.

"Explosives ready in five, four, three, two, one...GO!" Robert yelled as the explosive operator hit the switches in pre-determined sequences.

An incredible blast shook the surrounding buildings. Glass from the deserted factory windows exploded out, pieces of concrete and other loose materials flew up into the air and rained down around the two performers who had been thrown to the ground by the force of the explosion. A gigantic ball of flame and smoke rose above the building that crumbled to the ground like a huge wounded beast.

Something's gone wrong, Kris thought as debris fell down further away from the blast than anticipated. Onlookers behind the fences ran away from the site as big chunks of bricks and concrete fell around them. The technical crew closest to the explosion site ran to get undercover, leaving behind the cameras still filming.

When the falling debris let up, Kris sprinted to the stunt performers lying on the ground. She knelt beside them as they slowly rose to a sitting position and inspected them for any major injuries. "You guys okay?" she asked. Both nodded as they brushed the concrete dust off their clothes.

"What the hell happened?" Claudia asked, a bit shaken. "We weren't supposed to get bombarded by debris."

"Somebody's balls are in trouble," Mario, the young stuntman, grumbled. "I bet those explosive techs are really nervous right now."

Kris helped them up and once she was satisfied that neither had suffered any serious injuries, she looked around for Robert. Somebody was going to pay for this foul-up. "Get the medics to clean those cuts," she told the stunt performers and headed off to both directors and the producer.

After ripping her headset off her head, Kris handed it to a gopher walking by. A panic took hold of her as she remembered that Nicole had been standing among the crew in the area where a lot of debris had fallen. She turned around to look for the small blonde.

"Nicole?" she called out, trying to find a familiar face and ask about her location. When Kris spotted a group of technicians surrounding somebody sitting on the ground, she sped up her pace, her heart beating in her throat.

Some distance away, Robert was arguing violently with Watts, his face crimson with rage. "What do you mean it's not your fault?" he screamed, veins bulging in his throat. "Don't you dare put the fault on your assistant. You're the one who hired those amateurs."

"Just cool off, okay?" the director said. "Nobody got seriously hurt, just a couple of scratches that's all. Besides, we got great shots."

Robert turned around and took a few steps away from the director, wanting so much to hit him. The only things that mattered to that asshole Watts were his shots. It didn't matter if people got injured, even though they weren't seriously hurt. He looked around at all the debris littering the ground and at the firefighters battling the flames that blazed from the crumbled building. A movement caught his attention, and he turned in time to see Kris run towards a group of people. Forgetting Watts and the producer, he ran after the dark-haired stuntwoman.

Pushing people out of the way, Kris saw that it was her friend who sat on the ground, blood running down the side of her head and jaw. "Nicole!" she exclaimed with a shaky voice.

Slightly dazed, the young blonde looked up at the sound of the familiar voice and saw her friend push people away and kneel down beside her. "Kris?"

"I'm here," she said softly, as she brushed a lock of hair away from Nicole's bloodied face and put it behind her ear. "I want the medics here, *now*," she ordered the technicians and turned her attention back to Nicole. "How are you feeling?"

"I'm okay," she assured the stuntwoman. "Just a little dizzy, that's all."

Noticing Alex for the first time, Kris asked the seemingly uninjured woman, "How about you?"

Alex, upset by her cousin's injury, held onto Nicole's shoulders. "No problem," the brunette said. "Is there anything I can do?"

"Yeah, get everybody away from here," the stuntwoman ordered. Alex nodded, then stood up and backed people away from the women. Noticing that Nicole was shaking, Kris wrapped her arms around her and pulled her close. "You're going to be all right. Shhh," she whispered in her friend's ear, gently rocking the smaller woman back and forth. Tears formed in her eyes at the thought that her friend could have been more seriously injured. She should've insisted that Nicole not be present on the site. Even though the accident wasn't her fault, she couldn't help but feel responsible for what had happened and for her companion's injuries.

Nicole tightened her hold on the stuntwoman and felt the strong arms around her. *I'm okay, Kris is here now. Everything's gonna be all right*, she told herself. Aside from the cut she had received when a small piece of concrete had hit her on the side of the head, she wasn't that badly hurt. Taking a deep breath to calm her nerves, she relaxed in Kris' arms. She felt tremors through her friend's body and looked up at her closed eyes and tear streaked cheeks. "Hey," Nicole gently wiped the tears away with her fingers. "Kris?"

"You could have been seriously hurt. I'm so sorry," she said, her voice cracking.

"It's not your fault. It was an accident," Nicole said gently to the dark-haired woman. "I wanted to be here. I didn't want to miss the show."

"But you got hurt," Kris said as another tear slid down her cheek.

"I'm okay," she softly reassured the stuntwoman. She gave Kris a small kiss on the lips and whispered again, "I'm okay."

A medic knelt beside them to examine Nicole. Kris reluctantly let her go so that the technician could do his job properly, then stood up, keeping her eyes on the smaller woman.

Robert lightly touched Kris' arm and smiled. "They're going to take care of her. Let's go have a talk with Watts."

"No," she said, still watching the medic examine her friend. "I don't want to leave her alone."

"Kris, I'll be fine," Nicole said with a smile. "Go take care of business. I'll join you soon after the medics done." The tall woman hesitated. "Go on, Tiger, go kick some butts."

Kris smiled and then chuckled. "Okay, I'll be right back." She bent down and kissed Nicole, not caring if anybody was watching. She stood up and started walking, then stopped and turned back to look at the woman on the ground. "Tiger?" she mouthed, causing the young blonde to smirk.

"I think it suits you." Robert smiled, but quickly lost it

when Kris glared at him. "Or maybe not."

Kris shook her head. *Tiger.* Nobody had ever given her a pet name before and it felt...nice, she decided with a smile as they headed to the nervous looking Watts and his producer. She was in a perfect mood to kick some butts as Nicole had put it so well.

Chapter 11

"Do you think you had enough?" Kris asked with a grin. The table was littered with Chinese food cartons, most of them emptied by her friend.

Nicole pushed her plate away with a sigh. "Oh yeah," she said while rubbing her stomach. "Couldn't have another bite." She started to get up to clear the table. "Thanks for having me over for..."

Kris stood up and took the plates away from Nicole. "I'll do that. You just relax okay?" She cleared the table and put the dishes in the dishwasher. "The doctor said to take it easy for awhile. How's your headache?"

"I'm fine." Nicole shook her head. Ever since they got back from the hospital, Kris hadn't stopped fussing over her, making sure that she was comfortable. "I appreciate all the attention though." She grinned at her friend as she was guided out of the kitchen to the living room.

After taking a pillow from the sofa, Kris fluffed it and put it behind Nicole's back once she sat down. "I just want to make sure that you'll be okay." She fussed with it just a tad longer before stepping away, satisfied.

"Are you always this caring with slightly injured friends?" Nicole teased.

"Only with the ones that I really care about," Kris answered as she sat down beside her. "And there aren't that many."

"Thanks for the pillow, but I'd rather have you." Nicole smiled as she leaned onto Kris. "I'm going to miss you this weekend."

Kris had planned a working weekend at a horse-breeding stable some distance away from Montreal, wanting to check out the latest techniques and equipment. Having horses perform stunts also meant having to deal with all kinds of injuries. She had promised the veterinarian who worked full time at her estate that she would look into specific equipment for their needs.

"I'm not going," Kris finally said.

Nicole sat up and looked into Kris' eyes. "Why?" she asked. "I'm going to be fine. I promise that I'll be careful, okay?" She took the larger hand in hers and gave it a squeeze. "I know this visit is very important to you, and you had so much trouble getting an appointment with these people. Also, you don't have much free time left before you start teaching at the stunt school." She smiled at the tall woman and leaned back against her. "Besides, I have some housework to do before Sunday."

"That's another reason why I don't want to spend my weekend away from you," Kris said, as she brushed her fingers through Nicole's hair. "Your father's coming back, and it'll be difficult to see each other like we've been doing."

Nicole didn't want to lose the incredible feeling of inner peace and being loved of the last two weeks, and she was damned if she'd let her father get in the way of it. She was afraid of his reaction to her moving out of the house, but she couldn't continue living in fear. Kris had shown her that she could live as an independent woman, in control of her own destiny. It was about time that she did something about it. A smile crossed her lips.

"We'll have plenty of time to see each other," Nicole reassured her. "I'd like to come and stay with you, if the offer's still open that is."

Kris held her breath. Did she hear right? She shifted so she could better see Nicole's face. The young woman smiled at her, waiting for an answer. Her heart beat wildly against her chest. "Really?" she softly asked. The blonde silently nodded. "Of course, the offer is still open," she exclaimed in joy and gave Nicole a hug. "It'll give you a chance to get away from your father and..." Soft fingers touched Kris' lips and she blinked at her companion in surprise.

"I'm not asking to move in with you to run away from my father. I'm doing this because I want to be with you." She moved so she could look at Kris better. "You made me realize that I need to do things because I want to, not because I'm ordered to. I want to work with movie cameras and go back to school to learn about the proper techniques. I want to be able to have friends come visit me and not be afraid of him going nuts." She looked into the blue eyes and smiled. "I want to be able to live my life with a loved one, even if it means for a short amount of time." She paused and took a deep breath. "Kris, I want to live."

Kristina didn't know what to say. Words couldn't express what she was feeling. So she did the next best thing and wrapped her arms around Nicole and held her close. *How can I leave this woman behind when I go back to Austria?* she thought. Nicole had become such an important part of her life, making her feel so alive. She didn't want to leave that behind. She had loved before, but this time it was different, she was *in love*, head over heels.

Nicole smiled as she rested against Kris, lovingly wrapped in the long and muscular arms. She could hear the older woman's fast heartbeat and feel her warm breath caressing the side of her face. She didn't know what the future held for her or for them, but she knew that she had made the right decision. "Kris?" she asked softly, breaking the comfortable silence.

"Hmm?"

"Promise me that you'll go to the stables in Quebec City and enjoy yourself over the weekend?" she asked as she trailed her fingers on the woman's stomach.

"But don't you need help moving your things out of the house?" she asked softly, loving the effect the young woman had on her. Nicole's moving fingers gave her a nice tingle all over her body.

"I don't own much," Nicole sadly said. "Mostly clothes and books. Alex said she would help get most of my stuff out before my father arrives Sunday."

"But..."

"Promise me?" Nicole asked as she gently poked Kris in the stomach. "I mean it. I want you to have a good time this week-end, even if it's not a pleasure trip. I'll be fine."

Kris sighed. She hated to leave Nicole alone with her maniac father. At least Alex would be there to help her. She also knew that Nicole could count on her uncle if anything happened, but she'd feel so much better if she could be with her. "I'll prom-ise you only if you'll do something for me, okay?"

"Okay."

"I gave you my cell phone number before, right?" Kris asked and Nicole nodded. "So you give me a call as soon as you're out of the house or especially if something goes wrong, alright?"

"Nothing will..." Nicole started.

"Is it a deal? I'll go for the weekend, and you give me a call no matter what's going on?"

This went better than I thought, Nicole smiled to herself. "It's a deal," she agreed.

"Also, promise me that you'll be careful? Run out of there if he goes nuts," Kris insisted.

"You're a real mother hen, you know that?" Nicole chuck-led, then turned serious. "I promise I'll be careful."

Satisfied, Kris leaned back more comfortably in the sofa and brought the smaller woman closer to her. She wished that she could be there with her, but she understood the need for Nicole to face her father with her decision. It was Nicole's first step toward being an independent woman.

"How about if we watch a movie?" Nicole asked.

Kris nodded, accepting her friend's silent wish to change the subject. She reached for the remote control and switched the TV on. It would be their last evening together before everything happened, and she wanted Nicole to relax and enjoy herself. Things could get rough fast enough.

****

Nicole wandered about the house, trying to see if she had

forgotten anything. Alex had helped her pack her books and CDs, as well as her TV and CD player; her clothing was already at her uncle's place. All that remained was a small travel bag filled with little things she found as she searched the rooms. Things like her mother's favorite coffee mug that was still in the cupboard, and the pictures that she had on her night table. The mug was all she had that belonged to her deceased mother.

It had been a long and lonely weekend without Kris, but the tall Austrian had called her twice on Saturday and three times already that day, wanting to know if everything was okay. Kris was happy that her business trip was a success and told her that new equipment had been bought for her two stables, and that it would be shipped to Austria soon. Nicole couldn't wait to be with her friend again on Monday and smiled as she remembered telling her that she missed her.

Nicole's heart stopped when she heard a car door slam shut. She quickly hid the travel bag beside the front door and waited for her father to come in.

McGrail barreled into the house and dropped his suitcases at Nicole's feet. "Bring those bags to my room," was the greeting he gave his daughter and marched into the kitchen. She silently grabbed the bags and did as she was told. This was not the time to make him angry. After dropping the suitcases into the room and closing the door behind her, Nicole took a deep calming breath and walked to the kitchen.

Her father had made himself a cup of coffee and sat at the table reading papers that he had brought in with him. A good sign that he was angry or in a bad mood would have been his going into his office directly. Seeing him sitting in the kitchen gave Nicole courage enough to inform her father of her decision.

She took a few hesitant steps forward and stood some distance away from the table. "How was your trip, Father?" she asked with a soft voice.

"Hmmphh, what do you want?" he tersely asked, never lifting his eyes from his papers.

She swallowed a few times and held her hands in front of her to stop them from shaking. "I came to tell you goodbye."

McGrail looked up briefly at his daughter. "You're going to

bed early?"

"I'm not going to bed, Father. I'm leaving to go live on my own." She held her breath as her father slowly put his coffee mug on the table and stood up.

"What did you say?" he asked in a deep rumbling voice.

Don't quit now, Nicole told herself as she stood a little straighter. "I'm moving out. I'm eighteen years old, it's about time that I start living on my own."

"Who put those ideas into your head, girl?" he asked as he slowly stepped forward.

"Nobody did, Father," Nicole fearfully replied. "You gave me food and shelter all my life, and for that, I'm grateful." She took one step back to match her fathers steps. "But it's time that I do this on my own now."

"And how are you going to live? You don't even have a job."

That question surprised Nicole. She expected her father to rant and rave but never to ask a legitimate question like that. "Uncle Robert said he would give me a job at the studios. He would also help me go back to school."

"And would my dear brother also give you a place to live?" McGrail asked, crossing his arms over his massive chest.

There was no way that she would implicate Kris in this, but she didn't want to lie to her father either. "I'll have my own place eventually." She watched him for any signs that he was losing his temper but found none. He looked calm and collected, and she started to feel a little more comfortable. "I want to go to school and become a camera operator. I want to travel the world and see places that I've always read about."

"But I want you to go to school, too. I already talked to a friend of mine so you could start your lessons next semester," he calmly explained. "I want you to have a good, stable job that will give you a future, not make you some kind of drifter hopping around the world aimlessly," he said as he slowly approached his daughter.

"But, Daddy, courses in management aren't what I want to do. I want to learn the techniques of filming movies and go on location. Alex applied to be part of a crew that will be filming in

Central Africa. I'd like to do that, too, and..." His calm features turned into a frown and then became hard.

"So, it's Alex who turned you against me," he said in a low, dangerous voice. "I told you to stay away from that dyke. She will only cause you trouble."

"Alex had nothing to do with this, Daddy, I swear," Nicole said as she took another step back, away from her furious father. "I just want to live my life..."

"I gave you everything that you needed. Food..." McGrail took a step forward while Nicole took one back. "...shelter..." another step, "...clothes..." and another. "Everything that you wanted. You know what you are? You're just a little ingrate, that's what you are, just like your mother!" he spat.

"That's not true, Daddy, I always apprec..."

"Are you calling me a liar, girl?" he hissed as he swung his arm and hit Nicole across the face, sending the small woman bouncing off the kitchen sink and collapsing to the floor.

Nicole lifted a shaky hand to her lip and drew it back to see blood on it. She looked up at her father through teary eyes. "Why?" she asked as he towered above her. "Why do you keep hitting me?"

"Because you deserve it, you little bitch!" He reached down and grabbed both of Nicole's arms and dragged her to her feet. "You're just like your mother! All you women are all the same!" he screamed as he shook Nicole like a rag doll. "You tease men by flirting with us, wear clothes that should get you arrested, promise to spend the night with us, and then laugh as you leave us behind to go into the arms of...of another woman!" He slapped Nicole, sending her reeling against the refrigerator.

The man's clearly insane, Nicole thought. *I don't know what the hell he's talking about.* Did he mean that her mother left him for another woman or was it somebody else? He took a few steps towards her, and she quickly moved out of the way.

"Enough!" Nicole screamed, surprising him. "I've had enough of you hitting me," she said through clenched teeth. "I don't want to live like this anymore, I'm leaving," she stated with confidence before she turned around and headed to the front door. She looked back when a loud noise sounded behind her and she saw that her father had thrown a chair against the wall and was coming after her. She ran, quickly grabbing her travel bag on the way and tore through the door.

"Come back here, you bitch!" He yelled. She didn't stop. She knew that if she did, he would probably kill her. Nicole kept running, needing to get away from her insane father.

After a while, she looked back and saw that her father wasn't following anymore. She ran down another street and ended up at the general store two blocks away from Kris' house. She headed for the public phone and reached into her jeans' pocket for a quarter. After pulling a crumpled piece of paper out of her pocket, she wiped her eyes dry of the tears and angled the paper towards the light so she could see the number scrawled on it. She picked up the receiver and inserted the money into the slot and dialed the number. As she listened to the rings, Nicole looked out for any signs of her father. She sniffed a couple of times, trying to get her tears and breathing under control. It wouldn't do to start crying again with Kris three hours away from Montreal.

"Hello?" Kris answered.

How good it was to hear her voice. "Kris, it's me," she said, trying to keep her voice steady. She gingerly touched her lip with her fingers and saw that it was still bleeding.

"How are you?" Kris asked. "You sound nervous, is everything alright?"

"I'm okay, Kris. I'm..." The tears returned and she swallowed a couple of times to keep herself from crying. "I'm okay," her voice cracked.

"Where are you?" Kris asked, worried. "Did your father do something?"

"I'm at the corner store near your place in a public phone booth." Nicole sniffed. "He's nuts!"

"Listen to me. Go to the store and stay inside. Ask the clerk to make a call for you and tell your uncle to come and pick you up, okay?"

Nicole nodded to the phone and looked outside around the booth. "Okay," she said as she wiped her eyes with the back of her hand.

"I'll be with you as soon as possible. I'm leaving right now."

"Kris, you don't..."

"Go inside the store right now, Nicole. You'll be safer there," Kris instructed. "Listen, I'll call Robert myself. You just wait for him inside, okay?"

"Okay...Kris?" Nicole spoke softly. "Please be careful driving back? I'm fine now. Really."

"I'll see you soon, Nick." There was a silent moment before Kris continued. "I lo...See you soon."

"Bye," Nicole replied missing Kris' half-declared admission and hung up. She stepped out of the phone booth and took another look around but saw no signs of her father. She quickly entered store and gave the woman working behind the counter a shy smile. "Would it be possible to have a tissue or something?" she asked, fingering her bloody lip.

"Of course!" the woman exclaimed. "Come over here. Paul," she hollered, looking at the back room, "take the front desk will you?"

Nicole quietly followed the gray haired woman to the bathroom. Like Kris had said, at least she'd be safer indoors.

Somewhere in Quebec City, Kris packed her back pack and rushed out of her hotel room, stopping only at the registration desk to pay for her room. *If McGrail harmed Nicole in any way,* Kris thought, *I'll make sure he pays for it.* She climbed on her Harley and started the motor. She would ride all the way back to Montreal at breakneck speed even if it meant getting a few speeding tickets in the process. The tall, dark haired woman guided her motorcycle to the highway and then headed back to her friend, her new love.

Chapter 12

Nicole sat in the kitchen with Alex and her Aunt Michelle. The cut on her lip wasn't that bad and would heal fairly quickly. What bothered her the most was the nasty bruise on her cheek. Robert had gone into a rage after seeing what his brother had done and after driving his niece to his house, he took off with the car's tires screeching. *Probably to go "visit" her father*, Nicole thought.

Nearly two hours had passed since her father had gone crazy. The ring from the doorbell made everybody jump in surprise. It took a moment before Michelle stood up from the table and walked to the door. Looking out the side window, she sighed in relief to see that it wasn't her brother-in-law but Nicole's friend, Kristina. She unlocked the door and opened it for the tall Austrian to enter.

"How's Nicole?" Kris asked as she walked in and unzipped her leather jacket, her backpack still secured on her back.

Michelle took the stuntwoman's motorcycle helmet and gloves. "She's terrified that her father will come after her. Alex is in there with her," she said indicating the kitchen.

Kris marched into the room and came face to face with an angry Alex, her hand hovering above the hilt of a baseball bat on the kitchen table while her body shielded someone. The angry look was quickly replaced by one of relief.

"Are you planning to use this on me?"

"Of course not!" Alex took her hand away from the weapon. "I'm sorry."

"Kris!" Nicole exclaimed from behind her cousin and ran into her friend's arms. "I'm so glad to see you."

Kris held the smaller woman, not wanting to let her go. "I'm here now. Everything's gonna be okay," she softly said as she brushed her fingers through Nicole's hair. She was faintly aware of the others leaving the kitchen before she opened her eyes and looked down at her smaller companion. She noticed the cut lip and the bruise on her cheek. "Your father did that?" Kris asked in an angry voice. "The bastard! I'll..."

Nicole quickly reached for Kris' hand. "Please. Don't," she softly said, looking up into stormy eyes. "I've had enough of my father's temper, and then my uncle going after him. I don't need you going off like a bomb, too. Please...just stay with me?"

Kris' jaw muscles danced under the bronze skin before the tense features relaxed. The realization hit her in the face dead on. Nicole didn't need to share her life with another bad tempered person. Her temper was famous among the stunt people and crew. She didn't lose it often, but when she did, it was mostly to defend somebody in need, never to attack or play the diva on a movie set.

She usually calmed down fairly quick but never as fast as Nicole's presence enabled her to. The smaller woman had a magical touch. She looked into the green eyes as she took a deep breath, gave her a half smile then nodded. "You're right. I'm sorry."

"But I know you'd never hit me." She smiled then winced as her lip hurt. "You're not like my father."

Kris lifted her fingers and traced Nicole's lips gently. "I would never hurt you," she said as her eyes roamed over the beautiful face. "But I'd love five minutes alone with your father."

"I know." Nicole wrapped her arms around the taller woman's neck and kissed her. She had waited all weekend to do this, and she wasn't going to let a cut lip keep her away from

Kris' soft kisses.

"I took care of it, Kris." A voice from the doorway startled both women. "I visited my brother. He won't be bothering Nicole for some time," Robert said as he hid his bruised hand behind his back. "I'm sorry I interrupted," he added with a grin.

Kris smiled at Robert and gave Nicole a hug, keeping her in her arms. "Thanks for the help. I really appreciate it."

"Hey. It was the least I could do." He winked at the dark-haired woman. "Why don't you let us take Nicole's things to your place while you take good care of my favorite niece? Of course, I see you've already started doing that." He grinned at Nicole's blush as she buried her face into Kris' chest.

"Uncle, I'm your only niece," Nicole mumbled, making Kris and Robert smile.

"It doesn't matter. You're still my favorite." He chuckled. "Oh. Before I forget, we're having a barbecue tomorrow. We'd like to have the both of you over."

Kris looked down into Nicole's hopeful eyes. "We'd love to, Robert."

"Great!" Two other voices exclaimed from outside the kitchen. They turned to see Alex and her mother grinning in the doorway.

"Don't forget your bathing suits," Alex chipped in.

"We won't," Nicole said as she rubbed Kris' stomach. "Can we go now?"

"Sure." Kris grabbed the travel bag from the kitchen table and handed it to Nicole. As the blonde slung the bag across her back, Kris caught a small booklet that was about to fall out of the bag's pocket. It was a Canadian passport. Opening it while Nicole gave Robert a hug, Kris noticed that not one stamp graced the pages. She showed the official document to Nicole. "It's brand new."

Nicole nodded. "It's the first thing Robert insists that his crew have," she explained. "If we ever have to go outside Canada to film or something, everybody's ready."

"Wise decision." Kris smiled at the organized director.

"I do my best." Robert grinned. "Okay, everybody out and help me get Nicole settled."

The small group quickly filed out of the kitchen and each grabbed a box or item to put back into Robert's car and then drove to Kris' place. As he observed the stuntwoman help Nicole sit behind her on the beautiful Harley, Robert was struck with how happy both seemed to be.

He had seen his own daughter go from one woman to another, looking for a partner that would be willing to share her life with her. He wished that Alex could find somebody as caring and loving as Kris was for Nicole.

****

Robert was cooking the hamburgers on the grill while his wife, Michelle, fussed about, making sure that everybody had plenty to drink. Nicole sat on the edge of the pool, soaking her feet in the cold water, watching Kris and Alex play water volleyball in the deep end. Alex's girlfriend was working on her tan, away from the splashing swimmers. It was fun to see Kris' playful side with other people, which she usually reserved for only her. She smiled as Kris slapped the volleyball at Alex, causing the brunette to dive under the surface to avoid getting hit by the speeding ball.

Neilson approached Nicole and sat down next to her, his legs dipping into the water. "Hey, Neil, you're not joining in the fun?" she asked, indicating the two women in the pool.

"Nuh uh." He shook his head. "They play too rough for me." He smiled as he took a sip of his beer. Nicole couldn't keep her eyes off the tall woman. "She's something, isn't she?" Neilson asked gently. Nicole looked so happy. He was glad that his friend had found someone to love and be loved.

Nicole smiled and patted his leg. "She's great. I can't explain how I feel when I'm with her. She means everything to me, Neil."

Back home from Los Angeles, Neilson had heard about what happened between Nicole and her father from a message Alex had left on his answering machine. He had wished that he could've been there for Nicole. He never liked her father, the man gave him the creeps and he remembered with a shudder a conversation he once had with him. McGrail had insisted that Nicole would make him a very nice wife. Her father talked as if he was trying to sell a horse or even worst, a slave. The idea of marrying her had crossed his mind though, but that arrangement would have been only to take Nicole out of harms way. She was like the sister he never had, and he loved her as if she was.

Watching her now, smiling and giggling like a schoolgirl, he knew that Nicole had found the one person for her. He was happy that his friend had fallen head over heels in love, after he got over his surprise that it had been for another woman.

Nicole's smile widened, and he turned to see what she was looking at. Kris had stopped playing volleyball and was swimming to them. Alex had gone to join her girlfriend on the chaise lounges.

"Are you coming in for a swim?" Kris asked Nicole, putting both hands on each side of the blonde woman and easily pulling herself out of the water. She gave her a quick kiss before falling back into the pool.

"Go on, I'll see you later," Neilson said as he stood up and joined the others.

"Robert is cooking the burgers. We're about to eat." Nicole smiled as Kris playfully splashed her.

"We can swim until it's ready then. Come on." She opened her arms.

Nicole didn't waste a second and pushed herself into the water and into Kris' arms. She loosely locked her hands behind the taller woman's head and was towed away from the edge of the pool.

"This is nice." She smiled as Kris' hands slowly crawled up her body and she closed her eyes when the strong hands gently rubbed against her breasts. "Hmm...this is even better." Kris' soft lips pressed against hers and she opened her mouth, letting her partner's tongue enter. Nicole knew that people were watching, but she didn't care. She was in heaven, and nobody could take that away from her. Her hands roamed all over Kris' muscular body, and the stuntwoman's breathing became erratic.

Kris slowly pulled away from Nicole and smiled. "I think we'd better stop," she said as she gave a quick look at the smiling crowd.

"I'm sorry, I didn't mean to embarrass you," Nicole said as she looked down. A long finger lifted her chin, and she looked into sparkling blue eyes.

"I said we'd better stop, because otherwise, I couldn't be held accountable for my actions." She grinned, making Nicole smile. "I don't think you'd want that kind of a show for your family and friends, right?"

"I don't think so." Nicole shook her head as she blushed. "Kris?"

"Hmmm?"

"I want to thank you for not rushing me." Nicole lowered her voice. It was hard enough to say without having an audience too. "I mean, you've been so patient with me and..."

"Nick, what are you talking about?" Kris asked softly.

"Well, I know that you've been with women before and that I haven't and..." She sighed.

"Nick, I love you," Kris said, surprised she actually said it out loud. "I'm not hiding the fact that I dream about making love to you, but I told you that there was no rush, no pressure. We'll know when the time is right, okay?"

"I love you, too," Nicole said with tears in her eyes. She buried her face in the tall woman's neck and held on tight. "You've been so good to me."

"Lunch is ready!" Robert hollered.

Kris gave them a few more minutes to get their emotions under control and then looked into Nicole's green eyes. "Are you hungry?"

"What do you think?" Nicole returned with a laugh. "But you know what I'd love to eat?"

"What would that be?"

"Real Mexican food," she stated. "People say that what we have here is not as good as the real deal," Nicole explained as they climbed out of the pool.

"You never had the real deal?" Kris asked.

Nicole shook her head. "No. I only had the stuff from here. I'd love to be able to go to Mexico one day and be able to experience the atmosphere, walk through the streets smelling all the foods cooking and hearing the music," Nicole explained dreamily. "They say the beaches are incredible in Cancun. Have you ever been there?"

"No, I haven't. The only places I've been to in the Americas, aside from the United States and Canada is Argentina."

"Hey, you guys!" Alex called. "Are you gonna chat in there all night or are you coming out to eat?"

"We're coming, we're coming!" Nicole laughed and stepped out of the pool with Kris trailing behind her. "You can be so pushy sometimes."

****

Kris woke at four in the morning. She lay in bed feeling like a kid who couldn't wait to spring a surprise on someone. Having waited as long as she could, she nudged Nicole, who tightened her hold on her and mumbled incoherently, then gently shook her until she finally opened her eyes and blinked at her.

"Kris, it's only..." she started as she looked at the clock on the desk. "God, it's not even five o'clock yet."

"I know but Robert will be arriving soon." Kris gave Nicole a gentle kiss on the lips. "Good morning."

"Hmmm, good morning." She smiled as she lazily stretched.

Kris got out of bed and walked to the bathroom. The sound of the shower forced Nicole to reluctantly slip out from under the covers. "What is it again that Robert wants us to check out?" she called out.

Poking her head out of the bathroom, Kris said, "Some location or something. I'll make it quick so you can use the shower too."

"That's some precise information," Nicole mumbled good-naturedly as she watched Kris disappear into the bathroom then turned to finish packing her travel bag.

Both women were ready to leave by the time Robert arrived at the house and were soon on their way. As she looked out the car window, enjoying the light banter between Robert and Kris, Nicole frowned when she noticed they seemed to be headed for the airport. She had assumed that her uncle was driving them to a car rental place.

"Ah, Kris?" she asked softly. "I didn't know we were taking a plane."

"I didn't tell you?" Kris asked innocently. "I'm sorry, it must have slipped my mind."

Robert bit his lip, trying not to laugh. Looking into the rear-view mirror, he winked at Kris and parked the car in front of the terminal door. Everybody stepped out of the vehicle, took the travel bags out of the trunk and placed them on a cart. "Well, have a nice trip you guys." Robert smiled and gave Nicole a kiss on the cheek. "Try to have some fun, okay?" He said as he shook Kris' hand.

"I'll make sure we do that." She smiled. "Thanks for the lift."

"See you Monday." She waved at her uncle before he got into the car and drove off. Totally clueless about what was going on, Nicole was content to simply follow and walk alongside her friend into the terminal. "So, where are we going that we need to take a plane?" she asked as she looked at all the people walking past them, trying to guess their destinations.

"You'll see." Kris knew it was just a matter of time before she'd start with the questions.

Nicole looked up at the different airline names lining the halls and followed Kris as she headed to the Air Canada desk. She frowned when she saw the destination. "Ah, Kris?"

"Hmmm?" She looked innocently at Nicole.

"That's the line-up for Can..." Nicole suddenly stopped. She looked around and up at the board indicating the final destination. She looked back at Kris, her eyes big as saucers. "But...This is a flight for Cancun!" she exclaimed.

"Are you sure?" Kris asked, not moving from their place in the line-up.

"Yes. I think we have the wrong..." Then the realization hit her. Cancun, Mexico. She had mentioned it to Kris at her uncle's barbecue. *No, this couldn't be,* she thought as she stared at Kris who was now grinning from ear to ear. "Don't tell me...that I...that we...this isn't a joke, right?"

"It's not a joke, Nick." Kris chuckled.

Nicole stood still for a moment and then threw herself at Kris, giving her a solid hug. "I don't believe this!" she exclaimed. "Are we really going to Cancun?"

Smiling, Kris held up two airplane tickets along with two passports. "Yes, we are."

"Oh, God. I don't know what to say," she whispered, still holding on to Kris' waist.

"Just say thank you." Kris smiled at a bewildered Nicole. "I want this to be the most beautiful vacation you have ever had."

Nicole raised a shaky hand to her face and put a lock of hair behind an ear. "Tha...thank you." She closed her eyes as Kris wrapped her arms around her. "But...why?" she asked in a soft voice. *What did I ever do to deserve all this?*

Kris tilted her head and whispered in Nicole's ear, "Because you deserve to be happy. Because I want you to relax and have some fun, and because I love you."

"I love you, too." Nicole smiled and hugged Kris again, oblivious to the stares they were getting.

Chapter 13

Cancun, just an hour by air from Miami, nestled on the eastern coast of the vast, mysterious Yucatan Peninsula. The star jewel of the Mexican Caribbean, studded with luxury hotels, stunning beaches, jungles, and unfathomable ancient Mayan ruins.

Coming out of the gate at the airport, Kris guided Nicole through the throng of people, pushing their cart with luggage until they were clear of the human sea. She hated crowds, and she looked forward to getting into their car. Nicole, on the other hand, was enjoying herself immensely. She walked on autopilot, looking everywhere and absorbing the scenes playing around them with childlike wonder.

"Where do we go now?" Nicole asked, stopping to listen to a mariachi band.

"We try to find..." Kris started and looked above the crowd. "I found it. Follow me," the tall woman said as they continued through the crowd to the area reserved for limousine drivers waiting for their passengers. One of them held up a sign with "K.V. Deering" on it.

The man looked at the two women and smiled as Kristina showed her passport. He quickly took the two bags and walked to the exit.

"Wow." Nicole grinned at Kris. "It's nice to have somebody waiting for us. We don't have to go taxi hunting."

"Not if I can help it. Oh! I almost forgot." Kris opened her leather travel bag, took out a medium sized gift-wrapped box and handed it to Nicole. "You can't go on vacation without one of these."

Nicole took the box and frowned at her friend. "You are spoiling me rotten."

"You don't want it? Okay," Kris teased and reached for the gift but Nicole moved it away from her.

"Don't you dare." she smiled and unwrapped the box as they walked. "Oh!" She pulled a 35-mm camera out of the wrappings. "That's great. I'll be able to take pictures. Thanks." She studied her gift then looked up as Kris gently pulled at her arm. They were out of the terminal, and had been heading directly for a palm tree.

Kris chuckled. "Careful," she said as she put her sunglasses on.

"Oh, wow," the blonde exclaimed as she touched the tree. "It's a real one."

"I don't think they grow plastic palm trees around here, Nick," Kris said with a laugh, delighted at the way her friend marveled at everything, from her first plane ride to the sight of a palm tree. She waited patiently beside the driver who held the limousine door open. This was Nicole's vacation, and they would go at the young woman's pace. If it meant that they would stop at every little thing that caught her attention, then that's what they would do.

"This is so..." Nicole started as she turned around and saw the car. "A limo?" She approached the long vehicle and climbed into it with Kris right behind her. "You know, I must sound like a real tourist." she laughed as she took Kris' hand in hers.

"But we are tourists." Kris winked at her companion.

"I know that, but you don't react the same way as I do," Nicole said as she watched the passing scenery. "You're so calm and quiet, it looks like you've been here a dozen times before."

"Just because I don't say anything doesn't mean I don't enjoy it." Kris said. "To tell you the truth, I'm having fun just watching you."

Nicole turned to the taller woman. "I must be acting like a child," she said softly.

"No. You make me smile because I see all the joy you're feeling. It shows on your face." She put her arm around the smaller woman and pulled her against her. "You're showing me that life can be fun, too. It doesn't have to be so serious all the time. I've forgotten what it is to enjoy the simplest things in life." She gently kissed the blonde head under her chin. "Don't ever change, Nick."

Nicole smiled and closed her eyes. Here she was, worried that she was acting too childlike, and Kris was worried about being too serious. *One thing's for sure,* she thought, *we're both going to have the best time of our lives.* "I won't change, I promise."

****

A gentle nudge woke Nicole up. She sleepily opened her eyes and saw that the car had stopped at a marina. "Are we at the hotel already?" she asked as she rubbed her eyes.

"Not quite. We still have a ways to go, but I think you'll like this," Kris said as she stepped out of the limousine and held a hand out to help Nicole. A member of the marina crew had taken the bags from the driver and was headed to a speedboat that was moored not too far away. A beautiful sailboat caught Kris' attention. So many things to do and so little time. *We'll just have to make the best of it.*

"Are we going for a boat ride?" Nicole asked, all excited.

"Not just a ride, but this will take us to our place for the next few days," she said as she climbed aboard and helped Nicole in. "Were going to Isla Mujeres. It's about twenty-five minutes by boat northeast of Cancun," Kris explained as the boat navigated out of the dock and into the sea. "It's a small island, about five miles long and less than a mile wide. I'm sure you'll love it."

"I can't wait to see it."

Once out of dock, the small boat gathered speed and headed

east into the Caribbean Sea.

They arrived at Puerto Isla Mujeres, an exclusive and intimate resort as well as a deluxe yachting club. Sailboats, yachts and boats of all kind and sizes offered a beautiful sight. "This is incredible," Nicole breathed as they walked up to the registration desk.

"Why don't you take a look around while I get the keys for the villa, okay?" Kris said, as a resort employee handled their bags. "It shouldn't take long."

"A villa? You mean we don't have a hotel room?" Nicole shook her head. She knew that Kris had money, but this was getting ridiculous. "The next thing you'll tell me is that you bought a boat for us to sail around in." She chuckled and stopped, seeing Kris grin. "No, you must be kidding."

Kris laughed at her companion's expression. "Don't worry, I didn't buy it...I just chartered it for two days." She winked at Nicole.

"Don't you think..." Nicole started but Kris put a finger on the blonde's lips.

"Nick, I can't remember the last time I had a real vacation. All the travel I do is work related. I never get a chance to enjoy the places I visit," Kris explained softly. "Let me do this, okay?" Nicole silently nodded and Kris took her hand in hers. "How often do you get a chance to go on vacation and not worry about money?" She gave Nicole a quick kiss. "I'll be right back."

Nicole watched the tall woman walk away. She was really excited and thankful to be in this paradise with the most beautiful woman that she had ever met. But she felt a little awkward about how much it must be costing her friend.

In the past month, Kris had opened up more, and Nicole had been surprised to find out that she had very few friends. She knew a lot of people, of course, but nobody was close enough to her to merit the title of friend, until Nicole. She was touched by Kristina's trust, but was saddened by the fact that most of the stuntwoman's days were spent working, with very few people in her life.

Things will change, Nicole thought. She would make sure that Kris really enjoyed herself and that this little trip would be the best ever.

She looked out at the emerald water. The boats bobbed with the gentle waves. A little farther down the shore, people tanned themselves on the white beach, played or swam in the sea. Nicole had dreamed of being in a place like this, but to actually live it, and with such a loving person as Kris, was too good to be true. Just thinking about the tall, dark-haired woman caused hers heart to beat wildly against her chest.

She had initially thought that the reason she reacted that way to Kris was because it was the first time that anybody had given her so much attention. Now she knew she was madly in love with her. A jingle of keys brought Nicole out of her reverie, and she turned to her smiling friend.

"Are you coming?" Kris asked. "Our bags are already there. Let's get our bathing suits on and go for a swim."

"Great idea," Nicole replied with a smile. *Yes,* she thought. *This will be a vacation to remember.* She hooked arms with Kris and they headed to their villa.

****

Both women strolled on the quiet beach as the sun made its descent. Most of the swimmers had already left to get ready for the evening. Kris enjoyed this time of day as much as she enjoyed the early mornings. It was the best time to stop and think about what had happened so far and what needed to be done. At that moment, all she could think about was her young companion walking beside her in comfortable silence. It had been a long day traveling from Montreal, but Nicole seemed to be in fine shape. Maybe the small nap she had taken in the limousine helped.

A small hand gently nestled into her larger one and she looked down as her companion gave it a little squeeze. The simple touch warmed Kris' heart greatly. She couldn't get over the fact that a squeeze, a hug, or the simplest of touch from Nicole could cause her breath to catch in her throat and get her heart beating so hard it hurt. She was so used to her presence that she couldn't imagine life without her.

What's so special about Nicole, she thought, *is the fact that she seems to know what I want before I know it myself.* Kris had found that out the first time the small woman had been assigned as her assistant. Unlike other people, she never pried deep into her life, even though Kris knew she longed to know more about her life in Innsbruck. Everything Nicole did was from the goodness of her heart with no hidden agendas. She gave and expected nothing in return. Maybe that's why she was so happy to treat Nicole to things such as this vacation.

As they walked back to the villa, Kris slowed down to enjoy the view. Nicole gently tugged on her hand, smiling.

"Why don't we sit for a little while?" Nicole asked as she sat down on the sand. She smiled and waved to the house girl assigned to them. The girl waved back and then headed towards their villa.

The tall woman smiled as she sat behind Nicole, who shifted to sit between Kris' legs, then leaned back against her chest. She wrapped her arms around the petite blonde and rested her chin on her shoulder. "Did you have a nice day?" she asked, in Nicole's ear. "Are you tired?"

Brushing her hands on Kris' arms, Nicole closed her eyes as the taller woman hugged her tighter, enjoying her friend's voice vibrating through her body. "It was wonderful," she said. "And no, I'm not tired, I feel just fine. I could stay like this forever. How about you?"

"I feel the same," she said close to Nicole's ear and kissed it softly. "All this would be worth nothing if you weren't here with me."

They watched the last colors of the sun fade from orange, to red, and then to purple before it finally disappeared into the sea.

Nicole turned in Kris' arms and knelt before her, softly brushing her hand against the woman's cheek. "This is so incredible, finding myself here, with you," she said. "It feels like a dream." She bent forward and with a soft kiss, whispered, "Come on, I've got something for you." She smiled as she stood up and helped her friend to her feet. She tugged on the taller woman's hand, and they headed to their villa's private terrace. Pulling the sliding door open, she let Kris enter first and smiled when the woman stopped walking.

They were met with the enchanting view of lit candles floating in water filled glass bowls. Soft music playing in the background teased their ears. Mesmerized, the dark haired woman turned to a smiling Nicole who closed the door and slid the curtains shut.

So that's what Nicole was planning, Kris thought. She remembered seeing her young companion talking to the housemaid earlier in the day, making the girl smile and nod excitedly.

"I see that you've been very busy," Kris said, noticing that the bed was ready for the night. Nicole walked up to her and wrapped her arms around her neck.

"I wanted tonight to be a very special night," Nicole softly said as she kissed her, and Kris' strong arms slowly surrounded her. Guiding the tall woman as she walked backwards, Nicole gently pushed Kris onto the bed and laid her small body on top of the muscular one. "Did I tell you that I love you?" she softly asked, kissing her way from Kris' lips, stopping to nibble at her ear, and then continuing down her throat and neck.

Nicole could feel and hear her friend's rapid breathing and smiled as she undid Kris' blouse then kissed the soft flesh under her roving hands, surprised that she didn't feel at all nervous.

Everything seemed so natural to her, so...right. Nicole closed her eyes as Kris' hands reached for her T-shirt and slowly pulled it out of her shorts, then she hummed in pleasure as they moved under the shirt and across her back. Straddling the muscled thighs, Nicole's breath caught in her throat as the large but soft hands moved to softly brush against her breasts.

A small moan escaped her lips, and she leaned into the tall woman's touch. "Kris," she murmured, her breathing out of control, "make love to me...Please."

Kris briefly closed her eyes at the request. How she loved this gentle, passionate woman. She sat back up and pulled the T-shirt off of Nicole, then ever so gently wrapped her arms around the blonde and kissed her.

"I love you, Nicole," she said softly as she gently turned and laid the young woman on her back. "You mean everything to me." Kris brushed blonde hair away from her lover's face and kissed her again, this time more passionately. Feeling more nervous than she appeared to be, she slid her hand down Nicole's chest and cupped a breast, gently teasing a nipple with her fingers. She smiled as it hardened under her touch, and became more excited when she heard her partner's soft moans.

She had to take it slow, knowing that it was Nicole's first time making love. After leaving a trail of kisses all over her slim body, Kris softly kissed the other breast before taking the nipple in her mouth and softly sucking on it.

Nicole tried to keep her eyes open, wanting to see Kris make love to her, but the sensations running rampant through her body made it impossible. She ran her fingers through the raven hair, guiding her, urging her. Her heart was beating wildly, her breathing ragged and erratic. Nicole thought her heart would stop when Kris gently sucked her breast and her tongue sensually flicked at the hardened nipple. She had to bite her lip to keep from moaning too loud.

Looking up at Nicole, Kris noticed her reaction and stopped. "Are you okay? Do you want me to stop?" she asked worriedly. Green eyes opened and blinked a couple of times, confusion on her face.

"Why did you st..." Nicole said, out of breath. "Why do you say that?"

"I thought that...you looked like..."

Nicole gently caressed her cheek, and smiled. "I was biting my lip because I didn't want to make a sound," she explained sheepishly and laughed when Kris relaxed.

"We can make all the noise we want, Nicole," Kris reassured the smaller woman. "In fact, I'd really like it if you didn't hold back."

Nicole hesitated and murmured shyly, "You would, huh?"

"Yes, I would." Kris smiled. "Are you sure you want to do this? I mean I..."

Nicole put a delicate finger on Kris' lips. "This is my first time, I'm the one who's supposed to be nervous. What's your excuse?" she teased the older woman.

"I don't..." Kris stopped and swallowed nervously. *What's wrong with me?* "I guess I don't want to scare or hurt you," she explained softly.

"I know." Nicole nodded. "Kris, there's nothing I want more than this."

Kris took a deep breath and gently brushed her hand against Nicole's cheek. "But you've never...I mean it will hurt a little when...what I'm trying to say is..."

Nicole pulled Kris' head down and kissed her soundly, silencing the older woman. "Be gentle about it," she whispered with a smile. She knew what Kris meant, and she was a little nervous, having heard horror stories, but she also knew that her lover would be as gentle as possible. She trusted her with all of her heart. *My lover.* She reached for Kris' opened blouse and pulled it off of her shoulders, then reached around to unclasp her bra.

Kris smiled, now completely relaxed and slowly kissed the small woman, letting her tongue glide along the soft lips before entering her mouth and playing with her tongue. She caressed Nicole's chest and brushed her hand against a breast, softly teasing the excited nipple. She could feel her lover's increased heart beat as her hand wandered lower and as she slid her fingers under the elastic band on the young woman's shorts. She lingered a few moments giving Nicole a chance to change her mind, but the only reaction she got was a slight lift of her hips, urging Kris on.

Nicole wanted to scream for her to hurry, wanting to feel Kris inside, but she also wanted her to take her time, to make this moment last forever. She placed her hand on the dark-haired woman's and guided it lower, giving Kris silent permission to go on.

The simple gesture caught Kris by surprise. She looked up and saw so much love on the smaller woman's face. "I love you," she whispered and smiled as Nicole mouthed the words, "Me, too."

Slowly, Kris lowered her hand and brushed her fingers through the curly hair and ever so gently let her middle finger glide on the surface. The feel of her lover's wetness on her finger caused Kris' own juices to flow.

As the long fingers gently stroked her, Nicole's body

jumped at the new sensation. She didn't want to let go of Kris' hand. Holding her hand made her feel like she was taking an active part in the lovemaking. Matching her fingers on top of the long ones, Nicole could feel her every move, her every touch, discovering what was pleasing and where.

She couldn't stand it anymore and urged Kris' exploring digits to enter her, guiding her with her own hand. The sensation was incredible. The smooth movements caused her body to shiver in excitement, and she wished that she were completely naked. Impatiently, she started pulling her shorts down with her free hand.

"Let me," Kris softly said as she took up the task of lowering them along with her underwear and pulling them off. She trailed her hand all over Nicole's naked body, enjoying the shapely form before returning to her previous explorations, giving part of her attention to the small, firm breasts.

The young woman moaned breathlessly as her lover's fingers gradually moved faster, brushing against her excited bundle of nerves, going deeper with every stroke. The petite blonde reached for Kris' shoulders and held on tight.

"Oh...Kris!" she screamed as her body shuddered with intense spasms, riding the wave of passion until she climaxed in an explosion of pleasure.

The look of ecstasy on her young lover's face was enough to push Kris over the edge, and she came, along with Nicole. Her fingers slowed their movement and then stopped, waiting until Nicole's body calmed down before gently wrapping her arms around her companion. To her surprise, Nicole softly cried.

"Shhh, it's okay," Kris whispered, worried. "I'm sorry if I hurt you."

Moving to lay on Kris' chest, Nicole hugged the taller woman tight and put her head on her shoulder. "You didn't hurt me. I...didn't expect it to be so...intense," she said as she took a deep breath to calm her shaking body. She looked up at Kris and smiled. "I love you."

All the fears and worries flew away at those simple words. Kris hugged the smaller woman even tighter as her own tears fell. "I love you so much, Nicole."

Chapter 14

A slim body stirred under the blankets and green eyes blinked at daylight. It was morning already, and it looked like another beautiful day awaited them. Nicole gave a light squeeze to the naked body under her and smiled. What an incredible night it had been.

Kris had been so gentle and loving; something Nicole cherished in her lover. She smiled even more as she repeated the words in her mind, *My lover*. She'd wanted to please Kris but hadn't exactly known what to do. But her beautiful blue eyed partner had made it clear that last night's lovemaking was for her to enjoy.

Nicole grinned as she remembered how every little touch and kiss felt. With Kris as her teacher, she was confident she would be able to please her as much as the taller woman had, or at least she would do her best trying.

With her head resting in the crook of Kris' shoulder, Nicole's hand wandered all over the warm muscular flesh and felt her lover's breath catch as it moved lower. She lifted her head and saw a pair of hooded blue eyes looking back at her and smiled.

"Good morning."

"Hmmm, morning." Kris smiled and hugged the small

woman. "Sleep well?"

"Oh, yeah." Nicole nodded. "I had the most incredible dream," she said as she laid her head back down and her hand roamed all over the taut stomach. "I dreamt that I had the most beautiful woman making love to me all night and..." She brushed her thumb over a hardened nipple. "Oh! That's right, it wasn't a dream."

"Nick..." Kris playfully warned as she put her hand on top of the smaller one, stilling it. "We have less than an hour before we get aboard the sailboat." She smiled as she gently turned Nicole on her back and bent down to kiss her. "We need to take a shower and eat breakfast. We have a lot to visit today."

"But I want to stay in bed with you," Nicole pouted, putting a lock of raven hair behind Kris' ear. "I'd rather have you for breakfast." She blushed as soon as the words rolled off her tongue, causing Kris to laugh.

"You can have me as a late night snack then." She grinned and kissed Nicole. "You want to join me for a shower?"

The young blonde nodded vigorously, got out of bed, and followed her partner to the bathroom. She couldn't believe what she had said to Kris. She didn't expect being able to tease her that way, especially with one-liners so full of sexual innuendo. It was fun, especially since it made her friend laugh.

****

The sailboat Kris had chartered was a forty-one foot Beneteau 411. *A real beauty*, Nicole thought as she swung her backpack over her shoulder and got onboard.

The Captain, a woman named Isabella Lopez, who had been highly recommended by a friend of Kris', greeted them with a firm handshake and a smile. Isabella was a beautiful woman, slightly taller than Nicole was and as petite, but a closer inspection revealed the body of a lean muscled marathon runner. The Captain wore her short brown hair brushed back with her sunglasses sitting on top of her head. A pair of white shorts with a light green polo shirt and sockless feet in white running shoes adorned the rest of her body.

"Welcome aboard the *Chalchiuhtlicue,*" Isabella said as she took the two travel bags from Kris and led the way to their cabin.

"What does Chalchi...huh, Chal..." Nicole shook her head, making the Captain smile.

"Chalchiuhtlicue is the Aztec goddess of running water," she explained. "But I usually refer to the sailboat as just plain *Chalchi.*"

"Makes it much easier for us tourists." Nicole grinned, getting a light squeeze on her shoulder from Kris who smiled back.

The women followed Isabella as she gave them a tour of the sailboat, walking with an extra sense of security that the non-skid deck surface gave. The extra wide aft swim platform, walk-through transom, and cockpit shower made Nicole think of Kris in her bathing suit and decided that a swim in the Caribbean Sea was a must for when they dropped anchor.

Kris was amazed by the spacious and efficient layout below deck, making use of every nook and cranny. Many deck hatches, portholes, and dorade vents provided plenty of natural light and ventilation which flooded the interior and accented the rich, handcrafted, cherry stained, mahogany woodwork. Roomy companionways, large aft cabins and plenty of storage were found throughout the boat and as Kris entered the spacious salon area, she was glad to see it had up to six foot four headroom, plenty of space to allow her tall frame. The table could easily seat up to eight people and the gourmet galley was equipped with wide countertops, big double stainless sinks, and loads of storage.

Kris and Nicole looked at each other with a smile as they walked into the deluxe forward "masters" stateroom. A large double berth graced the area, and the upholstered port settee was perfect for reading and relaxing. There was a private access to the spacious forward head, which was well ventilated, fully lined with sink and shower unit.

Nicole tugged on Kris' shirt and whispered in the taller woman's ear, "This thing looks like a floating house."

"*Chalchi* is my pride and joy." Isabella smiled, having heard the blonde woman's comment and put the two travel bags on the bed then turned to go back on deck. "Just enjoy yourselves, and be sure to let me know if you need anything," the Captain said with a smile over her shoulder and left her guests alone.

"So, you like it?" Kris asked as she added both backpacks to the bags and gently pulled her young lover into her arms.

Leaning her head against Kris' chest, Nicole closed her eyes and wrapped her arms around the taller woman's waist. "I love it." She smiled and gave her friend a squeeze. "We're actually going to spend the night onboard?"

"Hmm mm," Kris acknowledged. "This way we can sail about, go to Xcaret to visit the nature preserve then come back to the boat for some more sailing and a swim." She looked at Nicole's sparkling eyes and chuckled. "Maybe later we could watch the sun set then come back here for a very nice evening, just you and me."

"Oh, I love your plan." She purred as she brought her hands up along Kris' chest to lock them behind the tall woman's neck. "Especially the evening part." Guiding the dark head lower towards her, *In fact, I could spend the whole day like this,* Nicole thought as she softly kissed her.

Kris hummed in pleasure as she caressed her young lover. Nicole seemed to be more comfortable with their newfound intimacy, and it warmed her on many levels. She also expressed a new boldness, which Kris didn't mind one bit. A movement of the boat told her that they were on their way.

"How about if we go on deck and enjoy the ride?" Kris suggested as she brushed blonde hair away from Nicole's face. "We could sit up front and get some sun." She saw Nicole hesitate a bit before silently nodding. "What is it?"

"Nothing. It's just silly, that's all." Nicole gave her a half smile before reaching for her backpack. She was stopped from going any further and lifted her head to look into a pair of blue eyes, one perfect eyebrow lifted in question. "It's just that...well, I..." Nicole sighed as a blush crept up her cheeks. "All I want to do is touch you all the time," she murmured as she looked down. "I mean, I want to hug you and I want you to hold me and..."

"And the problem with that is...?" Kris asked softly. "You know that I feel the same."

Nicole looked up at her companion and smiled sadly. "But,

the problem is once were out there, in public. I wish we could walk around like lovers do, just holding hands and stuff."

"What's stopping us?"

"But, what will happen if a photographer sees you and takes pictures? They might end up in magazines or newspapers or something." A booming laugh escaped Kris, and Nicole found herself in a tight hug. "What?" she asked, confused.

"Nick, that wouldn't be the first time." Kris smiled and said softly, "I'm just worried about you. Are you ready to let everybody know about us?"

"I can deal with comments or looks. I don't care what everybody says," Nicole stated. "If you don't mind holding hands in public, I'm all for it, too." She smiled and gave Kris a quick kiss. "The same goes for the Captain on deck." She reached for her backpack and took out her brand new camera.

Kris chuckled at the mention of Isabella. "I wouldn't worry about her," she said as she opened their cabin door. "Remember I told you she was recommended by a friend?" Nicole nodded. "Well, Isabella and Suzan have been lovers for eight years."

"Oh!" Nicole exclaimed then smiled. "Really? That's good then."

"Yep. Come on." Kris laughed and climbed the stairs to go on deck with Nicole following close behind her.

It was a beautiful day and by late morning the temperature grew hotter, but the cool breeze made the heat bearable. The sea was fairly calm, and it made for a nice sailing trip. Nicole took pictures of Isla Mujeres as they sailed away from the small island and took a few more of the boat and then of Kris who stood on deck, looking out at the retreating shoreline.

The taller woman wore a pair of khaki shorts with a beige tank top, making her look more tanned than she really was. Nicole chuckled at Kris' low cut hiking boots. No matter if she wore shorts or pants, the stuntwoman always wore boots, a habit she had since she was a child.

Nicole didn't often have a chance to just observe her lover, so she used the time to fully enjoy the view. Somehow, Kris always knew when she was being watched, but at that moment she seemed lost in her happy thoughts.

Moving slightly and crouching to get a full-length shot of her lover, Nicole smiled as the dark head tilted and a blue eye winked at her as she took a few pictures.

"You might want to keep some film for later," Kris teased as she left her spot by the railing and walked to Nicole. The tall woman lifted her eyes to the smiling Captain and nodded at a gesture the boat owner made to her.

"Give the camera to Isabella," she told Nicole as the Captain approached them. "She'll take a picture of us."

"That's a great idea," Nicole responded with enthusiasm and handed it to the skipper.

"Why don't you stand right over there," Isabella said, indicating a spot near the leather-covered steering wheel. "This way you'll have a good view of the boat," she explained.

Nicole smiled as Kris wrapped strong arms around her waist from behind and rested her chin on top of her head. The wind blew their hair back, mixing the gold with the raven locks. *Oh, this is paradise*, Nicole thought as she leaned against Kris after the Captain took the picture and looked up as her friend bent her head down. Just as they were about to kiss, Isabella took another picture.

"Oh, that'll be a very nice one," the Captain said, handing the camera back to a blushing Nicole. "You make a very nice couple." She smiled and went back to steering the sailboat.

"Thanks," Kris said, then grinned at the smaller woman. "Did anyone ever tell you that you're incredibly cute when you blush?" She laughed as Nicole backhanded her in the stomach and laughed herself.

****

Xcaret counted as one of the best nature preserves in Mexico. The wild Bird Breeding Aviary was a nursery and attraction, housing more than thirty different bird species from southeast Mexico, many in danger of extinction. Among the visitors' favorites were macaws, toucans, and flamingos. Nicole had a lot of fun taking pictures, especially of the very colorful birds. Right after the aviary, they visited the horse stable, the orchid farm, and the botanical garden. Nicole was already working on her third roll of film when they arrived at the caves.

All rivers in the Yucatan peninsula were underground. The gentle current carried people through the crystalline waters of the 1,590-foot underground waterway, allowing them to peacefully drift along the river, as they relaxed and enjoyed the magically sky-lit caves. Nicole was amazed to learn that this subterranean world, dating back to millions of years ago, formed part of the ocean floor.

After a quick snack, they came upon the area of the preserve devoted to dolphins. They walked through the educational section, hearing an audiocassette talking about the dolphins' world and learning about social and physical characteristics of bottlenose dolphins.

But the best part for Kris was watching Nicole's reactions. The young blonde loved dolphins, and it showed on her face. She was so captivated by the swimming mammals that the camera was forgotten in her hand. So much so that she didn't even realize it was missing after Kris took it away from her and snapped pictures while guiding her closer to the tanks.

The programs of the preserve consisted of the visitors standing on underwater platforms and participating in social interactive games with the dolphins. This activity allowed the visitor to discover the various abilities of the dolphins in how they swam, breathed, ate, and slept. Nicole nearly went out of her mind when she was asked to come out on one of the platforms to meet the dolphins, touch, and pet them.

Kris could have spent hours just watching Nicole play, she looked so happy. Not wanting to intrude, she stepped away from the tank and took more pictures, certain that Nicole would be thrilled to have such photographs as souvenirs. Already in her one-piece bathing suit, having taken off her shorts and T-shirt, Nicole was invited to swim with the dolphins. She let them drag her through the water and got a thrill as they jumped over her.

When she got out of the water, Nicole nearly ran to sit beside Kris. "Oh my God, that was so cool," she exclaimed, so excited her voice cracked. "I can't believe it. They're so smooth, so gentle. I...this was...oh...Wow!"

Kris laughed at her friend's excitement. She loosely laid her arm around Nicole's shoulder and gave her a quick hug. "I'm so glad you're having fun, Nick," she honestly said.

"Oh. I am." Nicole grinned, green eyes shinning, then she related her excited impressions of her adventure with the dolphins.

Kris just sat there and listened to her young lover. She couldn't remember when she had ever been that excited over anything. It was refreshing to see such unguarded emotions coming from someone, especially Nicole. The blonde eventually calmed herself and once her bathing suit had dried, slipped back into her shorts and T-shirt.

"It's nearly dinner time. Are you hungry?"

"You bet," Nicole replied as she slipped into her running shoes. "I saw on the map that there's a Mayan village that way," she said, indicating the direction with her hand. "I'm sure well find something there."

"Okay." Kris smiled as she got up. "Lead the way."

The sound of a band could be heard from the entrance to the museum. They found the beginning of a "fiesta" of music and color at the Mayan Ball Game court. This legendary game found a place to spring up again in Xcaret on the modern terrain. The last construction of a Ball Game court in the Mayan culture was in 590 A.D. The area was 48 yards long and 39.3 yards wide and a game called Ulama was played with a nine-pound ball with only the players' hips. Two teams of six players each struggled for the points. What Kris found most interesting was that the game was more than 2,000 years old.

After this introduction to the Mayan, the women went on a mystical journey into the past, winding through underground passageways and ending up in the Maya Village, with a live performance of the New Fire ceremony.

The common people lived in houses built of wood and cord whose elliptical shape kept their interior fresh all year round. Their roofs, palapa, were thatched with palm fronds, which had to be cut by the light of the full moon so the sap reached the tip of the frond making the roof waterproof for almost twenty-five years.

Penetrating a jungle that pulsated to the rhythm of pre-Hispanic drums, they reached pyramids built by the ancients, which gleamed with the light of candles, where ceremonies that evoked ancient gods and past conquests were held.

They soon arrived at the open-air, hand-carved theater to watch one of the most beautiful folkloric shows in Mexico. Dancers and musicians gave the theater a festive air. Restaurants ranging from traditional Mayan and Mexican foods to the internationally known American foods lined the ways outside the theater.

Remembering Nicole's comment at her uncle's place concerning real Mexican food, Kris headed towards a restaurant where a Mariachi band played and the staff was dressed in traditional Mexican garb.

Nicole was happy to see where they were heading to eat. It smelled so good, and the plates looked so colorful. Both women were glad to sit down and finally relax after such a long day of walking. The first thing Kris ordered besides food was two shots of Tequila and Mexican beer. Once they were served their food, Kris watched with amusement as Nicole attacked her food mercilessly.

The women chatted, reliving the day's events with laughter. A noise in one of the restaurant's corners attracted Nicole's attention and she watched with a smile as a group of people surrounded an elderly woman as she tried to hit a Piñata with a stick while blindfolded, egged on by the laughter and cheers of the surrounding patrons. Once hit, the colorful toy broke apart, sending a shower of small toys and candy to the floor, where they were quickly picked up by the waiting children.

"Do you want to try?" Kris asked Nicole who hesitated a bit. "Come on, it'll be fun." Kris stood up and handed a few bills to a young waiter, indicating the remains of the toy with her hand. The young man nodded vigorously, smiling from ear to ear at all the money given to him and attached a new Piñata at the end of the rope.

Kris stepped back and took the camera out of her backpack. The young waiter put a blindfold over Nicole's eyes, then handed her a long stick. He spun her around a couple of times and with his hands on her hips, guided her in the right direction. Kris frowned at the boy's gesture, a burst of jealousy coursing through her body. *Whoa there, he's only helping her out,* she told herself and took a calming breath. Keeping one eye on the waiter, she snapped some pictures of her friend as she swung the stick, trying to hit the toy but managing to hit everything else instead.

The young waiter, trying to keep low so the flying stick wouldn't hit him, approached Nicole and guided her in the right direction. Finally, she successfully hit the toy and rewarded the waiting children with more surprises.

Kris walked towards the young man, glaring at him after noting that one of his hands still rested on the small of Nicole's back. Meanwhile, Nicole took her blindfold off in time to see the children and catch the look on her angry lover's face. The young waiter turned white in fear, and he let go of her.

He stepped back and turned around, doing his best not to run away. Nicole caught the light smirk on Kris' face and bit her lip so she wouldn't laugh.

"Protecting your territory?" she asked with a grin as she grabbed her backpack then walked out of the open-air restaurant.

"If anyone's going to play with your butt, it's gonna be me." She growled playfully, causing Nicole to laugh.

"I don't know about you, but how about we head back to the boat and just relax?" the blonde asked and Kris nodded in agreement. They went to the parking lot and climbed aboard a taxi, which drove them to the marina.

Chapter 15

It had been a beautiful day so far and Kris was happy to be finally back at the boat. Stepping out of the taxi and wanting to get away from the chatty driver, Kris slipped on the wet surface, twisting her back in the process. She quickly recovered and succeeded in masking the wince with a cough. Her back was giving her problems again, and she didn't want Nicole to worry about the old injury and ruin her vacation.

She glanced at Nicole as she emerged from the taxi and was relieved to see that she hadn't noticed the slip. After paying the driver, they went to the end of the dock where the sailboat was moored.

Waving hello to the Captain, Nicole took Kris' backpack and went down the stairs to drop off their packs in their cabin. With a nod towards Isabella, Kris continued walking to the front of the boat and sat down on the floor, leaning her back against the mast. She took a deep breath to try to calm her pain and closed her eyes.

Images of Nicole playing with the dolphins went through her mind, and she smiled as she thought of the young blonde's sparkling green eyes and bubbling laughter. The sound of soft steps coming closer made Kris open her eyes and look up at a smiling Nicole.

"You okay?" she asked and was answered with a small nod. She hadn't been sure, but she thought that she had heard a soft grunt coming from her friend as she stepped out of the taxi. With a smile, she took the hand that her partner offered and sat down between the taller woman's legs. She leaned against Kris' chest and smiled as the long, strong arms wrapped around her body. She offered her a sip of water from her bottle but Kris shook her head no. She twisted the cap off and took one long swallow. "You sure you're okay?"

"I'm fine," Kris whispered in her ear. "Just look at those colors." She nodded at the sun set. They watched as the sky changed from one tint of orange to a deeper color as the sun sank into the ocean. The seagulls flying nearby and the sight of the surrounding boats made for a perfect picture.

Nicole took another sip and put the bottle on the deck, but the angle was too steep, and the bottle risked rolling off the deck and into the water.

Kris quickly reached for it and grabbed it before it slipped away from her fingers. *Oh...that was a bad idea,* she silently growled as another painful jab in her back made her hold her breath.

A hiss from Kris made Nicole turn around and look at her friend. "You told me you were okay," she accused her lover. "Your back's bothering you?"

Kris sighed then nodded. It was useless lying to her. Either she fibbed about the intensity of her pain and risk Nicole's anger if she found out the truth or be honest and be pampered all evening. She had never been one to let herself be nursed back to health by anyone, but she had to admit that the thought of Nicole doing the pampering wasn't unpleasant. Besides, the last thing she wanted to do was to lie to her lover.

"I must have pulled a muscle or something. It's not that serious."

"But it causes you pain," Nicole argued as she stood up and held a hand out. "Come on, let's go to our cabin so you can lie down for a while."

"I'm just sore, Nick. I'm okay, really."

"I'll give you a massage," she offered with a grin.

"Now that's an offer I simply cannot refuse." Kris grinned as she gingerly stood up and followed Nicole.

With a grunt, Kris sat on the edge of the berth as Nicole rummaged through her travel bag and took out a small bottle. "Do you always carry massage oil everywhere you go?" She asked with a smile as she took her boots off then her tank top.

"You never know when it'll come in handy." Nicole grinned, as her eyes roamed over the half naked bronzed body before her. "But the real reason is that my shoulders give me trouble sometimes," she said more seriously. "I find it easier to rub the pain away with the oil." The blonde took a few steps towards her lover. "A full body massage is prescribed for you, my friend. Off with the shorts, too."

A raised eyebrow was Nicole's reply, but Kris readily complied with a smile of her own. She took off her shorts and underwear and last, pulled her socks off before lying down on her stomach, her head resting against a pillow.

Nicole turned on the radio, choosing soft music and sat down on the bed. She poured a portion of oil in her hands and massaged it into the tense muscles on Kris' back. *This feels so nice,* she thought as she felt the soft flesh under her hands. She only wished that Kris would ask her for a massage more often but then again, she could just offer to give her one.

"You've been having problems since when?"

"Since the big accident a few months ago," Kris explained as she closed her eyes and relaxed under Nicole's gentle touch. "You know, the one where I wrapped a car around a tree?"

"Ew. That must have hurt," Nicole said sympathetically as she loosened the shoulder muscles then worked her way down.

"Hmmm, that feels so good."

"Enjoy it." Nicole smiled as Kris relaxed. How she loved to be able to slide her hands all over the broad back. Her friend was always so relaxed and at peace when she gave her a massage. Times like these were precious to Nicole.

She lightly brushed her hands over Kris' butt cheeks and playfully gave them a squeeze and chuckled when her lover jumped in surprise at the sudden gesture. She then continued down to massage the muscled leg all the way to her foot while her eyes wandered over the beautiful woman's body, committing to memory every little detail. After she gently massaged the toes, Nicole slid her hands up on each side of Kris' leg, over her calf and then all the way up to the middle thigh.

A small shiver passed over Kris' body and a smile tugged at the dark-haired woman's lips as she enjoyed the sweet sensations.

Nicole repeated the action on the other leg, but this time her hands went higher than mid thigh, ending up barely touching Kris' center. She was amazed at the stuntwoman's reaction and smiled as her lover's breathing deepened and became uneven. Nicole never expected to have this kind of effect on Kris and she found it quite arousing.

"Everything okay?" Nicole teasingly asked as her hand lingered a moment longer, softly brushing against the dark, curly hair before going back down the leg.

"Hmmm." Satisfaction and desire mixed into one exclamation was the only thing Kris could utter. Her heart beat furiously against her chest as she tried to calm her breathing down to a more normal level. She couldn't get enough of Nicole. The gentle hands all over her body was something she had quickly become addicted to.

She hummed again when her young lover's hands slid up to the top of her legs, over her buttocks and then up her back to continue down her shoulders and down her arms. Kris' heart missed a beat when Nicole softly kissed each shoulder blade and tried her best not to turn over and take Nicole in her arms. She was determined to let her do this her own way, even if the slow touches were driving her insane with desire.

Nicole remembered every detail the loving attention Kris had lavished on her the night before and longed to be able to make love to her in the same way. Thankful that she had taken the time to remove her bathing suit as soon as she returned to their cabin, the young blonde smiled as she slipped out of her T-shirt and gently shifted Kris' hair to one side. She bent down and kissed her lover's neck, gently nibbled at her ear, her naked breasts brushing against Kris' back.

Kris' breath caught in her throat at this new sensation and

unable to behave anymore, flipped onto her back. Nicole knelt beside her on the bed, dressed only in her light green shorts. She took a moment to look at her lover's half-naked body and smiled. She reached for Nicole, but she backed away with a grin and a shake of her head. Kris frowned at the unexpected move.

"Nah ah," Nicole wagged her finger at the confused looking woman. "I want you to relax. Just put your hands above your head and enjoy." She straddled Kris' thighs and took the massage oil from the small table beside the bed, poured a little oil into her hand and gently rubbed it on the taut abdomen. Her lover closed her eyes and sighed, a beautiful smile on her lips.

Guess I'm doing better than I thought. Nicole smiled as she slowly moved her hands up each side of Kris' powerful body. Her partner's breathing increased, and an image crossed her mind. It felt like she had lived this scene before. The décor, the situation, the older woman's reaction to her touch, then she remembered a dream she once had about making love to Kris. She smiled as the details of that dream came rushing back to her. *Why not?* She leaned down to kiss Kris' stomach but quickly pulled back when the dark haired woman reached for her again.

"Do I need to tie you up?" Nicole teased and gave her a long and passionate kiss.

"But I just want to hold you," Kris explained with a puppy dog expression, making Nicole laugh. "So you want to tie me up, huh? I didn't know you were into B&D." She grinned at her confused lover.

"What do you mean, B&D?"

"It means Bondage and Dominance." She waited as Nicole processed this new information.

"Oh..." she said, and then Kris laughed as recognition flashed across Nicole's face. "Oh!" she exclaimed, a blush creeping over her cheeks. With a slight shake of her head, she bent down to whisper in Kris, ear, "I'll tell you what. I may not be into B&D, but if you'll promise to behave, I'll give you a reward." She smiled as the blue eyes regarding her grew wider.

"I'll behave," Kris softly agreed and put her hands above her head.

Knowing that the blue eyes were watching her every move,

Nicole softly kissed a nipple and watched in fascination as it became erect. Encouraged by her dream and the memory of Kris' love making, she grew bolder and circled her tongue around the hardened nipple and gently sucked on it, causing Kris to moan. She brushed her hand across the flat stomach and her fingers trailed up to the other breast, teasing the nipple between them.

Kris clutched a handful of the bedspread, trying not to move. She never thought that this kind of teasing could be so arousing. She closed her eyes, trying to relax, but reopened them as Nicole's hand slid down her body while she continued to lick and suck her nipple.

Kris swallowed a few times as her lover's fingers reached the dark pubic hair, felt them hesitate slightly and prayed that Nicole wouldn't stop. Wanting to urge her on without putting pressure on the young woman, Kris chose to encourage her by parting her legs, giving silent permission for her to continue.

Nicole didn't know if she was shaking because she was nervous, scared, or extremely excited. She knew the latter was true by her reactions to Kris' naked body and soft moans.

Encouraged by the silent invitation her lover gave her, the young blonde kissed her way down the muscled stomach and ever so slowly moved her hand lower and tentatively touched Kris' center. She was rewarded with a low moan and shifted her glance to lock eyes with the blue ones watching her intently. She slid a finger inside, doing exactly what her lover had done to her the night before and was amazed at how wet her partner was and smiled, knowing that she was the cause of it.

"Oh...Nic..." Kris breathed, lifting her hips off the bed, trying to get her partner to increase the pressure. "Please..." she urged her young lover.

"Tell me what you want, Kris," Nicole purred in a seductive voice.

"Yes," she moaned as Nicole touched a sensitive spot. "H...Harder..." Kris gasped as she grabbed the bed covers tighter. Ever since she had met Nicole, she had dreamed of this moment. Holding her in her arms was heaven, but to have Nicole explore her body like she was doing was enough to drive her over the edge in ecstasy.

Kris kept her eyes locked on Nicole's, and the smile the young blonde gave her went straight to her heart. Her body shook as the pressure from the impending orgasm building up so much that she was about to lose control.

The tall woman's body shuddered and the muscles tensed. Nicole moved her fingers deeper and faster until Kris' inner muscles tightened around them and her body shook with an incredible orgasm.

Nicole moved up to kiss Kris passionately and, this time, didn't say anything when she wrapped her strong arms around her and held her tight.

"Oh, God, I love you so much," Kris whispered as her body calmed, and her breathing returned to normal. She gently turned Nicole on her back and kissed her softly, before looking into the young woman's eyes and smiling.

"Was I okay?" Nicole asked tentatively, causing Kris to chuckle.

"You were more than okay," she assured the younger woman. She kissed her again and Nicole relaxed under her. "I love you."

Nicole smiled and locked her fingers behind her lover's neck. "I love you, too, Kris."

That definitely went better than I thought it would, Nicole told herself, as she ran her hand through the long, raven hair and brushed her thumb lightly against Kris' cheek. There was so much love on her lover's face that she nearly stopped breathing. Nobody had ever cared or loved her this much. She wasn't sure anymore how she would deal with Kris' departure for Austria. Her sad thoughts were quickly put aside and she closed her eyes as Kris embarked on her own exploration. She knew that this would be another sleepless night, but she didn't care. All she wanted was to be wrapped in her lover's arms and be loved.

Chapter 16

I don't think it's even possible to have bad days here, Nicole thought idly as she stretched out on her beach towel on the deck of the *Chalchi.* She lay on her side, watching as her friend cast her fishing line into the sea. Not too crazy about fishing, she preferred letting her eyes roam over her lover's muscular body, clad in a bathing suit that left very little to the imagination. Nicole was happy to see Kris enjoying herself and she smiled as the dark haired woman wrestled with one fish after another, reeling them in like a pro.

Having docked at a marina in Cancun, the women headed to Chichén Itzá, one of the largest archeological sites on the peninsula with the most impressive Mayan ruins. The trip to the site took a few hours by car, but Isabella had promised them that it would be worth it. The mysterious temples and pyramids of the Maya rested deep within the jungles of Mexico and extended into the limestone shelf of the Yucatan peninsula.

Nicole was excited at the prospect of learning more about the long lost civilization. She had often heard and read stories about the Greeks and Romans as well as the Egyptians, but the Mayans remained a mystery to her. She listened with rapt fascination as their guide explained that the Maya had mapped the heavens, evolved the only true writing system native to the

Americas, and were masters of mathematics. They had also invented the calendars that are still used today. The mystery of the Maya was what had happened to such a well-developed society. The Mayan civilization had started to decline around 900 A.D. when, for reasons unknown, the southern Mayans abandoned their cities.

Kris walked silently beside Nicole, taking in the breathtaking sight of the surrounding temples and pyramids. It was still early in the morning, and tourists sparsely populated the area, which was fine with her. Roughly at the center of the site was the massive Kukulcán pyramid called *El Castillo*, the castle. They made their way towards the building and climbed the numerous steps, stopping once in a while as Nicole caught her breath.

Nicole looked up at her amused lover and smirked. "You think this is funny, don't ya?" she asked and laughed. "As soon as we get back to the island, I'll join you for your daily run. I really need to get in shape."

Kris shook her head and grinned. "It still won't help you now." She waited a few more seconds as Nicole took another deep breath before continuing their climb.

"Maybe not," she agreed. "But at least that way, I'll be able to keep up with you."

An evil grin tugged at Kris' lips. The chance to tease the young woman in public was too good to pass up. "You were doing great keeping up with me last night," she said. As guessed, a deep colored blush crept over her lover's neck and cheeks, causing Kris to give her young partner a gentle pat on her butt.

"At least, I'm in shape for that," Nicole finally replied with a grin.

The climb was quite a challenge and many visitors simply turned around and made their way back down. Those who made it all the way to the top of the pyramid were rewarded with a spectacular view of the Mayan City and the surrounding countryside. But the trip inside was the total opposite, Nicole thought as they walked into the dark and humid corridors and chambers. They quickly turned around and climbed back down to the ground.

One of the nice things about Chichén Itzá, Kris thought as

they walked among the dark portals, was that they were free to go into almost all of the ruins. Many still had the musty smell of the past, still present even after 1000 years.

"Now there's something for you," Nicole said, causing Kris to break out of her reverie. "It's called the Temple of the Warriors," she explained, just knowing that the name of the temple fit her tall, dark-haired companion.

Kris lifted an eyebrow at the petite woman, who was brushing her hand over the carved columns. "Something for me, huh?"

"Yep," Nicole easily replied. "You look like the warrior type; tall, strong, and have a commanding presence." Nicole paused and tilted her head, looking up at Kris. "And you're one excellent protector," she said as she thought of her friend's reaction towards her father's attack on her. "My knight in shining armor." Nicole smiled and then laughed at the blush on the tall woman's cheeks. "Oooh, that's so cute," she giggled and gave her lover a quick kiss on the lips.

"Humph," was all Kris managed to say and scratched at her jaw, not sure how to reply to that. "Come on, let's go," she finally said with a smile.

The Temple of the Warriors was the most awe-inspiring ruin on the complex. The structure was massively built and surrounded by hundreds of carved columns that continued on into the jungle. That part of the ruin was still unrestored, and it was unsettling to see how easily the forest had reclaimed the area.

The last ruin they visited was called the Nunnery. It was a group of ruins that contained some of the best-preserved structures in Chichén Itzá. The buildings looked like the living quarters for some of the very rich and powerful, probably the houses of the elite Mayans. Every square foot of wall was carved and had intricate paintings decorating them. The buildings were huge, and like most of the other ruins, Kris and Nicole were able to walk in and explore the interior.

"I would love to be able to go back in time and see who lived here," Nicole said as they walked the darkened corridors. "Just walk around and see people doing their daily chores, dressed in colorful clothes, to hear what type of music they played then, to be able to smell food cooking over fires. Did you know that all these buildings were built without any metal tools, beasts of burden, or even the wheel? How did they go from one place to another when they didn't even have horses?" *So many unanswered questions,* Nicole thought as she peered into a dark recess.

"You really love all that history stuff, don't you?" Kris gently asked. Nicole was an encyclopedia of information, always willing to share her knowledge and always eager to learn more whenever she could. Kris often saw her reading, from simple tourist brochures to history books.

"I do," Nicole replied simply. "Be it Mayans, Romans, Egyptians, or Greeks, I love hearing about the legends and myths surrounding those civilizations. Sometimes I find myself dreaming about those times and imagine myself walking the roads of ancient Greece." At that, she shyly smiled and looked up at her lover. "It's silly, isn't it?"

Kris shook her head and gently brushed her hand against Nicole's cheek. "No," she replied softly, "it's not silly." She understood the young woman perfectly. How to explain the images that went through her mind when she had looked at the ruins in Rome and Greece? The images had seemed so real to Kris—soldiers and horses on battlefields, yells and cries coming from wounded men lying on the ground, thoughts of Gods and Goddesses wreaking havoc on mortals.

Kris took a deep breath and shook her head. *I watch too many movies*, she told herself and stuck her head into the same dark recess Nicole was looking into.

"I wonder what's in there?" the young blonde said as she moved inside, curiosity getting the best of her.

"Go check it out," Kris told her with a grin. She knew that all of the ruins were safe, otherwise, they would have cordoned off the dangerous areas to keep the tourists out. "I'll wait here."

"You sure?" Nicole asked and the dark-haired woman nodded. "Okay." She turned her attention to the dark opening and walked deeper inside. Her heart beat against her chest, nervousness getting a hold of her, but the curiosity of finding out what lay at the end of the small corridor guided her ever deeper.

The walls gradually got closer to each other, and Nicole

soon found her shoulders brushing against the ancient walls. There were several intersections and turns that led to a dead end where a solid wall of limestone blocked the way. Disappointed at not having found any secret chamber or missed artifacts, Nicole sighed and reached a hand out to lean against the wall. Almost as soon as contact was made, something brushed across her hand heedlessly. That did it. With a small shriek, Nicole turned around and bolted out of the dark corridor, longing to be back in the bright sunshine and beside a very tall and muscled woman.

Kris had been studying some carvings on the walls when Nicole came running out of the corridor. She quickly reached her shaking friend and divided her attention between her young partner and the recess she had come from.

"What's wrong?" she asked as she tried to calm Nicole, who was out of breath and kept shaking her blonde head, her eyes fixed on the entrance. "Nicole, what happened? Did somebody scare you?"

The dark-haired woman's blood boiled at the thought of somebody trying to do anything to her friend. She had heard about young pickpockets that worked the streets of Cancun, like in any major city, but maybe they found it easier to work in darkened corridors, preying on unsuspecting tourists.

"Touched me...big...didn't see..." Nicole's words were jumbled as she struggled to get her breathing under control. She saw that Kris was getting angry and she tried to explain better. "It was dark...never saw..."

Kris turned and started to walk towards the dark corridor. *Whoever's in there is going to regret what they just did,* she promised as her jaw muscles jumped under her skin. A small but firm hand caught her arm, and she looked down at Nicole who was still shaking her head.

"No...wait," Nicole said and took one last deep breath and giggled nervously.

"What's so funny?" Kris asked a bit gruffly. Somebody had scared the daylights out of her and all she could do was laugh? "Let me go and check what..."

"It was some kind of...creature," Nicole spoke at the same time. Kris stared at her, her brows furrowed in concentration, then one shot up, and Kris looked at her in question.

"It was what?"

"This is sooo embarrassing." Nicole cleared her throat and looked up shyly at the still fuming woman. "Some kind of furry creature crawled over my hand," she explained in a whisper. "It surprised me."

Kris just stared at her, all thoughts of doing bodily damage to the invisible assailant forgotten. "A furry creature?" she repeated as she stared at the smaller woman, then took a deep breath to calm her nerves and crossed her long arms over her chest. Nicole looked like she didn't know if she should laugh or cry.

"I didn't mean to scare you," Nicole apologized. "It was dark and I put my hand on the wall and..." She frowned at Kris. Either the woman was shaking with anger, or she was trying her best not to laugh. A closer inspection revealed that her friend seemed to find the situation very funny. Nicole planted her fists on her hips and glared at the taller woman. "This is not funny, Kristina."

Kris couldn't hold it any longer and laughed, partly relieved that nothing serious had happened and partly because she couldn't keep the image of Nicole's reaction to the furry insect crawling over her hand out of her mind. Her laughter only got a frustrated sigh from her younger companion and Nicole stormed off towards the exit. The taller woman easily jogged after her.

"Hey, I'm sorry," Kris said, trying to stop laughing. She reached out for Nicole's arm and gently turned the smaller woman to face her. "I'm not laughing at you, love," she said softly. "I'm just glad that you're okay."

"I was really scared," Nicole murmured as she was wrapped in strong arms.

Kris brushed her hand over the blonde hair and glared at a couple staring at them. They quickly left the women alone. "Do you want to skip visiting the caverns?"

Nicole shook her head. "No. I'd like to go. But keep an eye out for a furry, multi-legged something, okay?" She grinned, feeling better already.

"I will." Kris chuckled and gave Nicole a hug before letting her go. "Come on."

East of the major Chichén Itzá ruins was a dark, underground world the Mayans called Cenoté. They were deep, water filled sinkholes formed by water dripping through the soft limestone above. Since the porous soil held little water, these underground bodies were extremely important to the Mayan City.

Kris entered the cavern through a vertical hole with narrow steps carved by the Mayans themselves. She made sure that Nicole followed close behind, looking back once in a while to check on her friend's progress. One misstep on the slimy ledges threatened to send them falling over twenty feet.

The air was thick and musty, but once their eyes got used to the dim light, handling the smell was worth it. The spectacle offered to them was breathtaking. Stalactites of blood red limestone seemed to ooze from the dripping walls, ahead was a strange green pool of glowing water. They approached the pool and noticed roots of the trees hanging before them. In their search for water, the trees had penetrated the ceiling, dropping fifty feet to the pool below, creating an eerie underground forest.

As they crawled under some low hanging stalactites, an incredible scene greeted them. A beautiful blue green pool of unknown depth stretched out before the women. A massive stalactite hung down just inches from touching the surface and above was a piercing beam of light that streamed in from the ceiling, illuminating the pool and the entire chamber.

"This is so amazing," Nicole whispered in awe after a few minutes of silent contemplation. She looked up at her companion and saw Kris looking as impressed as she herself was. A low rumbling was heard and Nicole smiled shyly as her stomach made itself known. "Guess it's lunch time already."

Kris looked down at her watch and frowned. "Hmm, no wonder you're hungry," she said. "It's passed dinner time."

"You're kidding, right?" Nicole pulled Kris' wrist closer to her face to see the time herself. "It's a good thing we ate before leaving or else I'd be dying of hunger!"

Kris chuckled. "Well, we visited most of the site already. We could grab something to snack on before we go back to the boat," she suggested, smiling as Nicole nodded vigorously.

"Then we could have a nice meal while we head back to Isla Mujeres."

"I'm looking forward to sleeping in a room that doesn't move up and down with every wave." Nicole grinned. "Don't get me wrong. I love the sailboat, but..."

With a smile, Kris guided the smaller woman back to the steps that would lead them outside. "I know what you mean. The next two days will be spent relaxing on the beach at the villa before we head back to Montreal, Sunday night."

"I can't believe this is only Friday. I've had such a wonderful time here." Nicole smiled warmly at her companion, lightly touching her arm. "Thank you so much."

"You're welcome. I had fun, too."

The women made their way to the surface and then to the marina where Isabella was waiting for them to sail back to the island resort. With a late flight on Sunday, they had nearly two full days to enjoy the sun and beaches in Mexico.

Monday would see both women starting new jobs. Kris would be teaching at the stunt school while Nicole would start as a camera assistant on a two-month contract where she would finally be doing what she had always dreamed of, learning and working behind the camera. That contract would also last until just before Kris was due back in Austria.

****

Mark Dunham shifted in his seat for the fifth time in five minutes. What he hated the most about traveling was the waiting to get aboard planes. He wished that the time he had just spent covering the boat race in Cancun had been longer. Even though he had worked all weekend, it had been a relaxing time, enjoying the sun, the sea, and all those women. But it was time to go back to do serious work. Sitting at the airport, he waited for his flight back home along with many other photographers from all over the world.

Trying to waste time, he had bought a magazine dealing mostly with European celebrities, interested in seeing who was the most popular in Europe these days. With many actors and celebrities coming for events or to film movies in Montreal from France, England, or Italy, it always helped the photographer to know who was most in demand. He would hunt them down to take pictures and then sell them for a hefty profit to different magazines.

He was leafing through the magazine when a fellow photographer from Germany sat down beside him. He nodded a greeting before returning his attention to the article before him. After scanning it, he flipped the page to gaze upon a picture of the most beautiful woman he had ever seen. Either the woman was very tall or the people surrounding her were very short. Her long, black hair cascaded over broad shoulders, the high cheekbones and angular face gave her an exotic look. But what impressed Mark the most were the incredibly blue eyes looking back at the camera.

"She's a beauty, isn't she?" his neighbor said, pointing at the picture with his chin. "She's one of the hottest celebrities in Europe right now."

Mark took another look at the woman and smiled. "She's a hot one for sure." He vaguely remembered seeing this woman before and couldn't figure out from where. He scanned the article for a name. "Kristina Von Deering," he muttered to himself. "She's a stuntwoman?" he asked the German.

Another photographer grabbed the magazine out of the Canadian's hands and leered at the picture. "She's just another dyke," he said with contempt and handed the magazine back. "I saw her and her new girlfriend a few minutes ago, she's a cute little thing. And here I thought that all dykes looked like truck drivers," the American snickered. "That blonde is far from looking like that."

"Kristina is here?" the German photographer asked. "Pictures of her sell very well. She's a real money maker."

"Yeah, I saw her and the blonde step out of a limo some time ago." The American shrugged. "Some people go nuts over her and her latest conquests. I much prefer hunting the Hollywood scene."

"I thought that she was in Montreal for three months," the German murmured to himself. "And with another girlfriend...Damn! That woman has had more lovers than a sailor." He reached for his camera. "I'm going after them," he said as he shouldered his bag and left in a hurry.

Mark watched the photographer leave and looked back at the picture. *She's in Montreal for three months?* he silently repeated. *Judging by the German's reaction, I'm sure I can make a few bucks out of following her.*

He leaned back in his seat and smiled. Kristina was right in his back yard, so to speak. Being a freelance photographer had its ups sometimes. He simply took the pictures and sold them. He didn't have to deal with boring assignments; he was his own master. He went where the money was, and right now, it seemed like it was with a certain woman named Kristina Von Deering. He had a good feeling about this.

His flight for Montreal was announced and he stood up, shouldered his bag and headed to the gate with his plane tickets in his hand. Something caught his attention and he turned his head and spotted the tall Austrian with a shorter woman walking beside her. *It's her!*

Kristina was laughing at something the blonde was saying, and he noticed the stuntwoman's hand gently brushing against the smaller woman's back. Mark smiled. Lady luck was on his side. Kristina and her girlfriend were on the same plane as he was on. It would make his finding her a lot easier. The only thing he had to do now was to follow her and see where she lived.

Chapter 17

The women stepped out of the limousine, unaware of the taxi that had stopped a few houses down the road, its only passenger watching them intently. The driver took the bags out of the trunk and put them down near the front door. Kris smiled as she handed him a few bills and took the bags herself, before walking into the house right behind the blonde.

Nicole blindly searched for the light, but before she found the switch, she heard the thump of the suitcases and then felt two strong hands gripping her hips. She closed her eyes as Kris leaned her chest against her back, and smiled when her lover brushed her hair aside to softly kiss her neck.

"Hmmm, that feels so nice," Nicole murmured. "But we have to unpack and..." Kris' hands moved up front and softly massaged her breasts, making it difficult to even think.

"Would you rather unpack the bags or go to bed?" Kris whispered seductively in Nicole's ear.

"What bags?" Nicole smiled as she took Kris' hand and led her lover to the bedroom. "I think the unpacking can wait."

Neither cared that it was late in the evening nor that both women were starting new jobs in the morning. What mattered was the comfort they found in one another's arms. Nicole had longed all day to hold Kris, but the sudden appearance of photographers at the airport in Cancun had made it difficult. They didn't want to feed the paparazzi, but the slightest movement of a hand on a shoulder or back and the smallest of smiles between them got the photographers snapping pictures in frenzy.

Kris had seen the worried and slightly scared look on the younger woman's face when the cameras' flashed. Thankful for their first class tickets allowing them to get on board first, the tall woman had guided them through the gate at the first call for their flight. Nicole had previously said that she didn't care who knew about their relationship, but the intense barrage of questions from the photographers had made her speechless. Kris had simply held one hand up at them and shook her head, refusing to answer their questions.

But they were far away from the paparazzi now and Nicole sighed in contentment as she settled comfortably against Kris, her head resting just under the taller woman's chin with her right arm and leg sprawled over the muscled body. Their breathing gradually returned to a normal rhythm while a thin layer of sweat covered their bodies.

The young woman smiled as she remembered Kris moaning her name as they made love. Nicole had quickly learned what pleased her lover and took great pleasure in putting her new knowledge into practice. She was obviously doing something right judging by the rapidly beating heart under her ear and the shaky breathing.

Nicole had been so worried about not being able to satisfy her, knowing that Kris had had many lovers before, but the older woman's reaction to her touch confirmed that she was doing everything right.

One thing kept nagging at her though as she silently repeated a question asked by a journalist at the airport, causing a few others to chuckle. *Hey Kristina! How long will this new girlfriend last this time?* She remembered Kris glaring at him, silencing them all. Only Nicole's gentle but firm pull on her lover's hand had saved the journalists from injury and destroyed property from the angry stuntwoman.

No matter how many times Kris told her that she loved her, Nicole kept wondering if their relationship was different from all the others Kris had previously. She wondered if this one would last for a long time or if she would eventually get tired and would start looking elsewhere.

Of course she'll find somebody else, a voice sounded in Nicole's mind. *You certainly don't expect her to stay celibate once she goes back home, do you?* Tears formed in her eyes at the thought of her lover and best friend with another woman in her arms, and she discretely wiped her eyes.

Kris caught the movement and heard a light sniffle. "Hey, what's wrong?" She gently brushed her fingers through her lover's blonde hair and frowned.

"I...was just thinking about the photographers and journalists at the airport," Nicole replied. *Better to say half a truth than a full lie.*

"They really scared you, didn't they?"

"How do you get used to that?" Nicole asked. "Why do they follow you like that?"

Kris took a deep breath and let it go slowly. *Why indeed?* "You never get use to it," she replied simply. "You just have to learn to deal with it the best way possible."

"I know actors and singers have to deal with this," Nicole said. "But I've never heard of stunt people generating this kind of reaction from them. Am I wrong?"

"No, you're not. Stunt performers don't usually get that much attention from the press but it seems that I'm one of their favorite targets," she explained sadly.

Maybe it had been a mixture of surprise at seeing all those people heading their way and the fact that Nicole was tired that had gotten to the younger woman. At least, the next time something like that happened again, Nicole would know what to expect and wouldn't be scared senseless.

"The journalists started hounding me about five years ago," Kris continued without being prompted. "A childhood friend of mine had starred in a German production. The night of the premier, she had an argument with her boyfriend and, not wanting to go to the premier alone, she asked me to go with her." She smiled at the memory.

They had been two young girls barely over eighteen, in a party mood with no adults watching over them. What an evening that had been. "Even though she was just a friend, the photographers wrongly assumed that something more than just friendship was going on between us."

Nicole shifted so she could look at Kris. "So, what happened?"

"After seeing the newspapers and magazines some time later, Sandra and I thought the stories were hilarious, but her parents didn't."

"But they knew she had a boyfriend, right?" Nicole asked.

"Yes, they knew. But the articles that were written, most of them lies, caused the big problem. Afraid that Sandra wouldn't get any future offers for movie deals, her mother told her to stop hanging around with me." The hurt crept back into Kris' soul at losing the only friend she ever had. "They moved to Los Angeles soon after that, and we never saw each other again."

"That's sad," Nicole said softly, seeing the hurt in her lover's eyes. "But you had other friends, right?"

Kris shook her head. "I had a lot of acquaintances, but none were close enough to call friend. Besides, it hurt too much when she left. I didn't want to go through that again, and I had no time for any social activities. I was getting more work as a stuntwoman so I gave it my full attention."

"But you have a friend now. Me." Nicole smiled, as her lover laughed, then, in a more serious voice, added, "I will never hurt you. I love you too much."

Kris softly kissed the blonde head. "But even though we never mean to, sometimes we unintentionally end up doing just that," she said softly. "It's getting late, and we have to wake up early." With her lover comfortably settled against her body, Kris wrapped her arms around the smaller woman and whispered, "I love you too."

Smiling, Nicole stretched a little to give her partner a kiss then went back to her original position, half-sprawled over Kris' body and holding on tight. "Good night."

****

After he wrote the stuntwoman's address in his pocket book,

the photographer returned to his car, wanting to be ready to follow if Kris or her girlfriend came out of the house, but all the lights remained turned off for the night.

Taking a chance that they were asleep, Mark drove to a 24-hour restaurant not too far away and ordered something to eat. While he was waiting for his food, he called his contact, Claire Gilbert, who worked at one of Montreal's best-selling show business magazines and informed her of Kris' presence in the city. Claire had mentioned something about wanting to interview the stuntwoman and that up-to-date pictures of the Austrian would be a nice addition to the article, so a verbal contract was quickly agreed upon over the phone for some shots. Not knowing Kristina's schedule, Mark hurriedly ate then went back to the house after his meal—ready to follow her anywhere she went just to take pictures.

The photographer became fully alert when, around five-thirty, the garage door opened, and the roar of a motorcycle sounded in the quiet morning air. The stuntwoman drove a Harley out of the garage while the blonde closed the door then joined Kristina on the bike.

Dressed in black leather jackets and jeans, the dark haired woman pulled her braided hair from under the collar and twisted on the motorcycle to speak to the smaller woman behind her.

Unable to hear them from his distance away, he lifted his camera and zoomed in on both women as Kristina gave her girlfriend a kiss before she put her sunglasses on, and they strapped on their helmets and got underway. The photographer waited for them to leave and then started up the car and followed at a reasonable distance.

The stuntwoman stopped the motorcycle in front of the Maisonneuve Studios where the small blonde got off the bike, removed her helmet and fastened it to the Harley. The photographer took more pictures as they talked then chuckled and he got a better shot of them kissing.

The blonde waved good-bye, opened the front door to the studios and walked in the building. Mark quickly scribbled the address, adding it into his notebook, and then put the car in gear when his target rode off.

Forty-five minutes later, Kristina arrived at the Canadian Stunt School just outside of Montreal. She parked her motorcycle in front of the large building that looked like a hangar, and walked in. Taking his camera and bag, the photographer climbed out of his car and walked around the area, wanting to know the layout of the school so he could find the best places to hide and take his pictures.

Mark only wished that the school managers weren't against photographers on their ground, it would make his job much easier. He remembered the story of the last photographer who had tried to get on the grounds without being approved. He had been accused of trespassing and was fined for it. Mark didn't have that kind of cash to throw away. Claire, the journalist he had spoken to, had promised him access to the school if Kristina agreed to an interview, but he couldn't wait until then. A lot of magazines were interested in having pictures of the famous stuntwoman, and he didn't want to let any good deals pass him by.

****

Kris watched as the students practiced and went through the newly learned routine, satisfied that the day had gone by without any problems. The students for the week were experienced stunters wanting to polish their skills. She didn't have to deal with rookie stuntmen this time, which made her job easier. That would come the following week.

Her job at the school was to teach stunts dealing with cars, such as controlled skidding, rollovers, jumps, and collisions, which meant racing on an obstacle course. Another aspect of her lessons was to teach the stuntmen how to get hit by a car without being injured.

The new instructors had been warmly welcomed that morning by the regular teachers, and Kris was happy to see that most of them were accomplished stuntmen and extremely good at their specialties. The school was well equipped and had plenty of space outdoors for performing. There was a hangar, providing rooms to teach the different stunts, high towers and walls to practice falls and climbing, and a full gymnasium to keep everybody in shape. Another area was set apart from everything and was reserved for the most dangerous of all stunts, those concerning fire and explosives.

Kris nodded with a smile as the students finished their routines and waved at her on their way to the locker rooms for a well-deserved shower. All that remained to do was to enter into the school's computer all the notes taken concerning the students. *Not the most interesting part of the job,* she told herself as she strolled towards the instructor's office.

As Kris walked past, the receptionist reached for a piece of paper and waved it at her. "Ms. Von Deering. You have a message."

Kris stopped and turned around to take the pink slip of paper. "Thanks." She continued down the corridor to her assigned desk and sat down in front of her computer. Looking at her message, she frowned at the name above the phone number.

She had expected the message to be from Nicole, but she didn't know a Claire Gilbert. As she was about to reach for the phone, the school director leaned against her desk and smiled at her.

"Something wrong?" Marcus asked, seeing Kris' frown.

"Somebody left a message to call back, but I don't recognize the name," she said as she handed the paper to the director. "Some woman from *Chatelaine.* Do you know who she is?"

Marcus looked at the name and nodded. "Yep, she's a journalist. She did a story on the school last year. Maybe she wants to do one about you."

"Why me?" Kris grumbled. "There are ten instructors teaching here, why can't she pick somebody else?"

"Maybe because you're the first stuntwoman to teach here in the past ten years?" He chuckled. He knew from her reputation that Kris didn't like to be singled out for interviews. "Besides, it's good publicity for the school, right?" He smiled, turning around and leaving her to make her own decision.

Kris was about to reach for the phone again when her cell phone rang. She quickly took it out of its leather casing. "Hello?"

"Hi," Nicole's cheerful voice sounded. "Am I calling at a bad time?"

Kris smiled, leaning back in her chair and closing her eyes. "Hi, love. No, your timing's perfect. How's your day?"

"It's great," Nicole said enthusiastically. "There's so much to learn here. I've been teamed up with a woman who's been working behind the camera for twenty years. She's very nice and told me that she would give me as much work as possible. She's willing to teach me everything."

"I'm glad that you like your new job," Kris said as she looked at her watch. "Are you on a regular schedule? What time do you finish working?"

"I start at six in the morning and finish at six at night, Monday to Friday. We have two talk shows to do, but I've been told it's pretty much basic shots. How was your first day?"

"Not too bad. I'm the only female instructor here, but the guys are fun, a bit on the rowdy side though." Kris looked up in time to see two instructors walk into the office and start pelting each other with paper balls, proving her point. "I have about one hour of paperwork to do, and then I'll be on my way to pick you up. Anything special you want to eat tonight?"

"Hmmm." Nicole was silent for a moment. "Yes...you," she purred.

A blush covered Kris' face at Nicole's seductive voice. She looked up at the stuntmen, who were watching her with smiles on their faces.

A tall and muscular stuntman elbowed his friend in the ribs and winked at Kris. "I don't know who's on the other end, but I sure would love to find out what's being said."

"Aw, just look at that face," the other chimed in. "Whoever can make the great Kristina blush that way must be real special."

"Guys," Kris growled playfully and turned her attention back to her giggling lover.

"So, I'm special, huh?" Nicole teased her. "I miss you," she said more seriously. "Can't wait to be home with you."

"I miss you, too." Kris smiled into the phone. "How about Chinese for dinner and me for desert?"

"Ooh, I can live with that. Well, I have to go. See you

soon?"

"You got it. Bye." Kris closed the connection and put her cell phone back into the leather casing attached to her belt. She looked at the instructors, who were still grinning at her, and she shook her head. "You guys are just like kids." She laughed and started working on the computer.

****

Having finished her work at the school, Kris left to get Nicole and then stopped at the Chinese restaurant to order and have the food delivered to the house. They ate and talked about their first day at work, sharing interesting events that had happened, and then settled comfortably in their bed to watch the movie playing on the TV.

"Did you reach the reporter that left you a message at the school?" Nicole asked as she cuddled against Kris, her hand slowly drawing figure eights over her lover's stomach.

"Hmm mm," Kris mumbled as she closed her eyes, enjoying the soft touch. "She'd like to come over to the school for an interview. Marcus, he's the schools director, said it would be good publicity."

"You don't sound like it's a good idea."

"I agree with the publicity for the school, they could use some. It's just that I don't trust reporters," Kris stated. "The interviews you give don't always sound the same on paper. What they usually want to know is your personal life. They don't care that much about the professional one."

"But if you don't answer the personal questions, you should be okay, right?"

Kris smiled at the question. If only it were that simple. No matter what she did, she couldn't control what the reporters wrote. If they wanted a story out, they would write it with or without her help. All she could do was keep her answers as simple as possible.

"Do you know anything about that reporter?" Kris asked as she gently ran her fingers through Nicole's hair.

"I don't know her personally," she replied. "But I've seen a couple of articles she wrote, mainly about women doing out-of-the-ordinary jobs. The interviews are very well done. She's not one of those gossip columnists."

"So, you think I should agree to the interview?" Kris asked with a smile. The blonde head lifted and green eyes looked at her.

"I know you told me that you weren't too fond of interviews, but I think Claire does interesting ones. I'm sure the school's director would be happy, too. When does she want to do it?"

Kris sighed and closed her eyes as her lover kissed her chest. "Marcus would prefer this Saturday. It would be less hectic than on a normal school day. He's going to ask for a couple of the best students we have to show up and do some demonstrations. Would you like to come to the school with me Saturday?"

"Can I?"

Kris nodded. "I'd like for you to be there with me."

"Great! I'd love to go," Nicole replied excitedly. "Will you be doing something for the interview? Even though it makes me nervous, I'd love to see you perform."

"You would, huh?" Kris asked with a smile. "Well, we could always prepare something." Effortlessly, she lifted the smaller woman off the bed and gently laid her on top of her, then wrapped her arms around the slim waist. "I'll let Marcus know that I agree to the interview and that you'll be there with me."

"Cool!"

"Enough talking," Kris growled playfully as she kissed Nicole, her hands wandering over her lover's back and buttocks. She smiled at the soft moan coming from Nicole and deepened her kiss.

Chapter 18

Claire Gilbert smiled when she saw the stunt school's grounds. The reporter couldn't believe her luck at the chance to interview the famous stuntwoman. So many people had tried, only to have their requests refused. *Why did Kristina agree this time?* She asked herself as she guided her car to the visitors' parking area. The short conversation on the phone with the Austrian had been pleasant at best, and the reporter found herself looking forward to meeting the dark-haired woman in person.

Noticing that the photographer was waiting for her not too far away, Claire nodded her greeting and approached a tall, dark-haired woman who was talking with a much shorter man. Looking down at the 8 x 10 photograph she had on her clipboard, she immediately recognized the Austrian stuntwoman.

Kristina's black, unbuttoned shirt, which revealed a white T-shirt underneath, was tucked neatly in faded blue jeans. Both of Kristina's hands were deep into her jeans pockets, and she scuffed one of her hiking boots on the ground as she listened to the man. Claire remembered him as being the school's director.

Standing beside the stuntwoman and Marcus was a petite woman. When Kristina put her arm across the smaller woman's shoulders, the blonde looked up and smiled, giving Kris a quick hug and then letting her go. Marcus laughed and scanned the grounds, finally noticing the reporter.

"Ms. Gilbert," he said with a smile as he walked to the woman, holding out his hand to shake hers. "Nice to see you at the school again."

"Thank you for the permission to do this interview." Claire looked over the director's shoulder at the tall woman walking towards them. "And thanks to you, too, Ms. Von Deering."

"Please, call me Kris." She shook Claire's hand. "And this is my friend, Nicole."

"Hi." Nicole smiled.

"Nice to meet you." Claire smiled back. "And this is the photographer who will be taking a few pictures today."

"Mark Dunham," he introduced himself as he showed his camera. "Just don't pay any attention to me. I'll be taking a few shots throughout the interview."

Kris nodded and returned her attention to the reporter. "So, how would you like to start this interview?" she asked, suddenly wishing it to be over with.

"Well, I toured the school the last time I came here so why don't we just sit somewhere and talk?" Claire suggested as she indicated a picnic table near a maple tree and started walking towards it. "I know you must be very busy, and I don't want to take too much of your time."

Kris smiled and nodded again. *I'm not going to argue with that*, she thought as they all sat at the picnic table. "You don't mind if Nicole and Marcus stay here with us?"

Claire smiled. "Of course not." She took her note pad out of her attaché case, put her recorder on the table and switched it on. "Before we start," the reporter spoke into the recorder, "I would like to have Ms. Kristina Von Deering's only condition to this interview be noted, which is that no questions concerning her private life be asked." She looked up at Kris and smiled. "Now that we have that out of the way, let's start this interview."

Nicole listened as Kris answered the questions about her career as a stuntwoman, and she understood why her friend wanted her to sit in on the interview. It was the perfect way to learn a little more about her and her career.

True to the reporter's promise, not a single question was

asked about Kris' private life. Claire stuck to questions concerning her professional life only, about the different movies and projects she had worked on and her present work at the stunt school. Nicole smiled as she remembered Kris' reaction when she was asked of all the people she had met, who had made the biggest impact in her life.

The dark-haired woman had smiled and gave Nicole a conspiratorial glance, before returning her attention to the reporter and answering. *How could she say I'm the one? We've only known each other for less than two months,* Nicole asked herself but didn't complain. She knew that the reporter had meant professionally, but it had felt so damn good to know that she was the most important person in Kris' private life.

By the time the interview was over, Kris was completely relaxed. The photographer had taken a lot of pictures, and Nicole was sure that she was in a few of them. She didn't mind really. It just felt weird to know that there was a chance her face would end up in a magazine.

Kris had warned her of that possibility, and the young woman said that if they chose a picture of the both of them together, she hoped that it would be a good one. The reply had made Kris laugh and had earned her a hug.

"Well, that was very informative, Kristina," Claire said as she shut the recorder off. "Thank you very much."

"My pleasure," the stuntwoman replied as she got up from the picnic table along with Nicole and Marcus.

"You mentioned something to me about hoping to see Kristina in action, right?" Marcus asked the reporter. This was the first time he had spoken since the beginning of the interview. He had asked to be present just in case Kris needed help, but the Austrian had done very well by herself. She had even surprised him with her knowledge of the school and its history.

"I'd love to see a demonstration." Claire smiled as she looked at Kris. "If it's not too much to ask."

"No trouble at all," the dark haired woman said. "If you'll follow me."

The small group headed towards a waiting helicopter. Not too far away, some of the school's instructors and students were making the last minute preparations on a fifty-foot square air-bag. The crew had started inflating the bag with the help of electric blowers as soon as the interview was finished, and they saw Kris head their way. The photographer continued taking pictures as the stuntwoman made a check of the rigging, the huge plastic sack used for high falls being the most important. She talked briefly with the crew and helicopter pilot before turning to Nicole.

Kris was possessed with an unrealistic wish that the photographer, the reporter and the whole crew would leave so she could have a private moment with Nicole. She sighed, as she looked at her then smiled. "Hey, you okay?" she asked gently, seeing the worried look on her lover's face.

Nicole looked up at Kris. *No. I'm not okay,* she wanted to scream, *and I changed my mind. I don't want to see you throw yourself out of a helicopter to land on top of a huge pillow.* "Just nervous, I guess." She gave her a little smile.

"Everything will be okay. I've done this stunt many times before," Kris said reassuringly. "It's just a demonstration, I'm not after a world record," she joked, hoping to ease Nicole's nervousness.

She started to reach for Nicole's cheek but stopped in mid movement when she heard the distinct clicks of pictures being taken. A hard stare in the photographer's direction made the man swallow hard and take a few steps away from the women. She turned her attention back to her friend.

"It'll be over before you know it." She smiled as she took an elastic band out of her jeans' pocket and tied her hair back so she wouldn't be blinded in mid fall.

All Nicole wanted to do was to hug her friend and never let her go. *Get over it, Nick!* She scolded herself. *This is her job, she's used to this. Everything is done as safely as possible. She won't take unnecessarily risks.* "Please, be careful?" she said in a shaky voice as she softly touched Kris' arm.

"I always am." She grinned and gently laid her hand over Nicole's then heard another picture being taken. She shook her head and sighed. "Photographers," she mumbled. With a light touch of her fingers against Nicole's cheek, Kris smiled then turned around and walked to the waiting helicopter.

Nicole watched Kris go and tried to get her nerves under control. She knew that she would be nervous watching her lover perform, having been nervous during Neilson's stunts, but she never expected to be a nervous wreck. Her heart was beating so fast it hurt. *Kris is a professional stuntwoman,* she told herself over and over again. *Everything will be okay.*

Kris put a headset on and adjusted the microphone, then grabbed the harness near the helicopter's door. With a wink, she waved at the small blonde.

Nicole waved back as the aircraft slowly lifted off the ground with the stuntwoman standing on its outside skid. She went to stand next to the reporter, who was listening to Marcus' explanation of the stunt.

"Since we don't have any buildings several hundred feet tall on the school grounds," Marcus explained, "Kris will fall out of the helicopter and onto that bag over there." He indicated the inflated sack.

"Isn't it too high of a fall for such a bag?" Claire asked.

Marcus shook his head. "Some stunt performers have done falls of three hundred feet with such a bag, so this isn't out of the ordinary."

Oh my God! Nicole exclaimed silently, *I didn't realize it would be so high.* She watched as the helicopter hovered above the landing site with Kris hanging on to the seat strap, leaning over, and looking down. She had her back against the open door and was making hand gestures, *probably giving the pilot directions,* Nicole thought.

"Recent techniques make it possible to do high falls without a catcher of any kind," Marcus continued. "We call it a ratchet fall. It's done with a small but powerful mechanism that pays out steel cable and seizes up at a predetermined length, leaving the stunt performer dangling in a harness. The stop is abrupt but, if done properly, it doesn't harm the human being or machinery."

"Why didn't Kristina do something with this ratchet mechanism instead of using a bag?" Claire asked as she kept her eyes on the helicopter above.

"The ratchet takes a long time to setup properly. This is

much simpler."

"But this is more dangerous, right? I've heard about stuntmen breaking their necks when they land," the reporter said.

"Yes, I'm sorry to say that's true," the director agreed. "But Kristina has done this stunt regularly. She knows what to expect."

I really didn't need to hear that, Nicole grumbled to herself and stepped away from Marcus and the reporter. All she wanted was for the stunt to be done and go back home with Kris in one piece.

The stuntwoman looked down and directed the helicopter pilot to move slightly to the right. "Okay, hold!" she yelled into the microphone so she would be heard over the sound of the rotors above her and the wind. She could see the safeties surrounding the airbag below, mainly the school's instructors staying close to the bag with keen eyes looking out for trouble. The medical team they had hired for the stunt waited close by in case something did go wrong. Shifting her eyes away from the landing bag, Kris noticed the photographer still taking pictures, Claire and Marcus standing together then Nicole, standing by herself, looking up at her.

Usually the stunt coordinator was the one who worried about a coming performance. In Kris' case that usually meant her older brother, Franz, but she was touched by her lover's nervous reaction. Kris was sure that Nicole hadn't seen too many stunts being performed, at least not enough to get used to it. *I wonder if she'd ever get used to that no matter how many stunts she saw.*

She shook her head and tried to focus on her performance. Thinking about Nicole right now was the worst thing she could do. She needed all of her concentration on the stunt, not lingering on the smiling young woman waiting for her below. That smile and sparkling green eyes, those gentle hands and soft skin...

"That's enough," she chastised herself forgetting that she had a headset and microphone on.

"What was that?" the helicopter pilot asked.

"Move slightly left," Kris replied, upset at her lack of control where Nicole was concerned. "Okay, hold!" She slipped her headset off and handed it to a waiting crewmember aboard the helicopter, then took another deep breath and went through the movements mentally one last time. She stared down at the black center mark on the white airbag and relaxed her body, preparing for the fall.

Nicole held her breath as Kris lifted her left arm up into the air. *This is it,* she told herself with a mix of nerve-wracking nervousness and excitement.

Her lover smoothly let herself fall off the helicopter skid and plunged headfirst towards the airbag. Kris' fall was so graceful that she looked like she was flying. Both of her legs were kept close together while her arms were stretched out on either side of her body. Nicole could see the beginning of a roll as the stuntwoman let her body tumble head over heels, preparing to land on her back.

Kris loved this kind of stunt. She loved the sensation of falling, free of any harnesses or cables, just the wind and air brushing against her body and face. Nothing holding her back, no fancy equipment to rely upon save for the airbag waiting for her below. She felt like a bird every time she performed this way, but the sensation only lasted for a few seconds, and she gave her body an angle, preparing for her landing.

A slight tilt of the head forward, a gentle hunch of her shoulders and her body turned upside down, ready to land on her back on the inflatable bag. The only downside of this kind of stunt was the landing, which could steal your breath away. Relaxing her body as best as she could, Kris fell gracefully and waited for the coming impact.

The only sound was the regular hum of the electrical blowers constantly pushing air into the airbag and the noise of the helicopter still hovering above. All of the crew watched the free fall, silently counting the seconds before Kris hit the bag. Nicole, the reporter, and Marcus were spellbound as Kris strong body toppled and shifted position in mid air. Only the photographer kept his camera aimed at the stuntwoman and took continuous shots of the stunt being performed.

Kris hit the airbag with a violent crash causing the vents

along the sides to split open on impact letting air escape the bag. The sack deflated immediately, and the crew ran towards it, trying to reach the stuntwoman in the middle of the floating plastic sack.

Kris kept her eyes shut and tried desperately to get some air into her lungs. The force of the impact, as predicted, left her gasping for air. She was faintly aware of shouting voices around her, knowing that it was the safeties trying to reach her to check for any injuries. Feeling her body sink in the middle of the bag as it deflated, she slowly moved her arms, legs, and neck to see if everything was all right.

The sound of Kris' body hitting the airbag had been too much for Nicole, and she ran towards the working crew. She watched nervously, biting her lower lip as she waited for news about her lover, faintly aware of Marcus standing beside her. A loud call came from somewhere on the bag and then silence. Nicole shook as the seconds turned into minutes, the wait seeming interminable.

"She's going to be okay, right?" Nicole asked the director without taking her eyes off the crew. Another call was heard, and the medics approached the completely deflated bag with a stretcher complete with medical cases and oxygen bottle. "Oh, my God!" Nicole started to move towards the group, but strong hands held her back.

"Let them work, Nicole," Marcus said softly as he kept his eyes on the crew. "This is normal procedure," he explained as one of the medics made his way through the assembled men. A loud cheering rose up, and he smiled.

Having gotten her breathing back under control and after making sure that nothing was broken, Kris slowly stood up and nodded weakly to the assembled crew. The men whooped in relief and clapped her on the back. She smiled as she made her way out of the plastic bag, helped by a medic, her only thought was to find Nicole and let her know that she was okay.

Nicole broke free from Marcus' grasp and ran to Kris, who opened her arms and wrapped them around her lover's slim waist.

The photographer quickly lifted his camera, but was stopped

by Marcus. "Give them some time okay?" the director said in a voice that bore no argument.

"Oh, God," Nicole whispered with her face deep in Kris' chest, both arms locked solidly behind the taller woman's neck. "Are you okay?" Tears formed in her eyes, as the tension in her body broke loose.

"I'm fine," Kris softly replied and gently kissed her head. "I got the wind knocked out of me, but that was expected." Neither woman moved, giving each other time to get their emotions under control.

The stuntwoman lifted her eyes and saw the approaching reporter. It was too late to break the embrace. Kris was sure that Claire now knew they were more than just friends, but she didn't care. Nicole needed her right now and that was all that mattered.

Claire smiled at the women. She had seen their exchanged looks during the interview, and had guessed that something was going on between them. The reporter gave them a few more minutes before she addressed the stuntwoman.

"That was fantastic, Kristina," she said as Nicole lifted her head. "I saw some incredible stunts the last time I was here, but this was awesome."

Nicole started to take a step away from Kris only to be held in place by the strong arm around her waist. Startled, she looked up at her lover, who smiled back at her. *I guess there's no reason now to try and keep our relationship a secret.*

"I'm glad you liked the show, Claire." Kris gave Nicole a little squeeze and then smiled at the reporter. "If we're done with the interview, we'd like to be on our way." Her eyes locked with Claire's. Would she keep her promise to abide by Kris' conditions or would she lower herself to the rank of a gossip columnist?

"Yes, we're done. Thank you for your time, Kristina," she said as she shook the stuntwoman's hand. "I'm sure it will be a very good article." Claire then turned her attention to Nicole who had her arm around Kris. "It was also nice to meet you, Nicole." Looking back at the Austrian, the reporter saw a worried expression on the beautiful face. "You don't have to worry. The article will only be about your professional career," Claire said and Kris relaxed. "But I'd love to be able to write your personal story. It would be nice to read the truth instead of all those rumors."

Kris laughed. "Always looking for a good story, eh? I'm afraid my life would be pretty boring to most readers. Not enough juicy events."

"Well, if you ever change your mind, give me a call," she said as she handed Kris her business card. "Take care, you two." The reporter walked away with the photographer trailing behind her.

"That was interesting," Nicole said as she gave Kris a hug, happy to finally be able to do so. "What did she mean by wanting to write the truth?" she asked as they walked to the picnic table where Kris had done the interview. They sat down, and the taller woman played with the splintered tabletop, deep in thought. *Maybe it hadn't been the best question to ask*, Nicole thought.

So many false stories had been written about her, mostly about her many lovers all over the world. Kris shook her head at the thought. She did have a few lovers in her life but nothing like the press claimed she had. They made her look like a female Casanova. Most of the people she had been photographed with had been acquaintances only. Ironically, her true lovers had never been photographed with her, until Nicole anyway.

On the other hand, some of what had been written was partly true but exaggerated quite a bit. She had never acted like a spoiled celebrity on any movie set. Yes, she did have a bad temper and easily lost it, but only when faced with gross stupidity of a crewmember that put people at risk. And the reason she rarely attended show business parties wasn't because she was a snob, but because she couldn't stand all that hypocrisy. She had more important things to do than to participate in half lies and idle chitchat.

Kris looked at Nicole. Why would she want to hang around artificial people when she had such a sweet and gentle woman that loved her? The last thing she wanted to do was introduce Nicole to that type of crowd. She sighed and shrugged her shoulders.

"It's just that so many rumors have been written, most of

them total lies. I guess Claire believes that my real story would be interesting to the public. I'm not sure I want them to see the real me."

"You mean you don't want the world to know that you're a warm, gentle, and caring human being?" Nicole grinned and laughed the blush on Kris' face. "You prefer to keep that bad girl image, huh?"

"Hey there," Marcus chuckled as he sat at the table. "Are you guys coming to the party later on? We're all going to Henry's."

The slightest frown on Nicole's brow told Kris the answer to that question. "I'm sorry, Marcus," she apologized with a smile, "but we have something planned already."

"That's too bad," he replied, a little disappointed. "It would have been great if you'd join us." The director stood up and patted Nicole on her arm. "It was great meeting you. Hope I'll see you again."

"Thanks for having me here."

Marcus nodded and then turned to Kris. "And I'll see you on Monday. Have a good weekend. Great stunt, by the way." He smiled as he walked back to the waiting crew.

"So," Kris said as they stood up. "You ready for some shopping?" she asked, putting her arm across Nicole's shoulder and tugging the smaller woman closer as they walked to the black Harley.

"Don't you want to rest a little bit after a stunt like that?" Nicole asked. "I'm sure we can go for the party supplies a little later on."

Kris smiled and shook her head. "Nah, I feel fine. Besides, Alex's going away party is tonight. It doesn't give us much time to get ready."

"I'm going to miss her," Nicole said in a small voice. "I hope that everything will go well for her in Africa."

"I'm sure it will," Kris assured the younger woman. "Movie crews on location have everything they need with them." She could see that something besides missing her cousin was bothering her. "Hey." She gently lifted Nicole's chin to look into her eyes. "What is it?"

Nicole opened her mouth, but closed it, then tried again with the same results. She shook her head unable to meet Kris' intense gaze.

"What is it?" she softly repeated.

Nicole took a deep breath and looked at her friend. "It's just that...it reminded me that you'll also be leaving soon." Her voice cracked and she bit her lip. *Damn. I promised myself I wouldn't say anything.* "I'm sorry, I didn't mean to bring it up."

"Well, I'm glad you did," Kris said softly, "because there's something I'd like to...well, I want to..." she stammered, nervously. She never thought she'd be asking this one day, but as she looked at Nicole, she knew that she was the only one for her.

"Hey," Nicole said, suddenly worried about her friend's serious expression. "I'm sorry if I..."

Kris took the smaller hands in hers. "When I came here, I had a job to do," she started as she looked down at their entwined hands. "I was going to perform the best way I knew how and spend my free time working on my horse breeding program until I went home." A small smile tugged at Kris' lips, and she looked up onto green eyes. "But I didn't expect what happened after I got here."

Nicole struggled to keep down the panic at Kris' serious tone of voice and her smile added a layer of confusion to the panic. "But, Kris..."

"Please, let me finish," she said gently. "You're the most important thing that has ever happened to me, Nicole. Your friendship is such a great gift to me, I don't know what I would do if I ever lost that." She took another deep breath and squeezed Nicole's hands. "But now things have changed..." Kris saw the instant panic on Nicole's face and she gave her a calming kiss. "What I mean is, what I feel for you is so much more than just friendship. I'm in love with you, and I don't want to let you go."

Tears formed in Nicole's eyes and her chest tightened at the love on her friend's face.

"I know that we've only been together for a couple of months, but I feel like we've known each other forever." Kris lifted Nicole's hands to her lips and kissed them. "What I'm trying to say is..." She cleared her throat nervously. "But I want you to really think about what I say before you decide anything, okay?"

The only thing Nicole could do was to nod silently, unable to take her eyes away from Kris' face.

"What I'd like...if you want...is for you to...I mean, I..." Kris closed her eyes to get her shaking body under control. She never thought it would be so hard to say. Not because she didn't want to, but because her strong emotions made it hard for her to express herself. *You're also afraid she'll refuse. Admit it, Kris.*

"Just say it," Nicole said softly. Her lover's body relaxed, and her eyelids opened to expose sparkling blue eyes.

"I want you to come live with me in Austria." *There. I said it.*

Nicole wanted to scream with joy. Did she really ask her to move to Austria with her? She had thought her hope of being asked to go with Kris was just a dream too good to come true.

"I know you want me to think it over, Kris, but you won't get rid of me so easily. I want to stay with you, love." A relieved Kris wrapped her in strong arms. "I love you."

"I love you, too," Kris whispered in Nicole's hair. She didn't know what she would have done if her lover had declined her offer.

They still had a few weeks left together in Montreal, to give the young woman a chance to be completely sure of her decision. Moving to a foreign country would be another big step toward the life she wanted to live.

"Come on, we have a party to prepare for." Nicole smiled. She was also anxious to let Alex know about the news. She needed her cousin's assurances that she was making the right decision. She wished she had more self-confidence but life with an overbearing father had stripped that away from her. Why couldn't she have the confidence of Alex or Kris?

They climbed onto the motorcycle and drove to the house, lost in their own thoughts, but happy with the outcome of their conversation.

Chapter 19

They took the newly rented Pathfinder out shopping for the party supplies. Originally, renting a vehicle for the time she'd spend in Montreal had been the last thing Kris wanted to do, figuring that bringing her Harley Davidson from Austria was enough. But with Nicole living with her, it made more sense to have a vehicle where they could talk without having to scream to be heard.

After shopping, they decorated the playroom in the house with brightly colored balloons. All the guests were bringing their own food specialties, and Nicole had explained that it was more fun because you never knew what to expect to eat. She was certain that her aunt Michelle was bringing her famous chicken wings, Robert his Irish stew, and Neilson, maple sugar pies.

Knowing that she couldn't offer anything to the potluck with her very limited cooking skills, Kris had insisted on buying beer, wine, and soft drinks for the party.

The guests arrived at the house by seven o'clock. When the party was in full swing, Nicole stood on the sidelines with an amused grin on her face as Kris beat her uncle at another game of pool. The poor man had lost three games in a row and swore that this time he was going to win. The tall woman chuckled as she prepared the table for another round while Rober''s wife,

Michelle, sat close by and teased him about his lack of skill at playing pool. Comfortably sitting in the corner of the room, Neilson made everybody laugh when he accused Kris of having too many skills. With a grin and a wink towards Nicole, the blue eyed woman simply agreed with the statement, causing more laughter to erupt.

From her place on the sofa, Nicole noticed Sophie's attempt to get a conversation going with Neilson's girlfriend, but Anne was always in a permanent state of grumpiness and didn't look too interested in being at the party. Giving up, Sophie shrugged as she stood up, and sat beside Michelle to watch the pool players. Nicole wondered what Neilson ever saw in Anne. She was everything he wasn't.

A strong hand squeezed her shoulder, and she looked up at a smiling Alex.

"Hey." Nicole grinned. "How do you like your going away party?"

Alex shook her head and laughed. "You do know that I'm coming back after the shooting is done, don't you?" she teased. "You make it sound like we'll never see each other again." She expected a witty retort from her cousin as it was her habit and frowned slightly when none came. Alex scanned the room, and seeing that everybody was busy watching the pool game, she gently grabbed Nicole's hand and gave it a small tug. "Why don't we go outside for some air, okay?"

The women walked to the lakeshore and sat on the grass, listening as the small, moon lit waves broke against the rocks and the light wind gently ruffled the leaves in the trees.

After a few minutes spent in silence, Nicole took a deep breath and closed her eyes. "Kris asked me to live with her." *Please tell me you agree with this.* She shyly looked at her cousin and saw a confused look on her face.

"Hmm, Nick? You've been doing that for some time now," Alex joked.

"In Austria," she added as she distractedly pulled at the blades of grass. "She wants me to move in with her in Innsbruck."

Alex softly whistled. "Wow!" They fell silent again and

looked out at the lake for a while. "How do you feel about that?"

"Thrilled...and scared," Nicole replied honestly. "Thrilled to have a chance to do something I always dreamed of doing. Not only to visit another country but to actually live there. And I'd be living my life with the most beautiful woman I ever saw, with somebody who really loves me. What else can I ask for?"

"Then why do you say you're scared?" Alex asked gently.

She sighed. "Because I'd be leaving everything behind," Nicole replied softly. "My friends, my family..."

"Listen to me," Alex said as she knelt in front of her friend and cousin. "Do you want to live with Kris?"

"Wh...yes, I do. But..."

"Do you think you'd be happy with her over there?" she continued.

Nicole didn't hesitate. "Of course, I would, but..."

"Then, go for it, girl," Alex said simply. "Nick, something wonderful is happening to you. Grab the chance. I know you'll miss your friends here, but we can always talk on the phone and e-mail each other every day." She grinned. "As for the family, I'm sure Mom and Dad will be thrilled for you. They really like Kris, you know?"

Nicole gave her a small smile, but Alex knew what she was thinking. "As for your father," she continued, trying hard not to let her hate for the man show on her face, "after what he did to you, he has no right to tell you how to live your life. You're an adult now, and you're allowed to make decisions by yourself. If you make good ones, they will be your own successes, nobody else's."

"But what if I make the wrong ones?" Nicole asked softly.

You mean what if it doesn't work with Kris, don't you, my friend? Alex thought. "Then you'll be able to say that you learned something." She smiled. "And by learning from experience, it only makes us stronger. Don't ever forget that you have people here who love you, Nick, no matter what."

"I won't forget. Thanks, Alex," Nicole said sincerely. But she couldn't help thinking about her father. Even after all he had done, he was still family, and she loved him. He hadn't always been like that. She remembered a gentler man, a loving father, and a happy family life from when she was a child. Nicole hoped that she could see that again if only once before she left to start a new life with Kris.

"Hey," Alex said, causing Nicole to break out of her thoughts. "There's a party happening in there. Maybe we should go back before they discover that the guest of honor has disappeared."

"You're right."

"I still have one week before I go. Let's see how much trouble we can cause in the meantime." Alex grinned and both laughed as they got up and walked back to the house where they could hear laughter and gentle ribbing going on. "I think Dad lost another pool game. Kris is amazing, you know that?"

"Yep, I sure do." Nicole smiled dreamily.

"So I guess that she really does have many skills, eh?" Alex asked with a grin, not missing the blush on Nicole's face. "Let's go back to the party." The brunette chuckled as she shook her head. *Ahh, what love can do!*

****

One more store to go to and then I'm done, Alex told herself as she drove her car into the parking lot. She was doing last minute shopping for her two month trip that would take her all over Africa. She smiled as she imagined life on location with a movie crew. *What an adventure that will be. Just like Nicole is about to live her own.*

She smiled when she thought back to the past few days spent in the company of her cousin and her girlfriend. Knowing that there were only a few days remaining in Montreal, Kris had invited her to spend some time with them, wanting the two cousins to have as much time together as possible. It had been very thoughtful of Kris, especially since Nicole would be gone by the time she came back from Africa.

But the rest of the week had gone by too fast, Alex sighed as she stepped out of her old, beat up Mercury Topaz and closed the door behind her. Trying to remember what else she needed to do before going back home, she missed seeing the man walking by suddenly change direction and head her way.

"I picked up Mom's stuff and Dad's suit from the dry cleaners," Alex mumbled as she ticked the list off her fingers. "Sophie asked me to..." She stopped as a large hand grabbed her arm and spun her around roughly. "What the fu..." she exclaimed in irritation and then the blood drained from her face when she looked into the enraged face of Nicole's father.

"Where is she?" McGrail growled. "Where did you hide the little bitch?"

With alarmed eyes, Alex looked around her and spotted a few people looking at them. She lifted her chin defiantly, feeling braver by the fact that they weren't alone in the parking lot. "First," she said, pulling her arm out of his grasp, "don't you dare touch me. Second, I don't know a little bitch," she spat and looked him straight in the eyes. "Only one tall bastard."

His jaw clenched and he swung his hand back, ready to strike her.

"Don't you even think about it," Alex warned. She knew that she couldn't do anything against the big man, especially if he decided to hit her, but at least it would give her a reason to strike back.

"You're the one who filled Nicole's head with crazy ideas, aren't you?" McGrail asked as he took a step closer to his niece. "She would've never left the house otherwise."

"She left because you treated her badly," Alex replied as she clenched her fists. "If you had been a good father, none of this would've happened."

"How dare you tell me how to raise my own daughter," he yelled, causing a man walking by to stop and watch.

"You beat the hell out of her!" she screamed back, her body shaking with anger. How she wanted to punch him in the face, *Just once.* "Why don't you let her live her own life?"

McGrail noticed the people gathering around them and took a step back. "If that's what she wants to do, fine," he told her. But in his mind, he said, *This is far from being over. She's coming back home with me, want it or not.* He then pushed his way through the small crowd.

"Are you okay, Miss?" one of the onlookers asked gently.

Alex nodded and took a shaky breath. *Wow. I can't believe I did that. Feisty little Amazon, aren't you?* She smiled at the stranger and nodded again. "Yeah, I'm fine, thanks," she replied, keeping an eye out for her crazed uncle. She still had a few places to go to and the last thing she wanted was to see him again. *Every family has a weird member, I guess.*

McGrail stomped across the parking lot and entered the general store to buy some cigarettes. He grabbed the morning paper and absentmindedly scanned the front page. Seeing his niece brought back the memories of the night when Nicole left.

He had guessed that his daughter had gone to his brother's house, and he was on his way there to bring her back when Robert showed up at his door. They had fought and he may have lost that round but the war wasn't over yet. Robert didn't understand the importance of having Nicole back at the house. All he wanted to do was keep an eye on her until she got married and gave birth to a baby boy. That's all he had ever wanted in life, a boy. He didn't care that the child wasn't his son, a grandson would do just fine.

Many years before, he had been thrilled to find out that his wife was pregnant and looked forward to being a father. He had made so many plans for his son, already seeing him as a hockey or baseball star. Had even picked out a college for him. But his wife had given birth to a girl, Nicole. He had been so disappointed. Girls were much more trouble than boys he had told himself. He still had the hope that one day, his wife would give him another child but that never happened.

He eventually got used to the child, but it wasn't the same. Years went by without the birth of a boy. His wife spent less time at home, and he had grown more aggressive by her absences. He had decided to follow her one evening and what he found angered him to the point of beating her senseless. All that time, he thought she was having an affair with another man, only to discover it had been with another woman.

He had followed her for days, watching the two women, going to the movies, shopping, or taking walks. *What else could they have been but lovers?* He had asked himself. No wonder his wife didn't give him another child, she was a damn lesbian.

Since that day, his life had become a nightmare. The few women he had tried to pick up later on had only managed to ridicule and laugh at him for reasons unknown to him, doing exactly what his wife had done.

He had become angrier when he had thought about the girl child back at the house, thinking that the only thing she would cause him, once she was grown up, would be more trouble.

Women, they're all the same, McGrail grumbled as he shook his head, trying to forget the bad memories, and glanced at the other newspapers on the shelves. He picked up a copy of the *Financial Post,* and as he was about to leave, his eyes fell on a magazine. He didn't recognize the dark-haired woman on the cover, but what caught his attention was the blonde standing in front of her.

"It can't be!" he breathed as he picked up the publication.

The picture showed Nicole smiling up at the woman, her hand resting on her arm. The taller one was reaching for Nicole's cheek. He quickly opened the magazine to the article and looked at the pictures.

The article was about an Austrian stuntwoman named Kristina Von Deering and her work at the Canadian Stunt School not too far away. He quickly scanned the article but no mention was made of Nicole.

He paid for his newspapers and the magazine along with a pack of cigarettes and walked out of the store.

All this time I thought you were hiding at Robert's. I bet you're with her! He opened the magazine to search for the reporter's name, then glanced at the pictures and found, right under them, the photographer's. *Well, now I have two people I can contact. Thank you for telling me where the bitch works.*

****

Kris' rented house came into view as the stuntwoman took one last curb on the paved path and pushed herself a little more as she jogged towards it. When she had awoken in the morning, Nicole was sound asleep. The previous night was Alex's last evening in Montreal and the small party had lasted until an early hour in the morning. Kris had wanted for her lover to sleep in, so she had gotten ready and quietly left the house to run for a couple of kilometers.

The stuntwoman slowed her pace to a stop then went through a last series of stretching exercises to cool off. Silence welcomed her as she entered the house, and she headed directly for their bedroom to check on Nicole. She smiled when she saw the young woman sprawled across the bed still deep in sleep.

It's the weekend. Why don't I let her sleep for awhile? She thought and left her sleeping lover to take a quick shower.

It was a beautiful sunny morning and with the day being not too warm, Kris decided on washing and polishing her motorcycle. As much as she enjoyed Nicole's company, she appreciated the time she spent alone, giving her the opportunity to think.

So many things needed to be done for her partner's moving with her to Austria. She wanted for Nicole to be able to go to school in Innsbruck so she would learn the proper way to handle video cameras and do some studio work. At least, her lover's present job gave her the chance to get a little practice. She smiled as she remembered Nicole's enthusiasm about her job as a VidCam assistant. Kris felt that the young woman could become a very good camerawoman one day, if given half the chance.

But the most important thing to do was to get the legal papers that would allow the Canadian to stay in Austria and not just as a tourist.

Kris couldn't believe that she had asked Nicole to come and live with her. That was so out of character for her. She had always thought of herself as a solitary person, actually liking the fact that she was mostly on her own. But the small blonde had stirred something deep in her soul that asked, no, that demanded that they share their lives together.

She smiled at the notion of having somebody in her house, especially somebody that loved her, willing to share their days and nights together. It would take some getting used to, but Kris knew that with a little bit of work on her part, she'd be able to make it work.

Still, some part of her was a little hesitant. Kris didn't question her love for the small woman, but she couldn't help her dark and negative side questioning her actions. *Does she love me as much as I love her? Is she moving to Austria because she loves me or is it because she wants to escape her father?*

Kris then remembered the conversation they had when she first asked Nicole to move into the house with her. *"I'm not asking to move in with you to run away from my father." Nicole had smiled at her. "I'm doing this because I want to be with you."*

She stopped polishing her bike, lost in thought. Others had wanted the same thing too; most of them lovers, but all had managed to hurt her. The only thing on their mind had been to tap into her large bank account.

But Nicole isn't like that. She scolded herself then relaxed as an afterthought crossed her mind. *She can't be. She was even embarrassed by all the things I bought her.*

The only dark thought that remained in Kris' mind was how much did Nicole really love her? Of course, the young woman had often said that she did, but Kris also knew that she was Nicole's first love. Relationships were so nice and perfect when they started, but as the novelty wore off, things often changed. It had happened to her before, and Kris prayed that it wouldn't happen again, not sure if she could survive another failed relationship, especially since she felt that this time, she had found her soulmate.

Chapter 20

Nicole woke up and found herself alone in the large bed. She knew that Kris had gone running, having seen the stunt-woman do that every morning since they had started living together. She stretched her neck to look at the time, and noticed that it was close to noon.

With a sigh, she got out of bed, wishing that her lover had come back to bed with her. She went into the bathroom to brush her hair and teeth then searched the house looking for Kris, but the woman was nowhere in sight. She looked out of the window at the lakeshore where she knew her friend often went to relax, but she wasn't there either.

Maybe she just decided to go for a ride on her motorcycle, Nicole thought. It wasn't Kris' habit to leave without telling her first or at least without leaving a note, but she decided to check if the Harley was still in the garage. She walked outside and stopped, having found her lover.

Sitting on the grass, Kris faced her motorcycle, a bucket of soapy water beside her. She was barefoot, dressed in shorts and wore a torn, cut off sweatshirt, her hair done into one neat braid that went down her back. The Harley was parked on one side of the driveway, and the dark haired woman just sat on the ground, a rag forgotten in her hand, and stared at the bike.

Wondering why her friend had such a serious look on her beautiful face, Nicole slowly approached and spoke softly so she wouldn't startle her.

"Good morning."

Kris blinked at the voice and turned to Nicole. She smiled at the sight of her lover, her good humor fully restored. "Hi. I thought you would spend the rest of the day in bed."

"Well, if I had some company when I woke up, maybe I would've." She winked. "Everything okay?"

"Oh, yeah." Kris nodded, not wanting to worry Nicole with her dark musings. "What do you want to do today?"

Nicole thought about that for a moment. She sensed that something was bothering Kris so she decided to do something that would make her relax and have fun. The blonde smiled as she spotted the garden hose on the ground and picked it up.

"I can help you wash your motorcycle." She grabbed the hose nozzle and was about to squeeze the trigger when Kris jumped up and pointed a warning finger at her.

"You can hose down anything that you want but not the Harley," Kris said as she stepped away from the bike and towards Nicole.

"Hmmm." She thought for a minute and then grinned. "Anything?"

"Why don't you water the plants over there." Kris pointed to the flowerbed. "Or if you really want to wash something, we can always work on the Pathfinder."

"Or I can always water..." Nicole said with an evil grin, "...you!" She aimed for Kris and squeezed the trigger, causing a powerful jet of water to hit the taller woman on the chest.

"Don't you..." Kris tried, unsuccessfully, to get out of Nicole's aim.

The young woman laughed at her lover's attempts to dodge the spray of water. She knew that Kris could easily get out of the way and was puzzled when she doubled back and stood beside the Harley. Nicole let the trigger go so she wouldn't hit the bike by mistake and her smile faded when Kris picked up the bucket of soapy water and flung the contents at her.

Kris laughed as her companion dropped the nozzle to push

her soaked and soapy hair away from her face.

Damn! That was the last thing I thought she would do. Nicole silently chuckled to herself, spitting out a mouthful of water. "Okay, you got me good," she admitted as she stuck her tongue out at the taste of soap in her mouth. She wiped her eyes and opened them. Kris stood in front of her, with the garden hose in hand and a very evil grin on her face.

"Hi there," the dark haired woman drawled.

"Huh." Nicole slowly stepped back and away from her advancing friend. "We're even...huh, you can put the hose down now...I, ah...Kris!" she warned as her lover squeezed the water out of her braided hair with one hand, the hose in the other.

"But you're so soapy," Kris chuckled. "What you need is a good...rinse cycle!" She lifted the hose and squeezed the trigger, completely soaking Nicole before she had a chance to get out of the way.

Sounds of laughter could be heard on the front lawn of the house as the two women ran after each other and then as they tried to wrestle the offending garden hose out of the other's grip. It was no use trying to run away anymore, since both were drenched from head to toe. Miraculously, the Harley stayed dry throughout the water fight.

After putting the motorcycle in the garage, they went to the back of the house and sat down on the grass to dry out in the sun.

Nicole smiled as she put her head against Kris' chest, sitting between the tall woman's outstretched legs. "Now, this is what I like to do," she said, looking out at the passing sailboats on the lake.

"You mean you like wearing wet clothes and getting chilled by the wind?" Kris teased as she leaned her back against a tree and distractedly played with Nicole's wet hair.

"No, silly," Nicole laughed. "What I mean is just relaxing with you like this."

"Yes, it is nice," Kris admitted. She was so used to working all the time that she had forgotten how good it felt to relax and do nothing.

"That's what I would like to do today," Nicole stated in a half serious voice. "Stay like this and enjoy the view."

"Hmm, that's an idea," Kris agreed as she softly kissed her way across her lover's temple, cheek and lips. "But you know what we could do?" she whispered in her ear.

"What?" she whispered back, smiling when she caught Kris' mischievous look.

"We could also go take a shower together then come back here and enjoy the view once we're nice and dry."

"Oh...I like your idea better," Nicole said as she stood up and pulled at her partner's hand. "Come on."

Blue eyes twinkled in amusement as Kris let the small woman pull her up. Judging by the grin on Nicole's face, she was sure that it would be some time before they got out of the shower, and frankly, she didn't mind one bit.

****

The photographer couldn't believe his luck. He had taken so many pictures of the Austrian stuntwoman that he was sure he would make a nice profit from them, especially the ones of Kristina and her little girlfriend. Now all he had to do was to find a buyer. He had contacted a lot of magazines, both American and European, a few had returned his calls saying they were interested, but nothing was definite yet.

Mark had spent the whole morning watching Kristina, but all she did was run along the lake and then wash her motorcycle. He had been about to leave when the small blonde walked out of the house.

After the women's little water fight, he had found a good spot on the beach to take pictures of them as they lounged in the back yard. He especially liked the shots of them leaning against each other and of them kissing. All the photographer saw while taking the pictures were dollar signs in his head. Without her knowledge, Kristina was going to make him a lot of money.

Mark was getting ready to leave after both women went inside the house when his cell phone buzzed in his pocket. He took it out and flipped it open. "Yeah?"

"Mark Dunham?" a man's voice asked.

"That's me. What can I do for you?" he asked as he put his

two cameras in a black leather bag.

"I contacted the magazine you work for. They tell me you're also a freelance photographer," the voice said. "Are you for hire, Mr. Dunham? I can make it worth your while if you are."

This is interesting, Mark thought. "It depends on what you want me to do. Who is this?"

"Your questions will be answered later," the man replied in a low growl. "If you accept, there will be a thousand dollars waiting for you when we meet. The rest will come with your delivery of the pictures." The man paused to let the words sink in. "Then, if I'm really pleased with your work, there's a fat bonus for you."

The promise of a large amount of money was very tempting. "Okay," the photographer finally said. "Where do you want to meet?"

The man gave him a rendezvous time and location, and Mark was surprised to find that it was only a few blocks away from where he was. He closed his cell phone connection and smiled. *One thousand dollars even before I start taking pictures. This man must be desperate.* The photographer looked at his watch and decided that he had enough time for a beer before he met his mysterious employer.

Not too far away, McGrail smiled as he hooked the receiver and stepped out of the public phone booth. *My plan is now under way.* He chuckled to himself.

****

Mark checked the time to make sure he wouldn't be late as he went to the meeting place. The chosen area was a secluded spot some distance away from the bicycle path that stretched along the lake. The area was quiet for a private talk but busy enough if something went wrong. He had no idea who he was meeting after all. The man could be a murderer for all he knew. *But if he were, why would he hire a photographer?* Mark chuckled nervously as he sat on the park bench. *This is starting to look like a bad* X-Files *episode.*

He shook his head then looked up as a tall, strongly built

man approached him. He was dressed in gray dress pants with an open collared white shirt, a black windbreaker completing his outfit.

Mark swallowed nervously at the intense look on the man's face and he put on the best, bored expression he could muster. *No sense in looking too eager for this project.* The photographer watched as the man sat down.

"Mr. Dunham?" McGrail asked and smiled when the man nodded. "I know your time must be valuable, so I'll be brief. I need you to take pictures of two women. You took some already when you worked on that stunt school interview."

"You're talking about the stuntwoman Kristina Von Deering and her girlfriend?" Mark asked and caught the man's expression as his jaw momentarily tightened at the mention of the name.

Her girlfriend? McGrail silently growled. *How could Nicole do this to me?* "That's them," he said, trying to keep the anger out of his voice. "What's the blonde's name again?" Deep down inside, he hoped that it wouldn't be his daughter. He didn't want to deal with another lesbian. His wife had been enough. *What's wrong with the women I come in contact with? Are they all goddamn dykes?*

The photographer searched his memory for the name. "Oh, I remember now. Kristina introduced her as Nicole. I don't think she mentioned a last name though."

The man closed his eyes for a moment and then took a deep breath. When he opened them, Mark was staring into hard, hazel eyes. For a second, he thought about refusing the contract, wanting to have nothing to do with the strange man, but the promise of a lot of money was too tempting.

"They share a house a few blocks away from here. I took some great shots of them this morning. I could always sell you a few if you want."

They're just a few streets away from me? McGrail's temper rose, but the last thing he wanted to do was scare the photographer away. "Yes, I know where they live," McGrail lied, doing his best to stay calm. "But the pictures I want are specific shots. Are you interested?"

He's offering a lot of money. Go for it! "Yes, I am. What do you want from me?"

McGrail pulled an envelope out of his windbreaker pocket and handed it to the photographer. "This is for you, then."

Mark took the yellow envelope and looked inside. It contained a large amount of money and a slip of paper. He took it out and looked at it. It stated the amount of the cash inside, what would be given to him for the pictures and what the bonus would be if the job were more than satisfactory. Mark whistled at the money he would make out of this project.

"I want to make something very clear. There will be no questions asked," McGrail said and waited until the photographer nodded. "What I want you to do is get the best compromising pictures you can take of the stuntwoman. Leave her...girlfriend," he almost spat, "out of it. I want the Austrian. Take pictures of her with men or other women, I don't care. I want them to look like she's got another lover. You got that?"

Mark nodded quietly. As much as he wanted to know what the pictures would be used for, for some reason he didn't want to make the man angry. There was a lot of money to be made, and he didn't want to screw this up. "I got it."

"Good," McGrail said as he stood up. "I'll contact you again to check on your progress." He turned then stopped. Tilting his head, he stared at the photographer. "One piece of advice. Don't try to screw me over. I could make your life a living hell." The younger man swallowed nervously. A satisfied McGrail walked away.

What did I get myself into? Mark looked down at the envelope. "But there's so much money to be made here." He smiled and stood up. His girlfriend wasn't the only one able to get shady deals. "Just wait until she sees what I'll get for a couple of lousy pictures." He laughed as he returned to his car.

****

The drive back from work was a quiet one. Kris spent most of the time thinking about the incident at the stunt school and the student that had almost caused another to get seriously injured. She didn't mind teaching people the art of performing stunts, in fact she loved it, but she didn't have any patience with thrill seekers. That student had been trouble since the very first day at the school. He had little regard if any for security procedures and never listened to the instructions given to him. All he wanted to do was to throw himself off the towers and drive cars at breakneck speeds. Kris had yelled at him when he did a maneuver on the driving range the wrong way and rolled his car over, barely missing the other students who were watching. The car had been totaled and one student had been slightly injured by a flying piece of metal.

Kris had lost her temper when the student had gotten out of the car then laughed at her when she reprimanded him. It had taken a couple of men to keep her from throttling him. After she had a long talk with the school's director, Marcus had agreed to give the student his money back and expel him from the school. Performing stunts was a serious business, and Kris refused to deal with people who didn't want to do the job safely.

Her cell phone rang, causing Kris to break out of her thoughts. She flipped the phone open as she kept her eyes on the road and gruffly answered, "Yes?" She listened silently for a while then replied in her native tongue.

Sitting next to her, Nicole looked at her friend. She couldn't understand what was being said, but it looked like trouble judging from Kris' facial expression. Her lover had been unusually quiet ever since she picked her up at the studios. A hello with a quick kiss had been the only thing from Kris in the past half hour. Nicole felt that she needed some quiet time and so had left her friend to her thoughts.

Kris let out what sounded like a curse, and the dark-haired woman's jaw muscle tightened. After speaking a few more words, she closed the connection and dropped the cell phone on the dashboard. Nicole had seen her this way twice before and the only thing she could do was to keep out of her way.

"Kris?" Nicole asked softly.

"Hmm?" she replied absently.

"Why don't you take a nap once we get home. I could wake you up when dinner's ready." She was starting to believe that Kris wasn't going to answer but the older woman finally sighed and gave her a small smile. *She looks so tired,* Nicole thought.

"I'm sorry," Kris said as she lightly squeezed her lover's thigh. "It's been a bad day, and that phone call didn't help any."

"Is there anything I can do?"

"Not really. Thanks for offering though." Kris turned her attention back to the road. "I need to get online as soon as we get home. There's a very important buyer interested in doing business with the Arabian stable, but he's also very difficult. Nobody wants to risk losing the contract, so I decided that I'd take care of it personally."

"Will you be working late tonight?" Nicole asked as Kris guided the Pathfinder into the driveway then shut the motor off.

She leaned her head against the headrest and closed her eyes. "Probably." Kris sighed. "I'll also be working late at the school this week. Marcus wants us to test some new equipment. I'm afraid we'll have to drive separately to work," she said with a sad smile. "You can take the Pathfinder if you want, I'll ride the Harley to school."

"I can take the bus to go to work, I've done it for a long time," Nicole said as they got out of the vehicle and walked into the house. "You don't have to chauffeur me all the time. I'm a big girl, you know, I can take care of myself." She grinned, but caught the flash of hurt on Kris' face before it was masked with a nod and a smile. "I'll get the dinner started."

"Do you mind if I eat later? I'd like to start working as soon as possible."

Nicole shrugged and went to the kitchen, disappointed that she'd be eating alone tonight. She had planned on a quiet meal with soft music and do some cuddling in front of the TV later. Guess she had to find something else to do.

Kris sighed as she watched the small woman leave then headed for her office. Sitting down on her chair, she booted her laptop and linked into her stable's computer in Innsbruck. *I'll make it up to Nicole later*, she promised.

Nicole tried twice to get Kris to eat something, but she shook her head both times and continued working. Nicole finally gave up and ate alone, sitting in front of the TV. She knew that once Kris started working, she would only stop when everything was done. Feeling a little bored, she decided to go for a walk along the lake and informed Kris of her decision so she wouldn't worry.

Half an hour had passed when Nicole realized that she was near where her father often came when he had some thinking to do. A pang of fear gripped her heart at the possibility of meeting him, and she turned around to go back home.

But standing ten feet away from her, was the man she desperately wanted to avoid. Her father looked calm, and he even smiled a little, which confused her. It wasn't the smile she had learned to expect right before he hit her, but instead it seemed to say that he was happy to see her. He made no move to get closer to her. His hands were stuffed into the pockets of his pants, and he cocked his head as he looked back at his daughter.

"Hello, Nickie," McGrail said softly. "How have you been?"

Nicole didn't know what to do. She wanted to run, but on the other hand, her father seemed to be genuinely happy to see her. "I'm fine," she replied cautiously.

"Listen, I know that I did bad things..." He started to say, moving towards her but stopped when Nicole took a step back. "But I wanted you to know that I'm getting help," McGrail said as he looked down and sighed. He looked up again, and gave her a small smile. "I know that I can't ask you to trust me right now, not after everything I've done to you, but I'd like it if you could find it in your heart to give me a second chance."

Nicole couldn't believe it. It sounded too good to be true. Part of her was screaming to run away, that this was just a trick, but another part was hoping that it was true, that he was really getting help. She always loved her father, even with his bad temper and the occasional beatings, but he was the only immediate family she had. She always hoped that they could go back to the happy family life they had so many years ago. It would be so nice to be able to make peace with him before leaving to start a new life in Austria with Kris.

"I'm not asking you to meet me at the house," McGrail continued. "We could talk here in the park where there are a lot of people. I don't want you to be afraid of me anymore, Nickie."

Nicole nodded and gave him a small smile. "I'd like that

very much," she said softly.

McGrail smiled. "Good. How about meeting here tomorrow? Same time?"

Nicole took a deep breath and let it go slowly. She was nervous about meeting him, but if he really was making an effort to control his temper, she could at least listen to him. "That would be good."

"Okay, then. See you tomorrow," he said. "Thanks for giving me a chance." He turned and walked away, leaving his stunned daughter behind. McGrail smirked as he thought about his naïve girl. *You were always so easy to manipulate. A couple more meetings like this and I'll have you eating out of my hand.*

Nicole watched her father go. He looked sincere enough. *What harm is there in meeting him in a public place?* She asked herself then decided to give him a chance. If things didn't work out, at least she could say that she tried and have a clear conscience. *But I can't say anything to Kris. She's got enough problems already without her having to worry about me.*

She walked back home, lost in thought. She had to find a way to get out of the house without Kris knowing about her meeting. A sudden thought crossed Nicole's mind and she remembered that her friend would be working late at the school. With that in mind, she smiled at the possibility of having a chance at a more normal relationship with her father.

Chapter 21

For several days, Nicole took long walks alone after dinner and ended up meeting with her father. She was happy to see that he had really started to change. Not once had he raised his voice at her or gotten upset. They talked about everything from her new job to the latest events happening in the world. Surprisingly, he hadn't asked where she lived or if she had anybody in her life. Nicole wasn't sure if she could have talked about her life with Kris anyway, certain that he wouldn't understand.

Kris wouldn't understand either. Nicole wanted so much to tell her lover about her father and the fact that he was doing his best to change, but she was afraid of her reaction. The older woman never hid the fact that she despised him. Nicole had even heard her tell Robert that she would hit her father if he ever touched her again. She felt bad about keeping something from Kris, but it was the only thing she could do. She didn't want to ruin the progress she had made with her father, and having Kris hovering behind her like a bodyguard was the last thing she wanted.

Early in the week, she had thought that her friend knew about her father. Kris had come home one day and asked where she had been. There had been a moment of panic from Nicole before Kris added that she had called a couple of times, but nobody was home. She had smiled and explained that when she had taken a walk after dinner on Monday, it had been so relaxing, that she wanted to make it a daily routine, especially since she was going to work late. The excused had been accepted without any problems.

One evening, McGrail and Nicole sat on a bench facing the lake, each lost in their own thoughts, the time spent in a comfortable silence. One thing kept nagging at her and she needed to reassure the part of her that still believed he was and would always be a violent man.

The only way she could prove to herself that he had changed was to provoke him. Nicole could have chosen to tell him about Kris, but she had decided to let him know about her leaving the country instead. She braced herself for any kind of reaction as she talked about her decision.

It had taken every bit of control he could muster not to blow up. McGrail was sure that the stuntwoman was responsible for Nicole's decision, even though she never even mentioned the dark-haired woman. He took a couple of breaths as he stared out at the lake, trying to calm his raising temper. McGrail had thought he had plenty of time to win Nicole back, but now he needed to get his plan moving faster. He looked at his daughter and gave her a sad smile.

"Why do you want to move?" he asked softly. He saw Nicole relax visibly and mentally snickered at how she was so easily fooled. He knew that she now believed him when he told her that he was doing his best to change. *Stupid girl!* "Aren't you happy here?"

Nicole had taken a gamble and won. Her father even looked sad about her leaving.

"It's not that I'm not happy here, but I have a chance to travel and see the world. I've always wanted to do that," Nicole explained. Her father nodded and smiled. They talked for a while longer and, after wishing each other a good night, went their separate ways.

****

Sitting behind the wheel of the Pathfinder, Kris rubbed her

eyes as she waited for the light to turn green. It had been another long day at the school, and she was looking forward to spending the evening and weekend with her lover. The past week had been a little strained between them, and she knew that it was mostly her fault. But all the hours spent online with the Arabian stable in Innsbruck and the many conversations on the phone with the potential client had paid off. Kris had succeeded in convincing the man to sign a contract. Not only would the new client bring in a lot of money, but it would also make the breeding program better known on the international market.

Once home, the dark haired woman took the grocery bags out of the truck and headed for the kitchen to put them on the counter then went to the living room, letting herself fall like a rock onto the sofa and closed her eyes. The house was silent and seemed so empty without Nicole. She was glad that her lover had started taking walks every day, but she wished that she were able to join her once in a while.

Nicole had seemed so distant all week, and Kris wondered if something was bothering her. For a fleeting moment, she thought back to her last ex-lover, and couldn't help but remember that their breakup had begun the same way. She shook her head. *If something's bothering her, she'll tell me...Right*? She just hoped that her partner wasn't getting tired of their relationship. *Maybe Nicole just needs some time alone.* They had been together every day since they had met and it was only normal to have a need to do things on their own, but she wished that Nicole was home at the moment.

Kris stood up and went back to the kitchen. As usual, the room was spotless and everything was neatly put away. She opened the door and stepped out onto the deck and lit the barbecue. She never bothered to do much cooking. Oma, her housekeeper in Austria, did most of it when she was home. Otherwise, Kris usually ate in restaurants. It was much simpler that way. But once in a while, she would prepare something when she felt like it.

She took the two steaks she had bought out of their wrappings and put them on the grill then prepared some potatoes and vegetables for cooking. Earlier in the day, Kris had called the studios where Nicole worked and had left a message for her to call back. Wanting to give her friend a break from cooking, she had told her that she would take care of it that night. Nicole had seemed a little hesitant at hearing the news.

"You mean you'll be home early?" Nicole had asked with a hint of hesitation in her voice.

"Yes, I will," she had answered, a little disappointed at not finding Nicole more excited than that. "With me working so late for the past week, I thought that maybe we could have a nice dinner together. Did you have anything planned?"

"Huh...yes, I mean...no. I was only going for my walk that's all. Dinner would be nice, Kris," she had said, her voice returning to her normal excited tone.

"Maybe we could go for a walk after we eat?" she had offered, not wanting for Nicole to skip her daily exercise.

"Okay. Listen, I have to go back to work. See you tonight?"

"Sure."

Kris stopped cutting the vegetables and took a deep breath as she closed her eyes. A common accusation came crashing back to her, sounding so real in her head that she almost turned around to see who was saying it. *You're never home, you're always working. Don't you see what it's doing to us? Don't you care anymore?* Kris shook her head as she tightened her jaw. She had heard that accusation before, uttered by another frustrated lover. But it hadn't been from Nicole...yet.

"No!" Kris muttered. "I won't let work destroy another relationship," she said as she clenched her hands. She had been working late all week, which can happen sometimes, she rationalized, but she knew her working habits and realized that once she got back into the routine, no relationship could survive her long work schedule. Kris could see the signs already. Nicole was distant and seemed quieter than usual. The walks that she had started were getting longer every day, and she had stopped asking what they were going to do in the evenings.

There was no way that Kris would let anything come between them. She loved Nicole with all her heart and soul and she would do anything within her power to keep it that way. *Unless Nicole gets tired of you and leaves like everybody else did before her,* a voice said inside of her.

"NO!" Kris yelled as she hit the table with her fists. "Nicole isn't that way," she said as she let herself drop into a kitchen chair. *She might find somebody else,* the voice taunted. *Or you might scare her away with your temper. You're just like her father,* the voice accused. "No, I would never hurt her," she said then looked at her tightly fisted hands. "Oh, God!" Her voice choked. "I'd leave before I'd do anything to her."

Kris stood up at the sound of a door opening, and she gruffly scrubbed her face. As much as she was in complete command of her professional life, she hated being so insecure with her personal one. *I should give Nicole more credit. If something's wrong, I know she'll tell me.* She nodded to herself as she continued preparing the dinner.

"Hi," Nicole said cheerfully as she walked up to Kris and wrapped her arms around her lover's waist, giving her a hug. "I missed ya."

Kris smiled and hugged her back. "I missed you, too." *Does she sound like she's tired or scared of me?* She silently asked. *I don't think so.*

"Need any help?" the blonde asked as she washed her hands.

"Sure. Why don't you continue with the veggies while I cook the steaks?" She smiled as Nicole winked at her and took the knife away from her hand.

"Shoo. Out of my kitchen," she said as she gently pushed Kris towards the door.

"Okay. Okay." The tall woman laughed and grabbed the spices before walking outside.

****

The evening was perfect for a nice long walk along the lake and Kris was glad to see that the usual crowds decreased as darkness fell. The time spent together had been fun with both of them relaxing. Nicole was back to her chatty self and whatever had bothered her young friend seemed to have been pushed to the back of her mind.

Kris couldn't help but feel that she was part of the reason why Nicole had been so quiet all week. She was certain that the long hours at school and extra hours spent in front of the computer at home had something to do with it.

Having shoved her hands into the pockets of her jeans, Kris absentmindedly played with the loose change in them as she thought back to the past week. She really didn't want to ruin the beautiful friendship she had with Nicole and with a curt nod, she made up her mind.

"Nick?" she called softly.

"Hmm?"

"I know that I've been working a lot this week," Kris started, looking more at her feet than at her companion. "I still have a couple of days left to do, but..." She stopped walking and looked out at the lake where the last traces of the setting sun could be seen. "I promise that after this project, we'll get back to our routine. I'll drive you to work, and we'll both come back at the same time. No more overtime at the school."

Nicole smiled and wrapped her hand around Kris' forearm and gave her a little squeeze. "I understand about your work, but it'll be nice to be able to spend more time together," she replied honestly. "It's been a while since we did anything."

Kris took one hand out of her pocket, rested her arm across Nicole's shoulders, and pulled her close. "That's true," she agreed, trying to keep the guilt she was feeling out of her voice. "I'm sorry." Nicole brushed her hand against her back before she hooked a finger on her belt. The dark-haired woman took a deep breath and smiled. "Tomorrow's your day," she stated. "Where would you like to go?"

"Kris, I didn't say that because..." A long finger made her stop talking. Nicole looked up in time to see Kris bend down and kiss her softly. She closed her eyes and her knees weakened as a soft moan escaped her lips. No matter how many times they kissed, Nicole couldn't get enough of Kris' soft and full lips against hers. She sighed as the contact was broken and blinked at smiling blue eyes watching her.

"Where..." Kris asked again as she softly kissed Nicole's

forehead, "...would you..." a kiss on a cheek, "...like..." the other cheek, "...to go?" she finished as she kissed her lover's nose.

"You mean besides staying in bed with you?" Nicole grinned.

"We can work on that as soon as we get home," Kris whispered seductively in Nicole's ear. "I have one last phone call to make to the stables in Innsbruck tonight, and then I'm all yours."

Nicole was glad the darkness hid the blush that crept up her neck and cheeks. Kris was such a seductress, she smiled and then froze as images of the journalists they had seen at the Cancun airport and their questions concerning Kris' lovers came crashing back to her.

A jolt of lack of confidence hit Nicole as she wondered what Kris ever saw in her to want her move to Austria and live there. She shook her head, trying to get rid of those thoughts and looked up at her friend who seemed to be waiting for an answer.

"I'm sorry," Nicole said softly, silently cursing her lack of confidence and self doubt. "I was just thinking." She smiled and took a chance at answering Kris' question. She hoped that it was still about what to do this weekend. "Horseback riding."

It was the first thing that crossed her mind. After all, horses were an important part of Kris' life, and since she was going to live near dozens of horses, she thought she should learn how to ride.

"But you once told me that you've never ridden a horse before," Kris said softly. "Are you sure?"

Nicole nodded. "Yep. I couldn't ask for a better teacher than you." She smiled. "How 'bout it? I really want to learn, and I know you love horses so..."

Kris thought about it for a moment, and when she saw the grin on her lover's face, she couldn't help but laugh. "Okay. You got it."

"Cool," Nicole exclaimed and gave her companion a hug. "That'll be so much fun."

"Come on," Kris said, chuckling. "Let's go home." They happily turned around and walked back to the house.

****

With a quick phone call to one of the instructors at the stunt school, Kris decided they would go to the ranch that had been recommended by him. The center was only two hours from Montreal and in the mountains.

The sky was still overcast, but Nicole was happy to see that it finally stopped raining. The storm the night before had put a damper on her excitement, thinking that maybe they couldn't go horseback riding after all, but as they headed north, the sun broke through the clouds.

Kris was a little nervous about teaching Nicole to ride. She had seen too many accidents with experienced riders that she shuddered at the thought that something could happen to her lover. *If only we were at my own ranch,* Kris thought as she guided the Pathfinder along the gravel road. *I would know exactly which horse to give her for her first time.*

Upon exiting the 4x4, Kris looked around the center and nodded her approval. The place was well kept, and the horses that were outside looked healthy and well cared for. A young man, about Nicole's age, walked up to them with a smile. He was dressed in faded blue jeans with tan chaps, a beige flannel shirt, brown boots, and a black, beat-up cowboy hat.

"Hi. My name's Tommy. You must be Kristina and Nicole, right?" he asked as he shook their hands.

Nicole gave him a friendly smile. "That's us," she said and looked around at the horses tied to the gate. "Wow, they're so big," she said as she spotted a grey mare that another guide was walking out of the stable. A group of tourists waited nearby for their mounts. "Are we going with them?"

"No. Uncle Dan told me to give you a private ride. He said that you would appreciate the peace and quiet." Tommy smiled as he looked at the tall stuntwoman. "Big groups like that can be very noisy sometimes."

"Dan's your uncle?" Kris asked surprised, thinking of the instructor at the stunt school.

"Yep. He's the owner too," Tommy stated as he walked to the stable. "Come with me. I'll get you your horses, okay?"

Seeing that Nicole was occupied with brushing the nose of a saddled horse, Kris took two long steps to catch up with the young man. "Listen, I'd like for you to give Nicole the most tame horse you have. She's never ridden before."

"Oh don't worry," Tommy said. "They're all very nice and well behaved." His arm was suddenly grabbed in a solid lock. He looked up at the serious expression on the dark haired woman's face.

"I'm serious," Kris said, not letting Tommy go. "I want a tame horse for her."

The boy swallowed nervously as he stared into the woman's icy blue eyes. He slowly nodded and gave her a nervous smile. "Of course...no problem," he said, looking from Nicole, who was still petting the horse, to the tall woman glaring down at him. *Damn, she's tall,* Tommy thought, as he craned his neck to look up at her.

Having made her point, Kris stepped back as Nicole walked to them and watched the boy hurry to get the animals.

The horse that was chosen for Nicole was a golden, nine year old Saddlebred. Kris walked up to the mare and patted her, letting her expertise take over in assessing the animal. Satisfied as best as she could that the mare was a tame one, Kris smiled at her friend and handed her the reins.

A beautiful chestnut Morgan, nearly fifteen hands tall was brought out of the stable for Kris. Tommy guided the horse toward her and shyly said, "Uncle Dan told me you were an expert rider and said you'd appreciate Artemis."

"I've never tried a Morgan," Kris said looking the horse over. "She's a beauty." She smiled at Tommy who beamed back at her.

"What's my horse's name?" Nicole piped in as she scratched the mare's jaw.

"That's Gabby. Did you see her mane? It almost matches your hair." He grinned as he flirted with the young woman. "But your hair is much nicer."

Kris stepped next to Tommy and gave him a back off glare. The boy quickly looked away and started doing a last minute check on his own horse's saddle. She watched him a couple of seconds longer, and after tying her horse to the fence, checked on her friend's saddle. She wanted to make sure that everything was set properly.

"What?" she asked Nicole, who was grinning at her.

"That was so cute. The poor guy was only making small talk you know," she said as she patted Kris' arm.

"Well, I didn't like the way he was looking at you," Kris replied, trying to keep the edge out of her voice. *What's the matter with me? He was only being nice.* She looked at Nicole and shyly smiled. "It's just...I don't..."

"It's okay." Nicole stretched up and gave her lover a quick kiss. "If anybody gets too fresh with me, I'll let you know, okay?" Kris nodded. "Now, what do I have to do to get on this thing?"

Tommy was about to answer but quickly stopped at the look Kris gave him. He shrugged and turned back to his own horse and waited until the dark-haired woman finished explaining the basics of horseback riding. He sat on his horse and listened. *She definitely knows her stuff,* Tommy decided after Kris had explained everything to Nicole and as she expertly sat on the Morgan. For once he wasn't dealing with weekend cowboys. That was the term he used for riders that had absolutely no skills when dealing with horses but always claimed the contrary. It would be a very pleasant ride.

"Everybody ready?" he asked. He received a silent nod from Kris and a big smile from Nicole. "Okay, let's go."

They entered the forest, going single file with Tommy leading the way on his Appaloosa, Nicole in the middle, and Kris bringing up the rear. Tommy's dog, a small terrier named Buddy, ran excitedly beside the horses and into the forest once in a while to chase after a shadow or creature.

Kris briefly closed her eyes and let her body relax with the sounds of nature. The sun had finally come out and the smell of the horses, mixed with wet vegetation and earth, brought memories of a family outing when they had gone horseback riding in the Alps. Realizing that her horse had slowed down, she hurried to catch up to Nicole.

Hearing a fast trot behind her, Nicole turned around. "Everything okay?" she asked as the tall woman brought her horse beside her, her question answered with a nod. "This is so much fun," she said excitedly. "I thought that it would be harder than this. It's just like sitting on a chair."

"Hmmm. Except your chair doesn't throw you off if something happens," she said, ducking her head as she passed under a tree branch.

Tommy turned to the women behind him. Nicole seemed to be enjoying herself, while Kris silently rode along. "So far, so good?"

"Oh yeah." Nicole laughed. "It's great."

"How 'bout if we do a little trotting?" Tommy asked.

"Do you feel comfortable enough for that?" Kris asked Nicole.

"Huh." She hesitated for a few seconds then softly asked, "Will you show me how?" Kris answered with a wink and explained the proper way to ride the horse so her back wouldn't get too sore. "Let's try it before I change my mind."

"Okay. Let's go." Tommy smiled as his horse took off at a trot. Either the tall woman was very protective, he thought or she didn't have enough confidence in the young blonde, but Nicole was doing very well so far. Much better than some of the first timers that came to the center.

He glanced back and saw that Nicole was following him with very little trouble. "Just relax in the saddle. Follow the horse's pace like Kris showed you." After a few minutes of trotting along, he looked back again and nodded with approval. "That's very good."

"I'm gonna have a sore butt tomorrow," Nicole said as she concentrated on her movements. Trotting looked much easier than it actually was.

"All you need now is practice. That way, you won't get too sore. You're doing great, Nick," Kris said proudly.

"Thanks." Nicole beamed at the unexpected compliment. "I'm lucky to have a very good teacher."

They came to a wider section of the trail, and Tommy stopped and waited until Nicole walked her horse beside him. The area was clear of low branches, and the trees were cut away from the sides of the trail. "How is it going so far?"

"I love it. I never thought it could be so much fun," Nicole said and looked back at her friend, who was busy with a piece of equipment.

The right stirrup had been bothering Kris since they had left the stable and she couldn't adjust it properly. It was either too high or too low. "No wonder so many people are fussy about having their own saddles," she mumbled to herself.

"Well," Tommy started as he got a good grip on his reins, "since you're doing so well, how 'bout we do some galloping, okay?" he asked Nicole then quickly glanced at Kris.

"Huh." Nicole hesitated briefly then grinned at him. "Yeah, sure, why not. That'd be fun."

"I don't think so," Kris replied. "Why don't you take it slow, okay?"

"Ah, come on." Nicole looked back at her partner. "It's been going great so far, I'd like to try it."

"I'd much prefer if you tried it with a horse I know better."

"I assure you that this mare is one of the tamest we have," Tommy said. "She's even trained to obey by whistles."

"Kris," Nicole pleaded, "just once?"

"I don't know," she mumbled, but her resolve melted under those emerald eyes blinking at her. "Oh, all right." Kris gave up at her lover's puppy dog look then turned to Tommy. "We'll take it slow, okay?"

"Yes, ma'am!" the young guide replied with a bright smile.

Once more, Kris explained the proper way of settling on the horse in order to gallop. She bit back a smile at the serious look on Nicole's face.

"Just remember that whatever happens, don't let go of the reins. That way your horse won't trip over them and won't send you flying over its head."

"And if it makes you feel safer," Tommy joined in, "you can always hang on to the saddle horn. You ready?" he asked Nicole.

"Oh, yeah," she replied as she held the leather straps tighter in her hands.

"Okay, let's do this slowly," Tommy instructed as they cantered at an easy pace down the trail. They continued that way for some time with both Kris and Tommy keeping an eye on Nicole. The young woman seemed to enjoy herself as her laughter sounded in the forest. "Everything okay?"

"It's great," Nicole replied, smiling from ear to ear.

"How about if we go a little faster?"

She hesitated. "Huh...okay."

Kris shook her head. "Nick, I don't think..."

"Okay, let's do it then. YEAH!" Tommy yelled as he pushed his horse to a gallop.

"NO! Wait..." Kris warned but wasn't quick enough to stop Tommy. She watched helplessly as the guide's sudden yell spooked Nicole's horse and caused it to bolt after the Appaloosa. Cursing under her breath, Kris took off at fast gallop, trying to reach her friend before anything happened.

Nicole hung on for dear life as her horse quickly passed Tommy's. She had no idea how to stop the animal. The trees flashed by as they sprinted down the trail and she remembered what Kris had told her before she climbed on the horse. *"Just remember that whatever happens, don't let go of the reins. That way your horse won't trip over them and won't send you flying over its head."* Nicole gripped the leather even tighter and grabbed the saddle horn at the same time.

Tommy's eyes widened in panic as the Saddlebred ran past him and pressed his horse into a faster pace trying to reach Nicole. Thankfully the horse was trained to obey different whistles. Tommy put two fingers into his mouth and blew a command to stop. The Saddlebred slowed down enough for him to catch up, grab the reins from Nicole and slow the mare to a stop.

"I'm so sorry," he blurted out as he dismounted. "I don't know why she reacted that way."

Kris sped towards them and barely stopped before she jumped off the Morgan and ran to Nicole.

"I'm okay," Nicole shakily said and slowly dismounted, helped by Tommy, his hands firmly around her waist. She closed her eyes as she stood on rubbery legs and grabbed the saddle and rested her forehead against it, wishing for the ground to stop shaking. She could feel Tommy's hands still holding her tight and she nodded with a weak smile. "You can let go now, I'm fine," she said but kept her eyes closed. *First thing's first. Get your breathing and heartbeat under control.*

Kris was furious. She grabbed Tommy's shoulder and spun him around to face her, breaking his hold on Nicole. "Get your hands off her!" she growled as she glared at him. "What the hell were you thinking?" she demanded, pushing him against the Saddlebred and grabbing two fistfuls of his shirt. "I told you to wait!"

"I...I'm sorry!" Tommy stammered with fear in his eyes. "I didn't know that the horse would..." The vibrant blue of Kris' eyes had suddenly been replaced by two pieces of ice staring back at him. He swallowed nervously as the hands grabbing his shirt shook with barely controlled fury. "I didn't mean..."

"She could've gotten hurt," Kris said between clenched teeth and pulled her arm back as she made a fist ready to strike him.

Taking one last deep breath, Nicole opened her eyes as she felt her legs become stronger under her. She turned in time to see her friend ready to slug the young man. Fear coursed through her body at the rage she saw on Kris' face. The only time she had seen that look had been on her father's face just before he lashed out at her.

"Daddy! Don't hit!"

Kris froze in mid swing. She stared at the trembling young man then at her hand grabbing his shirt. *She called me Daddy...Oh, God.* She breathed shakily as she let go of the guide. *I'm acting exactly like her father.* She took a step back and whispered, "I'm sorry."

Nicole took a cautious step forward and gently touched Kris' arm. She gave her friend a small smile but knew it must have looked more like a grimace than something that was meant to reassure.

"I'm so sorry, Nicole." Kris said with a quavering voice, "I didn't mean to lose my temper like that."

She looked down at the shaking small hand holding her arm, not knowing if the trembling was due to her adventure with the horse or if it was a reaction to her anger.

"Are you okay?" Kris asked softly and Nicole nodded. The dark haired woman then turned to Tommy, who was still plastered against his horse. She made an effort to smile, trying to ease the tension. "How far are we from the stables?" The boy visibly relaxed with the question.

"We're not too far away."

Kris looked back at Nicole and spoke softly. "Do you want to walk the rest of the way?" she asked, wishing her young friend would say something, anything.

"I'd like that," Nicole finally replied, as Tommy took hold of her horse.

Kris walked past him, paused and turned to the young guide. "I didn't mean to lash out like that. I was afraid she'd get hurt."

"Hey, it's okay." Tommy smiled. "I would've reacted the same way if it were someone I cared about."

They silently walked on, lost in their own thoughts. Kris cursed her temper and vowed to get a better grip on it. The last thing she wanted was to scare Nicole. She remembered something she had promised herself the day before: *You're just like her father, the voice had accused. "No, I would never hurt Nicole," she told herself then looked at her hands that were still on the table, tightly made into fists. "Oh God!" she whispered. "I'd leave before I do anything to her."*

Nicole could feel the conflict within her friend. She understood that her lover was only trying to protect her, but her violent reaction on her behalf had been a shock to see. Kris had a temper; she had seen it on a few occasions, mainly while she was talking on the phone, but it had been the first time that she had seen her nearly hit somebody. Nicole suddenly wondered if she wasn't getting out of the proverbial frying pan and into the fire. But deep down inside, she knew that Kris would never hit her, she wasn't like her father.

Chapter 22

Somewhere in Montreal a cell phone rang, startling its owner. He sleepily reached for it and flipped it open as he looked at the clock on the nightstand. They'd been in bed for only a couple of hours. His girlfriend grumbled as she put her pillow over her head.

"This had better be good," he mumbled. "What do you want?" he barked into the phone.

"That is no way to talk to your employer, Mr. Dunham," a voice calmly replied.

The photographer sat up and wiped the sleep out of his eyes. "I'm sorry. I didn't know it was you."

"Do you have anything interesting for me?" McGrail asked.

Mark hadn't looked forward to this phone call. What he had so far wasn't worth the money promised to him. "I did get a few shots of her talking with some guys at the stunt school," he started. "But nobody gets close enough to her to get the type of pictures that you want."

"I want results, Mr. Dunham," McGrail warned. "I want you to find a woman that will do something for me."

Mark thought about that for a moment before his gaze shifted to his sleeping girlfriend. "I may have somebody for you."

"I want her to follow my instructions precisely. There will be an interesting amount of money for her if she does. If not..." McGrail waited and smiled when he heard the photographer swallow nervously. "If not, you'll be the one responsible for the screw up."

Mark nodded vigorously at the phone. "I'll make sure everything goes well."

"Good," McGrail drawled. "Meet me in one hour at the same place as before. I'll give you the instructions," he said then closed the connection.

Mark looked at the silent phone and hung up. "This is getting weirder by the moment."

****

Nicole had suffered no injury from her adventure with the horse except a good scare. The young guide kept Kris in his line of sight as they walked back to the stable, but the woman was silent all the way. She didn't look angry anymore. In fact, she looked like she had lost her best friend.

The drive back home was a quiet one, with Nicole occasionally glancing at Kris. She had never seen her partner look so sad before. She knew what was bothering her, and she bit her lip, trying to find a way to approach the subject. They silently walked into the house, and Nicole gently took Kris' arm, causing the taller woman to turn around and look at her.

"I'd like for us to talk," she said with a smile. She caught the guarded expression on her lover's face and a glimpse of fear, too. She gently kissed Kris' lips. That single action made the stuntwoman relax and even smile a little. "I'm making myself a cup of coffee. You want one?"

"Sure." Kris sighed and walked into the living room, stopped at the glass door, and looked at the stormy lake. The wind had picked up and judging by the gathering clouds, it looked like another storm was on its way. She closed her eyes and leaned her forehead against the glass door.

What would she do if Nicole decided that she couldn't deal with her temper? The young woman had become such an important part of her life in such a short time, Kris didn't know if she could survive without her. She had never felt that way with anyone before.

A small hand gently brushed against her back, and she opened her eyes to Nicole's worried look. The two mugs of coffee sat on the table in front of the sofa. *How long was I standing like this?* She gave Nicole a small smile, took the offered hand in hers and followed her lover to the sofa.

Nicole sat down beside her partner and faced her. "Kris," she started, searching for the right words, "I know that you feel bad about what happened today. But I would be lying if I told you that it didn't scare me to see you that way."

Kris was prepared to hear the worst, but the gentle hand holding hers confused her. Nicole wasn't screaming like her ex-lovers had done when something went wrong. She saw only love in the emerald eyes looking back.

"I know why you reacted the way you did. It's because you were afraid that I might have gotten hurt, right?" Nicole asked gently.

"Yeah," Kris agreed softly. "But I should've been more careful." She gave Nicole's hand a light squeeze. "You shouldn't have to deal with another mean tempered person. You don't need me acting like your father."

"You're nothing like my father," Nicole stated firmly and touched Kris' cheek, making her look at her. "Would you hurt me?"

"No!" Kris exclaimed. "God, I could never do that. I love you so much, I couldn't even think of doing such a thing."

"And I knew that, too." Nicole smiled. "I just wanted you to realize that for yourself," she continued as she scooted closer.

"I was so sure that you were going to leave me," Kris said softly. "I promise that I won't let my temper get the best of me again."

Nicole leaned against her lover and wrapped her arm around her waist. "I know," she said gently. "And you won't get rid of me so easily. I love you too much." She smiled at the soft kiss on top of her head.

She gently brushed her hand over Kris' shirt and pulled it

out of her pants, letting her fingers slide under it and over the warm skin. Her lover's breath caught in her throat as Nicole brushed her fingers against her bra, feeling the firm breast underneath.

Nicole sat up and straddled her partner's thighs. While looking into blue eyes, she undid her own blouse, starting with the last button and slowly working her way up. Kris swallowed in anticipation, unable to keep her eyes off of her lover's nimble fingers. They suddenly stopped their movements and Nicole waited until Kris looked up and, as expected, raised an eyebrow. The blonde winked at her, finished opening her blouse, and let it fall off of her shoulders onto the floor.

The blood rushed through Kris' body, the sound deafening in her ears, loving the unexpected show her lover was putting on. She slid her hands around her partner's waist and slowly brought them up to unhook the delicate brassiere, letting it glide down her arms, and dropping it on top of the blouse. She gently pulled Nicole closer to her and kissed the offered breast, her tongue slowly circling the erect nipple, softly sucking on the sensitive flesh.

A moan escaped Nicole as she tilted her head back and closed her eyes. She firmly wrapped her hands behind the taller woman's head and pulled her lover even closer to her while Kris' strong arms held her tight, losing herself in their connection. She could spend the rest of her life locked in an embrace like this. Nicole smiled as Kris moved from under her and tightening her arms around her waist slowly stood up, pulling the small woman up with her.

"Going somewhere?" Nicole asked seductively and nibbled at her lover's ear.

Kris smiled as she closed her eyes, allowing the warm feeling to run all over her body. "Anyplace in particular you'd like to go?"

"Hmmm, someplace nice and comfortable," Nicole replied as she kissed her. "I have a feeling that we won't get much sleep tonight."

"You're right." Kris winked at her and walked to their bedroom.

****

Working on a Sunday wasn't what Kris wanted to do, especially not when she had Nicole waiting for her at home. But it was a small price to pay when she knew that the project was almost finished and that she would soon get back to their normal schedule and routine. She was looking forward to driving Nicole to and from work again.

The extra days working overtime at the school had been spent on preparing a new section where brand new equipment had been installed. Air rams and ratchet systems had been assembled and tested where students could train with the latest devices on the market. The equipment allowed the stunt performer to be launched into the air, activated only when they either jumped on it using the air ram or stepped forward with the help of the ratchet system. Compared to the previous equipment, the new unit didn't have any buttons or wires connected to the performer and didn't have any airborne radio or IR signals. This new technology reduced the risk of accidental activation by requiring at least the full body weight of the stunt person to activate the system.

It was Marcus' pet project, and he had looked forward to having it fully operational at the stunt school. Kris watched with amusement as every instructor tried the new system. She looked at her watch and she saw that it was nearly dinnertime. Knowing that the work was done for the day and that the instructors were mostly just goofing around, Kris waved goodbye to Marcus and drove home.

It had been a fairly calm day, Nicole thought as she came back from her daily walk. Her father had seemed to be in a good mood, in fact, she couldn't recall him smiling so much. The phone rang as she entered the house and she hurried to answer it.

"Hello?" Silence answered her, and Nicole shifted impatiently on her feet. "Who's this?" she asked, then the connection was broken. "Wrong number, I guess."

She turned around and looked at the time. If everything went well at the school, Kris would be home in two hours. She decided to wash her hair and take a long, hot bath wanting to relax. It still bothered her to have to sneak around in order to meet her father. She wished that she had told Kris about it even if her lover didn't agree with it. After spending a few days meeting with her father, she was certain that he was indeed seeking help. It showed in his attitude when they spoke together.

No matter how Kris would react to the news, Nicole wanted to get this secret out in the open, but today wasn't the time to do it. She wanted to prepare a nice meal and relax with her lover, maybe even watch a movie at home.

Coming out of the bathroom, Nicole heard the phone ring again. Thinking that it was Kris, she ran for it and answered. "Hello?"

"Hum," there was a slight hesitation on the other end. "Kris?" a woman's voice asked.

"I'm sorry, she's not here right now. Can I take..."

Click.

Nicole looked at the phone in puzzlement. "...a message. Well, that was rude," she said as she hung up and shrugged, trying to think of who might be calling Kris. If it was business related, she usually gave her cell phone number. "If it's important, she'll call back."

As she prepared dinner, Nicole caught the unmistakable sound of an approaching Harley and smiled. The front door closed as Nicole set the table and she heard the sound of booted feet sounding on the wooden floor and then silence. A bit of shuffling told her that her friend was putting her leather jacket and helmet away then heard two thumps and assumed that it was Kris' boots hitting the floor. Nicole walked up to the chilled bottle of wine and poured two glasses.

Seeing that her partner wasn't coming in the kitchen, Nicole figured that Kris probably believed that she was alone in the house. The first thing her lover usually did upon arriving home was to kiss her hello, the second was to go into her office and check her e-mails. Being careful not to make any noise and wanting to surprise her, Nicole carried the two glasses and went in search of her friend. The dark-haired woman was sitting at the computer with her elbows on the desk, her head resting into her hands.

"Another hard day?" Nicole asked from the doorway.

Startled, Kris turned around. "Hey, I thought you were still out walking."

"I went earlier than usual," she explained as she handed one of the glasses she was holding.

Kris took a sip before putting it on her desk. "Thanks for the wine." She smiled and tugged on Nicole's free hand, pulling her closer.

"You're welcome." Nicole smiled. She stepped behind and leaned over Kris to put her own wine beside the other glass. "Everything okay?" She asked as she gently massaged the tense muscles in her friend's shoulders.

Kris closed her eyes as Nicole's gentle fingers soothed her and she sighed, feeling her body relax under her lover's caring hands. *No matter if I'm tired, sad, or upset, she manages to calm me.* "You've got a magic touch, Nick," she said and was answered by a small chuckle.

"There's nothing magical about it," Nicole said softly. "It comes from love." She bent down and kissed Kris' neck. "You ready for dinner? We can continue this later." She grinned and winked at her smiling lover. "Come on." Nicole took Kris' arm and led her partner out of the office.

Something seemed to be bothering Kris, and Nicole realized that she hadn't answered her question. Maybe she was just tired, especially after all those long hours at work. *One things for sure, I'm gonna do my best to make her relax tonight.*

****

The beginning of the week came and went but on Wednesday, Kris was more than upset to find out that she had to spend another day working at the school after teaching due to an unexpected problem with the equipment. The stuntwoman had seen the same problem while on location in Germany and had successfully fixed it. If Kris didn't repair the unit, a specialist had to come from Los Angeles to do it and the school couldn't afford to take the time for him to get there. Fortunately, it took less time than she had figured to fix the problem and although she was still upset about working late, Kris was happy that it was fairly early in the day.

I guess Nicole is about to go on her daily walk. Maybe I should go and meet her. Kris smiled to herself, her mood improving with her plan.

Knowing that Nicole always walked the same trail, Kris drove slowly along the lakeshore in search of her blonde friend. Spotting a familiar form sitting on a park bench, she parked the Pathfinder, climbed out and walked towards the young woman. A man sat beside Nicole and she engaged him in an animated conversation. Kris couldn't recall having seen the man before. Maybe he was a friend of hers or maybe not. Nicole was the only person she knew who could start a conversation with a stranger.

Kris slowed her pace, watching Nicole's hands trace patterns in the air as she explained something. The man nodded and made signs of his own in response, which caused Nicole to burst out laughing. She playfully slapped the well-built man.

"Oh, come on, Dad!" Nicole exclaimed.

Kris froze in place. *Dad?* Everything stopped existing around her as she processed this information. A mixture of fear and anger slowly built within her as she continued walking toward the couple. What was Nicole's father doing there? Was he threatening her? Was she okay? Then the sound of Nicole's laughter came back to her, and she stopped once more. *But...she's laughing!*

She wanted to know what was going on, but she was damned if she would ask her in front of her father. A look around the populated area showed Kris that it was fairly safe for Nicole, so she walked back to the Pathfinder and drove home.

Looking at the time every five minutes, Kris paced the living room floor, wrestling with her emotions not to go back to the park and confront McGrail. Normally, Nicole would be back from her walk in another twenty minutes. *If she's not here in twenty-five, I'm going back there. I don't trust that man.*

She heard the back door open and close and nearly collided with her friend when the small woman walked around the corner.

Nicole stifled a scream with her hand. "Jeez Kris...you scared me half to death! You're home early," she said as she put her Walkman on the coffee table. Her smiled faded at the serious expression on Kris' face. "What's wrong?"

"Why didn't you tell me?"

"Tell you what?"

Kris walked to the glass door, crossed her arms over her chest, and blindly stared outside. "Did you meet anybody while you were walking?"

"What's going on?" Nicole asked, her beating faster. "What are you getting at?"

"Did you meet anybody?" Kris demanded more forcefully, then remembered her promise and did her best to keep her temper under control. She closed her eyes and leaned her forehead against the door.

Nicole opened her mouth to speak but no words came out. She tried again, certain that her voice would crack with the tension she was feeling. "What do you want to know?" she asked softly

"Who were you sitting with on the park bench?" She opened her eyes, seeing Nicole's reflection in the glass door as the younger woman shifted on her feet.

Nicole stopped breathing. Her worst fear had come true. *Damn you!* She cursed herself. *Why didn't you talk to her like you were supposed to do yesterday?* She tried to calm her nerves. "I was with my father."

"Why? Did he follow you?" Kris asked as she turned around to face Nicole. "Did he try to hurt you again?"

"Calm down, Kris. We were just talking." The jaw muscles clenching under Kris tanned skin, told Nicole that her partner was doing her best to control her temper. "Nothing happened."

"That's what you told me the last time he hit you," Kris replied as she ran a shaking hand through her raven hair.

"We were just talking," she repeated. "We've been meeting like this for the past week and..."

"What?" Kris exclaimed. "You've been seeing him...You never...Nicole, what do you think you're doing?"

"He's getting help," Nicole explained.

Kris turned around and closed her eyes. "The only help he needs is a good swift kick in the..."

Nicole grabbed Kris' arm and spun her around so the older woman would look at her. "This is my father we're talking about. I know we don't have the best relationship, but he's trying to change. " As an afterthought, she added, "What were you doing in the park? Were you spying on me?"

Seeing the anger in Nicole's eyes, Kris did her best to calm her by keeping her voice gentle. "No, I wasn't. I left early so we could spend some time together. I didn't know you were going to be with him."

"Look, we met last Monday. You were too busy to even have dinner with me so I left the house to take a walk, and he happened to be there," Nicole started, wanting to get everything out in the open. "He always went there to relax and think." She took a calming breath and sat down on the sofa. "Listen, he asked me for a second chance and we've been meeting in a public place. It's not as if I was completely alone with him."

"Well, I don't like it, something doesn't feel right," Kris stated not sure why Nicole would believe him after all that he'd done to her. "He's up to no good, can't you see that?" she asked as she squatted in front of Nicole.

"No, I don't," she replied. "Kris, I knew that you were going to react this way, that's why I didn't want to say anything." Nicole winced at the hurt in Kris' eyes and spoke softly. "I wanted to see if he really changed. I even tested him. I wanted to see if he was going to lose his temper. He didn't. It almost broke his heart, he looked so sad."

Kris listened to her partner's trembling voice. She hated the man for the lifetime of abuse he had given his daughter and would never forgive him like Nicole seemed to be able to do. She just hoped that she was wrong and her friend could prove to her that he was doing his best to change his ways.

"Kris," Nicole said softly, resting her hand on her lover's muscular arm, "I didn't mean to hurt you. I just thought that for once in my life I could make my own decision about what I wanted to do and that's to give my father a second chance."

The dark-haired woman reached for Nicole's hand on her arm. For a frightening moment, Nicole thought that Kris was going to brush her hand away, but the older woman gave it a squeeze and looked up at her.

"You're right." Kris gave her a small smile. "You have every right to make your own decisions, Nicole." She stood up from her crouched position and sat beside her friend. "I just don't want to see you get hurt, that's all."

Nicole was so relieved to see that Kris wasn't angry anymore, she cried. The next thing she knew, she was solidly wrapped in a pair of long arms.

"Shhh, I've got you. Everything's gonna be okay." Kris couldn't shake the feeling that Nicole's father was up to something. *No matter what you do, you can't keep a rattlesnake from biting.* If Nicole really believed her father, all she could do was to make sure that nothing happened to her.

Chapter 23

Since morning, Kris hadn't been able to concentrate. Too many times, she had caught herself mentally drifting from her students, and now she had been staring at her computer screen for the past twenty minutes trying to do her evaluations. She couldn't get her mind off of Nicole and her father.

She understood Nicole's need to have a normal relationship with him and her partner seemed to really believe that he was seeking help. Obviously, she saw a difference with his attitude towards her or else she wouldn't have met him so many times.

Kris closed her eyes and rubbed her temples, trying to get rid of the headache that had steadily grown ever since her discussion with her lover.

A strong hand squeezed her shoulder and with a quick movement, she stood up, kicked away her chair, and spun around to face the person foolish enough to grab her from behind. The dark-haired woman glared at the man, ready to strike.

Marcus froze at Kris' reaction and the blood drained from his face. Coming back to his senses, he lifted his hands and took a step away from the stuntwoman. "Hey, Kris, chill out. I didn't mean to startle you."

"Don't," Kris growled, "ever do that to me again." She stretched to her full height, towering over the man and took a calming breath. If there was one thing that she couldn't stand it was to be touched, especially from behind. Memories from a long time ago rushed back to her.

Her whole family, starting from the grandparents all the way to the grandchildren, had always worked as stunt performers. Helmut Von Deering had been a well known stuntman in the silent movie era and had continued working as the "talkies" hit the silver screen. That's how he had met his future wife, Louisa, one of the first stuntwoman in the movie industry. After they got married and children were born, the whole family slowly got into what was later referred to as the family business and every member of the Von Deering clan became an accomplished stunt performer.

The training had been long and hard. Since the family didn't want any specialist in the business, everybody was trained in all disciplines, which basically meant car stunts, falls, fire, and fight scenes.

Young Kristina proved to be very capable in hand to hand combat and not wanting to be limited to staged fights, had asked and received approval to get professional training in martial arts. That decision saved her life nine years later.

Her developing body, already showing the signs of a beautiful woman in the making, caught everybody's attention, especially with her height and piercing blue eyes. The Von Deerings had been working on a TV project in Vienna when Kristina was barely fifteen. Without her knowledge, three young men followed her on her way back from the TV set.

They had seen the beautiful young woman before and decided to have a little fun that day. As soon as she was hidden from view, one of the men caught her from behind, pinning her arms along her body while the others grabbed her legs and covered her mouth.

Kristina's training took over as she kicked and threw her opponents everywhere. Realizing that they hadn't chosen a weak and defenseless victim, the young men ran away clutching at their numerous injuries, leaving a torn-clothed, but otherwise uninjured girl behind.

Ever since that day, Kris disliked anybody touching her, and the people who had done so from behind quickly learned not to do it again.

Putting her memories away, Kris picked up her chair and mumbled. "I'm sorry. You just surprised me."

With a nod, Marcus sat on the edge of her desk. "It's okay, no harm done. You don't seem like yourself today, Kris. What's up?"

She shook her head and sat down. She hated to talk about her private life, and she was not about to do it with a man she barely knew. "I'm fine."

Marcus snorted. "Yeah, right. And I'm the Queen of England." Kris gave him a look and saw the beginnings of a smile tugging at her lips. "Listen, it's been a long day, and everybody's hot. Since the students did very well today, I decided to cut the day short," the director said as he stood up. "The instructors and students are all going out for a cold beer. You promised you'd come with us the next time we do something. How 'bout it?"

Kris looked at her watch and saw that it was only two o'clock. She still had some time before she picked Nicole up. One beer sure wouldn't hurt. "Sure." She smiled as she shut down her computer. "I'll join you guys."

"Great! Suzan will be happy to hear that," Marcus said as they walked out of the instructor's office.

"Who?"

"Suzan Shelby. One of the two female students we have at the school," he explained. "Don't tell me you forgot about her already." He laughed, about to clap Kris on the back but stopped when he remembered the look she had given him earlier.

"Oh..." Kris shook her head. "No, I didn't forget."

A new batch of students had arrived at the beginning of the week and one of them had been Suzan. The woman was, as she called herself, Kristina's number one fan. The Austrian had been the reason why the tall, shapely brunette had enrolled at the stunt school.

Knowing that her idol was teaching, and especially since it was in Montreal, Suzan had decided to go for it. She wasn't one of the best students and so the instructors had to spend extra time with her to explain the simplest of movements, not that the men were complaining about it. Suzan was very pleasant to look at, and the guys didn't mind getting close to her at all.

Kris suffered a lot of teasing from the other instructors about her *fan*, especially since Suzan followed her around the school grounds like a little puppy whenever she could. The stuntwoman sighed, knowing that somehow the brunette would find a way to sit next to her. *At least, I'll only be at the pub for a couple of hours.*

****

Some time later, Kris stood up from the table and took her keys out of her pocket while the instructors sitting nearby voiced their objections at her departure.

"Come on, Kris," Marcus complained. "It's still early. Why do you have to go?"

Kris smiled and finished the rest of her beer. "You know that Nicole will be waiting for me at the studios." She took a quick look around and grinned at Marcus. "And I have a clear way for the door."

"Running away from Suzan, huh?" The school's director chuckled.

"Yeah, well, that's the type of worship I don't need right now." Kris smiled and waved to the rest of the guys. "See you all tomorrow," she said and walked out of the pub.

Two cars away from her Pathfinder, Kris noticed a car with its hood up and Suzan standing in front of it looking at the motor. Debating between driving off or helping the young student, she shook her head and walked to the brunette. "What's up?"

"I have no idea." Suzan sighed as she crossed her arms over her chest. "It's just a piece of junk. I should buy another one, but I can't afford it."

"Did you leave your lights on?" Kris asked as she checked the engine.

"No, I didn't. Things like this always happens when we're in a hurry, don't they?" Suzan asked as the dark haired woman walked to the driver's side and climbed into the car.

Kris tried to start the motor, but the car wouldn't cooperate. "I can't find the problem, sorry. Do you want me to call a tow truck?" She asked as she unclipped her cell phone off of her belt.

"No!" Suzan responded a bit too quickly. "I mean, I'm in a hurry, and I don't have time to wait for it." She smiled shyly. "Could you give me a lift? It would really help me."

Kris sighed. *Why did I know that this was coming?* She looked at her watch. She had an hour left before she was due at the studios. "What about your car?"

"I'll have my brother take care of it," Suzan said.

Guess there's no harm in helping her out. "Alright, I'll drive you. Come on," she said as she walked to the Pathfinder.

Letting the hood of her car slam shut, Suzan pumped her arm in victory. She would finally spend some time alone with her idol, even though it was only for a short while. Making sure that Kris wasn't looking, Suzan quickly shoved the wires she had cut from her car's engine into her pocket and smiled as she trotted after the Austrian stuntwoman.

Later the same evening, Nicole headed for the microwave and put a bag of popcorn in it. *A quiet evening watching movies with my lover. What else can I ask for?* She smiled. Kris had left twenty minutes before to rent a couple of films and was due back any minute. The phone rang, and she jogged to the living room to answer it.

"Hello?"

"Can I speak to Kris?" a female voice asked.

"She's not here right now," Nicole answered. "Do you want to leave a message?"

"Oh," the woman replied, sounding disappointed. "No, it's okay. I'll see her tomorrow then. Thank you," she said, then hung up.

See her tomorrow? Nicole frowned and replaced the receiver on its base. *I wonder who that was,* she wondered as she walked back into the kitchen, hearing the microwave beep.

****

Nicole loved her job as a camera operator. She was lucky enough to be the assistant to a wonderful woman who wasn't afraid to show her all the tricks of the trade. She was learning fast and showed a lot of potential. Nicole spent her working hours observing D.J., the camerawoman she was assisting, taking notes, and asking a lot of questions when they weren't filming. More often than she should've allowed, D.J. let the young woman handle the camera for less critical shots, wanting her protégé to learn as much as possible. The crew quickly got used to the small woman's questions as she went from one technician to the other, wanting to know as much as possible about the business.

But that day, the crew found Nicole very quiet, more distracted than upset or angry. A few concerned techs tried to talk to her during the lunch break, but she responded with a simple, "I'm fine, thanks," and returned to her technical books.

In truth, Nicole had been staring at the pages for a half hour. She knew that she shouldn't make such a big deal out of it, but the phone calls to Kris were bothering her. They were always from a woman, and they never left a message. The voice seemed to sound the same, but she couldn't be sure that all the calls were from the same woman.

Kris knew a lot of people and many called the house, so why did those calls bother her so much? Was it because they came from a woman who refused to identify herself? Nicole shook her head in frustration. She hated feeling so damn insecure. *If only Alex was here. I'd have somebody to talk to about this.*

A bell rang in the studio, indicating that lunch was over. Nicole closed her books and stood up, wondering what her cousin would say about the calls. *She'd probably say it's all in my head and stop making such a big thing about it.* Nicole smiled as she could almost hear her spirited cousin's voice. Knowing that it was probably true, she decided against talking with Kris about it and went back to work.

Later in the afternoon, a car parked not too far away from Kris' house while two occupants silently sat and watched. Their eyes followed as a Pathfinder entered the driveway and a petite blonde woman step out of it and closed the door. She briefly talked to the driver, and then waved before the vehicle backed down the drive and continued down the road.

The occupants of the parked sedan smiled at each other when the blonde entered the house, alone. Waiting another minute or two, the driver took his cell phone, dialed a number, and passed the phone to his passenger. The woman grinned as she took it and listened to the rings. The call was picked up after the third.

"Hello?" A female voice answered, out of breath.

"May I speak to Kris, please?" the passenger said, smiling into the phone.

"Kris just left," Nicole replied. "She'll be back shortly. Do you want to leave a message?"

"Yes," the woman drawled and spoke with a sultry voice. "Would you thank her for the wonderful time we had? Thank you so much," then hung up. The passenger looked up at the man, and both laughed. "How was that?"

"You were wonderful." Mark smiled and kissed his girlfriend. "You know something, Alice? We could make a lot of money taking contracts like these." He grinned as he started the car and drove home.

****

Nicole stared at the phone in her hand. "What the hell was that all about?" This was getting a bit too much for her. *What did she mean by a wonderful time?* "Enough is enough," Nicole grumbled as she dialed Kris' cell phone number and waited. She jumped in surprise as a ring sounded from her attaché case. With a sigh, she remembered that while they were driving back from work, she had kept the phone after she made a call to the technician who was repairing her CD player.

Nicole hung up in frustration. She had no way to reach her partner and ask her about the phone call. "What the hell's going on, Kris?" She stomped out of the living room and walked out of the house, trying to calm her shaking body.

Having picked up Nicole's CD player and a few snacks for the evening, Kris reached for her cell phone on her belt and found it missing. "Damn, Nick has it." Knowing that her lover was probably taking her daily walk, Kris drove to where Nicole usually stopped for a while to relax. *And talk with her father,* she added silently. All she wanted to know was what kind of movie Nicole wanted to see. *If she's with him, I can always make sure that she's okay.* She put the Pathfinder in gear and drove to find her friend.

"Hey."

A soft voice interrupted Nicole's thoughts, and she looked up at her father who had a worried expression on his face. With Alex gone in Africa and both her Aunt and Uncle on vacation, Nicole had nobody to talk to about the way she was feeling. But she realized too late that calling her father wasn't such a good idea. Not only had she never mentioned Kris to him, but her father would never understand her relationship with her.

"Is something bothering you?" McGrail asked as he put a gentle hand on Nicole's lap and smiled when he saw that she didn't avoid his touch. *Good, she trusts me now.*

"I'm..." Nicole started but bit her lip. Could she take the chance and tell him about Kris? If she did, it would be the best test she could think of to see how her father would react. "I've been living with a friend, and things...well, it's not as rosy as it once was," Nicole said as she looked down at her shaking hands.

"Are you living with Neilson?" he asked with hope in his voice. "He's a real nice boy. What happened?"

"No." Nicole shook her head, suddenly wishing that she had called her childhood friend instead of her father. "It's not Neilson. I...live with a woman. Her name is Kristina." She instinctively cringed, expecting a violent reaction from her father. She slowly looked up when nothing happened and saw the dumbfounded look on his face.

"A woman?" he repeated. "She's just a friend, right? I mean you two aren't..." He smiled inwardly as Nicole shifted nervously on the bench. *Let the games begin.*

"Please understand, I love her very much," she said and grew more confident at her father's lack of reaction. "It's just that there are a few things that we need to work out, that's all."

"Who is this...Kristina?" he asked, trying hard to keep the

disdain out of his voice.

Well, you started this, you better go all the way now, Nicole told herself. "She's a stuntwoman I met while working with Uncle Robert. She's the one I'm going to live with in Austria."

"Austria?" McGrail asked, "You're not talking about Kristina Von Deering are you?"

Nicole could hear the worried tone in her father's voice. He never read anything concerning show business. How did he about Kris? "Yes, it's her. But..."

"Nickie, do you realize how much trouble that woman is?" he asked softly.

"What do you mean?" Nicole looked confused. "She's been very nice to me."

"Of course, she is," he replied as if speaking to a child. "Nicole, do you know how many lovers that woman has had?" he asked, taking her cold hand in his. "While I went to buy a newspaper, I saw many magazines that mentioned it. One of those lovers talked about Kristina's bad temper and possessiveness. Nickie, Kristina's a womanizer." He bit his lip trying to keep himself from grinning. He could see by Nicole's reaction that he had hit the bullseye. "You can ask Neilson, he's a stuntman, too. I'm sure he knows something about her."

Nicole stood up and closed her eyes, running shaking fingers through her hair. She knew that her father was speaking the truth. Kris did have a temper, and in a way, she was over protective, but that was only because she cared. What she wasn't sure about were Kris' lovers. The stuntwoman had never exactly talked about them, and she wasn't even sure if what was written in those magazines was the truth. Probably not, Nicole thought.

She opened her eyes and looked at the calm lake for a moment then turned around to face her father. Something caught her attention, and she shifted her eyes and saw a black Pathfinder in the parking lot not too far away.

"Dad, would you mind if I ask you to leave so I can think about all of this?"

McGrail smiled and stood up, knowing that he had succeeded in planting a seed of doubt in Nicole's head. "I don't mind. If you need to talk again, give me a call, okay?" He gently brushed his hand on his daughter's hair and left the park. *This calls for a celebration.* He grinned, barely holding back a laugh.

What do I do now? Nicole thought as she sat back on the bench and stared at the lake. Was Kris spying on her? Did she have so little confidence in her that she felt the need to come here and guard her? *I thought that we had agreed when we discussed my father. I guess I was wrong.* Nicole turned as she heard somebody approach.

"Hey, how are you doing?" Kris asked as she sat beside Nicole and quickly lost her smile when she saw the upset look on her face. "What's wrong? Did he do something?" She looked at McGrail's retreating back and then at Nicole.

"What are you doing here, Kris?" she asked. "I thought that you trusted me enough to be alone with my father."

Kris looked confused. "I do trust you, Nicole. I was just..."

Nicole stood up and faced her. "Then, why are you here?" she demanded.

"I wanted to know what movie you wanted to see tonight and..."

"You couldn't have waited until I was back home to ask me?" she asked as she put her fists on her hips. "You know, Kris, I'm not a child, I don't need a babysitter when I'm meeting people."

Now Kris was totally confounded. Why was Nicole reacting this way? Sure, she had been watching them, but it was because she didn't want to intrude on their time together. "I was not spying on you," she tried to explain. "But why is it so wrong for me to see if you're all right?" she asked. "I just don't want to see you get hurt."

"Stop being so protective, Kris," Nicole exclaimed. "I can take care of myself. My father's been real nice and everything's okay but you know something? No matter what he does or say, you'll never like him. But he's my father, and I'll meet with him whenever I feel like it no matter what you say. End of discussion." Nicole turned and left Kris speechless, sitting on the park bench.

Chapter 24

Neilson entered the *Café des Berges* and looked around for Nicole. The sound of her voice when she had called him on the phone had him worried. He spotted her sitting in a corner, alone. *Where's Kris?* He wondered as he walked to her. Even in the dim lit room, he could see that Nicole had been crying.

"Hey, Nick," he said gently as he pulled out a chair and sat across from her. "What's wrong?"

Nicole looked up with a small smile and wiped her eyes with a tissue. "I'm sorry I've bothered you, Neil. I didn't want to mess up your plans for tonight."

"You never bother me, Nick." He smiled as he patted her hand. He indicated Nicole's half-empty glass of Coke and held two fingers up to the approaching waiter. "The only plan I had tonight was watching TV alone, the same thing that I've been doing for the past two weeks. So, don't worry about it, okay?"

"Where's Anne?" Nicole frowned.

"Who knows?" Neil chuckled. "I was tired of her constant pouting and complaining. So, I told her it wouldn't work between us. It's been over for a few weeks now."

"I'm sorry," Nicole said sincerely.

"I'm not," he replied with a smile. "So, what's up? Where's Kris?" He bit his lip at the look on Nicole's face. The question nearly caused her to start crying again. "Hey, I'm sorry. I didn't mean..."

"No, it's okay," she said. "We...I..." Nicole sighed and shook her head. "How much do you know about Kris?"

The question caught Neilson by surprise. "Well, not as well as you that's for sure." He grinned, trying to make Nicole smile. "I don't know much about her," he confessed, then paid the waiter for the drinks and turned his attention back to his friend. "I've heard a lot about her from stuntmen who worked with her. She's a real professional, and she's well respected."

"No, I mean, do you know anything about *her*, the woman."

Neilson thought about that for a moment, then shook his head. "I told you before, Nick, you know a lot more about her than anybody else does. All we know are the rumors written by newspapers and magazines, and God knows we can't trust those." He moved his chair a little closer to her and squeezed her hand. "What's going on, Nick?"

She looked down at their entwined fingers and smiled. Neilson was such a good friend. Aside from Alex, he was the only person she could fully trust. She just wished that she could feel the same with Kris. She used to trust her, but with all the questions she had lately, she wasn't sure anymore.

"I think Kris is seeing somebody else."

"What?" Neilson exclaimed. "Why would you say that?"

"I've been receiving phone calls at home. They started with the caller hanging up, then the woman asked for Kris," Nicole explained in a soft voice. "She never left a message...until today."

Neilson didn't like the sound of this. Was it possible that Kris was fooling around? He shook his head in disbelief. He was usually a good judge of people, when they weren't his own girlfriends, and nothing showed him that Kris was that kind of a woman. She looked and acted like she loved Nicole dearly. Why would she bother to invite Nicole to live with her in Austria if she didn't?

"What message did the woman leave?" he asked.

"She wanted me to thank Kris for a wonderful time." This time, Nicole couldn't hold her tears back.

Neilson shifted his chair to sit beside his friend and cradle her in his arms while she cried. He didn't know what to say to make her feel better, and so he waited until Nicole relaxed in his arms.

"I know it's a bit naïve of me to think this, Nick, but that message can be taken many ways."

Nicole sat up and sniffed. "What do you mean?"

"Well, we know that Kris allows some interviews, and she does like to perform." He knew his explanation sounded lame, even to his own ears. "I know the last reporter loved the interview she did with you guys."

"She doesn't do many interviews, Neil. She hates them," Nicole replied as she brushed her tears away. "Besides, she would have told me about it."

Okay, let's go for the direct questioning. "What tells you that Kris is having an affair, aside from the phone calls you've been receiving? Do you have a real proof that they come from another lover?"

Nicole thought about that for a moment. When they weren't working, most of their free time was spent together. Kris did do a lot of overtime in the past weeks, but every time she had called the school, her friend had been there to answer, except yesterday.

"I called Kris at the school, and the receptionist told me that she had already left for the day," Nicole said as she played with her glass. "It was only two-thirty when I called. She picked me up as usual, but she never told me where she had gone for the rest of the afternoon."

"Did you call her on her cell phone and asked her where she was?" Neilson asked gently.

Nicole silently shook her head no. She did talk to her during the afternoon break then had gone back to work, forgetting all about calling her again. Nicole frowned as she thought back to a few phone calls Kris had received on her cell.

"She went outside the house a few times to talk with callers, but she never told me who they were."

"Do you always tell Kris what you do or who you talk to?" Neilson asked with a smile.

She looked at him and blushed. She knew where he was going with this line of questioning. "I...I try." Kris dealt with a lot more people than she did, and her partner didn't really need to tell her everything, did she? "But...I've gotten used to her telling me everything that she does. Now, it seems like she's telling me less."

"Nick, you can't expect Kris to tell you everything she does every moment of the day," he said while patting her hand. "Especially, if those things are insignificant or personal to her."

"But she had a few lovers before me. How do I know it's not one of them calling now?"

Neilson couldn't stop the laugh that escaped his lips. "I'm sorry, Nick," he said when Nicole glared at him. "I'm not laughing at you. But if the fact that Kris had lovers before makes you suspicious of her having an affair, my last girlfriend could have said the same thing about me." He gently squeezed her hand. "Yes, she could be talking to one of them, but, Nicole, there's no law against that. They could still be friends."

"I don't know what to think anymore, Neil."

"Do you love her?" he asked gently. "Do you want your relationship to continue?"

"Yes, I do."

"Did you talk to her about your fears and concerns?" She bowed her head and shook her head. "I suggest that you do, Nick."

Nicole knew that it was the only thing she could do. How would Kris welcome her after the way she had left her in the park? Would she be so upset that she would leave her? What would she do if Kris decided it wouldn't work out between them after all? So many questions needed to be answered. Taking a deep breath, Nicole looked up at Neilson and smiled.

"You're right. I'll speak to her. Thanks, my friend," she said, and kissed his cheek.

Neilson smiled as Nicole stood up and squeezed his shoulder. "Anytime, Nick," he replied and watched her leave. So much had happened to Nicole, the good as well as the bad. He hoped dearly that everything worked out between both women. He didn't want to think about what would happen if Kris stepped out of the picture. He knew for a fact that McGrail wouldn't leave his daughter alone if she did. In fact, he was surprised that he hadn't said nor done anything since Nicole left his house.

He smiled as he remembered a talk he once had with Nicole after she had suffered one of her father's occasional beatings. Very seriously, he had told her that they should get married since it was what her father wanted. That way, she would be out of the house and away from his violent temper. Nicole could then finally start living normally without any fear of a beating. Marriage wasn't something he wanted, but knowing that McGrail wouldn't approve of anything less, he would gladly do it if it meant saving his best friend from her own father.

****

Unable to say anything, Kris watched Nicole leave the park in an angry huff. She tried to figure out what she had done wrong and couldn't come up with anything. All she wanted to do was ask Nicole a simple question.

She drove to the house, all thoughts of a movie and dinner forgotten and went to the back yard, sat on the grass and looked out at the lake. *What's going on with Nicole? Is she getting tired of me already? Am I getting on her nerves?* Kris knew that her friend was right when she accused her of being overprotective. If she didn't care and love her so much, would she even bother to do that?

Wrapping her long arms around her knees, Kris rested her forehead on them and bit her lip. So many emotions ran rampant through her. She was angry at not knowing what the hell was going on, and she was hurt that if something was wrong, Nicole wasn't talking about it.

She knew that her lover's aggressiveness had nothing to do with the long hours at the school. Her partner understood the need to get the equipment up and working, and she also understood the long hours spent at the computer to take care of the stables in Austria. Nicole had told her so.

So what happened?

Thinking back to the past weeks, things started to go wrong ever since Nicole's father came back into her life. Kris was torn between believing Nicole and her own distrust for the man. Maybe she was right when she said that he was really seeking help and was a changed man, at least he was making an effort to be. But what if her father was playing a game with his daughter? What was his plan?

Kris knew that he was a violent man and had seen his handiwork on Nicole's body, but why would he act like the repentant father? Was it to lure Nicole in and then beat her up? It simply didn't make any sense.

But where's Nicole now? Where did she go after leaving the park? Kris would have bet she was at Alex's if her cousin wasn't out of the country. Maybe she was there, talking with her Aunt and Uncle. Had she gone back to her father's? The idea made her shiver. What would happen to their lives together if she did? Would he let her go a second time and permit her to move to Austria with her? Did Nicole still want to move? Kris had so many questions hitting her from all sides that it gave her a headache.

She didn't know how long she sat staring out at the peaceful water, lost in thought. The sun was setting, and she felt a chill but didn't want to move. She simply didn't know what to do.

The sound of feet on the gravel made Kris turn around and she saw her friend standing there, with her hands deep in her pants pockets. Kris was glad that she had come back, but fear crept into her heart as she waited for her to say something, anything.

Nicole was about to leave when Kris turned and looked in her direction. The older woman was probably angry at the way she had left earlier, although she looked pretty calm and was afraid that her lover didn't want to talk to her.

I probably deserve her silence, she thought and took a few steps forward and stopped, gauging Kris' reaction. Her friend didn't make a move to leave. The mixture of hurt and apprehension on Kris' face shocked Nicole. She swallowed nervously and continued walking.

They sat side by side, lost in their thoughts. Finally Nicole turned to Kris. "I...I think we need to...talk," the blonde said softly.

Kris looked at her partner, fearing the worst.

Nicole hesitated. "Are you...Are you having an affair?" she

finally asked, unable to look at the dark haired woman.

The question caught Kris by surprise. "What?" Kris choked. "What are you talking about?"

"I received a phone call today at the house from a woman," Nicole started with a shaking voice, fighting back tears. "She asked me to give you a message."

Kris watched as Nicole fought with her feelings. She wanted to take her in her arms, but she feared that her touch would make the younger woman move away.

"She told me to..." Nicole stopped to take a shaky breath and wipe her eyes as tears glided down her cheeks. "She thanked you for a wonderful time." Nicole broke down and cried, letting her built up emotions break free.

Kris' heart stopped. What was going on? Who was the woman that called? She lifted her hand and hesitated before she gently touched her friend's cheek. "I don't know what you're talking about," Kris said softly and scooted closer to the younger woman. "I'm not having an affair, believe me." Taking a nervous breath, she opened her arms and waited.

The blonde looked at her partner through eyes full of tears. Feeling a strong need to believe her, she wrapped her arms around the stuntwoman's waist.

Thank me for a wonderful time? Kris silently repeated. Who could have said such a thing? The only women that had called her had done so on her cell phone, mainly the reporter that had done the interview, wanting a few details concerning Austria and the school's receptionist so she could give Kris her messages. Very few people had the phone number from the house. Nicole's uncle had it and Marcus had it written in her file at the school along with her cell number.

Thank you for a wonderful time, she kept repeating as she gently rocked Nicole in her arms. The only other woman she had spent some time with was Suzan Shelby. *But I only drove her home.* She gently kissed the blonde head under her chin and murmured.

"There's no one in my life but you."

Nicole shifted in Kris' arms, sat back and looked up at her. "No one but me?"

"You're the only one," Kris assured her with a smile. "Why didn't you talk to me before all this started?"

"I...I'm not used to...I mean, I don't handle confrontations very well." She smiled shyly as she wiped her wet cheek.

"Discussing isn't a confrontation, Nicole." Kris said softly. "It's normal to disagree sometimes, but it's not right for you or for me to keep something like that to ourselves, especially when it causes so much worries. Talk to me, okay?" Kris gently scratched her neck.

The smaller woman closed her eyes and leaned into Kris' touch. "I'm not used to talking about things like that," she whispered then looked at her partner. "It's my first relationship. Give me some time to get used to this serious kind of talk, okay?"

Kris nodded with a smile and stood up. "Come on, it's getting chilly," she said as she held her hand out for Nicole. "Are we okay?"

"We're okay," Nicole confirmed with a smile. "I'm sorry for the way I reacted. I hate having fights like this."

"But fights do have a good side," Kris said with a crooked grin. "Making up makes it worthwhile."

****

People ran out of the way as Kris skidded the truck to a halt, climbed out of the Pathfinder and slammed the door shut behind her. She marched straight to the instructors' room and threw her bag on her desk scattering papers everywhere. Most of the instructors had already arrived for the last day of teaching and were talking excitedly about the new students due to arrive on the following Monday. They stopped talking and watched in apprehension as Kris got ready for her day of teaching.

Joey, the youngest instructor, stood up and walked to her. "Hey, everything okay?" he asked and gulped as Kris glared at him.

"Who is Suzan scheduled to work with today?" she asked brusquely.

Joey shifted his feet nervously. "She's at the towers with me." *When things are stressed, try humor,* his mother had once told him. He smiled and looked at the tall woman. "What's the matter? Problems with your pet student?" His laugh faded as Kris took a step towards him. *Very bad thing to say, very stupid,* he told himself and backed up.

"That," she growled, her blue eyes turning gunmetal grey, "is not funny. She is *not* my pet."

Marcus entered the room and seeing the rage on Kris' face stepped between the two instructors. "What's going on here?" he asked. Kris looked like she wanted to kill. *Not a fun way to end the week.* He sighed and indicated Joey's desk with his chin. "Sit down," he instructed him then looked at the stuntwoman. "Kris, come with me." He turned and headed to his office.

"Go get Suzan and bring her here," Kris told Joey in a calmer tone. "I want to talk to her." The instructor quickly nodded and left the office in search of the student.

Once inside Marcus' office, Kris closed the door behind her and slumped in the chair in front of his desk. The day hadn't started yet, and she already had a headache. She rubbed her temples and sighed.

"Wanna talk about what happened?" Marcus asked as he opened his thermos, poured coffee into two mugs, and handed her one. "I know you don't like to talk about your personal life, Kris, but sometimes it helps," he said as he sat down behind his desk. "Ever since you started teaching here, I've never seen you so upset."

"Did you ever give my phone number to anyone? The one at the house?" she asked tiredly. All night, unable to sleep, Kris had thought about the phone call Nicole had received. She took the coffee mug and took a sip, letting the warm liquid slide down her throat.

Marcus thought for a moment and shook his head. "I have your number written in my address book, and it's also in your personal file, but no, I never gave your home number to anyone."

Kris looked at the filing cabinets along the wall and noticed that one was slightly ajar. "Do you lock your files or your office door?"

Marcus frowned at her. "I don't. There's no sensitive information in here. Nobody comes in here anyway." He shifted in his chair and leaned his elbows on his desk. "Why?"

"Well, maybe you should lock everything." She sighed and ran her hand through her hair. "Somebody called the house and left a message for me that almost caused a breakup with Nicole." She swirled her coffee in her mug. "I suspect that Suzan had something to do with it."

That caught Marcus by surprise. "I know that she's a big fan of yours, but I don't think she'd do something like that. Why would she anyway?"

"Never heard of stalkers, Marcus?" Kris asked wryly. "She follows me everywhere at school, and her only subject of conversation when she talks with the other students is me. She told me about all the stuff she's got in her collection and even has pictures of me all over her house. Hell, Marcus, she even has an old helmet of mine sitting on a dresser in her bedroom."

"You saw her bedroom?" he exclaimed. "What the hell were you doing there?"

"Relax, Marcus. I never even stepped into her house." She put the mug on the desk, stood up, and paced around the office. "After we all went to the pub, I saw that Suzan was having problems with her car, and I offered her a lift home, that's all. She told me all that on our way there. As soon as she got out of the car, I left to get Nicole at her work."

The director relaxed and shook his head. The last thing he needed was for one of his instructors to get involved with a student. "What kind of message did she leave?"

"She wanted to thank me for a wonderful time." Kris blew out a breath and looked out the office window. "Damn it, Marcus. All we did was talk." She spun around to face him. "Nicole didn't like the message at all."

"I guess not. It can be taken so many ways," he replied and looked up at a knock on the door. "Come in."

The door opened, and Suzan poked her head into the office. "You wanted to see me?" She entered as the director waved her in and closed the door behind her. "Hi, Kris." She beamed at her idol.

"Please, sit down, Suzan," Marcus said and peeked at Kris, who had her arms crossed and was glaring at the student. *I hope you're right about this, Kris, or else you'll have one hell of an apology to make.* "Suzan, did you call Kris at home this week?"

The question caught her by surprise. She swallowed nervously when she looked at the dark haired woman who was not smiling. In fact, she looked downright hostile. "Huh, yes...I did. Did I do something wrong?" she asked, looking at both instructor and director.

"How did you get her phone number?" he continued and warned Kris with a shake of his head as she straightened, ready for the answer.

"The...the receptionist gave it to me," she stammered, knowing she was lying. She watched as Marcus opened his address book, picked up the phone, and dialed a number.

"Hi, do you have Kris' phone number handy, please?" he asked the receptionist and waited. Checking in his address book, he shook his head. "No, not her cell phone, I need her house number."

"For that I'd need to go in her personal file, sir," A young voice replied. "Do you want me to get it for you?"

"No, it's okay. Did anyone ask for that particular number?"

"No, sir. Nobody did."

"Thank you." He hung up and looked at the student who was squirming in her seat. "Would you mind telling me again where you got that phone number?"

"I only wanted to thank you for your help," Suzan said to Kris with tears in her eyes. "You were so nice to me at the pub and driving me back home. I didn't mean to cause any trouble."

"But you did," Kris said, pushing herself away from her spot by the window. "Where did you get my number?"

"The files," Suzan whispered, unable to look at either one of them. "I got it from the files here."

"She's your problem now, Marcus," Kris said as she opened the door. "I've wasted enough time already. I've got a class to teach." She walked out of the office, leaving the crying student with the director and closed the door behind her.

Stopping at her desk, Kris thought of calling Nicole to tell her about her discovery but decided otherwise. Her partner didn't need to relive this event. They had talked the night before, and everything was almost back to normal between them. They still had a few things to discuss, mainly about trust and communication, but that would come with time. She picked up her clipboard with her students' files and headed out of the now empty instructors' office.

Chapter 25

Two weeks remained before they would pack their bags and leave for Innsbruck. Even though Kris enjoyed Montreal, Nicole knew that the stuntwoman was looking forward to returning home. She'd be lying if she said that she wasn't nervous about the move. Not that she wasn't looking forward to seeing her lover's home or starting a new life, but her lifelong insecurity caused Nicole to ask herself some questions.

Her relationship with her father had never been better, and she had a job that she had always dreamed of having. Her contract was nearly completed at the studios, and having proved to be a quick study, another contract had been offered to her. She had turned it down, explaining that she would be moving to Austria. It was with regret that they heard the news, but they had made it clear that if she ever wanted to work for them again, she would be welcome.

What made Nicole nervous was that she was about to leave everything behind and launch herself into the unknown in a new country, with another language, and no friends. But as long as Kris was with her, everything would be fine, right? *But what will happen if she's not there or if she leaves?* Nicole's insecure side asked. *What if she gets tired of you and finds another lover?*

"Earth to Nicole, come in," the camerawoman teased.

Startled, the blonde woman looked up at D.J. She smiled at

her co-worker and took a bite from her sandwich. "Sorry, I was just thinking," she mumbled.

"Lunch is over. Are you coming back to work?" The older woman grinned.

Nicole glanced at the time and scrambled to her feet. "I'm so sorry," she exclaimed. "I didn't notice the time." She gathered her papers and technical books and took another bite of her sandwich. "Is everybody waiting for me?"

D.J. chuckled and shook her head. "Nah, we're waiting for the sound crew to finish their adjustments. But they're almost done. Come on."

The crew was on location in Quebec City for three days. It was a weird feeling for Nicole to be on her own and away from Kris, but she knew that the time they spent apart would make their reunion all the nicer and she smiled at the thought of being wrapped in her lover's warm embrace.

She really enjoyed her time with the crew, and much to her surprise, had been chosen to be second camera for the on-location project.

Nicole nodded at the camerawoman and tried to put her thoughts and worries about her new life in Austria in the back of her mind.

****

Marcus smiled as he hung up the phone. He walked out of his office and found Kris at her desk. "Hey, are you busy this afternoon?" he asked as he sat on the edge of her desk.

Kris looked at the director and rubbed her aching eyes. "Except for that," she said indicating the files on her desk, "I don't have much to do. Why?"

"I need a favor. I need you to go to the airport for me and meet somebody there. She'll be in between flights and will give you something."

"Sure." Kris nodded as she pushed her chair away from the desk and stood up. "It'll give me a chance to clear my mind from all the paper work."

"Thanks, Kris," Marcus said as he handed her a piece of

paper. "This is where you'll meet her." He winked at his instructor and left the room.

"But how will I..." Kris started but the director had already left, "...know it's her," she finished to an empty room. She looked down at the note and silently read it. *She says she knows you.* Kris shrugged, took her keys and left for the airport.

Outside the stunt school, Mark Dunham, sat in his car wondering what to do next. It had been weeks since he had received the contract from the mysterious man, and so far, all the pictures were not what his employer wanted. The stuntwoman wouldn't let anybody get close to her. *How the hell am I supposed to take pictures in that case?* He grumbled. There was only one person who was physically close to Kristina and that was her girlfriend, Nicole, but his employer gave strict orders to leave the blonde alone.

The photographer looked at his collection of pictures, certain that his employer would reject them as he did the others. Mark's cell phone buzzed, making him jump in surprise. He put the photographs aside and flipped the phone open. "Yeah?" he barked.

"I'm getting very impatient with you, Mr. Dunham," a deep voice rumbled.

The unmistakable voice made Mark swallow nervously and shuffle through the pictures on the passenger seat. "I'm doing the best I can. She's not the easiest woman to catch in a compromising situation." A movement caught his attention. The stuntwoman was walking out of the school and getting into her vehicle.

"She's leaving soon. I don't care how you get them but I need those pictures before that, Mr. Dunham," McGrail growled. "You better provide what I paid for, or else, I'll take more than just my money back," he warned then hung up.

Mark flipped his cell phone closed and threw it on the seat in frustration. "Easy for you to say," the photographer complained. He started his car, put it in gear and followed Kristina at a reasonable distance. "Where are you going now?"

Maybe I'll ask Alice to help me. She could always throw herself at her or something. He thought of the phone call his girlfriend had made to Kristina's house and smiled as a plan formed in his mind.

The photographer followed the Pathfinder to the airport and parked not too far away from it. He grabbed his two cameras and trailed Kris into the terminal, easily following her through the crowd without being noticed.

Walking through the airport, Kris took another look at the note Marcus had given her and changed direction for the American Airline information counter. "Now, how am I supposed to know who I'm looking for?" Kris muttered.

"Well," a female voice behind Kris said. "You're so damn famous now, you don't even say hello anymore?"

Kris spun around on her heels. A huge grin broke out on the stuntwoman's face, and she opened her arms to welcome the visitor. "Marianne!" She laughed and hugged the woman. "What are you doing here? Aren't you supposed to be in Los Angeles?"

"Yeah, I'm in between flights." Marianne grinned. "It's good to see you. I missed you so much," she said as she hugged Kris and gave her a kiss on the cheek. "I see that Marcus was true to his word. He didn't tell you I was coming." She laughed as she kept her arms loosely wrapped around the tall woman's waist.

"You're the one I was supposed to meet? Just wait 'til I talk to that little sneak," Kris growled playfully. "And you're one, too, you know that?" She planted a gentle kiss on Marianne's forehead and smiled. "How much time do you have before your next flight?"

She sighed. "Oh, only two hours," Marianne replied with disappointment in her voice. She rested her head against Kris' chest and gave her a squeeze. "We all miss you."

"I do too. How about we go for a coffee and talk for a while?" Kris asked and guided the smaller woman to the bar, their arms around each other's waists.

Mark couldn't believe his luck. *These pictures will save my neck,* he chuckled, giddy at the thought that he'd finally supply his employer with the merchandise and that the mysterious man would finally be out of his life.

****

The photographer waited impatiently on the park bench where he usually met his client. This time, Mark knew that the man would be satisfied with the photographs. He nervously fingered the yellow envelope as he watched the sailboats on the lake then glanced at his watch for the third time. It was almost time for their regular meeting.

With no way of reaching his client, Mark had to wait impatiently for two days with the developed photographs until either the man called or until they met at their usual meeting time. He turned his head as his employer approached and sat down on the bench beside him. With a smile, Mark handed him the envelope.

Without a word, McGrail took it and pulled some photographs out. He went through the pictures and frowned. "What's this shit you've given me?" he angrily asked. "This is useless to me." Most of the pictures were taken at the school showing some of the instructors assembled around Kristina. McGrail studied several other photographs. *This is better, but it's not what I'm looking for,* he thought as he looked at pictures of Kristina talking to a shapely brunette in a parking lot and another photo of both women getting into the stuntwoman's Pathfinder.

"From what I heard, this was one of Kristina's students at the stunt school. Her name is Suzan Shelby," Mark said as the well-built man looked at another picture. "This one was taken when Kristina drove Suzan to her place." The picture showed the brunette standing outside Kris' vehicle on the driver's side and talking with the stuntwoman.

"I don't give a damn who she is," McGrail growled throwing the pictures back at the photographer. "These are not good enough." He stood up and faced the now shaking man. "You are such an incompetent asshole." McGrail grabbed at the photographer's shirt, not caring if anybody was watching, and pulled him to his feet. "I told you not to fuck with me."

"Wait!" he begged. "I have more pictures for you. There's a second envelope beside the bench on the grass."

Mark was sure that the man was completely insane. He tried to keep from falling on the ground when the man shoved him out of his way. Mark's shoulders sagged as his chance of making more money with the last photographs went up in smoke. For some stupid reason, he had hoped that the pictures with the brunette would be satisfactory enough, and he would be free to sell them to others.

McGrail wasn't stupid, and he saw right through the greedy photographer's plan. It had been a bad mistake to try to hide anything from him. He picked up the second envelope and took a few steps away from Mark. McGrail slipped the photographs out and looked at them. The first one was of the stuntwoman smiling broadly as she held her arms open to a smaller, dark-haired woman. The second one showed the woman giving Kristina a kiss on the cheek while the stuntwoman held her in her arms. McGrail sifted through the pictures with a growing smile on his face. More photographs showed the two women talking and laughing. But the last two pictures were the best. One showed the Austrian kissing the smaller woman's head while it rested against Kristina's chest, her arms wrapped around Kris' waist. The other photo showed the women walking away with their arms wrapped around each other's waists.

I've got you now. McGrail smiled evilly as he put the pictures back into the envelope. He turned to the photographer and indicated the scattered photographs on the ground. "Pick those up and give them to me." McGrail glared at the nervous man and as he scrambled to gather the pictures.

"What about the rest of the money you owe me?" Mark asked nervously as he handed over the photographs. "What about the bonus you promised?"

McGrail laughed, the sound devoid of any humor. "You are either very greedy, Mr. Dunham or very stupid. I honestly think you're both. The second half of your money will be sent to your house." He snickered when the photographer froze. "Yes, I know where you live. Do you think I'm stupid enough not to inquire about you?" McGrail asked and smiled as Mark shook his head. "As for your bonus, it was promised only if I was satisfied with your work. The pictures are interesting, but your work is less than acceptable." McGrail stopped him from commenting with a raised finger and a glare. "I wouldn't say a thing if I were you,

Mr. Dunham. It took forever to receive what I wanted, and you tried to screw me by keeping the pictures away from me. Just be happy that you'll receive the other half of the money." McGrail slowly and menacingly stepped towards the shaking man. "Get out of my sight, you worthless piece of shit."

Mark didn't need to be told twice and he ran. *This is the last time I take private contracts.* The laughter coming from the mysterious man behind him sent chills down his spine. *Never again,* he promised himself.

****

Nicole stepped out of the car and waved at D.J. as the camerawoman backed out of the driveway and drove away. They had returned from Quebec City earlier than planned, and wanting to surprise Kris, Nicole came straight home without telling her lover. The past days had been hard on her. Working as second camera had made her nervous but everything had gone well, and she had received a lot of praise for her work. She only wished that her lover had been there with her. She had tried a couple of times to call Kris, but she either got a busy signal or didn't get through because the cell phone was shut off. Only once did they succeed in talking to each other.

After stepping inside the house, Nicole dropped her travel bag in the living room and called out, "I'm home." The house was silent, and judging by the state that the house was in, either Kris did a complete cleanup or she hadn't stayed in the house for a long period of time. Disappointed, Nicole picked up the phone and called her father, wanting to see how he was doing. The phone rang twice and was picked up before the third.

"Yes?" McGrail answered brusquely.

"Hi, Dad, it's me." Nicole frowned at her father's tone. "Is something wrong?"

McGrail made a great effort to calm his voice and to sound worried. "You can say that. I need to see you as soon as possible, Nicole. Can you come here?" he pleaded as he fingered the photographs next to the phone. "I know we always meet in the park but...what I have to show you...well, it's kind of private."

Nicole hesitated. Her father sounded worried and upset, not angry but more like sadness. "When do you want me there?" she asked. Something was wrong, she could feel it. What did he have to show her that was so private?

"As soon as you can. You really need to know this." McGrail bit his lip to keep from chuckling. His daughter was so easy to fool. From now on, everything would be child's play. "I'm really sorry to ask you this, Nickie, but I don't know what else to do."

"It's okay. I'm on my way now." Nicole hung up and grabbed a pen and paper to leave Kris a message, even though she would probably be back before her friend arrived from wherever she was at the moment. She took the house key and walked out the door to meet her father.

McGrail smiled as he hung up the phone. His daughter was on her way back home and soon, he would be rid of that dark-haired bitch.

Nicole arrived at the family house and nervously rang the doorbell. How strange it was for her to do that when she had lived there all her life. *He's come so far since the last time I was here.* The door quickly opened, and her father stood there with a look of sorrow on his face.

"Please, come in," McGrail said as he stepped back to allow his daughter to enter. "I...I don't know how to start." He looked at his hand, trying to act as nervous as possible.

"What's going on, Dad? Are you ill?" Nicole asked as she touched his arm.

"No, I'm fine. I..." McGrail sighed and scratched his jaw. "I was at the airport this week and..." He blew a frustrated breath and shook his head. "I'm sorry, this is hard for me to do." He walked into the living room and stopped in the middle, looking at the envelope on the TV set.

"Dad, what's wrong?" Nicole asked nervously.

"You know I was wrong when I did all those horrible things to you, and you know that I'm doing my best not to do them again, don't you?" he asked with pleading eyes.

"I know that you're doing your best to change. It shows so much." Nicole smiled as she gave her father's arm a squeeze.

"The last thing I want is to see you get hurt," McGrail said as he looked down at his hands. "If it ever got out to the public, I don't know what I would have done."

"What are you talking about, Dad?"

McGrail took a deep breath and looked up at his daughter. *Show time.* "Some pictures were taken when I was waiting for a friend at the airport. I bought the whole roll of film from the photographer because I didn't want them to end up in magazines. You can check my bank account if you don't believe me, they cost me a fortune and..."

"Wait! Hold on." Nicole held a hand up to stop her babbling father. Her mind was reeling. Pictures taken at the airport? They certainly weren't pictures of her. The last time she had been at the airport was for her trip to Cancun with Kris...*Kris? Oh my God, could the pictures be of her?* "What pictures?"

McGrail took the envelope and handed it to her. "I'm sorry you have to see this, Nickie. It's better that you know now."

Nicole fearfully pulled the photographs out and looked through them. He silently screamed victory as tears formed in her eyes and fell down her cheeks.

"I asked around before showing you this. Kristina has been seeing this woman for some time now."

"No," Nicole moaned. "It can't be." Little things that had been bothering her came back to her with a vengeance. Phone calls, anonymous messages, absences from the house without knowing where Kris was, and now this. "She said there was no one but me," she whispered, unable to tear her eyes away from the incriminating evidence. "She lied to me. I thought she loved me." She cried unable to control her emotions any longer.

"It's not the first time that she did that," McGrail said softly. "You were just a play thing for her. If she really loved you, would she do something like this?" He handed her a new set of photographs.

Her whole world came crashing down on her at the sight of the new pictures. Were the past three months just a game to Kris? How could she be so cruel? She closed her eyes, not wanting to believe what she was seeing. She had never felt such pain in her life. All she wanted to do was to lie down and die. Nicole bit her lip as tears fell freely down her cheeks.

"Why?"

Nicole opened her eyes and took a shaky breath, trying to see through her tears. She stared at the picture of Kris holding the woman tenderly in her arms. *Just like she used to hold me.* Tears of anger and fury replaced her tears of sorrow.

"Why?" Nicole screamed and tore the pictures apart and ran up the stairs to find refuge in her old bedroom.

McGrail looked down at the shredded pictures on his living room floor and smiled. Everything had gone as planned.

Chapter 26

Kris was satisfied with her day. All the arrangements had been made and her Harley-Davidson was ready to be shipped back to Innsbruck. Since she wanted Nicole to enjoy one of her remaining weekends in Canada, she had leased a cabin in the mountains so they could spend some time together. She had missed her the past few days and was looking forward to seeing her lover again. Feeling a bit lonely, Kris had spent the time as busy as possible getting ready for the move to Austria and preparing a romantic weekend.

Nearing the house, Kris noticed a taxi in the driveway and smiled at the thought of Nicole being home. She gave the driver a moment to back up the car and frowned when the taxi didn't move out of the driveway. Kris turned the motor off, stepped out of the vehicle and walked to the taxi. The trunk was filled with bags, and the driver stood next to the house's opened door.

"What's going on?" she asked the driver who only shrugged. "Nicole?" she called out loud as she walked in. "Where are you?" Her heart pounded when she realized that, for some reason, Nicole was leaving. She practically ran from room to room, trying to find her partner and found her crying in the bedroom. "What's wrong?" Kris asked worriedly and took a step forward to touch her arm.

"Don't touch me!" Nicole screamed with a fresh flood of tears. "Just...don't."

Kris pulled her hand back as if burned. "Wha..." she started. In shock, she stared as the younger woman put the last of her clothes into the bag and zipped it closed.

"Get out of my way, Kris," she said through clenched teeth, her vision blurred by the tears. Nicole took her bag and moved towards the door. Kris did not move. "I said move!" she yelled and grabbed the first thing that came into her hand and threw it at the taller woman.

Kris, through her haze, barely had enough time to duck as the plug tore out of the wall and the lamp flew past where her head had been. The lamp broke against the wall in a shower of glass and porcelain.

"I loved you so much. How could I have been so wrong about you?" Nicole wailed as she ran out of the room, the strap of her bag slung over her shoulder. "What a mistake I made," she cried as she ran down the hall.

"What did I do? Nicole, talk to me!" Kris pleaded, the pain tightening her heart and soul. Something had gone horribly wrong, and she had no idea what it was. "*Nicole!*" she screamed as she ran out in time to see the blonde woman closing the door of the taxi, and the car pulling out of the driveway. "Please...wait?" she choked, but the car didn't stop.

Her legs finally gave out, and she sat on the front lawn with a thump. What just happened? Why did Nicole leave this way? Kris couldn't think straight. The sound of her racing heart and the blood pumping through her veins made it hard for her to think. She wanted to get up and go after Nicole, but her legs wouldn't obey her.

Kris hit the ground with her fist in frustration. Determined to find out what had happened, she scrambled to her feet like a drunken sailor.

"It can't end this way!" She closed her eyes as images of her previous breakup came back to haunt her. "Don't do this to me, please," she whispered, hoping that when she would open her eyes, Nicole would be standing in front of her. Reeling from the emotions hitting her from all sides, Kris opened her eyes to see that her wish hadn't come true.

"Where could she have gone?" she mumbled as she headed

for her vehicle parked in the street. "Her uncle...She must have gone to Robert's."

A few minutes later, Kris ran up the driveway and to the front door. She rang the doorbell and waited impatiently for somebody to answer. She rang twice more and when no one answered, she jogged to the back yard to see if anybody was there. Nobody seemed to be home. Running shaking hands through her long hair, she turned around and noticed the empty driveway. Every time she had been at Robert's house, there had always been a vehicle parked in the driveway. Her shoulders slumped in defeat as she walked down the path back to her car.

She sat in the Pathfinder and put her forehead on the steering wheel. "What am I going to do now?" she asked as she closed her eyes. "Where are you, Nicole?" Kris leaned back and rubbed her palms against her aching eyes. She started the engine and drove back home. *Hopefully, she'll call me once she calms down.*

It was too quiet. Kris walked throughout the house aimlessly, trying to figure out what had happened. She repeatedly called Robert's house hoping that someone was at home, but Kris only succeeded in reaching their answering machine. She left a message asking them that if they talk to Nicole to have her call home. Her fifth and last message was a plea for Robert to call her as soon as possible. All evening she waited by the phone, hoping Nicole or Robert would call.

"I need a drink," Kris said as she walked into the kitchen. She wished that she had something stronger than beer but decided against getting drunk. That wouldn't solve anything. Reaching for the fridge, she noticed for the first time a note stuck to the door and pulled the paper from under the colorful magnet. Her heart raced as she read it.

Hey honey,

If you read this note, I guess that means you came back before I did. My father needed to talk to me so I left to see what he wants. I'll be at his house but don't worry okay? I'll be careful. See you soon.

I miss you!

Love, Nicole

Kris closed her eyes and put the note to her lips. Her partner had seemed fine when she wrote the note so whatever went wrong happened while she was at her father's place.

"Her father's..." Kris repeated and tightened her jaw. Anger swelled inside her as she realized that maybe McGrail had something to do with what had happened. She grabbed her keys from the counter and raced the Pathfinder out of the driveway and headed over to the family house.

The furious stuntwoman ran up the stairs and didn't even bother to ring the doorbell. She banged her fist against the door, letting the tension out of her system. "McGrail! Open the damn door!" she yelled and kicked the door when nobody answered. "Where is everybody?" she screamed in frustration. A curious neighbor looked out at her, but a glare sent the man cowering back into his house. She had no idea where Nicole was and neither Robert nor McGrail were home. She headed back to her house, hoping for a phone call. It never came.

After a night of tossing and turning, Kris went on her run earlier than usual before heading to the stunt school. Her lack of concentration caused her to nearly ram the car in front of her twice on the road and as she parked the Pathfinder, she misjudged the distance and the vehicle jumped over the small cement block that indicated where the parking space ended. Kris shook her head and climbed out, leaving the car where it was.

A few students and instructors chuckled at seeing Kris' mistake, but their smiles quickly faded at her pale and drawn face. She silently entered the school without even looking at them. Usually, she stopped to chat before the day started even when she wasn't feeling well.

Marcus excused himself from the group and followed the stuntwoman. The director waited until she settled her briefcase on her desk.

"Kris, can I speak with you?" he aasked with a smile and entered his office. She nodded, never looking up at him and headed his way. He closed the door as she walked past him and sat on a chair in front of his desk. Kris was staring at her hands, and if he didn't know her better, he could have sworn that she was ready to cry.

The school director pulled the second chair close to her and sat down. "I've never seen you like this, Kris. What's going on?" For a long moment, Marcus believed that she wasn't going to answer, but she sighed and shook her head.

"I don't know what happened," she whispered. "She's gone. Nicole left me." Kris bit her lip to keep the tears from falling. She still couldn't believe that her partner had packed her bags and left.

"Well," Marcus hesitated, "maybe all you need is to talk with her. I'm sure if you do, everything will be okay."

"I don't even know where she is," Kris said as she planted her elbows on her thighs and put her head in her hands. "I tried to find her. I looked everywhere I could think of. She's nowhere to be found."

"Kris, you look exhausted. Why don't you take some time off and work things out with Nicole?" Marcus asked gently. "I can find another instructor to replace you."

"I'm fine, Marcus, I just need..." She looked up when the director touched her arm.

"You're in no shape to teach, Kris. Would you let a stuntman perform if he was feeling the way you are?"

"I'm not performing, Marcus, I'm just..."

"Your concentration isn't there," he stated, holding her eyes with his own. "Find her and talk to her. Give me a call once your head is clear, okay?"

Kris knew that Marcus was right. She nodded and stood up. "I'm sorry about this."

"Hey, don't worry, okay? I just want to see the two of you together again. Nicole's a very nice woman." He opened the door and smiled at her.

"Yes, she is." Kris forced a smile. "Thanks." She walked back to her desk, picked up the phone and dialed a number she now knew by heart. "Is Nicole McGrail there?" she asked the receptionist at the studios.

"I'm sorry. She won't be coming to work for a few days. Would you like to leave a message?"

"No," Kris said with disappointment in her voice. "Thank you." She hung up and left the instructors' office carrying her briefcase with her.

****

Kris spent the next couple of days driving back and forth between Robert's house and McGrail's. No one had shown up yet. Kris, exhausted from lack of sleep, patrolled the lakeshore in hopes of seeing Nicole. She had even gone to the pub where she knew some of her friends hung out, hoping to see a familiar face, but she had no luck. She learned from the studio where Nicole worked that a crisis had happened in her family, and nobody was sure when the young camerawoman would be coming back.

One early morning Kris finally found someone home at Robert's house. She parked the car and as she was about to step out, she noticed the time. It wasn't even six yet. Wanting to give them a chance to sleep, she drove three blocks away to get a coffee and came back to wait for a more appropriate time to wake them up.

An hour later, Kris couldn't stand the wait any longer and walked up to the house and rang the doorbell. Michelle opened the door after three rings. Kris caught the look of surprise on Michelle's face before it was replaced by a smile.

"Hello, Kris. What brings you here so early?" Michelle greeted as she held the door open for the stuntwoman. "Please, come in."

"I'm sorry to show up this way but..." Kris quickly looked up at the sound of footfalls coming down the hall, but her shoulders sagged when a sleepy Robert poked his head in.

"Hi, Kris," he said as he looked from his wife to the dark-haired woman. "What happened to you? Are you okay?" Robert frowned at the tall woman and gently guided her to the kitchen and made her sit down. "You look awful."

"Robert!" Michelle exclaimed. "You don't say things like that." She then turned her attention to Kris. "Do you want a cup of coffee or something to eat? You look like you could use some."

"No...thanks." Kris nervously played with her hands, trying

to stop them from shaking. "Did you...Have you spoken to...to Nicole lately?"

Michelle was about to answer when Robert gave her a look that made her stop. She turned around to serve her husband and herself some coffee. He pulled a chair next to Kris, who was still looking down at her hands, and gently touched them. "We heard the messages you left on the machine."

A dark head rose and blue eyes pinned him where he sat. "Then why didn't you call me like I asked you?" Kris shot back, her temper rising. "You could have told me if you had seen her or something."

"We came in very late last night. I didn't want to wake you up," Robert said defensively.

"You knew that you could call me anytime, Robert, you've done it before on many occasions, none of them as important as this is to me." Kris took a deep breath and let it go slowly. "I'm sorry. I didn't mean to get upset at you."

"It's okay, don't worry about it. You look like you haven't slept in days. What happened?"

"I don't know. I honestly don't know," she whispered. "She...I've been looking everywhere for her." Kris stopped and closed her eyes. She was so tired her emotions were threatening to explode at the slightest thing. She looked up at Nicole's aunt. "Is she here?"

The look on Kris' face was so gut wrenching it almost made Michelle cry. "No, she's not here," she said softly and gently squeezed Kris' shoulder.

Kris looked at her with pleading eyes. "If...if you see her, can you tell her that I would like to...talk to her?"

"We will," Michelle and Robert agreed as Kris stood up.

She nodded with a look of utter defeat. They walked the tall woman to the door and watched her get int her car and leave.

"Do you believe what Nicole said about Kris?" Michelle asked. Their niece had left a message on their answering machine, telling them briefly what had happened and the name of the hotel at which she was staying.

"No, I don't believe it," Robert replied. "If she didn't care that much about Nicole, would she be searching for her like she is?" He turned to his wife. "You know Nicole, she's very insecure, and she quickly jumps to conclusions. I'm sure it's just a misunderstanding."

"I'm concerned about Kris though," Michelle said. "She looks like she's about to collapse. Should we get involved?"

Robert shook his head with a sad look on his face. "No. Nicole needs the time to think about all of this. I'm sure when she comes back from our country house, they'll talk."

As was her routine of the last few days, Kris drove past McGrail's house. A car was parked in the driveway, and she nearly drove the 4x4 onto the grass in her hurry to reach the house.

Lack of sleep and very little food made Kris almost lose her balance as she climbed out of the vehicle and ran up the stairs to the door. She banged on the door with her fist until it was finally opened. A tall, well-built man answered the insistent knocking with a frown.

"What's going on?" he asked with irritation. "Don't you know how to use a doorbell?" McGrail demanded as he looked at the tall, dark-haired woman. She looked like she hadn't slept in days. Her hands shook either from her weakened state or by the barely controlled fury reflecting in her eyes. *Well, well, well, if it isn't the great Kristina herself.* He silently snickered. *She doesn't look so great now. Trouble sleeping? I wonder why?*

"Where is she?" Kris growled, trying to take a look inside the house.

"Who are you talking about?" McGrail asked in a calm voice. The woman was close to losing her temper. *That could work. She hits me, I have her arrested, and she goes back to Austria. End of story.* He smiled as she clenched her fists.

Kris' eyes went down to slits as she glared at him. "Where...is...Nicole?" she asked, her voice a dangerous rumble.

"She's not here," he replied truthfully and started closing the door only to be stopped by the stuntwoman. Her arm had shot out and blocked the door. "What are you doing?" he exclaimed, playing the outraged citizen. "I told you Nicole isn't here."

"Do you mind if I don't believe you?"

"If you feel this way, come right in and see." McGrail made

a big show of inviting the woman in. He grinned as she inspected the rooms, finding nothing. "I told you, but you wouldn't believe me." He chuckled at the frustration on Kristina's face. "The last time she was here was a couple of months ago," he said with a touch of anger in his voice. He tried his best to control his temper, wanting so much to get this dyke out of his house. "You should know, you're the one who stole my daughter away from me."

Kris stopped her search and whirled around, facing him. "She hasn't been here for a few months?" she asked incredulously. Nicole's note had been clear; she was heading to her father's. Either Nicole had never made it or McGrail was lying.

"It's been weeks since I've talked to..." His eyes bugged out as the stuntwoman grabbed him by his shirt and pushed him against the wall.

"You lying son of a bitch!" Kris yelled as she lifted a fist to hit him. "You talked to her last weekend. Nicole was coming here because you wanted to see her. Tell me where she is."

"And what are you gonna do about it, dyke?" He laughed then winced as Kris bounced him against the wall. "Hit me until I tell you where she is?"

"That's an idea," Kris growled, seriously considering it then shoved the man away and stepped back breathing hard. She closed her eyes and tried to get her temper under control, but McGrail's laugh made it difficult.

He pulled at his shirt and tucked it back into his pants. "Come on, you want to hit me, don't you? You're just like me." McGrail taunted her as he walked close to Kris. "Admit it."

Kris turned her back on him, almost daring him to do something. *I'm nothing like you,* she thought as she ran shaking hands through her hair.

"It's hard to control the temper, isn't it?" McGrail continued, keeping his voice on a calm level. "I've had to control it so much, first when she mentioned she was moving, then when she said that she was living with *you,*" he spat. "You know that you're just like me."

The dark-haired woman spun on her heels to face the snickering man. "Don't even put me in the same category as you."

"Well, you are, considering that you would love to hit me right now."

Kris glared at McGrail and clenched her fists. "I might have a temper, but I will never stoop to your level," she said, doing her best to calm her raging fury and walked to the front door. "I'm going to find her, whether you like it or not."

"I don't think so. I made sure that you never do."

Kris stopped and frowned at him. "What do you mean?"

"Do you honestly think I'm stupid enough to tell you?" McGrail chuckled.

She took long strides towards him. "You'd better put it into that thick skull of yours that I love Nicole and that you won't come between us anymore. I'll find her." McGrail grabbed Kris' arm and she yanked it out of his grip. "Don't you *ever* touch me again."

"Fine. I'll make you a deal. I won't touch you, and you'll never touch Nicole...or else."

"Is that a threat?" Kris asked dangerously.

"Let's just say that if you don't stop looking for her, I'll make sure that she never speaks to anybody again. Have a nice day," McGrail said with a smile and closed the door on Kris.

Now what? She stared at the closed door. *What am I supposed to do now?* Defeated, she returned to her vehicle, got in, and drove away, not knowing where she was going. *Do I continue looking for her and risk the threat coming true? Will I be able to protect her if he does hurt her? Whose need should I take care of first? My need to find her and talk to her? Or letting her go and keeping her away from harm? Can I be so selfish and risk getting Nicole hurt?*

"No. I can't do that," she said out loud. A decision had to be made, and Kris knew that it wouldn't be an easy one. She found herself at the stunt school half an hour later and walked inside to talk to Marcus.

"I'm sorry, Marcus, I know my contract isn't finished yet, but I've had it. I'm going home."

"Are you sure about this?" he asked. "Did you talk to Nicole?"

Kris shook her head. "I couldn't find her, and it's the only thing I can do now. I know I promised you to stay until the end, but I can't deal with what's going on."

"But you could at least stay as a..." he started, stopped when Kris raised a hand. He hated to see her look so beaten, and the last thing he wanted was for her go this way.

"No, Marcus. I can't," Kris said softly. "You asked me before if I would let a stuntman perform the way that I'm feeling. The answer is no, I wouldn't. Don't ask me to do it."

Marcus nodded. "I understand. If you ever need anything, let me know. You've been such a great help to me and the school, I'm really sorry your time here had to end this way."

She nodded and stood up. "Yes, there is something you can do for me. I'd like for you to take the Pathfinder back to the dealer. All the papers are in the glove compartment, and everything has been paid." She handed over the car keys.

"Sure, I can do that. Can I drive you back..."

"No, thanks. I'll take a cab," Kris said as she opened the door to Marcus' office.

"Are you sure?"

"Yeah, I'm sure. I need some time alone. Thanks for everything. Tell the guys that I'm sorry, I just can't face anyone right now."

"No problem, Kris. Take care, okay?" Marcus said as he shook her hand. "It was a pleasure working with you. You know that you're welcome to come back here to teach anytime that you want."

She gave him a small smile and nodded. "Thanks."

As soon as she arrived home, Kris called the airline and made preparations for her departure. "Yes, I'd like a ticket for your next available flight to Innsbruck, Austria...my name is Kristina Von Deering, I had an open ticket...yes, that's my credit card number...no, that's not too early, that would be fine...no, just one ticket...yes, thank you." She hung up and looked around the silent house and sighed.

Three months ago, these preparations would have been normal to Kris. But now, knowing that Nicole wouldn't be joining her, made packing difficult. She made one last call to a courier company to pick up the two large boxes that had already been packed. All that was left to do was pack her suitcases.

Kris' heart beat furiously when the phone rang, and she raced to answer. It was the owner telling her where to leave the key. It would be picked up later. Kris called for a taxicab to drive her to the airport, and then to go home, alone.

Epilogue

During her first week home, Kris threw herself into her work at the stables, making sure that all her waking hours were occupied with something. It still hurt to think about Nicole, and she wondered where she was and if she was safe. Kris had no way of knowing if her father would keep his side of the bargain, that if she left, he wouldn't hurt her.

Nobody knew what had happened to Kris, but her siblings didn't want to pry into their sister's affairs. She wasn't the most talkative person, but her sullen and sad mood was out of character for her. Offers of help were quickly refused. After a while, they simply left her alone to heal from whatever had happened. The only one who dared talk to her was her housekeeper, affectionately called Oma.

Oma was like a grandmother to the Von Deering family. Everybody went to her for advice and comfort, and it hurt the housekeeper that Kristina didn't seek her help. The dark-haired stuntwoman stayed alone all day and barely ate. Oma had tried to bring Kris out of her depressed state by cooking all of her favorite foods but nothing worked.

Having unpacked Kris' suitcases as soon as she had arrived from Canada, Oma found photographs of her with a small blonde woman. They looked so happy in those pictures and hoping that it would raise Kris' spirit, Oma chose the best one and put it in a frame. She quietly walked up to the tall woman, finding her looking at her trophies and special pictures in the spacious living room.

Kris examined every item on the shelves as she fingered the small colorful braid that was still fixed to her hair, thinking back to the day spent in Old Montreal. Before her were trophies from all kinds of competitions, pictures of her with actors and celebrities from all over the world and special events that had happened in her life. Maybe she could add the braid to them, a reminder of the only time she had been madly in love.

She turned to the housekeeper as she entered the living room, and she gave her a small smile. As much as she wanted to be alone, especially away from her questioning family, Kris was glad to have Oma close to her. She knew that she wasn't ready to talk about what had happened, but she also knew that she would eventually talk about it, and the first person to know would be Oma.

"Can I do something for you?" Kris asked softly as she spied the older woman's arms locked behind her back.

"Not really." The elderly housekeeper smiled. "It's more what I can do for *you.*"

Kris frowned. The older woman was up to something. "Oh? And what's that?"

"While I was unpacking your suitcases, I found some pictures," Oma started. "I thought that you might want to have one of them up there in your collection," she said as she handed Kris a framed photograph. "It's the best one of the lot." She patted her arm with a smile and turned around, leaving the younger woman looking at the picture.

Kris held her breath. The photograph was the one taken in Cancun of Nicole and her aboard the sailboat on the Caribbean Sea. She closed her eyes as memories of the trip came back to her. She could almost smell the fresh air of the sea and feel her lover's body in her arms. She opened her eyes and let go of her breath in a shaky motion. She ran trembling fingers over the picture, wanting to touch Nicole one last time. Her vision blurred as a single tear slowly slid down her cheek.

"No matter what happened, I'll always love you, Nicole," Kris said. She pushed two pictures aside to make room for the latest addition and put it on the shelf. "Always."

To be continued in Daredevil Hearts...

Available soon from
Yellow Rose Books

Meridio's Daughter
By LJ Maas

Tessa (Nikki) Nikolaidis is cold and ruthless, the perfect person to be Karê, the right-hand, to Greek magnate Andreas Meridio. Cassandra (Casey) Meridio has come home after a six-year absence to find that her father's new Karê is a very desirable, but highly dangerous woman.

Set in modern day Greece on the beautiful island of Mýkonos, this novel weaves a tale of emotional intrigue as two women from different worlds struggle with forbidden desires. As the two come closer to the point of no return, Casey begins to wonder if she can really trust the beautiful Karê. Does Nikki's dark past, hide secrets that will eventually bring down the brutal Meridio Empire, or are her actions simply those of a vindictive woman? Will she stop at nothing for vengeance...even seduction?

Other titles to look for in the
coming months from
Yellow Rose Books

Prairie Fire
By LJ Maas

Lost Paradise: Book Two - Daredevil Hearts
By Francine Quesnel

Many Roads To Travel
By Karen King and Nann Dunne

Ricochet In Time
By Lori L. Lake

Love's Journey
By Carrie Carr

Second Chances
By Lynne Norris

9 781930 928121